True Sisters

Also by Sandra Dallas

The Bride's House

Whiter Than Snow

Prayers for Sale

Tallgrass

New Mercies

The Chili Queen

Alice's Tulips

The Diary of Mattie Spenser

The Persian Pickle Club

Buster Midnight's Café

True Sisters

Sandra Dallas

St. Martin's Press
New York

TRUE SISTERS. Copyright 2012 by Sandra Dallas. All rights reserved. Printed in the United States of America. For information, address St. Martin's Press, 175 Fifth Avenue, New York, N.Y. 10010.

www.stmartins.com

ISBN 978-1-250-00502-1 (hardcover)
ISBN 978-1-4668-0224-7 (e-book)

10 9 8 7 6 5 4 3 2

To my own true sisters

Donna and Mary.

There is no bond as powerful as that of sisters.

ARRIVAL:—Cap. Edward Martin and Company, it being the last hand-cart company of this season, arrived on the 30th of November. As was to be expected, they have suffered considerably from storms and inclement weather, and several have had their feet and hands more or less frosted, but are now comfortably housed and cared for.

—*Deseret News*, December 3, 1856

True Sisters

Chapter 1

July 28, 1856

The two sisters leaned forward, their hands flat against the rear of the handcart, waiting, fidgeting, impatient. It was late in the day, and they had been ready for hours, had stood there behind the spindly cart that was piled with all their worldly goods, listening for the command or maybe the sound of the cornet that would send them on their way. Already, the horn ordered their lives, waking them at five in the morning, calling them to prayers twice a day, sounding again at ten at night for the fires and lights to be extinguished. For three weeks, their lives had been ordered by that clarion call, and the sisters thought it had grown a little tiresome. But now the young women strained their ears for the sound, hoping the notes would begin the procession.

"Will the horn start us off, Andrew? Will it, do ye think?" Ella Buck called to her husband, who stood between the two shafts, ready to pick up the crossbar. At nineteen, Ella was the elder of the two women, and taller—an inch taller and a year older than her sister, although the two looked as much alike as two roses on a bush, both plump, round-faced, with hair the color of straw at dusk, hair that curled into ringlets in the damp Iowa air.

"Och! I told ye I dinna know," Andrew replied. It was the same answer he'd given his wife a few minutes earlier and once before that, and he sounded put out this time.

"Why do we skitter about? We are three weeks late," Ella continued, ignoring her husband's tone. "Why couldna we hae left at dawn?"

"I dinna know, I say. You've small patience. There's a reason we haena started. Ye can count on it."

"What reason?" Nannie Macintosh, Ella's sister, asked.

Andrew didn't answer, perhaps because he didn't know, or maybe he was afraid that his own impatience would show. After all, he had awakened them before the first sounding of the cornet and insisted they eat a cold breakfast so they would be ready to go at dawn. Now, he picked up the crossbar that was connected to the two shafts of the handcart and began to examine it. There was a knot in it, and Andrew told his wife that he hoped the wood wouldn't split before they reached Zion.

The cart was made of green wood. They were all constructed of green wood, and put together by the Saints themselves. The handcarts were to have been waiting for them when the converts arrived from Europe, but to Nannie's disappointment, they weren't, and the men had gone looking for seasoned lumber, only there wasn't any. So the carpenters among them fashioned the handcarts themselves from the poor wood that was available, made them to the Prophet Brigham Young's own instructions, to look like the carts the peddlers and dustmen pushed in the cities at home. While a few of the travelers had carts covered with canvas hoods, Andrew had been assigned an open cart with two wooden wheels, some four feet in diameter, with hoop-iron tires. The vehicle was the width of a wagon track so that it could roll along easily on the ruts of the trails. Between the wheels was a sort of wagon box or platform made of four or five planks, about three feet wide and four feet long, to hold bedding, cooking utensils, clothing, flour, and other provisions that Nannie and Ella stored there. The planks were nailed to two frame pieces that extended forward to form the shafts. Fastened to the two shafts was a crossbar. The space between the shafts accommodated two persons, but Andrew would pull the cart himself, while the women pushed. The cart, empty, weighed sixty-five pounds.

Andrew had said that the handcarts were a brilliant idea, proposed by the prophet himself, that allowed even the poorest among them to make the journey to the Great Salt Lake Valley. Andrew, Ella, and Nannie never could have paid for the trip to the Promised Land if they'd had to lay out three hundred dollars for a team and wagon. But a handcart for the three of them cost less than twenty dollars, and what's more, the church loaned them the money for the journey, which they would pay back once they were settled in Utah and Andrew found work.

It wasn't just the cost, however. The three emigrants knew

that the carts would make the trip faster than any wagon, because the people would not have to worry about livestock—hitching up the oxen each morning, gathering feed, hunting for the animals if they wandered off. Moreover, the handcarts wouldn't have to carry all the supplies needed to reach the valley, since resupply stations would be set up along the way. So with the other Saints, they could average fifteen miles a day across the thirteen hundred miles of prairie and mountains from Iowa City to the valley. That meant a trip of less than three months.

"But we canna walk all that way? I've never walked more than five miles at a time, and down a country lane outside Edinburgh at that. How can ye ask it?" Ella had inquired when she first heard about the carts.

"The exercise and the fresh air will strengthen you," the missionary speaking to the gathering in Scotland had replied.

"What if I get taken in sickness or break my leg and hae to hirple?"

"There will be wagons for the lame and infirm as well as the elderly."

"But I'm . . ." Embarrassed, she looked down at her stomach, which was still as flat as a flatiron.

"Of no consequence, sister. Other women, much further along, have crossed the prairie, some all the way to California. And as I told you, there will be the wagons for those who can't walk."

Ella discovered in Iowa City that there were only seven wagons, filled now with supplies and freight, for the infirm among the 650 emigrants, however. Still, Ella believed the elder who had spoken, since this group—called the Martin Com-

4

pany, for its leader, Edward Martin, a Mormon missionary who had served in England and Scotland—was the last of the five handcart companies to cross the prairie that year. The Willie Company had left two weeks earlier, not long after Andrew, Ella, and Nannie arrived. Ella said the shortage of wagons must mean that the elders were sure in the knowledge that few fell sick on the Overland Trail. The Lord would give them strength, a missionary promised her. As Ella stood behind the cart, waiting for the signal to move, examining a splinter that had worked its way into her hand, she thought again of walking the hundreds of miles and hoped the missionary was right.

The sisters heard shouts then, a creaking as the first carts, some lined up on the road, others spread out across the prairie, moved forward in a jumble, cries as parents called to their children, shouts of praise to the Lord, a few prayers. Ella had thought they would move out with a song, a trill of the cornet, a flash of lightning, or a boom of thunder rolling across the prairie, something to herald the momentous occasion, but there was nothing. With no ceremony at all, the first carts began to move, and then the ones behind them.

"Andrew," Ella called.

"I can see," he said, although he had been studying the poor piece of wood in his hand instead of watching the line of carts. Now he looked up at the procession of conveyances in front of him, his face as open and shining as the sun above them, and turned to his wife and her sister. All traces of impatience gone, he grinned and called, "Ready to roll on, are ye? Ready to roll to Zion?"

"Aye," Ella and Nannie cried, and as Andrew strained to

push the crossbar, the two women leaned hard against the back of the cart, and the awkward wheels began to move.

Ella and Nannie smiled broadly at each other, and the older girl touched her sister's arm. "You will love it in Zion. Wait and see. Ye'll be with God's people. No one will jeer at us, call us dirty Mormons. We'll be with our own." She added, although she should not have, "Ye'll meet someone there, a man worthy of ye." And then she repeated, "Ye'll love it, Nannie."

Her sister nodded. "I will love it because ye are there, Ella."

"Ye'll wear your red shoon, Nannie. Before a year is out, ye'll wear them." Ella stumbled a little as the wheel of the cart bounced over a rock, then checked to make sure that nothing had fallen out. She looked up at the dozens of carts in front of them, the dozens behind, and caught the eye of a woman pushing a handcart with a little girl perched on the top, thinking she would remember the woman, remember the day, July 28, 1856. "We're off," Ella shouted above the din.

The woman didn't smile, but she shouted back, "We're off to the Salt Lake indeed!"

Ella looked again at her sister. "I shouldna hae said that about the shoon. If your boots wear out, ye'll need the slippers before we reach Utah."

Nannie shook her head, her round cheeks already red from the exertion. "They're for my wedding. I won't wear them until I'm married, even if I hae to cross the mountains barefoot. That's why I bought them. And if I never marry, why then, the shoon will never be worn."

Ella turned away, hoping her sister had not seen her eyes cloud over with pity. The shoes had been bought for Nannie's wedding. She had been betrothed to Levi Kirkwood, a shop-keeper from London. They had set a date, and Nannie had made her wedding dress, gray silk with a sprinkling of red flowers, then lavished a week's wages from her job as a chambermaid on the shoes, fragile red silk with kid bottoms that would not survive half a dozen wearings. "I'll put them on for my wedding, then set them away and wear them again on our fiftieth anniversary. Then I'll be buried in them," she had told Ella.

And then on the day of the wedding, Levi sent word that he had changed his mind, that he cared for another. Nannie sold the dress. "What does a chambermaid need with a silk dress?" she asked. But she had saved the shoes, the wedding shoes. And she'd brought them with her to America. "I know I'm a bampot to bring them, what with the little we're allowed to take. But they don't weigh much, and they take up such a small space in the cart. Why, I could even carry them in my pocket or hang them around my neck," Nannie explained to Ella.

She did not know until she gathered with the other Saints in Iowa City that Levi Kirkwood and his bride, Patricia, had taken an earlier ship, had waited in Iowa to join the last emigrant train, and now they were part of the procession of carts that made up the Martin Company. Filled with anger and humiliation, Nannie hid her face in her apron when she first saw him in the camp and asked Ella, "Did ye know? I would not hae come." Ella shook her head, but Andrew turned away, and Nannie saw him look over at Levi, and she realized that Andrew had known. "How could ye?" she asked him, and Andrew replied that it was Levi's doing, not his.

"Do ye think he shouldna gather to Zion just because he—ye turned him down?" Andrew asked, repeating the bit of fiction the family had spread to save face for Nannie. "Zion is for the sinners amongst us, too."

"But I would hae waited until next year rather than cross with him."

"And done what, pushed a cart by yourself?" Andrew asked, and Nannie knew he was right. Although others had made the journey alone, she did not believe she could do it.

"Besides," Andrew added with gentleness, "Ella needs ye." And Nannie knew he was right about that, too.

When Andrew questioned the wisdom of putting the shoes into the cart while so many other things had had to be abandoned, Ella told him to hush. "We're allowed seventeen pounds each, and if Nannie wants the shoon in her poundage instead of tossed in the midden, who are we to say nay?"

The rigid weight limit was a surprise. The emigrants had known at the outset that there would be little room in the carts for their belongings and had been told to pack only what was necessary. Then when they arrived, they were informed that they could take even less than they had expected, just seventeen pounds for each adult, less for children. And the possessions would be weighed to make sure no one cheated. It was for their own good, the people were told. Once the journey was under way, they would be glad for every pound they didn't have to push across the prairie.

So the pioneers went through their things, casting aside precious items, selling them to the local people in Iowa City at a fraction of their worth or abandoning them at the campground. The sisters sold their small trunk for fifty cents, a bed quilt for a dime, their extra bonnets for a nickel. One of the missionaries accompanying the group paid Ella a quarter for her mirror, which was framed in gold. Then he put it into the supply wagon for the trip to the valley, and Ella brooded that the weight limit didn't apply to the church leaders. The mirror had been her prized possession, but she had no need to view herself each day after tramping across the prairie.

The sisters pared down their wardrobes, so that each had just three dresses, two for the journey and the third to wear for the handcart entrance into Great Salt Lake City, where they expected to be met by a brass band.

There was not much demand in Iowa City for the Saints' belongings, however, so what Ella and Nannie and the others couldn't sell was abandoned on the ground—clothing, china plates and copper pots, volumes of *Pilgrim's Progress* and *Robinson Crusoe,* an ear trumpet, a china dog, a warming pan, a bird-cage whose tiny door was open, as if the bird had been allowed to fly off; embroidered pillow slips and striped ticks that were already ripped open, their feathers blowing in the breeze. They might have burned the discarded treasure that the Gentiles of Iowa City were too parsimonious to purchase, but waste was not the Saints' way, and so they left their things in great piles to be scavenged.

Nannie glanced over at her sister, who was straining as they pushed the cart up a hill. Ella's face was red and wet from the exertion, and the back of her dress was stained with perspiration. The dress stretched across Ella's stomach, gently rounded now, and Nannie thought her sister's exhaustion was due more to pregnancy than from pushing the cart. She hoped the baby would not come before they reached Utah. "I'll push by myself awhile," Nannie told her sister. "Ye walk alongside."

"I'll do my part."

"Of course ye will. But there's no reason for both of us to push just now. We'll take turns. Ye walk for a time. Then we'll trade places." She glanced at her brother-in-law, his hands against the crossbar, propelling the cart, and whispered to Ella, "And if Andrew disna notice, we can both stop pushing." The sisters laughed.

Ella took her hands off the cart, examining a blister that had formed already on one palm. "When we stop tonight, I'll get out my gloves. My hands will be ruined by the time we reach the valley. And my clothes," she added, glancing down at the dark cotton of her dress. The sisters had hemmed their skirts to above their boots to keep them from dragging on the ground, but already, the hems were dirty. "I'll rest for only a minute. I'll catch up with ye." Ella sat down on the limb of a fallen tree.

Nannie centered herself in the back of the cart. The vehicle really was not difficult to push, and it rode easily along the rutted road. Other carts passed them, traveling alongside on the prairie grass, but Andrew kept to the trail, where the going was easier. He glanced back at Nannie and said over his shoulder, "That was good of you. The baby moves. Ella disna sleep well."

"She will tonight."

"Aye."

He turned back to the trail, and Nannie studied his narrow back and lean arms, his body as lanky as a coatrack. He had once been a strong lad, but years of working in a mill had weakened him, and she worried about his lungs. Still, she knew her sister's heart fluttered at the sight of him, for Andrew was blond and blue-eyed, a fine catch for any girl. He worked hard, too. She had to give him that, although he was a little too pompous, a little too self-important, too ready to make clear that he was the head of his household and would make the decisions. Well, what newly married husband wasn't? Ella asked when Nannie mentioned that Andrew seemed full of himself. Ella was right, of course, and after that, Nannie found Andrew's attitude more amusing than annoying. He was like a boy playacting his role as master of his home. Besides, Andrew loved her sister. He loved her so much that he'd promised Ella before they married that he would never take another wife.

The three of them knew about polygamy, had known about it before they agreed to go to Utah Territory. In 1853, not long after they joined the Church of Jesus Christ of Latter-day Saints, they learned that Joseph Smith had revealed to his people that the Lord had told Mormon men to take second and third wives. Some might have even more. The Lord Himself commanded it of His people, the prophet had said. After all, the patriarchs of old had been polygamous.

Ella and Nannie had been stunned and then disgusted when the news arrived in Scotland, had even considered leaving the church. "The Lord's way is never easy," one of the missionaries said after the young women shared their misgivings. "The Lord does not test us with a life of ease." So many more women than men had joined the church, and it was unfair to deny them husbands, he continued, and without a husband,

Ella and Nannie were told, a woman could not rise to the highest celestial kingdom. Besides, the missionary confided, only a select few of the Saints—mainly church leaders—practiced plural marriage, and most of them did it out of compassion, taking up women who were old and feeble. But Ella was not reassured, and when Andrew asked her to marry him, she hesitated, telling him she feared he might someday enter into celestial marriage.

Andrew was shocked—and then offended. The idea sickened him, too, he said. The two of them had known each other since they were children living in a small town not far from Edinburgh, and he had never imagined taking anyone else for a first wife, let alone a second. He told her, "We can be good Saints without living the principle." The *principle,* that was what it was called. "Look at the missionaries. They have only a single wife at home," he added. Still, Ella was fearful and had insisted they wait. Even on the day of the wedding, she was troubled, and so Andrew wrote in their Bible, "My wife is Ella Macintosh. I will take no other."

Nannie witnessed the declaration, and she knew that Andrew meant what he wrote, and that whatever his faults, he was a man to honor his promise.

He had been the first among them to join the Saints. Like the other villagers, the Macintoshes and the Bucks had attended the Presbyterian church, with its solemn worship and threats of a dour hereafter for the wicked, which included almost everyone. Then two Latter-day Saints missionaries called on Andrew and told him about the new American religion. The church's founder, the prophet Joseph Smith, had been singled out by the Lord to restore his gospel. In 1823, the angel

Moroni appeared to Joseph Smith, a poor farm boy in New York, telling him about the Book of Mormon, the story of an ancient people in America. Jesus had appeared to these believers nearly two thousand years before, but they had descended into wickedness and been destroyed. Four years after he saw the angel, young Smith was shown where the ancient record was hidden. He translated it and had it published in the spring of 1830.

Andrew learned that the prophet Joseph Smith had been martyred. Persecuted by men who coveted the Mormons' land and belongings, Smith's people had journeyed to Missouri and Illinois, pursued by *mobocrats,* as the Mormons called them, who beat them and burned their houses and farms. Eventually, these vengeful men murdered Joseph Smith and his brother Hyrum. The Mormons fled once again, under the leadership of Brigham Young.

Andrew smiled when he heard that part of the story, because he knew that without Young, the Mormons might have dispersed, dooming their new religion. Instead, the Lord Himself directed Young to lead the Saints across the Mississippi River and through Iowa Territory, and across the wide Missouri to a place they called "Winter Quarters." And then in 1847, Young and a few of his followers journeyed all the way to the Salt Lake Valley, which Young declared would be the new Zion. Now, not quite ten years later, the Saints had a kingdom in Utah Territory and tens of thousands of converts, most of them poor, many from the British Isles and Scandinavia, and, like Andrew, Ella, and Nannie, they were being gathered to Zion to join with the Lord's chosen.

Andrew had studied the Book of Mormon, had been

entranced with the story of the Saints, but even more, he had loved the joy of the new religion, the idea that he was blessed of God, and so he had been baptized. Ella joined the church not long afterward, along with the other members of the Buck and Macintosh families, all excepting Nannie, who worked in a hotel in Edinburgh and knew nothing about the missionaries at work in her town.

In fact, she did not know about the conversions at all until another maid told her that Nannie's family had joined the Saints. Nannie denied it and wrote her parents to warn them that vicious lies and rumors were being spread about them. "Ye must not come in contact with those vile Mormons for fear people will believe ye are amongst them. I write to warn ye that your reputation is in danger. Beware!"

And then she went home and discovered the truth for herself. "Ye, too, Ella?" she asked her sister, for the two had always been close. "Most of all, I canna stand it that ye are one of them."

"Ye don't know the blessedness of it. It's the pure religion our Lord founded so long ago, before it was fouled by the preachers with all their rules and rituals. Come to a service with us," Ella replied, and Nannie did so, if only to be better prepared to show her sister the error of her conversion. Ella introduced her to the shopkeeper-missionary Levi Kirkwood, an early British convert, who talked of going to America one day. After Levi told her about the teachings of the church, told her as the two walked the country lanes, Nannie, too, was baptized. The Holy Spirit had entered her, Nannie believed, although she might have been taken in a little by the youth and vibrancy of the missionary, so different from the gray-bearded patriarch of the local kirk.

At first, she was careful not to let anyone in Edinburgh learn of her conversion, but she was filled with such happiness that her friends in service at the hotel immediately knew something about her had changed. They wondered if she had become engaged, and indeed, Nannie had great hopes for a life with the young missionary, who told her he had been taken with her earnestness. She confided her desires to two or three girls, admitting to them that she had become a Mormon. Then a maid at the hotel discovered Nannie's secret and told on her. Nannie was summoned by the housekeeper, who said she would allow no Saint to work in the hotel, proselytizing and corrupting the other maids. "Renounce the Mormons or ye'll seek work elsewhere, my girl," she told Nannie.

Jobs were not easily found, but Nannie would not deny her religion. She saw the demand as the first test of her faith, and all but gloried in being dismissed, telling Levi that she'd starve rather than denounce her religion. He praised her for it, telling her he loved her for her pure and noble nature, and then he asked her to marry him.

Unlike her sister, Nannie did not ask her fiancé to promise in a Bible that he would not take a second wife. She believed he was too honorable to follow the principle. Now that she had found him to be false, Nannie wondered if he might turn out to be one of the polygamous ones after all. Perhaps it was better that he had abandoned her in Scotland instead of taking her to America, where one day, she would have had to share him with other women. Of course, she would not have made the trip with Andrew and Ella if she had known that Levi would be going to the valley with the handcart company. She would have stayed behind and come the following year or the year after that, when the rest of her family hoped to emigrate. But Andrew had wanted her to come, had said that she could help prepare a home in Zion for her parents. Ella, he told her, would need her.

Nannie and Levi had not exchanged a word since she discovered he was in Iowa City. She did not let her eyes linger on him if she spied him in a crowd, and because of that, she did not know if he looked at her. But she thought perhaps he did. At times, she felt someone staring at her, but that was foolishness. And so what if he did? He was married to another, a beautiful girl with golden curls, so very fine and fair, with skin as translucent as a butterfly's wing, but one who was clingy and childish and who did not appear to be up to the journey. While still in Iowa City, Nannie had heard Patricia whine about the hardships. And the real hardships, everyone knew, hadn't even begun.

Perhaps Levi was sorry he had married Patricia. And then Nannie had the appalling idea that Levi might be considering her for a second wife. The idea disgusted her, but she also found it amusing. She thought of how curtly she would turn him down if he asked. She would tell him she did not fancy half of a man—and half of a very poor man at that.

"I'll push now," Ella said, coming up behind Nannie, and because Nannie could see that the carts in front of the train had stopped and several of the Saints were already putting up tents, she agreed. "Ye were lost in thought. What were ye thinking?" Ella asked, taking Nannie's place at the back of the cart.

Nannie gave a bark of a laugh. "I was thinking, What if Levi Kirkwood asks me to be his second wife?"

"Nannie!"

16

Nannie shrugged. "Well, he might."

"Och! He might. That one will be amongst the first to live the principle, and, dare I say it, three times or four. Ye were right to leave him at the altar."

That fantasy about just who had forsaken whom at the altar had been repeated so many times by their family that Nannie wondered if her sister actually believed it. No, she decided, glancing around, her eyes stopping on Levi's wife's hair shining in the sun. No one would believe that.

Anne Sully could barely contain her annoyance when she saw that the carts in the front of the train had stopped and the men were putting up the tents. At the rate they were going, they wouldn't reach the Great Salt Lake until the back end of the year. She had waited for hours for the procession to begin, and now after such a short time, the people were quitting for the night. She and John and the children might just as well have spent the day in the Iowa City camp and caught up with the train in the morning. Now they would need to unpack the cart and build a fire, and she would have to prepare supper and mend Joe's pants, which the four-year-old had ripped in the first hour of the walk. And she ought to wash out the baby's dress, which was sour from where Lucy had spit up. The baby, nearly two years old, was blotchy and cranky from the heat and clung to Anne as she tried to go about her chores.

Anne herself, well along in her pregnancy, was tired and cranky, too. She marveled at the other women in her condition who appeared oblivious to the hardships. So many women of child-bearing age seemed to be pregnant, and those who were not had babes at the breast. She was humiliated at having to push the cart like some beast of burden. With every step, she expected someone to cry out "Gee" or "Haw." Her ankles were swollen and she was afraid she had the beginning of one of the headaches that had plagued her since she was a child. Walking in the dust and heat the next day with the pounding in her temple and the churning in her stomach would be unbearable. On the trail, she had held her handkerchief across her mouth and then a scarf to keep out the dirt that the handcarts and ox-drawn wagons accompanying the Saints threw up, but they had made breathing more difficult. Lucy wouldn't be the only one to vomit. There were wagons for the sick, but Anne was too proud to ride among the toothless old people, their minds as brittle as the dry prairie grass, who babbled about how blessed they were to be going to the Promised Land. Besides, who knew what she might pick up and give to her children, sicknesses from the dirty urchins whose families had joined the Mormon Church. She had reason enough to fear their illnesses.

"A good day's start. We travel first-rate," John said. The obvious excitement he had felt all day now that the handcart migration was under way seemed to have turned into a sense of satisfaction, and he appeared oblivious to his wife's ill humor. "It wasn't so hard, was it now, Annie?" He put his arm around his wife's waist, and despite her annoyance, Anne leaned against him, feeling glad for his strength. He didn't understand her feelings. He never would understand them.

Now, looking at her husband, Anne sensed that all he felt just then was the joy of going to Zion, just like those other demented Saints. If she complained about the trek, he would tell her she was better off than most, and she was. Many of the women, some with six or eight children or even more, were widows, with no men to help them push their carts. But if she were a widow, she wouldn't have come to America at all, would she? She would be at home with her children. She wouldn't be making this ghastly trip across the snuff-colored plains.

Anne put those thoughts from her mind. She and John had argued until she was worn-out, had argued until the day they boarded the ship, and what good had it done? Besides, she had agreed to come on this journey to America, so she must share the blame, although what choice had she had? Only the choice of joining the emigrants or staying home in London with her children—and maybe without them, because John had threatened to take them along. His mind had been made up. He was going to America despite her pleas. Would he really have taken the children? Anne had asked herself that question a hundred times before they left Liverpool and again on the long trip by ship and by train to Iowa City. She didn't know the answer. Could she have stopped him from leaving with the little ones? No, she knew she couldn't have. John might have left her with the girls, but he would have taken Joe. John was as stubborn as the missionaries themselves when he made up his mind about a thing. Just look at the way he had defied her to embrace this strange new religion.

Before he met the missionaries, John had never been much for churchgoing. He had attended the Church of England, but that was to please her and especially to please her father. John had been employed in the fashionable gentlemen's clothing shop in London that Anne's father owned. At first, he had stitched on the coats and pants and jackets, but he had a way with the patrons, and in time, he'd begun measuring the dukes and earls and even members of the royal family who summoned him to their homes. The clients liked John's amiable manner, his suggestions for fashions that made them appear a little thinner, a little taller. He convinced Anne's father to stock accessories and at a huge markup, as well as form an alliance with a boot maker, who paid for referrals. The shop prospered, and so did John, who married his boss's daughter.

It might have been a marriage of convenience for both of them. The connection certainly was a step up for John and a way to ensure that someday he would take over the shop. For Anne, whose outspokenness and lack of deference to men brought her few suitors, it was a marriage to a temperate and ambitious man and one far handsomer than a plain woman like her deserved. A big man, John had thick black hair brushed back off his broad forehead, a trim mustache, and steel blue eyes, while Anne had a fulsome figure and a placid face that belied her intelligence. Her hair, too light to be brown, too dark to be blond, was so lank that she could only part it in the middle and pull it back into a knot.

But, in fact, the marriage had been a love match between two people who were as complementary to each other as any young couple could be. When the father died, leaving the shop to John, as was proper, the husband told Anne the establishment belonged equally to her. He appreciated her intellect and business acumen and the way she took over the bookkeeping, sending out bills and gentle reminders, ordering materials, haggling with tradesmen and suppliers. Together, they redecorated the shop with dark paneling and gilt embellishments, added a fireplace and comfortable chairs, and offered whiskey and sherry. They set aside a small room where servants and drivers could sit over a cup of tea, instead of waiting outside in the weather. The patrons appreciated the cozy atmosphere, and their attendants, grateful for the rare courtesy the shop offered, took to flattering their employers in their new clothes. Within two years of inheriting the shop, the two had doubled its business. Even after their children came, Anne continued working with her husband, hiring a nurse to care for the little ones upstairs in the rooms they lived in over the shop.

It had been a wonderful eight years, Annie reflected, as she unloaded the cart. At least it had been until the missionaries came into the shop and took advantage of them. One of the men had ripped his coat and stopped to ask for a bit of thread and the loan of a needle. They were so young, so earnest, and the place was deserted that afternoon. So Anne asked John if he would mend the coat himself while she fixed them a tea. And John, good-hearted as he was, agreed. Oh, if only she had given them needle and thread and sent them on their way! Better that a till frisker had entered the shop and taken their money! Anne wondered later if the Mormon had marked John as a potential convert and torn his coat on purpose, because as John stitched, the men devoured her scones and talked about their religion. When they left, they invited John to attend a service.

"Not likely," Anne retorted as she collected the plates, on which not so much as a crumb was left.

"Oh, I don't know. I admit to being intrigued with what they said, and they are such likable fellows. What harm is there in going? If you're right, we can laugh about it later. Won't you come?"

"I am as I was made. You know right well I do not go in foolishness," she replied.

So John had attended the meeting without her, for Anne would have none of it. He had gone back a second time and a third, and Anne discovered the Book of Mormon in a drawer in which John kept trimmings. "Surely you'll not waste your time reading it when there is work to be done," she said.

"I wish you would come with me and listen to them," John replied. "I would value your opinion. Their religion throws off the ecclesiastical trappings of the church and lets the Mormons deal directly with God."

So because she wanted to quash her husband's interest in the new religion (and because she was easily flattered when her husband mentioned her intelligence, which she knew was her greatest asset), she went with him to the service.

"What did you think?" he asked as they walked home.

"The people are nice enough," she replied after a time, and held her tongue so that she did not add, "the deceivers."

"They are. I thought you might like it that the women participate more than they do in the old church," he said. "But what about the religion?"

"There is naught to it."

"You didn't feel the spirit?"

"'The spirit'? Surely you aren't serious. If there is a spirit in those people, it is one of fraud."

"How can you say that?" John stopped under a gaslight and looked Anne in the face.

She could see his disappointment, but she would not be stopped. "You can't believe their story about God giving a poor American farmer seer stones to read golden plates! It's a fairy tale. I've never heard anything so preposterous."

"Is it any more preposterous than God giving Moses stone tablets with the Ten Commandments written on them?"

"That's different."

"How so?"

"Moses is in the Bible. Mormonism is foolishness, and I want no part of it." And she refused to have anything more to do with the sect.

But not so John. Despite Anne's disdain, John continued to attend the services, and one evening he returned elated, saying that he had been baptized in the church. "The Church of Jesus Christ of Latter-day Saints has complete possession of me," he announced.

"They have snared your soul? You are a *Mormon*?" Anne cried. "Against my will?"

"It is God's will."

"It is demagoguery." They argued over his decision, John begging Anne to join and save her soul, and Anne ordering John to quit the church for fear of losing his. But after a time, they wore themselves out with the fighting, and they agreed to say no more about Mormonism. John would continue to attend services but would no longer expect Anne to go with him.

That had been an uneasy truce, but one that Anne could live with. Sooner or later, John would see on his own that the religion was rubbish and give it up. But that had not happened. In fact, John began to neglect his duties in the shop to meet with the Saints and even drove away patrons with his proselytizing. She warned him to keep his religion to himself or lose the business. And then one night after supper, after the children were in bed, John sat down with her and took her hands. "I have made an important decision that affects us all," he told her.

She could not imagine what he was talking about. They had turned the business into a great success, despite John's recent lack of interest, and the two of them had talked about enlarging the shop, acquiring a new location or perhaps expanding it into their living quarters and moving the family to a new home. Anne wondered if John had found a house for them, hoping that was the case, for she was house-proud and did not want to live forever over the shop. She smiled and waited, thinking that not every husband was as solicitous of his wife and family. This was like the earlier days of their marriage, when John had burst with ideas for their future, telling them to her as they sat in front of the little grate in their parlor. "Well?" she asked when he didn't continue.

"We are going to America," John blurted out. "We are going to the Salt Lake Valley. Brigham Young has called the Mormons to gather in Zion." He trembled with excitement.

"We are *what*?" Anne asked, barely able to comprehend what her husband had said.

"The Lord has called us."

"Not my Lord. He hasn't called me." She could not stop herself from asking, "Are you mad, John?"

He was taken aback. "You'll like it. Wait and see. It will be a good life, where we won't be attacked for our beliefs."

"*You* won't be attacked. I believe no such thing."

"You'll come around after you get to know them. They are holy people."

"I *won't* get to know them. I have no use for Mormons. They're troublemakers. See how they've come between us. This is foolish talk. I'll have none of it."

"It's too late. I've agreed to go."

"Tell them you've changed your mind."

"No."

Anne was stunned and stood up and paced, going to and again over the carpet. That carpet, a good ingrain one, had been installed not long before the missionaries entered the shop, and Anne had thought then that she could want for nothing more. She had a beautiful home filled with treasures, a good husband and children, and they would be adding to the family in the fall. Anne put her hand on her stomach, where the tiny bit of life was growing. "When?" she asked.

"This year. We embark before the end of May."

"May! That's only a month hence!" Anne put her hands over her face and thought, and after a moment, she realized there was a way out. "Surely we can't leave when I am in this condition, John. You know how hard it goes for me. We must wait until next year."

"Other women in your state have made the journey. America is a healthy place. And we will be in the Salt Lake Valley before your time. Think of it, Anne. This child will be born in Zion."

"You would force me to go when I am like this?" She was incredulous that her husband would not take her fears into consideration, would make such a decision without consulting her, without accounting for her feelings. It galled her, too, that he believed she would embrace the religion once they got to America.

John looked down and studied the coals that glowed in the little grate. "No, Anne. I would not force you to go. You can stay here if you like. But I will go."

"You would desert me?"

"I'd go on ahead to prepare our home. You could come later."

"By myself? But why must you leave so soon? Stay here one year, and if you are still of a mind to go, I'll give in to you." A year, she thought, would be time enough for her to convince him that the new religion was a humbug.

"I cannot stay." He took a breath, and without looking at his wife, he added, "I have sold the shop."

Anne's face went white, and she sank onto a stool, because her legs were too weak for her to stand. "No, you would not have done that. You are just threatening me."

"I've signed the papers."

"But you can't have done so. The shop is half mine."

"It was mine alone. Your father left it to me."

"Left it to you so that you could take care of me. You said it yourself, that we owned it equally."

"It was in my name," he said stubbornly.

The truth of that stung Anne, and she doubled over, putting her face in her hands, but she did not weep. She never wept. Instead, she rocked back and forth, until John knelt on the floor beside her. "Give it a try, Annie. If you don't like it after a year, I'll bring you back here. It won't be so bad, I promise. There is enough money to buy a good wagon and teams of oxen. You'll be able to take your things—your silver and china, your dresses, the dresser that was your mother's, the Persian carpets. We'll be as comfortable as if we were riding in a railway car, and they say the Salt Lake Valley is as beautiful as the Alps. The children will grow up in sunlight and fresh air instead of in a city filled with smoke and rubbish."

She looked up at John but didn't speak, and he continued: "The people are the best I've ever known. In time, you'll see for yourself. You don't have to join the church. I won't insist on it. There may be others going who aren't Mormons."

For days, they talked of nothing else, sometimes pleading with each other, sometimes threatening. They argued over whether the children would go, how much money John would give Anne if she stayed in London. Anne asked how he would drive a team of oxen when he had never even saddled a horse, how he would earn his living once they reached the valley, for surely there was little need for tailors there. John countered each objection by replying that God would help him.

At last, Anne grew too weary to argue. With the shop gone, there was no way she could support herself and the children. And with a baby on the way, she would not be able to find employment, even if she had the skills to work, which she did not. Few tailoring shops needed a woman to manage them. So she gave in. "Not willingly, John, not willingly," she told him.

He had been grateful, solicitous, had told her he would do everything to ensure her comfort. She could pack her feather bed, her pillows, her blankets and shawls, the carpets, the trunks. He would buy her a sewing machine to take with them, for surely America did not have them, and he would fit up a bed for her in the wagon so that she could ride whenever she was tired. But nothing could assuage her dread.

They embarked on May 25 from Liverpool, sailing on the packet ship *Horizon* with a horde of poor converts from the factories and mines, their belongings tied up in bundles. The passengers crowded onto the ship, waving their ragged handkerchiefs at friends onshore who had come to see them off. During the voyage, Anne kept her three children close to her, but at times, Emma Lee, who was six, and sometimes Joe slipped off to play. When Anne complained to John that the children were liable to catch some disease, he soothed her. "It's no more dangerous for them than if they were at home. Besides, they have the sea air to breathe." But Anne was not convinced.

The ship was crowded. The five of them slept in a bunk no larger than a small bed at home. To her surprise, Anne found the expedition was well organized. The elders scheduled times for the women to prepare meals of salt pork and boiled beef, hard sea biscuit, oatmeal, peas, beans, rice, and tea, so there was no jostling or arguing over space in the tiny galley. In fact, there was little arguing at all, and that surprised Anne even more. The people were sharing, joyful. They felt blessed that the Lord was sending them to America, away from the filth and decay, the disease and starvation of their homelands, and they did not complain about the cramped accommodations, the rolling ship that kept many in their beds with seasickness. Each morning and evening, they gathered to praise the Lord and sing. The ship's captain told them he had never sailed with a finer group, that he would always be happy to transport Mormons. Anne had to admit that the Saints were good people, and kind—the women, especially.

"I had my doubts, too," Catherine Dunford, a convert from Glasgow, said after discovering that Anne had not accepted the doctrine. Catherine had befriended Anne, offering to loan her a tiny volume of poems she'd brought along, a book that Anne later saw lying in a pile of discarded items in Iowa City. "I thought it was nonsense, all that talk about Jesus preaching to the Indians. But the spirit came over me and told me it was the true religion, the one Jesus Himself started. I pray the spirit will move ye, too."

Anne murmured something unintelligible, hoping the woman would stop, because she did not care to be preached at, but Catherine would not be stilled. "Myself, I thought it was all the strangest thing ever I heard. I don't question that ye doubt. For the longest time, I wanted to embrace the faith, for my husband had, and he's a brilliant man. I thought maybe there was something wrong with me. It was only after I stopped trying to believe that the Lord called to me. He did indeed reach out for me. The faith isnae something you accept with your head, but with your heart."

"It is idiotic. I despise it," Anne blurted out.

The words did not shock the woman. "I am not surprised at your remarks, Sister Sully. You and your little ones have been taken from your home and are going to a country filled with savages. Since ye are not a believer, ye must hate your husband for it. I advise ye to rest your mind for a while. Do not grieve over your loss, but look on it as an adventure. And do not worry over your lack of faith. If God intends to make ye a Mormon, He will find a way. I won't speak of it further."

"You will be the only one."

Catherine laughed. "Yes, we do preach, don't we? It is

because we find such happiness in our religion that we want to share it with others."

"But I don't understand why you can't be happy with it in Scotland."

"Because the millennium is near upon us. It is in us to want to be collected to Zion. Every loyal Saint wants to go to the Salt Lake Valley."

Later, when John pressed her, as he had repeatedly since they boarded the ship, to consider joining the church, Anne repeated the woman's words: "If God wants me to become a Mormon, He, not you, will tell me."

The voyage was not a difficult one, with only a little rough weather, and Anne was entranced with the endless sea rolling around her, with the solitude of it, even though she was surrounded by noisy converts. When her children played or napped, she stood at the railing of the ship, watching the waves break around her, marveling at their power to move the ship. She liked staying on deck even when it rained, feeling the drops of water roll over her. Once during a storm, after she had taken cover and was watching the foam that was tossed about in the waves, she saw the sailors raise a sail and listened as one yelled, "Hoist higher."

"Higher," the men called to one another across the noise of the wind, "higher."

An old woman who was nearly deaf heard the shout and cried out, "Fire! Fire!"

A fire was what passengers feared most on a ship, and the Mormons ran out onto the deck, crying out to one another, looking for water buckets, only to learn there was no fire at all, only an order to hoist higher. Despite the panic, Anne found the situation comical, and she could not help thinking what fools the Mormons were.

One night midway through the voyage, she was awakened by Emma Lee, who slept beside her on the cramped bunk, as the girl tossed about and whimpered in her sleep. Anne reached over to still the child and discovered Emma Lee's forehead was as hot as a stovetop. She picked up the sleeping child and carried her out onto the deck, thinking the sea air would cool her. But the child began to cough and cry a little. "Wake up, Emma Lee," Anne said to the six-year-old, thinking the girl might have had a bad dream. But the child would not wake.

Anne found water and, using the hem of her nightdress, rubbed it on the child's forehead, but that did nothing to cool her. "Precious girl, wake for Mama," Anne whispered. She shook the child a little, but Emma Lee did not respond. Frightened now, Anne asked a man who was standing on the deck, looking out at the ocean, to stay with her daughter while she fetched her husband, then slipped back into the bowels of the ship to find John. He followed her to the deck and picked up the stricken girl, calling, "Emma Lee! Emma Lee!"

The man on deck disappeared and returned a few moments later with two elders. One of them, a physician, reached out and took the child, looked into her eyes and mouth, examined her chest. "We must bring down the fever. My wife will help." He nodded at a woman who had joined them. Without being told what to do, the woman fetched a pail of water and some cloths and began to sponge Emma Lee.

"I'll do it," Anne said.

"Then I'll pray," the woman told her, kneeling on the deck.

The men, along with John, got down on their knees beside the woman, and although she felt the prayers of Mormons carried no special weight with God, Anne nonetheless was touched by the earnestness of these strangers. In a few minutes, a dozen of the Saints, some in their nightclothes, were kneeling beside Emma Lee, asking the Lord to spare her.

One told Anne that she had saved an apple, which was stored in her trunk. "It might cool her throat. Would she eat it?" Anne shook her head, replying that the child was not con- scious. Another brought a bottle of cologne and poured it onto the girl's wrists, hoping to soothe her. Someone pushed Anne aside and told her to rest while she sponged the child.

Catherine came on deck and gave Anne a cup of water, and when Anne said she must check on Joe and Lucy, her friend told her that someone was already caring for the two children. "Has she been anointed?" Catherine asked. Anne looked dumbly at the woman, not understanding. "Anointed with oil. 'Tis our way. The elders must administer the ordinances."

Anne looked up at John, who nodded solemnly. "We must do it."

"Does that mean she's going to die?"

"Her life is in the Lord's hands."

Anne had never participated in such a ceremony before, and she watched dumbly as an elder took out a vial of oil, dipped his fingers into it, then touched them to Emma Lee's forehead. On board the ship, Anne had heard elders prophesy, knew they told those who were sick that they would not die but would live to reach the valley, and she prayed that someone would tell her that Emma Lee would be all right, but no one spoke. When the elders were finished, Anne sat down on the deck beside her daughter, taking Emma Lee's hand, and promised the Lord that if He let the child live, Anne would join the Mormon Church. If God would perform such a miracle, then surely that was the sign she needed to embrace the faith.

But there was no miracle. Emma Lee did not regain consciousness. She lay on a pallet on the deck all day while Anne and John fanned her and others took turns washing the girl with cool water. At dusk, Emma Lee died. She did not take a deep breath and expire. There was no rattling in her throat. She simply breathed her last and was still. At first, Anne was not aware that the girl was gone. The breathing had been so weak that she did not realize Emma Lee no longer took a breath. She did not know until John said softly, "It is over," and tried to raise Anne to her feet.

But Anne would not get up. Instead, she moaned and fell across the child's body, calling to Emma Lee to awaken, calling God to bring back her daughter. John tried to raise her, but Anne was deadweight in his arms, so he let her lie beside the girl, standing over her, tears streaming down his face. The other women attempted to comfort her, saying that Emma Lee's death was God's will and that the girl had gone to a better place. Anne did not reply, only thought that her daughter's death was not God's will at all but John's and that if they had stayed in London, Emma Lee would indeed be in a better place.

At last, Catherine sat down beside her and took Anne's hand in her own. "We must prepare the body," she said. And then as if she understood what Anne was thinking, Catherine added, "Ye must not blame him. He is fast bound in misery like ye. His heart bleeds, too. Let him comfort ye."

So Anne stood up and let John put his arms around her.

She reached up and wiped his tears with her fingers and nodded when he said, "I am sorry." His grief must be even greater than hers, she realized, because he would blame himself for the decision to go to America. But that thought did not comfort her.

There was a ceremony, with the Saints crowded around them, murmuring words of sorrow, and then the child was wrapped in sacking and placed on a board. The board was propped against the railing, and the little body slid into the dark sea. At first, Anne thought the little girl would float in the water, would bump against the ship and maybe even follow in its wake, but weights had been tied to her feet, and the body slipped under the waves.

The Saints dispersed, but Anne stood by the rail, staring at the spot where her daughter's body had disappeared, stared at it as the ship moved along, and after a while she could not be sure she was looking at the right place. She stood there a long time, thinking she might see some sign of Emma Lee, a ray of sunshine through the clouds, a dove rising from the ocean, but there was no sun. Nor were there doves in the middle of the sea. At last, John led her back belowdeck, whispering that Joe and Lucy needed her. "Think of your other children," he said. Anne turned away and could never look at the sea again without seeing her daughter's body sink into its depths.

Perhaps it was for the best that they were moving to America, Anne thought afterward. She could never go back to London without Emma Lee. A new country, a new life were what they needed to deal with the death of the child. And so she began to look forward to arriving in Boston, to moving ahead instead of going back. She talked to the children about the journey across the prairie, and although Lucy was too young to understand, Joe was thrilled to think he would ride in a covered wagon. Anne promised that he could name the oxen. "I'll call one Emma Lee—the prettiest one," he said, and Anne closed her eyes in grief at the tribute to her daughter.

She knew that the other emigrants would travel with handcarts, but not until after they docked in Boston and had begun the train trip to Iowa City did John take her aside and tell her about his decision. "It is not fair for us to journey to the valley in a wagon when others will push the carts," he began.

Anne looked at him a long time but did not reply.

"The cost of the wagon and teams will pay for a dozen handcarts."

"What are you saying?"

"I do not believe we can ride to Zion in a wagon like some potentate while our brothers and sisters walk."

"What have you done, John? Are you telling me that we ought to push a handcart so that we can loan our money to the others?"

John looked away. "Not quite."

"What, then?"

John took her hands. "I've given the money to the elders. They asked for it. We have so much, and the others have nothing."

"You *what*?" Anne looked at him incredulously.

"You heard what I said."

"You gave away our money! It wasn't yours to give. My father left it to us so that we could have a better life."

"And we will. Wait until we reach the valley."

"You had no right," Anne said.

"I have every right. As I have told you, the shop was left to me. If you would only try to understand—"

"Don't you think I have tried? Don't you think I've asked God why He sent us here, why He took Emma Lee?" Her throat constricted when she said her daughter's name.

"He's trying us."

"You maybe, but not Emma Lee. What right does He have to try Emma Lee?"

"It's not our place to question."

Anne looked around at the Saints in the railway car, those placid, happy people who, like John, accepted everything as the will of the Lord. She clenched her hands and thought she would not cry, would not let anyone see her distress. "And how will we return to London?"

John looked at her quizzically.

"You promised that if I didn't like Utah after a year, we could go back." When John did not reply, Anne knew he hadn't meant the promise. "I see," she said.

"Mama, look at the cows," Joe said, distracting her. The boy pointed out the door when the train stopped. "Are those like the cows that will pull our wagon?"

Anne turned to John, telling him to explain to their son that they wouldn't be going in a wagon. "We've decided to pull a handcart," John told Joe. "You and I will pull, and Mama will push, and Lucy will ride on top."

"We will be the oxen ourselves," Anne muttered, but John ignored her. "We will walk across America."

"Can I ride, too, if I get tired?" Joe asked.

"Of course."

"What about Mama? What if she gets tired?"

John looked at Anne, as if he had not thought about that, and she touched her swollen belly. "There will be wagons for the sick to ride in," he told her softly.

Anne wanted to reply that she was not sick, only pregnant, but too much bitterness had passed between them. She knew that she had no choice other than to push a handcart to Utah. She was pregnant, the mother of two small children, and their money was gone. She was dependent on John for everything, and she must make the best of it all. She must swallow her anger. "We will manage," she said.

John took her hand and whispered, "I will make it up to you. I love you, Annie."

Anne was grateful he did not bring up God's will again.

Anne's decision to keep her anger in check had been sorely tried in the days that followed. When they reached Iowa City, they discovered the carts were not ready and that the men had to make them from green wood, a job that put off their departure for three weeks. Anne was vexed, because the delay meant there was no chance they would arrive in the valley before the baby was born. She would not have even the privacy of a wagon, but would have to deliver the child on the prairie, in the shade of a handcart. She had already seen the prairie, so different from the lushness of England.

Just as disappointing was the order that emigrants would be allowed to take no more than seventeen pounds of possessions with them. So she discarded the rug that had been her mother's and sold the sewing machine they had brought for their home in Great Salt Lake City, both items that could have fit into a wagon but not a handcart. Then she abandoned a trunk of clothing, curtains, her books, the Delft plates, and a crystal castor. When that was not enough, she put aside Emma Lee's toys, because she knew there was no room in the cart for sentiment. Her two living children came first, and she must use the small amount of space for their necessities. She had hoped to save Emma Lee's wooden doll, the girl's prized possession. She and John had bought it for the Christmas Emma Lee turned five, and Anne had stitched clothes for it—a ball gown, a traveling dress. Emma Lee herself had made the apron and put it on the doll for the ocean voyage.

On the day before they left Iowa City, Anne, her hands shaking, set the last remembrance of her beloved daughter on a pile of clothing, hoping that some little girl would find it and love it as much as Emma Lee had. Catherine came up beside Anne to place her own discards on the pile. "It was Emma Lee's," Anne explained, her voice breaking. "I've packed and repacked the cart, but there is no place for it."

"What a pity."

"It's only a toy." But no, she thought. It was so much more than a toy.

Catherine bent and picked up the doll, examining the exquisite stitching in the dress, the crude stitches in the apron. "Such a lovely doll. What is her name?"

"Clara."

"Well, I believe I can find a place for Clara in my cart. Your other daughter shall have her when we get to the valley." Anne looked at her friend wordlessly, for she was too distraught to speak, and Catherine turned away.

Anne stared at the heap of discarded items for a long time. Then her eyes focused on the tiny book of poems that Catherine had placed there, and Anne picked it up and put it into her own pocket.

The following day, Anne spotted Catherine among the Saints waiting to begin the trek, and her heart filled with gratitude for this new friend. She felt her spirits rise a little as she thought of the kindness of other Saints. They might not be her people, but they were her husband's, and, like it or not, she had thrown in with them. She let herself feel a tiny thrill of wonder as the carts began to move forward and the people called out their praise. And when a woman she had seen on the ship, a woman who had cared for Emma Lee that last day, called out to her, Anne replied, "We're off to the Salt Lake indeed!" And then she thought how foolish she sounded. Of course, they were off to Salt Lake—the Mormon Zion. Where else would they be going?

Chapter 2

August 18, 1856

The hard rain that had plagued the Saints throughout the day, turning the prairie into ankle-deep mud, seemed to be stopping. At least Louisa Tanner hoped it was, because she was wet and chill and had the beginnings of a cold in her chest. She arched her back in hopes of relieving the soreness, as she and her father, Hall Chetwin, waded through the brown muck that stuck to the wheels of their cart. The bed of the cart was heavy with clothing, blankets, and cooking utensils. Louisa's sister, Huldah, pushed it, while their mother, Margaret, shuffled behind, shivering under her soaked shawl, the knitting she worked as she walked along shoved into her pocket now. All of them were drenched by the cold rain and exhausted from pushing the cart through the mud and sand that sucked at the wheels. Thales Tanner, Louisa's husband, who had gone on ahead, turned to scrutinize the little group.

Louisa, her yellow hair plastered to her tiny face by the

lashing rain, caught his eye and sent a mute plea for help. Instead, he gave her a nod and a tight-lipped smile of encouragement. She knew he had responsibilities beyond his wife and her people. He had told her so. Others in his hundred needed him more than the family, who would have to harden themselves if they expected to reach the valley, he'd said. Louisa had bowed her head in acceptance. She wished Thales was more understanding, but nonetheless, she was proud to be the wife of such a man of God.

Louisa knew her husband was someone of standing among the 625 emigrants who had departed from Iowa City on the journey west. Not all who had left England on the ship *Horizon* were continuing on to Great Salt Lake City. Others assigned to the handcarts had stayed behind, too sick to continue or frightened that the company's late start would mean traveling in foul weather, and they had remained in the East. A few had deserted in Iowa. Some had even abandoned the Saints on the trail. Good riddance to them—to all the deserters, Thales had told Louisa. The dropouts were too weak, too worldly to reach Zion. Only those who truly believed would be blessed with the Promised Land. The others deserved to be cast by the wayside. Although Louisa sympathized with those who pleaded age or sickness, Thales was unmoved. "The honest of heart will be assembled and the tares left in the field," he told her. She was glad that none of those who'd turned their backs on the church was a Saint whom her husband personally had converted during his mission in England. All of Thales Tanner's converts stood firm, including Louisa's family, although they might have wavered without his guidance.

Louisa knew, of course, that Thales would help any who

needed him, but those assigned to him were his especial responsibility. The Mormons were divided into groups of one hundred, with each hundred under the direction of a captain. She was proud that Thales, as one of the missionaries who had come from the valley, had been asked to captain one of the hundreds. He was charged not only with enforcing rules that governed the company but with looking after the elderly and sick, overseeing the tents and provisions that were in the wagon assigned to his group, settling disagreements and quarrels, and helping those whose carts broke down along the trail. Only two weeks out from Iowa City, the carts were beginning to fall apart. As the green wood dried, it shrank, causing wheels to break, axles to come loose. These people, these converts who had worked in factories and mills, Thales told Louisa, knew nothing about repairing carts, and they needed his assistance.

They were ill-prepared in other ways, she knew. So many were from slums and had worked in the dank factories, and they had no experience of the outdoors, had never slept on the ground, were not used to walking long distances. Some were old and in ill health, their lungs congested from years of living in the damp and smoke of Europe's cities. They would have had a hard time of it even if they'd been in wagons. Now, they were expected to walk thirteen hundred miles, pushing the laden carts, and some could not keep up. Louisa had passed them on the trail. Already, there were those who did not arrive in camp until after evening prayers. Even without Thales telling her so, she suspected that not all of the converts would live to reach Zion.

Louisa and her father stopped their cart beside Thales, who had paused to help an old man whose conveyance was stuck in the wet sand. "You pull. I'll push," Thales told Robert Amos, taking his place with the wife, Maud, and a young couple behind the cart. When the vehicle was free, Robert said, "We asked God for help, and you came along. Truly, He listens to our prayers."

Louisa's heart swelled when Maud took Thales's hands and asked, "Is it true you knew Joseph?"

"I did," Thales said, affecting the attitude of humility he showed whenever he was asked the question. Louisa knew the truth was that her husband had not really *known* the prophet. He had been only sixteen when Joseph Smith was murdered, but he had seen Joseph in town, in church, had doffed his hat to the prophet and in return had been greeted by name. Well, actually, it was his brother's name, Thales once admitted to Louisa, but many others got the two mixed up, too.

Louisa never ceased to be thrilled when her husband told the story of the Tanners' early conversion, how they had followed Joseph from place to place until they ended up in Nauvoo, Illinois, where Thales's father was a stonemason working on the temple. After Joseph's death, Thales's father and others labored to finish the temple so that the Mormons could use it to perform the sacred rituals they called "endowments," before they were driven west across the Mississippi. At a meeting to select Joseph's successor, the elder Tanner spoke up for Brigham Young, and later, the Tanner family had camped with the new leader at Winter Quarters in Iowa, where the Saints waited before the push to the Great Salt Lake. If the elder Tanner was anything like his son, Louisa thought, his voice would have sounded like the prophets of old.

She was proud to learn that in 1847, Thales, then twenty,

had been among those select few chosen to accompany Brother Brigham on that first trip into the Salt Lake Valley. Even the converts in the handcart company knew Thales's family was Mormon royalty, and Thales himself a crown prince. After all, Brother Brigham had once given him a blessing that foretold Thales would rise to the highest level of the kingdom.

And Louisa would be beside him!

When Louisa first heard an English convert ask, "Did you know Joseph?" she observed that her husband was uneasy and said the two had been only acquaintances. But she, like others, believed that Thales was being modest. She had been thrilled to meet someone who had walked with the prophet. That connection gave him an air of authority, and it was natural that the converts, Louisa included, were awed. With gentle eyes and a soft voice, she pleaded to know more. She would have loved Thales if he had never seen Joseph Smith, but his closeness to the church founder raised his esteem among Louisa and her people. He had not expected to take a wife among the converts, he told her when he proposed marriage, but he had been smitten at once by Louisa's sweet oval face, the bloom of youth still on her, and her manifest faith. Besides, he'd confided, he was twenty-eight years old, and a man, even a man of God, had his needs.

"It's true, then. I had heard so," Maud, the woman at the cart, said. "You did know Joseph."

"Bless you, Sister," Thales replied, turning away before Maud could ask for details, for stories. The questioning could go on for hours.

Maud reached out a hand, touched his sleeve, but Thales did not stop. He turned back to Louisa, who said, "Father cannot push farther. You must help." Thales appeared annoyed, but he shoved the older man aside and joined his wife behind the crossbar. They did not have far to go, and Louisa was grateful Thales was there, because they would need his help in setting up the campfire. Despite the days on the trail, Louisa's family did a poor job of it. Louisa was not such a good cook, and she could barely manage over an outdoor fire. Her mother and sister were no better.

Pushing their way past the carts that had bogged down in the thick mud, which made every step an effort, Louisa and Thales came upon her two nephews, Dick and Jimmy, eleven and eight, the sons of Louisa's widowed sister, Huldah Rowley. As they walked along, the two boys had played a game with sticks, pushing a rock back and forth to each other and laughing. They were young, still children, but old enough to help, and Thales let go of the crosspiece and grabbed the two by their shirt collars, propelling them along. "Where have you been? There will be no idle hands while I am in charge of this family. You are shirkers. You could stand a good hiding."

Dick, the older boy, stood in front of his brother, as if to protect him in case Thales made good on his threat. "It's all right, Jimmy," he whispered.

Louisa thought to protest that the two were only boys, but Thales had made it clear from the beginning that she was not to question him. Besides, there would be hard work for them to do once they reached Utah. Thales had told her he was serving the boys well by insisting they do their chores now. He was a hard taskmaster, but he never asked a member of Louisa's family or any other Saint to work harder than he did himself. She believed that it was Thales's hard work, along with his faith and his practical bent, that had caused him to be chosen a leader of one of the hundreds.

"We can park the Tanner cart over there," Dick said, pointing to a vacant spot under a tree. By rights, it ought to have been called the Chetwin cart, for Louisa's father, who was head of the family, but Hall Chetwin deferred to Thales now, and rightly so, Louisa knew. Hall had been so humiliated by the incident in New York that he had let Thales take charge. They all—the sister, the in-laws, the nephews, and Louisa most of all—considered Thales Tanner to be their leader.

Thales ordered the boys to unload the cart, then walked off, saying he must see to his hundred. As soon as he was gone, Louisa shooed the boys away, telling them to go and play but to be careful that Brother Tanner should not see them.

Louisa and her family had arrived in America well ahead of other members of the Martin Company. They had embarked from Liverpool in December on the *John Boyd* with an earlier group of converts, landing in New York City in February. Thales, who had been called back to America the previous year, not to the valley but to Iowa to help with the handcarts, was to reunite with them in Iowa City for the last of the handcart treks to the valley that year.

The trip across the ocean was a difficult one for Louisa, whose sister, Huldah, along with their mother, Margaret, spent most of their time tossing on the bunks while Louisa and her father ministered to them. Hall was not well himself, suffering from a congestion in his lungs. Only the two boys traveled well, and they taxed both sisters, who took turns leaving their sickbeds to look after them.

Badly debilitated by the time they reached New York, the family decided to stay there until they recovered. Louisa wrote Thales to tell him they would travel overland to Iowa City in the summer, with the last of the handcart companies. She was disappointed, she wrote, for the two of them had been wed only a short time before Thales departed for America and she was anxious to join her husband. But without rest, her mother, Margaret, would never survive even the trip to Iowa, let alone the journey from Iowa to the valley.

Once on land, Louisa's family, all except her mother, re-gained their energy, and, abhorring idleness, as did all the Saints, they found jobs. While Huldah took care of her mother and her sons and did the cooking in the boardinghouse in which they lived, which paid for their quarters, Louisa found work as a chambermaid. Although Louisa protested, her father, worn-out by the ocean voyage, nonetheless took a job in an oyster house.

They all liked America, their large rooms in Brooklyn, the fresh air, but most of all, they liked the money they made. And after a few weeks, Louisa suggested it would be best to stay in Brooklyn and wait a year to make the trip to Utah. Not only would her parents be in better health, but the family would have saved enough money to outfit a wagon. Margaret would be able to ride to the valley instead of walking next to a hand-cart. Besides, the wagon would hold everything they had brought with them as well as what they expected to purchase with their wages—linens and crockery, a bureau, even a rock-ing chair. With such riches, they would be better prepared to set up housekeeping in the valley.

Louisa wrote to Thales in Iowa City, telling him of the decision.

It is a splendid plan, is it not? With the money we will make, we will not have to go to the Salt Lake Valley as beggars. And by then, Mother will be recovered from her disabilities. At this time, she can scarce walk a half mile, and I do not believe she could ever manage fifteen miles every day. Mother is so convinced of the rightness of our plan that she says she must have a revelation before she will make the journey this year.

Then she added:

I have talked with the church authorities here, and they seem to have no objection to our decision. Could you not inquire there whether you could join us in Brooklyn? Surely there is much work to be done here among the Saints, and you would be welcomed. You and I could be together, and I would not be so lonely for my dear husband.

She was sure that Thales would approve of the decision to remain in Brooklyn. After all, he was a man of strong appetites, and the separation was hard for both of them. In fact, so confident was Louisa that she inquired of the woman who owned the rooming house whether there was a small room that she and her husband might share.

Louisa was stunned, then, when she received Thales's reply.

I can scarcely believe that my wife, whom I never would have married had I known she prized the comforts of Babylon over her faith, has betrayed me by wishing to remain among the ungodly. I am resolved never to condone such an action. We are commanded to gather in Zion, and yet you are so weak that you place money before your duties to the Lord. I am ashamed that my own wife would wish to live amongst the heathen in that place of wickedness instead of with God's chosen people in Utah.

He rebuked her further.

Does your mother not believe that God ordered her to make the journey when she joined the church? Does she demand more of Him? Does she believe our God speaks directly to her instead of through her betters? If she has only as much faith as a flaxseed, she will arrive in the valley without the least sign of sickness. It is only those who lack faith who perish by the wayside.

And then, most hurtful of all to Louisa, Thales blamed her father.

I put this at Hall Chetwin's feet. He has not so much as one atom of the spirit of Zion but has much of the spirit of apostasy. He would make a shipwreck of his salvation. I had thought to write this letter to him, but I am so filled with anger that I do not trust what I might say.

A stricken Louisa told her family, "Thales says we must go."

"What does he write?" her mother asked, reaching for the letter.

Louisa would not give it up. Instead, she said, "It is personal. He says only that we are not to stay in New York, but must prepare to leave from Boston when the converts on the *Horizon* arrive."

The parents would not be put off, however, and her father insisted on reading Thales's words himself. Hall turned white as he read the letter and grabbed on to the edge of a table to steady himself, then fell into a chair. "You must not read it, Mother," he said, tears streaming down his face. But Margaret took the missive and read it, her face lined with grief when she was finished, because it was obvious to the others that she blamed herself for Thales's outburst.

"You are not weak in your faith, Hall," she insisted. "Thales can have no reason to say that. But he is right in prophesying that the Lord will strengthen me for the journey. We will go ahead. I want no one to question your commitment to the Lord."

The three agreed not to show the letter to Huldah but instead to say they had changed their minds and were ready to leave. But Huldah found out the contents, because Thales had sent a second letter to the president of the church in New York, warning the elders that they must double their efforts to send the converts to Zion, that even his own family was being seduced by the wickedness of New York City.

My wife's father, Hall Chetwin, is as close to being an apostate as any man I ever knew. He has convinced my family to remain in that place of sin instead of gathering with the holy in the Salt Lake Valley. I fear the devil has his clutches in him so deep that he will fall into hell.

Thales did not ask the president to show the letter to others. He told Louisa after they were reunited in Iowa City that he had written it only because he was concerned for her father's soul and hoped the authorities would take him in hand and show him the error of his ways. But that had not been necessary. Hall was so disturbed by the charges that he asked to be rebaptized, and to show his humility, he turned over the responsibility for the family to Thales. The harsh letter accomplished its purpose: The family had gone at once to Boston to await the arrival of the *Horizon,* and then they had traveled with the converts to Iowa City. Her husband had been right to write such a letter. Louisa did not question that. But then, she never questioned the rightness of Thales's decisions. After all, his orders came from the Lord.

Jessie Cooper watched Brother Thales Tanner rush by, his head high, as if he were in charge of the whole world, instead of just one little group of a hundred people. He was a little shorter than average, but he was broad in the back and as strong as the bull the Coopers had left behind on the farm. And if he did not have the fair face of her brothers, he at least was not unpleasant to look at. There was an air of assurance, sometimes of godliness about him. After all, the man had converted the three of them—Jessie and her brothers, Ephraim and Sutter. She felt a thrill when she recalled the way he'd talked that first time, the thunder in his voice, the fire, the cadence of words. His voice was the voice of mighty God, and Jessie felt as if the Lord Himself had been speaking directly to her.

Although a cousin, Rebecca Savage, had joined the strange church years before and gone off to America to live with the Saints, the three Coopers had not expected to be caught up with the Mormons. In fact, Jessie had thought her cousin demented. She and her brothers had attended the meeting out of curiosity, not religious zeal. She had expected to be entertained by the foolishness of the doctrine. It would be fun to laugh at the Mormons later on. The three of them had gone because it was a nice evening to walk down the lane, past the blooming lilacs with their sweet perfume, to the Chetwin cottage. Margaret Chetwin might serve tea and nut scones, and the Coopers were all tired of Jessie's cooking.

But to their surprise, the three had been intrigued by the missionary. They had been skeptical, had asked questions, had not been converted so quickly as the Chetwins. But they went back, and over many weeks, they were taken up with the Book of Mormon, which told of a church like the one that Jesus had founded, a simple, honest church unencumbered by the pomp and rituals of the Church of England, for which they had no use. They were taken by the idea of leaving the used-up tenant farm for the virgin land of America, too. And there seemed to be a place for women in the young church, which appealed to Jessie. Eventually, Ephraim, then Sutter, and finally Jessie were baptized by the missionary Thales Tanner.

Thales had led their way to the true church. Jessie would always be grateful to him for it. He was a holy man. She would give him that. But Jessie did not like him much. He had called at the farm more than was necessary after the Coopers' conversion, and her brothers had teased her that when the three made the trip to Utah, Jessie would go as Thales's bride. Indeed, it was obvious to everyone that he was interested in more than Jessie's soul. But she did not care for his domineering ways, his humorlessness, his assurance that he was right in all things, even beyond religion, although he rarely spoke about anything other than religion. "I bet he knows the number of whiskers in the prophet Brigham Young's beard," she told her brothers.

After a time, Jessie did not encourage him, and so Thales courted Louisa Chetwin. Those two were a better match anyway. What Jessie considered blustery in Thales, Louisa found authoritative. While Jessie thought Thales pompous, Louisa believed him inspired. Louisa was a timid little thing who would cling to a husband, while Jessie worked side by side with her brothers and was a match for both of them. Louisa had a fair, lovely look, a tidy figure, and curls the color of sunshine, and she was as nice as a sunny day, too. Jessie, whose hair was as black as the loamy earth she worked, was as broad as Thales, and almost as strong, since she did her share of plowing and harvesting. Her face, with its wide brow and high cheekbones, would have been handsome in a man but was too strong for a woman. Her mood could be as dark as a winter storm. Indeed, Louisa, who was obedient and as fragile-looking as chinaware, was far better suited to the missionary.

The two girls, both of them twenty-two years of age now, had been friends all of their lives, and Thales might have come between them by what was perceived by some as his tossing Jessie over for Louisa. Besides, it was clear that Louisa thought Thales such a fine catch of a husband that she preened in his company. But Jessie was relieved by the match, so she said nothing, even letting Louisa think that she had stolen Thales from her, for she valued Louisa's friendship that much. Jessie attended the wedding, of course, and was the first to congratulate the married couple, telling Louisa what a stunning match she had made, and Thales that he was as lucky a man as ever lived.

But she thought Louisa was not so lucky, and she was saddened to see how Thales dominated her friend, expecting her to wait on him and to accommodate the Mormon elders he brought home unannounced. Thales criticized Louisa's cooking, her housekeeping, even the color of her bonnets, and he did not always do so in private. But Louisa didn't seem to mind. "He is so patient in pointing out the error of my ways," Louisa confided. "Am I not lucky to have such a husband?" Jessie held her tongue.

Jessie tried to concentrate on Thales's good qualities—his knowledge of the Bible and the Book of Mormon, his earnestness in prayer, and his zealotry in living the faith. Thales was, she knew, a decent man, who would give a poor Saint his own cloak if it was raining or go out in the night to help a neighbor in need. There was an air of spirituality about him, of holiness. And something else. Jessie thought of him when she saw the hogs rutting.

Now, watching as Thales gave the Chetwins directions for setting up their camp, Jessie once again was grateful he was not her husband. He might hold sway over their spiritual needs, but Jessie and her brothers would never let him control their lives. In their lighter moments, her brothers sometimes made fun of Thales, imitating his speech as they ordered each other around. "I believe if you had married him, you would have come to wish him to embrace the principle of plural marriage," Ephraim told his sister, "else you would have to have him all to yourself the day long." He asked, "Was he ever known to smile?"

Still, the three knew that they were lucky to be in Thales's hundred. "He runs it shipshape," Sutter observed. The tents were orderly, the carts repaired at each stop, and Thales saw after his people, settling disagreements, admonishing the Saints to help one another, chiding those who failed to attend prayers each morning and evening.

For that last reason, the Coopers tried not to camp too close to the Tanner cart. The three were strong in the faith, but they did not believe that everything out of the elders' mouths was ordered by God. They were not as dumb as cattle, Jessie thought, looking out at the herd of animals that accompanied them. One of those things they doubted was the everlasting prayer sessions that deprived them of sleep in the morning and work on the cart at night. One each day was plenty. The Coopers' cart was among the poorest, and every evening they were taxed to strengthen and repair it. The other thing they believed was not God-ordained was the endless sound of the cornet that called them to their duties several times each day. "If I ever see the instrument unattended, I'll make sure we never hear it again," Sutter threatened. But to the Coopers' regret, and that of many other Saints, the musician kept the horn closely guarded.

Prayers were still an hour or more away, so Jessie built a cooking fire that evening and began preparing their meal. The food was monotonous—bread, salt pork, greens they picked beside the trail, if they were lucky—but the simplicity of their diet did not bother her. She liked not having to prepare a large meal, bending over the hearth to tend heavy pots hanging from cranes. She didn't care for cooking, never had, but it had been her lot. As a girl, she had worked in the fields and the barn with her brothers, both older, who had taken over the farming following their father's death. But then their mother died, and the housekeeping fell to Jessie, who did it grudgingly. Fortunately for her, her brothers did not care about the food as long as it was plentiful. Nor did they remark on the disorder of the house. Jessie finished her chores quickly so that she could labor outside, doing the work of a man. Now, while other women complained about the inconvenience of cooking over a campfire, Jessie enjoyed it. The easy duty gave her more time to roam the prairie beyond the Saints' tents.

The trip had been a lark for the young woman. She loved walking along the trail, taking her turn at the cart. The hot sun that beat down on the Saints some days and robbed them of energy felt good on her back, and the rain refreshed her. Jessie joyed to see the vast land, so wide and open, so different from the landscape of the farm, with its copses and hedgerows. She gathered bouquets of sunflowers with their brown ox-eye centers, and sometimes she picked up handfuls of dirt, smelling it and letting it sift through her fingers, wondering what crops could be planted there. "I never saw a country I liked better in my life," she told Ephraim. "The earth is as young as a baby, while at home it was as aged as an old man."

"You haven't seen but one other country," he reminded her.

She liked the sunsets most of all. They stretched across the prairie from horizon to horizon and were glorious, with rays of pink and gold against a sky the hue of Wedgwood, or else were violent—a streak the color of blood separating the black earth from the blue sky.

She wanted to stop and talk to the farmers they passed, ask

them what they raised. She would have if Thales had not told them to have no truck with the local people.

The curious inhabitants came out of their houses to stare at the Saints as they passed, making fun of their awkward carts and joking with their neighbors. "It's the Mormons. Lock up your daughters," said one, and another called, "My ox is named Joe Smith!"

"I thought all you Mormons had gone to hell," one man called, and Ephraim answered him gaily, "The Lord has made no such requisition."

Several well-meaning villagers begged the Coopers to winter there, telling them that they had started out too late in the year and would run into snow before they got to the Salt Lake. "You'd better say your prayers if you keep on, Mormons," one called. He was rebuked by Sutter, who retorted, "Your Babylon has no claim on us."

Many of the people were friendly, and despite Thales's warning, Jessie sometimes stopped to exchange a word with the onlookers. A woman sold her a pail of milk for a nickel. Another offered a glass of buttermilk when the Coopers stopped to repair a broken spoke. Sutter and Jessie had tied the broken ends together with a rag, intending to replace the spoke later with a tree branch, but a farmer offered a seasoned piece of wood that he said would work better. And because they knew the green wood used to build the cart was the source of their troubles, they accepted.

Thales came along then and reprimanded the two, saying, "We need no help but that which we receive from God." The Coopers and the farmer smiled at one another, and after Thales moved on, Sutter said he considered the farmer an instrument of the Lord and the lumber a gift from God, and he placed the board in his cart.

"We have a preacher here. He, too, has the misfortune of doubling for the Almighty," the farmer said, and they all laughed.

Jessie heard the songs of birds over the creaking of the carts, songs she could not identify, and looked for the birds that made them. She found wildflowers that grew among the prairie grasses, coarser and taller than the grasses at home, and picked up rocks that intrigued her, putting them into the cart. When it was Sutter's turn to pull, he threw out the stones, remarking that Thales would contend the three had gone over their allotment of seventeen pounds each.

Sutter had been the one who had balked at going to America. Looking across their familiar English farm, he had said to his brother and sister, "We've made this the best farm for miles around. Why should we give it up?"

Jessie and Ephraim were taken with the idea of starting life in a new land among other Mormons, however, and they believed that despite their efforts, the farm was worn-out. Thales had talked as much about America as he had about religion, and Jessie was convinced the land was as rich as Eden. When their brother resisted the move, Jessie and Ephraim did not talk about Sutter's soul or the church's call to Zion. Instead, Ephraim asked, "You want to work this piece of land for the rest of your life? Don't you intend for nothing more than that?"

Jessie added, "Supposing you or Ephraim should marry. You'd have to divide the farm."

"Or Jessie," Ephraim said. "By rights, she should have a third."

"By rights, but not by law," Sutter replied, correcting him.

"You'd deprive her?"

"No, I would not. I'm just pointing out the fact of it."

"And if you had a wife, would she agree to let Jessie have a third of the land?"

"This is the sort of argument we'll get into one day if we stay here," Jessie said.

Their arguments made Sutter doubt the wisdom of remaining, he told his sister later on. He admitted he'd asked himself if he really wanted to repeat each day's chores for the next thirty or forty years. One morning when he went out to slop the hogs, he came back inside to tell his sister that the thought of staring into the face of a pig for the next ten thousand days was daunting. He didn't want to feel the chill that went into his bones each winter morning as he rose from his bed, and then, he asked Jessie, did he want to marry one of the dough-faced girls in the village and raise a brood of brats who would follow him into the fields as he had followed his father, and his father his grandfather? So he agreed with his brother and sister to go to the Salt Lake. It did not occur to any of the Coopers that life in American was likely to be as repetitious.

The Coopers gave up the farm, sold their belongings, and despite the admonitions from the elders, they did not turn the money over to the church. Instead, they purchased the seed and implements they expected to use to start farming in the valley. Like the other Saints, they had expected to take a hundred pounds of baggage apiece with them to Zion, discovering only when they reached Iowa City that they were limited to seventeen. So they went through their belongings, setting aside coats and shoes and dresses, crockery and silver, keepsakes. They ripped their parents' silhouettes from their frame and cast aside the frame. Their books, even those on farming principles, went into the pile of discards, along with the diary that Jessie had written in since their departure from Liverpool. Other Saints, including Ephraim, considered their diaries as sacred as their Bibles and kept them even later, when the carts were lightened further. But Jessie did not want hers to add to the weight. Even at that, they had had to cast aside some of those things they had thought indispensable. Like other women, Jessie put on several layers of clothing, so the garments would not count against her on weight, and she tied the bags of seeds under her skirts so that they did not have to be left behind. "I do not believe Thales Tanner will look for them there," she told her brothers.

"I thank God, then, that you did not marry him," Sutter told her slyly. "You would have packed a different seed with you."

His sister swatted Sutter for his impertinence, but she turned aside and laughed to herself.

Now Jessie was setting out the three tin plates and three forks, all that was left after the purge at Iowa City, when she looked up and saw Louisa standing beside the cart, her skirt muddy from the trail. Jessie rose and greeted her friend, glad to see her, because the two had had little time to talk on the journey, and even then, Thales had been nearby. She looked around for him, but Louisa said, "I am alone. I felt the need for a little walk."

"After walking fifteen miles already today?" Jessie smiled.

Louisa shrugged. "Sometimes I need to be alone with my

thoughts. You remember how I used to hide out by the grind-stone when we were girls. Of course, Thales would be dis-pleased if he knew I wanted to be alone. He thinks it is a sin to be idle. There are so many sins. . . ."

"More for women than men, I think," Jessie said.

Louisa gave a wisp of a smile and then frowned. "Thales would not like such a joke about the church."

"Oh, I'm not talking about the Mormon Church. The old church, too, had a preponderance of sins for women. All doc-trines do that are written by men."

"Living a righteous life is not easy, and I must learn to be obedient. How fortunate I am to have a husband who helps me."

"Oh, bosh, Louisa. You're as good a person as ever lived. Thales is picking at motes."

Louisa looked stunned for a moment, then relaxed. "Thales does go on sometimes, doesn't he? I know you think that." Per-haps shocked that she had criticized her husband, Louisa added quickly, "But he is such a good Mormon. You would not be critical if you heard his prayers, the way he gives his testimony, admitting to God so many weaknesses. If Mormons believed in such things, Thales would beat himself with whips and wear a hair shirt. Did you know he fasts one day each week?"

Jessie did not. She also did not care. "You look tired," she said.

"I have sad news. Sister Esther Smalls died not more than an hour ago. There will be a service after prayers. We've wrapped her in her counterpane, and Thales has asked some men to dig a grave. Brother Martin will conduct a service."

Jessie took her friend's hand. "She was so good to us. She taught even me to love poetry."

"She was a grand teacher, oh yes. Why, did you know that

61

she had not intended to teach at all, but when Mr. Smalls died, she had those three small children to raise, and as no one else wanted the job of teacher and she was willing to work for half the pay, she was given it. No one expected her to achieve success."

"But she did. She taught us literature, music, philosophy, and even manners in addition to reading and ciphering. I had not planned to stay in school beyond the sixth term, but she captivated me, and I had more years of schooling than my brothers. I was pleased when she was baptized and agreed to go to Utah, although I knew she was distraught that her children did not accept the faith and that she had to embark on her own."

"I'd thought she would teach my children, just as she taught you and me at home," Louisa said.

Without thinking, Jessie glanced down at her friend's stomach, but Louisa shook her head. "How did she die?" Jessie asked. She had seen the woman on the trail, pushing a handcart with a young couple, but had not talked with her.

"She died praising God," Louisa replied.

"Yes, of course, but what was the cause?"

"She caught a cold. It went into her chest and turned into pneumonia. After they reached camp this evening, she begged to sit down for a few minutes, and when the others went to fetch her, she was in a delirium." Louisa looked away. "Thales says it was a lack of faith."

"How could he! The idea!" Jessie was indignant. "What does faith have to do with catching a cold?"

Louisa shrugged. "Thales says if our belief is strong enough, we will make it. God does not want to take into His kingdom those who question their faith."

"Mrs. Smalls was as strong a believer as you and I," Jessie said.

"Perhaps in her heart she was not."

"Perhaps, but not likely."

Louisa looked away. "I wanted to tell you. I know you loved her."

"Yes, I did." And I do not love Thales Tanner, Jessie thought. She watched her friend turn and walk back toward her own cart, wondering what would happen if Louisa fell sick. What would Thales say about her then?

She squatted down next to the fire, where the dinner was already burned. It wasn't the first time.

Prayers were over by the time Robert and Maud Amos reached the camp. In the darkening light, Maud looked at her old fellow. They were too aged to make the trip. They'd both known that. They'd had no children to tell them nay but plenty of neighbors to call them fools. Their friends of long years had questioned Maud and Robert's sanity in selling their few possessions and starting off on the long ocean voyage to America. And not even to a big city such as New York, but to a place nobody had ever heard of before the Mormons came into the Midlands village with their preaching—a valley in the far west of America without even the barest of creature comforts.

"In the going down of your years, Mrs. Amos! You ought to spend them on your settle in the chimney corner, toasting yourself by the fire," the cottager on the east side of her house told her. "And with Mr. Amos. The shame of it!"

"Lordy, Maud, if the wolves don't get you, the wild Indians

will. And where will you be buried? Do they even have cemeteries in that country?" the neighbor to the west asked.

"I expect so, unless Americans live forever, and in that case, we would fare right well," Maud replied.

"You're not much in the habit of traveling, I think. I've seen you walk down to the market, and you couldn't any more walk across America than you could fly over it. And pushing a wheelbarrow, too! You've took leave of your senses."

"A cart, not a wheelbarrow. And we're as sensible as we've always been," Maud insisted, although she and Robert wondered themselves how they could walk a thousand miles or more. In fact, they had asked the missionary that very question, and he had replied that if their faith was strong, the Lord would give them strength. And their faith was indeed strong.

The old couple had been good members of the Church of England before they met the missionaries, and at first, they were not inclined to pay attention to the doctrine from America. But they were kind people, and out of courtesy to the nice young men who called on them, they listened to the message about the Mormon Church and agreed to attend a service. The preacher wasn't as good as Thales Tanner, whom they met later in Iowa City, but nonetheless, they were caught up in his zeal. After the service, Maud told her husband that a heat like a coal fire had gone into her heart when she heard the brother speak, and Robert replied that he'd heard angels singing and a light had seemed to shine on the missionary, although they were crowded into a dark room with others, where only a lamp and the glare of the fire in the grate lighted the room. Could it be that at their age they were being called by the Lord?

Maud and her husband pondered the message of the Mormons and studied their book. Their pastor, a man almost as old as they were, told them that Satan had taken hold of them and was tempting them, that their souls would be lost if they embraced the Mormon faith. Why, he himself would hold open the door to hell for them if they joined the upstart church, he told Maud. "You would bring disgrace to your family name for joining such a cursed religion. You would be the devil's odd man."

The couple was wounded at that, because the minister had been their friend for many years, and they'd hoped they could trust him to counsel them. The two gave it time, because they did not want to be wrong and because one of them would not join the church without the other. They were always of one heart. But in the end, they would not deny that the Lord had spoken to them, and they were baptized.

They were faithful converts, donating their time to the church, welcoming elders into their home, tithing, for the church demanded much. It never occurred to them that they would ever be called to Zion, and at first, they demurred. "Our age," Maud said.

But the missionary would not be put off and insisted that if they sold their few belongings, they would have enough to pay for passage to America and a cart that they could push to Zion. "Others even older than you are going, and they have put their trust in the Lord. I had thought you firmer in the faith."

They talked it over then, for one never made a decision without first hearing from the other. The two were closer than most couples, perhaps because they shared the tragedy of five little children who had not lived to grow up. The couple was poor and hardworking, Robert still laboring in a carpentry shop, and they often worried what would happen to them if he became too infirm to work.

"We've never taken an adventure," Robert said one evening as they sat in their worn chairs in front of the hearth.

"What if we fall into sickness?"

"You heard the missionary. We must have faith."

"Faith may give us strength, but it won't help if you break your leg."

"And what if I do?" he asked. "What if I die out there? I won't be any more dead there than I would be here. Besides, there's a chance we'll make it all the way, and wouldn't that be something?"

"A fire to go burns inside of me," Maud said.

Robert took her worn hand, the skin dry and thin as paper. "Me, too. Old girl, we'll do it."

And so they boarded the ship at Liverpool and made it safely across the ocean. The fresh sea air cleansed the vapors from their systems, and they arrived in Boston feeling younger than their years. Then there had been the trip by train across the land, a journey that filled Maud with awe at the vastness of the country she would call home.

And finally came their arrival at Iowa City, the disappointment that they would have to wait weeks to embark, although they were cheerful and put the time to good use. Robert was skilled with his hands and helped manufacture the carts. Maud knew that if he had been by himself, he would not have been so selfish as to put extra work into his own cart, but he feared she would not have the strength to push, so he selected for himself one of the better-made vehicles, constructed with wood that was a little aged, and he made sure that the wheels and hubs were well made. "I would have bought iron hubs if I could have, but none are available, so I made them out of the hardest wood I could find," he told his wife. Still, he added, he did not know if they would last the trip.

While Robert worked on the carts, Maud made the rounds of the camp, tending children, sharing herbs for cooking and medicinal use, herbs she had grown at home, dried and bundled for the trip. She'd brought along seeds to plant in the valley, had stitched bags from scraps of fabric to store them. And since Maud was known to be a midwife, she'd been sought out to help deliver a baby in camp. Looking at the young women among the converts, she knew she'd be called upon again and again before the journey was over. The idea made her glow. She loved babies. It was a heavy burden for her that she had failed Robert in that way. But he had never complained. "We have each other. I couldn't wish for more," he told her often enough.

Now she glanced at her husband of so many years as he trudged off into the darkness to find wood for the cooking fire. Sometimes, they picked up a few sticks on the way, but the extra wood made the cart more difficult to push, and so they waited until they reached camp to look for fallen branches. By then, however, the area had been scoured by others, since the old people were among the last to arrive.

On that day, they were even later than usual, because they had stopped to pick gooseberries that Maud had spotted just off the trail. The gooseberries, along with wild plums, varied their diet. Maud took out the kettle and frying pan and food-stuffs and mixed up a pancake, folding in the tiny sour berries. They would have the scone with bacon. She ought to prepare more. Robert deserved better. But she was too tired, and besides, by the time they set up their campsite, both of them were almost too exhausted to eat. She hoped that when they reached the mountains, they could ride in a wagon. Or maybe a party from the valley would meet them this side of the mountains and carry them to Zion. Maud would like that.

While she waited for Robert, Maud made a fire with the sticks from the cart and set the kettle on top of it. The cake wouldn't bake through without more wood, but she could get it started. She sat down next to the fire, but before she could settle in, a woman touched her arm. "Sister Maud, my baby's sick. It would be a blessing if you'd take a look at her."

Maud smiled and rose stiffly. A baby, now that was reason enough to shake off the day's tiredness. She looked down at the dinner. The fire would die out before the pancake burned. If Robert returned before she did, he'd tend the fire, knowing she'd left for a reason. Maud followed the young woman across the camp, hearing the baby squalling before she saw him.

"I asked Sister Sharon for advice," the young woman said. "She told me it is nothing, but he's my first, and I'm afraid . . ." The woman's voice trailed off.

"Of course, you're scared. Who wouldn't be, out here with no doctor, no chemist. I would be myself." They reached the campsite, and Maud took the baby from the father, cooed and swayed a little with the child in her arms. She touched his forehead and examined the little body, then ran her finger inside the baby's mouth. As the boy's cries tapered off, Maud handed him to the mother, smiling a little. "He's teething. If you'll dip your finger in a little whiskey or wine and run it along the gums, that ought to settle him down."

"Whiskey?" the father asked. "No one in this place has spirits."

Maud cocked her head. "I expect many have it for medicinal needs. If you'll inquire of your neighbors, I believe the Lord may produce it for you."

"What do we owe you, Sister?" he asked.

"Not a thing, but if you find the whiskey, you might give my old fellow a tot." She turned and walked back to her campfire, anxious to find her husband and thinking a jolt of spirits would be a good thing for Robert.

Jessie and her brothers were nearly three weeks out of Iowa City, and they were seasoned. They, like the other Saints, were hardened by the heat that rose to more than a hundred degrees in the daytime and turned the tents into ovens at night. They waded through dust that came to the tops of their shoes, dust so thick, blowing into their skin and eyes, the pockets and seams of their clothing, that sometimes they could see only a few feet in front of them. Their skin was burned by the sun, peeled, and was burned again. When they weren't tormented by the sun and the flies and mosquitoes, they were chilled by cold rains that washed over them as they trudged along, the rain mixing with the dust in their hair and skin and turning it into mud. Instead of blisters, calluses now covered their feet.

The three were glad they had chosen to sleep in the open instead of being crowded into tents with strangers who snored and coughed and cried out in the night. Their stomachs had adjusted to bad water and to the food, which was either raw or scorched, doughy loaves leavened without saleratus and salt pork rancid from the heat. They had come to see it all as their due, as the Lord's way of trying them, of separating the chaff of unworthiness from the wheat of godliness.

They heard some muttering, of course—about the hard weather, the poorly constructed carts, the quality of the food, many asking where the provisions were that the church had promised along the route. One woman asked Jessie who had concocted the foolish handcart scheme—perhaps it was the devil himself—but she was silenced by Jessie's reply that Brigham Young had ordained it.

At the meetings Jessie and her brothers attended, they listened to the elders admonish the people, telling them that the Lord demanded a happy countenance in times of trouble, declaring theirs was an easy journey compared to that of the Saints who had been driven out of Nauvoo to live in cold misery in Winter Quarters. "You are soft. You are grumblers," Thales Tanner said, looking at Jessie, although neither she nor Sutter nor Ephraim had voiced a complaint. "We'll have no critics of Brother Brigham." Then he told the gathering, "If this complaining don't cease, sickness will get into your midst, and you will die off like rotten sheep. I counsel you to be humble and keep united so that the blessings of the Lord will attend you."

At that, someone began singing their anthem, "The Handcart Song."

Some must push and some must pull
As we go marching up the hill.
As merrily on the way we go
Until we reach the valley, oh.

And so the Coopers and the rest of the Saints marched on through Iowa with new conviction, for weren't they God's chosen people? And a people of joy, for at night when prayers were done, there was singing and laughter, and Jessie loved that. Men played fiddles and blew horns, and some danced jigs. There were even jokes, for the Mormon religion was a happy one. Singing might appeal to Jessie, who had a strong, if not melodious, voice, but she knew it did not dissuade all the converts from dropping out, and occasionally when the Martin Company passed through a settlement, she saw another handcart stop and not continue.

"You've a hard way of serving the Lord, by God," the villagers called. "We've jobs. Wait out the winter with us." Jessie waved and thanked them, but she was not tempted to stop.

One evening at camp, Thales Tanner told her that a cart pulled by a widow woman with five children had broken down, and that the woman had hired a man to take her back to a town the Saints had passed through earlier in the day. To Jessie's horror, Thales thundered, "She has betrayed the covenants!" And that night at the meeting, he urged the membership to excommunicate her. The missionary was the voice of God in matters of religion, Jessie knew, but still, she would not have voted to excommunicate the convert. Jessie had met the woman, who was not an apostate at all, but only a tired widow in poor health, with a blind son and another who was lame from where the wheel of a handcart had run over his foot. The sister had told Jessie she would winter in the town, taking shelter with her rescuer, and go on in the spring with the year's first handcart company. But Brother Thales said he would rather see her in hell than let her pollute the next year's converts. And so the Saints had voted to remove her and her children from the church. The decision left Jessie restive. Didn't the religion that brought her so much pleasure have room for compassion?

That day had been a long one for the Coopers, whose cart had broken down on the road. They were used to walking, but they were going farther each day now, and that was harder on the carts. At first, they'd pushed their carts only a few miles a day, but Brother Martin told them they must hurry to avoid being caught in the mountains when the snows came, and so they doubled and tripled the miles they walked, until that day, the Coopers had gone twenty miles, and without water.

Jessie saw Robert Amos change places with his wife, Maud, she pulling and he pushing. Robert refused the water they carried in the cart so that his wife could have his share, but she would not take a sip, saving her portion for him. The result was that neither drank. Instead, they placed small smooth stones in their mouths to keep down the thirst. In the late afternoon, their cart bogged down in the heavy sand, and only with the help of the Coopers did they and the young couple who pushed with them free the wheels. The task was hard on Robert, who, with failing strength, was forced to sit in the road and rest before he picked up the crosspiece again.

Then he stumbled and went down, the cart toppling and spilling its contents, the kettle that hung beneath the cart rolling across the prairie. The Coopers stopped to right the cart and pile the belongings back on top while the young couple only watched. "I'll pull for a little," Sutter offered, but Robert waved him off.

"If I can't pull it myself, I have no business going to Zion. I won't be a burden to you."

"No burden."

"There's no sin in accepting help," Maud told her husband.

Robert shook his head. "I'll just rest a minute and be as good as new."

"Then I'll pull with your wife, for I would talk to a woman instead of my brothers," Jessie said. "You should ride on the wagon tomorrow," she told Robert, who limped along beside her. He was an old man, his beard nearly all white, the skin on his face loose, and he was bony, his elbows sharp points, like the wings of a plucked chicken.

Maud looked at him fondly, saying, "My old fellow. We've got this far." They were close to the encampment now, because they heard the cornet, and they hurried along, parking the Amos cart beside that of the Coopers. The couple went off to join friends.

While the women unpacked the supper things, the men examined the carts. "The axle does poorly. I believe it was harmed when the cart tipped," Robert said.

"My brothers—" Jessie began, but Robert waved her away and went off to borrow a tool to fix it.

The two women bent over their campfires, but just then, Brother Thales passed by and admonished them. "Did you not hear the call to prayers, Sisters?" So with Ephraim and Sutter, the women left their suppers and followed the missionary to the gathering. "At least your husband won't have to attend," Jessie whispered.

When they returned to their campfires, they found Robert

working on the cart, which was lying on its side. "I was caught up in prayers, and afterward, there was preaching," Maud explained.

"And before you could start supper."

"Nay, it's in the kettle."

"The kettle's empty, 'twas empty when I returned."

Jessie gave a sad smile. She'd seen the scone Maud had made with a few berries and a little sugar; her mouth had watered over it, because the Coopers' supper was likely to be a burned pancake. Perhaps Robert had eaten it, then, abashed, denied the supper had been there.

Maud went to the fire and lifted the lid from the kettle, and indeed, it was empty of the scone. "I used the last of the sugar." The old woman sighed. "Someone's taken it. I hope whoever they are, they were hungrier than we. There's not the time to cook a new pone."

"You'll share our meal, such as it is," Jessie said.

"Nay, we've chokecherries."

"With no sugar?" the young woman asked. She reached into her cart and put a spoonful of sugar into a tin cup and handed it to Maud.

"Bless you, Sister," the old woman said. The couple ate the cherries, spitting out the stones, then spread their blankets on the ground, because it was too hot to sleep in a tent.

"I'll be a minute. I must finish the cart. I'll use the last of the tallow we bought to put on the axle, unless you want to save it to eat," Robert said.

"Use it," his wife said. She knew that the axles were made of wood, not metal, and grated in their wooden sockets without something to grease them. But the tallow used for grease collected dirt and pebbles, and they sanded away the wood as the cart moved along. Robert spread the tallow onto the wood with a palsied hand.

Jessie went to sleep to the sound of the old man's humming and woke at dawn, when she heard Maud mutter, "Is it made good now?"

The young woman sat up and watched as Maud reached for her husband, who was sitting upright, leaning against the cart wheel, as if he'd fallen asleep while working on the axle. Maud grasped Robert's lumpy fingers, and then she began to wail. There was a stirring among the sleeping Saints. One called out, "Hush," but Jessie crept to where Maud sat and asked, "What is it, Sister?"

"My husband's dead," she whispered. "He died in the night. He's gone. I didn't have the chance to say good-bye."

Jessie put her arms around Maud and tried to raise her, but Maud would not be moved. "A minute," she said, staring at her husband's face as if she were trying to memorize his features.

"I'll fetch my brothers. They'll dig a grave."

Maud didn't reply. Instead, she leaned over Robert's body and whispered, "You were a good husband, the best that ever was. I was blessed." As if her mind were muddled, she muttered gibberish, words of love and sorrow. Then at last, she asked, "What's to become of your old Maudie? How will I get to Zion without you?" She sobbed quietly, her shoulders shaking in her grief.

"We'll assign you to another cart. You will make it safely to the valley, Sister Maud."

Jessie had been about comforting the old woman, and now,

hearing these words, she looked up and found herself staring into the face of Thales Tanner, who took Maud by the arms and lifted her. Jessie stared at him darkly, waiting for him to tell the widow that Robert had died for lack of faith, but instead, the missionary said, "He was an honorable man, a good Saint. He is with the Lord our God, waiting for you, but you won't join him just yet," and he smiled at her. "I prophesy that you will reach Zion and live a goodly life there for years to come."

"It's best I stay with him. I would not want him to be cold," Maud said.

But Thales led her away. "I believe he would want you to reach Zion, would he not?"

Maud pondered the question, then nodded. Thales told her to collect her belongings while the Coopers wrapped Robert's body in a blanket. When Maud had selected her few things, she distributed Robert's clothing—his coat to a boy who had none, his hat to a man whose own had been blown across the prairie. She put aside the clock, a fine clock with the face of the moon on it. "What reason do I have to count time now?" she asked Jessie. "Time will go on without me," and she gave the clock to a woman who had admired it. The couple the Amoses had traveled with claimed the cart.

Then there was a hasty service, for the departure of the carts could not be delayed. Thales read from the Bible and asked the Lord to accept the soul of His faithful servant Robert, who had labored hard and was used up. He did not blame Robert's death on weak faith, and for that, Jessie was grateful.

After the service was finished and the men had shoveled the dirt over the body of the dead man, Jessie brought Maud a cup of porridge and told her to eat, because they had many miles to travel that day. So Maud accepted the cup and ate the contents, and when she was finished, she saw that Sutter and Ephraim had piled her things onto the Cooper cart.

Maud looked at the three young people, two strong men and a sister nearly as tough as they were, and said they did not need to take on the care of an old woman. She told them she could go along on her own, but Jessie Cooper put her arm around Maud's shoulders and said, "I've had it gruff from my brothers. I've a cousin in the valley. I wrote to her that we were coming. But until then, I could use a bit of company from another woman."

"I don't want to be a burden. I'd like to be serviceable to you."

"You will be. I tell you truly, I am no cook, never was. I saw the supper you fixed last night with nothing more than flour and water and a handful of berries. If you'll agree to do the cooking, I'll take your turn at the cart, and we'll both call it a good bargain."

"There's nothing I like so well as cooking," Maud said, turning to Jessie with damp eyes.

"Now, now. We'll have no tears," Jessie said. "You'll set me to weeping, too, and my brothers won't stand for a crying woman."

"Then neither of us shall do it." Maud then added, "Unless, of course, we can use the tears to have our way."

Jessie laughed, a deep laugh like a man's. "Sister Maud, I believe we have come to an understanding."

Chapter 3

August 23, 1856

After four weeks of pushing their handcarts across the prairie, Nannie, Ella, Andrew, and the rest of the Martin Company passed Council Bluffs and camped at Florence, the settlement that Brigham Young had once called Winter Quarters. Bone-tired, they pulled their carts into the encampment, grateful for a few days to rest, mend the broken vehicles, and replenish supplies. Andrew was anxious to move on, but his wife and her sister were thankful for a day or two of respite, glad for a time to bake pies and cakes and bread, to spend their hoarded pennies on precious amounts of cinnamon and clove that were available from the merchants, to kneel with other women on the riverbank as they washed clothes or sit a moment and gossip over their mending before the long push—a thousand miles more—to the valley.

"Sit ye, lass," Nannie Macintosh told her sister, Ella Buck, after they had unloaded the cart and sorted through their belongings to see what garments needed washing, which mending—everything, it seemed. "I'll scrub the clothes. When ye are rested, ye can bake the cake, a lovely cake with eggs and butter. We'll not have another till we reach the valley." They had bought the makings for the delicacy from a farmer who had come into the camp with a wagon loaded with produce and dairy products, an abundance the Saints had not seen since leaving Iowa City. Few had money for purchases, however.

Before Nannie picked up the dirty clothes, she helped Ella to the ground so that her sister could rest in the shade of a blanket that Andrew had stretched over tree limbs above their cart. The leaves of the tree quivered in the late-summer breeze. Ella reached out her arm, studying the pattern of sunlight that came through the leaves onto her skin, hoped Utah would have trees and meadows, grasses dark with dew in the morning, and wild roses. But of course it would. After all, they were going to the Salt Lake *Valley*. There might even be heather, Ella thought as she watched her sister walk away, wondering how she could have coped with both the trek and her pregnancy without Nannie. It had been a blessed thing that both of them had left the hard old religion that taught man was sinful and joined the Mormon Church, with its promise of eternal life. Ella stretched her legs and noticed that her slim ankles, of which she'd once been proud, were swollen, either from the walk or her condition—she wasn't sure which. She sighed and leaned back against the cart, and for a moment, she indulged herself in being bone-idle.

"I wish I could sit like that."

Well, of course, some self-righteous sister just had to come along to scold her for her indolence! There always seemed to be those who liked nothing better than finding shortcomings in their fellow Saints. But when Ella looked up, she saw Sister Anne, that strange, angry woman who had come to America with her husband even though she wasn't a Mormon. Ella remembered shouting "We're off" to her the day they began their journey in Iowa City.

"Then why don't ye?" Ella retorted, refusing to let the heretic make her feel guilty. Then she remembered that Anne had lost her daughter on the ship, and she softened, but only a little.

Anne studied Ella a moment, then replied, "No reason I know of, Mrs. Buck," and dropped heavily to the ground, setting Lucy, her little daughter, in her lap.

Anne's pregnancy was more advanced than Ella's, and with a family—Ella had seen her with a little boy, too—she undoubtedly needed rest. Still, Ella was not altogether pleased that the woman had joined her. She had hoped to have a little time to herself, something that was rare among the hundreds of emigrants. Nonetheless, she said, "I believe the Lord will forgive ye and me resting here, if it's not for more than few minutes and we don't get to blethering."

"He would indeed suffer such indolence if *He* were a woman, I think. Have you ever thought we would not have to endure pregnancy if God were a woman?"

Shocked, as any Saint would be at such a thought, Ella caught her breath at the blasphemy, then wondered if it were blasphemy if the sister was not one of them? Thinking over Anne's remark, Ella smiled, however, because she had to agree that the woman was right. "Then where would we get bairns?"

"Some better way. Maybe at the market, or we could pluck them out of a field. Perhaps we'd dig them up like potatoes."

"A bushel at a time?" Ella asked

"We could throw out the bad ones."

"Some there were on the trail that should hae been culled." The two women chuckled. "I wish just once a man would hae a bairn—and hae it through his ear. They would have respect for us then."

The two women burst out laughing, and Anne said, "I've missed women to talk to. I envy you having a sister."

"But ye've a friend in Sister Catherine. I've seen ye together."

"Yes, she is indeed an intimate, and I'm grateful for her. But she's so much older. I would like a friend who is nearer my own age, too."

"Then ye shall be friends with me and my sister, all of us together."

Anne blushed. "Oh, I didn't mean to intrude. I wasn't suggesting that I impose on you."

"Ye make me laugh, and sometimes I purely need to laugh. Besides, we are all one here."

"Not me." Anne ran her hands through her little girl's fine hair, removing a burr. "Perhaps you don't know that I'm not a Mormon."

"Aye, I dae know," Ella said, wondering if Andrew would approve of this woman. She knew Nannie would, because Nannie liked any woman who was outspoken, but Andrew believed women should keep their place. He would not have liked the comment about a man having a baby through his ear, and he would be angry at the remark about God being a woman. "Then why did ye come?"

"My husband is . . . one of you."

"Ye've heard the Gospel and tried to believe?"

"Yes."

Ella was perplexed. She could not understand why anyone who had heard the words come from the mouths of the missionaries was not converted. They made such perfect sense. Who could not be awed by the claim that Mormonism was the restoration of the church Jesus had founded for his saints in the first century, that today's church was the one God had restored for the saints of later days? The Book of Mormon itself was evidence of that, and was a witness to the ministry of Christ. But if this woman had listened to preaching from the likes of Thales Tanner and not seen its truth, she would not be convinced by anything Ella said, and so she dropped the subject. "We share the hard trail and husbands who direct our lives for us. That's enough in common for us to be friends."

Anne relaxed a little and looked out across the busy camp, the children playing, the Saints going about their chores. There was a certain order and purpose to it. "At meeting, I am told, they will discuss whether to winter here or go on to the valley. Summer is sleeping already, and it won't be long till winter. The air is nipping," she said. "What are your thoughts on it?"

Ella did not speak for a moment, not sure whether to confide in this Gentile. "I'm swithered. I'm anxious to reach Zion," she said.

"As are all."

"But I'm tired, too. I donna like to think of walking a thousand miles with a bairn inside me." She turned a little, because the baby she carried had made her uncomfortable.

"Nor do I. It's harder than suits me," Anne said. "We seem to travel backward and forward, and by the end of the day, I'm all in a swelter and wasted with heat. I've had trouble enough to get to camp, but instead of resting, I am charged with preparing supper over a campfire and attending to all the other chores that never seem to end. My husband does as much as he can. He is a good man and doesn't shirk, but still, there are things that only I can do."

"At least, ye do not hae to go to prayer meeting twice a day."

Anne looked up quickly, surprised at Ella's remark, and Ella grinned. "Being a Mormon doesn't mean we don't hae our complaints," she admitted. She looked around, then whispered, "Of course, it isn't wise to say them out loud. But ye being a Gentile, I guess I can tell ye. Not attending the prayer meetings, that's an advantage ye hae over the rest of us."

"You people do preach and sing."

"Aye, and there is joy to it. I love our worship. It is the best part of our trek. But we donna need to do it so often. There are times I would rather have sleep than joy. And times that I dinna care for the subject of the meeting."

"The woman last night?"

"Ye know about her, then?"

"Indeed." Anne nodded. "As does everyone in the company. I suppose you had no choice but to excommunicate her, although I wondered when I heard of it what happened to the doctrine of turning the other cheek."

"She was caught in adultery—twice—with a Gentile from Council Bluffs. She spent the entire night in the woods with him. Even her husband spoke against her."

"And what if he had been the one caught in adultery? Would she have demanded he be excommunicated?" Ella looked at her dumbly and didn't respond, and Anne added, "No, I suppose he would just take the other woman as an additional wife."

"We aren't all of us for celestial marriage. My husband's promised he won't hae any but me for a wife, even wrote it down in my Bible."

Anne gave a short laugh, but instead of arguing, she said, "I am not surprised at what that woman did." Anne set Lucy in the dirt, and the girl began to pick up leaves. "We camped near them one night. He is as cruel a man as ever existed and ill-used his wife. He threw their dinner on the ground because it was burnt and ordered her to make another. When she told him to do it himself, he struck her across the face and knocked her to the ground, saying she deserved it for stirring him to anger. And then he switched her and, when done, said she was lucky, for he could have given her more stick. I've seen bruises on her arms and face."

"That is not our way. An elder should speak to him."

"Some elders, I've noticed, do not interfere in what is between a man and his wife—unless it is the woman who is in the wrong."

"Then she must learn not to provoke him. We are counseled to be obedient. Obedience is a woman's lot."

"Is it?"

Ella looked at Anne curiously, wondering if she had been wrong to make this heretic a friend. "Don't ye believe it's a husband's right to discipline his wife?"

"With a stick and fists?" Anne took a deep breath and settled herself. "Her husband voted with the others to send her out of the camp, and he refused to let her take the children, one of them a babe at her breast. I think it is beastly." She stopped, thinking of Emma Lee and how heartbreaking it was to deprive a mother of her child. "But I believe you do not agree, so I'll say no more about it." She moved so that she could rest against the wheel, and the two sat quietly for a moment, watching Lucy as she shredded a leaf.

Ella thought over what Anne had said. She, too, believed it wrong to take away the children of even a sinful woman, but she would not question the leaders in such a matter, especially to a Gentile. That would be apostasy. Nor would she say more about a man's right to discipline his wife. She wondered what she would do if Andrew ever leathered her, but she could not believe he would do it. Instead, she said, "I've got two minds about wintering here. I want my bairn born in Zion, but what if the snow comes before we reach the valley? What do ye think about going on?"

Anne replied with a trace of bitterness, "I asked leave of my husband to let us stay here and go on in the spring. I told him I would voice no opposition if he would only wait until the baby is born. But he will not hear of it. My labor is so difficult. I dread giving birth by myself on the trail."

"Ye won't be alone. Ye will hae us—my sister and me—and Sister Catherine. And Sister Maud, who is a midwife—"

"And whose husband died a week hence. I daresay she won't make it," Anne interjected. "I lost my older girl on the ocean voyage. If I should lose this baby . . . Sometimes I think God has forsaken me." Anne closed her eyes and could not continue.

Ella had heard the women gossip that the death of Emma Lee was God's way of punishing Anne for not embracing the faith, but she did not believe it now. Nor had she then. She took her new friend's hand and held it for a moment. "God does not forsake us. He only tests us. The God we believe in is wise, and He is kind. I believe He is with us in our suffering."

"Perhaps you are right, but I've not seen it. Oh, I miss her so much!"

"Ye must give it more time."

"Do I have a choice?"

"Ye don't like us much, do ye?" Ella asked.

Anne didn't answer. Instead, she said, "I don't know you."

Ella grasped one of the spokes of the wheel to help herself rise and said she had rested long enough. "I've been lazy as a lord, and there's work to do. I am making a cake. We bought a dozen eggs and butter the size of a cobblestone. I bought a bit of cinnamon, too. Will ye and your family share it with us before tonight's meeting? I promise that Nannie and I will not try to convert you." She thought that over. "But I can't promise aboot Andrew."

"I would like that," Anne replied, turning over so that she rested on her knees, then used her hands to push herself up. "Don't worry about the preaching. I have been preached at so much since I left England that if it stopped, I would think I had gotten carried away by a group of Gentiles."

There were prayers and singing that night, the sacrament was administered, and then the Saints sat quietly while the leaders told them that questions had been raised about the wisdom of continuing on to the valley. Louisa knew that. In the villages they had passed through, the farmers and shopkeepers had warned her family that they were too late in the year to cross the mountains safely. And some of the members of the company who had been to Utah before said that they might encounter snow. Louisa knew the people had talked about it among themselves, so that during the first four weeks of the trip, there had been an undercurrent of disagreement about whether the Saints should stay the winter in Florence or go on. So many in a previous company had abandoned the trek in Florence that a woman remarked to Louisa that the Mormon apostates there were thicker than the lice of Egypt in the days of the Pharaoh. Thales had not liked the remark.

"Who will be first to speak in favor of staying here?" asked Brother Martin.

There was mumbling, but for a moment, no one stood, because, Louisa knew, it was the desire of those in charge to continue, and none wanted to be first to risk their ire. Margaret Chetwin moved a little and appeared ready to speak out, but she looked at her daughter, and Louisa willed her mother to be still. In fact, Louisa was horrified that Margaret might say something. Certainly, it was not a woman's place, but more important, Margaret was Thales Tanner's mother-in-law, and he would be furious, might even call her an apostate. Of course, Louisa sympathized with her mother and her sufferings. The poor woman had to force herself to rise each morning. Sometimes the journey was so tiring that she started off by herself before the carts were under way, so that she could rest at intervals, sitting on a rock with her knitting. She would join the Tanner cart when it reached her, but later on, she'd fall behind and Louisa or her sister would have to turn back to help their mother.

Louisa begged Thales to secure a place for Margaret in one of the wagons, but Thales insisted the wagons were for the truly sick, not those weak in faith. When Louisa argued that her mother's faith was strong, Thales reminded her how Margaret had plotted to stay in New York. Besides, how would it look if he put his mother-in-law into a wagon when others far sicker had to walk?

Now Louisa put a restraining hand on her mother's arm. Surely Margaret knew it would do no good and a great deal of harm if she spoke out. The leaders were of one mind about continuing the trek. Nothing a woman said would dissuade them. Margaret gave her daughter a sad smile and patted her hand. She would keep still.

Others would not, however, and after a few seconds, a man Louisa did not know stood and said he was for staying over. "If it was good enough for Brigham Young to winter at this place in 1846, I guess it's good enough for me. The prophet himself knew enough not to go on."

"The prophet wants us to winter in the valley," a Saint admonished him.

"Bust me if going on's not a poor idea! I've made this trip before. This time of year, too," a man Louisa knew as Old Absalom said. Although elderly, Absalom Schmidt, an early convert, had been tireless in helping the emigrants. He had suffered much for his religion, had been tarred and feathered by an angry mob in Illinois, thrown into the Mississippi to drown by another, and was much admired by Louisa and the other Saints for his steadfast faith. "Most times, we get on just fine this time of year in the mountains, maybe a squall or two, but not heavy snow. Still, that don't mean we won't get it. The Indians tell about such storms. We got womens and childrens with us, old folks, sick ones. It ain't easy for them to cross the mountains in good weather. How will they do if it snows? I say stay. We can go on to the valley next spring in time for planting."

"My wife's with child. I wouldn't like to see her give birth in the snow," Andrew Buck said, and Ella looked at her husband in surprise, because she knew he was anxious to reach the Great Salt Lake. Her heart warmed at his concern.

Some of the men snickered, and a woman muttered, "Humph!" Then a man said, "There's always women giving birth. I don't expect we can hold up the train just because some woman's about to foal."

A few of the Saints laughed at that, too, but Louisa's sister, Huldah, said, "For shame," and there was a murmur of agreement among the women. Louisa did not know if that was because the women wanted to stay or because they objected to the man's language. There was a certain earthiness in the way the people talked.

Then Old Absalom said, "Birthing a baby in the snow ain't a good thing, even for an Indian. For a white woman, it's death. We've already lost some of our people. We'll lose plenty more if we go on."

No one spoke for a moment, even those Louisa thought agreed with the old man, for what good would it do? Louisa was tired and wanted sleep. She knew how the vote would go, and she wished the meeting would conclude. What reason to continue the talk when in the end the leaders would make the decision? She knew that no matter what the arguments were, the company would march on. Beside her, Saints stretched and yawned, while children whined and babies cried. They had spent the day washing and cooking and repairing the carts, and they were weary.

A few, however, yet wanted a say in the decision. After all, their lives depended on it. A woman from Louisa's village suggested a secret vote, with each man putting down his choice. That would be the fairest way. But she was scorned. "We have no secrets," a man told her.

Then slowly, one of the church leaders at Florence went to the front of the gathering. Louisa looked at him with awe and not a little fear, because it was said that he was a member of the Danites, Brigham Young's avenging angels, the band of zealots who were rumored to kill men who opposed the Mormons. "How many of ye joined the Mormon Church for an easy life?" He glared at the Saints, many of whom would not meet his eye. "I tell ye, God don't want no sissies in His church, no fallbacks, and Brigham Young don't, neither. I know Brother Brigham, and I can say he spits on anybody that don't listen to the leaders. If ye won't mind them, then I say go on back to your coal mines and your tea shops. You're grumblers, pilferers, liars, and so forth, good for nothing but hanging. The Destroyer is among ye. You ain't worth the name of Mormon."

One or two Saints yelled their agreement, while those who were offended muttered softly, and Huldah whispered to Louisa, "I would not expose myself to that man's chastisement for all the horses in the land of God." But no one defied him openly.

"The wicked will die off. They'll go to hell across lots," the Danite prophesied, and went to stand by himself, scowling at the Saints. "Those of ye that think ye ought to stay, I say think on it again. Ye likely be destroyed! Long live the devil!"

"Are you for God or against Him?" one of the leaders asked the people after the old man was finished.

"I left home to go to Zion, and I intend to get there this year," called one young man, whose deep cough and ragged clothes identified him as a victim of the factories. "I joined up to go to Zion. I say we go on, and anybody that don't like it can stay behind."

"I'd rather go to hell than be left behind," a convert yelled.

When no one else spoke out, the people looked around, anxious, whispering. Then when it seemed that the leaders were about to call for a vote, Thales Tanner stood, and the Saints quieted. Louisa knew that some of the Saints revered her husband, a few found him pompous, but all agreed he was a man of God and that he spoke for Brigham Young. Although he was of less than average height, he appeared big because his body was square, his beard cut square on a rectangular face. He seemed taller than he was, too, since he loomed above the Saints who were sitting on the ground. The missionary looked out over the congregation for a moment, nodding at one or two whom he recognized. Then his eyes flickered as they lit on Louisa, and she felt a thrill of excitement, and she was no longer tired. This was the man she had fallen in love with, this passionate missionary who seemed to speak for God. At times like this, she forgave him his overbearing ways toward her and her family, for he truly could be inspired, and he was now, she knew. She glanced at her mother, who stared at her son-in-law with rapture, and Louisa knew that Margaret, too, felt his presence as a man of God.

Thales held out his right arm full length to still the crowd and waited until the gathering was silent, until the people were poised to hear what he had to say, and then he began in a voice as soothing as if he were talking to a baby. "My dear friends, we have embarked on a remarkable journey, a journey that has taxed even the strongest amongst us," he said, then stopped, and Louisa was taken by his choice of words. He did not berate the Saints. He did not even chide them as befuddled children, but instead, he made himself one with them.

"We are chosen of the Lord. We have seen the true Gospel and have pledged ourselves to it. God has singled us out and put His mark on us."

He paused as an undercurrent of voices gave thanks and praised God.

"Is there anyone here who does not feel blessed?"

"No, brother!" a man called, and the people voiced their agreement.

"Anyone who does not thank the Lord?"

This time, there were cries of thanks.

"Anyone who would not do what little the Lord asks of us in return for His great blessings?"

"No! No!" the Saints called.

Thales looked around for a moment, until his eyes lit on Louisa again, and she knew that later, when everyone was asleep, he would reach for her. He always wanted her after the spirit was on him, when he was taken up with preaching like this. A thrill went over her as she thought of his gentle hands caressing her. He was caring in bed, not demanding as he was in the daylight. She had not expected that.

Thales's eyes glistened, and he made fists with his hands, raising them in the air. "Then is there anyone here who would not go to Zion if the Lord and Brigham Young asked him to? Is there anyone so weak in faith that he would defy the prophet?"

There was a crescendo of response this time, women clapping, men jumping up and pounding their fists into the air.

"Then I say we go on." Thales's voice had a hard edge now. "I say let the cowards and the apostates stay. They will find a curse come upon them. But we will go Zionward, just as Brigham Young wills us. We will do as the Lord commands. We will go up into the high mountain. We will go to Zion!"

"Ho! For Zion!" a man called.

"The Lord will look after His people. He parted the Red Sea for Moses and the Israelites and led them into the Promised Land." Thales could not stop now, and his voice was like thunder. "The Lord our God will lead us into the land of Zion. We are His people, and He will turn away the storms while we pass by. It may storm on our right and on our left, but the Lord will keep open our way before us. I will eat every flake of snow that falls upon the Saints."

Louisa was so moved by Thales that tears ran down her face. He was indeed God's saint among the Saints. She could not be more sure of that if the heavens had opened and a voice from on high had anointed him. She glanced around the crowd, the people standing now, their faces beaming. But not all, she thought, her eyes resting on knots of emigrants who stood silently, not daring to catch the eyes of the joyful. Old Absalom stood off by himself, his head bowed, his arms folded, as if he were praying.

One of the Saints joshed the old man, demanding, "Ye stay behind with the other apostates, will ye, Brother Absalom?"

Louisa watched the people who were near the old man quiet to hear his reply, to see whether he would form a group of staybacks whose refusal to continue on with the handcarts might mean excommunication. She knew there were some who did indeed hope he would be their leader. After all, he was a man who had known Joseph, a man equal to any in the church. If Old Absalom stood with them, then surely Brother Brigham would not turn his back on them.

"Will you stay?" a woman asked him.

Old Absalom looked at her for a long time, then with his arm, he pushed her away a little. "I will go," he said. "If it's the will of the Saints to go on to the valley, then I'll be with you. And I'll help you through. But if the heavens open and the snows come, then Old Absalom can do nothing. You will be in the hands of the Lord."

Jessie and her brothers were among the Saints who were anxious to proceed. They were young and strong and used to the elements, and they might have gone on even if the rest of the party had voted to remain, for they were eager to claim their stewardship. They had not crossed the ocean and half of the American continent just to spend the winter in a tent on the Missouri River. So when the Saints were polled, the Coopers raised their hands and voted with those who wanted to continue the trip.

But what about Maud, the old widow woman whose care had fallen to them? Maud was tough, and she asked no sympathy from the three young people. Still, she was elderly, and Jessie had seen her stumble on the trail, had seen her sit down in the dirt beside the road and gulp air as if her lungs had collapsed. What would become of her if she chose to stay behind? Jessie sought out the woman and asked, "Will you be going along with us?"

"Yes."

"You don't have to. There are others wintering here. There is no shame in it, to my way of thinking. I don't believe Brigham Young will chastise you, despite the threats from Brother Tanner and that old zealot."

Maud frowned. "I have no desire to stay behind, Jessie. Me and Robert signed up to go all the way to Zion, and now I'm going for the both of us." Her eyes gleamed with conviction, and she straightened up. "Of course, when you think on it, he's beat me there. I just got to catch up." Then she paused as a thought occurred to her. "Is it that you believe I will be a burden on you? I can go on by myself if you don't want me. You can speak plainness."

"Of course, we want you. We never ate so well, even at home. Why, to keep you with us, my brothers would push you on the cart."

"They won't have to do that. I'll do my part. I'll make it on these old legs or perish in the trying of it." Then she stared at the young woman, who was watching her intently. "Are you wishing to stay yourselves?"

Jessie shook her head. "No, that's not what I'm thinking. We're game to go. A bull couldn't hold back the Coopers. I'm just wondering why you'd risk the cold and the snow when you could just as well go in the spring, when it would be easier on you. It's only a few months."

Maud wrapped her hands in her apron and stared across the prairie. "I might not have a few months. You young folks have a plenty of time. A winter spent here wouldn't mean a thing to you. But me, I'm so old, I might not live through the winter. So I have to go on."

Ella Buck beamed at her husband as they walked to their tent. "Andrew, I never knew ye to be so thoughtful of me," she told him. "But ye musn't worry. I can hae the baby fine. There's already others born on this trip, and that old widow woman, Sister Maud, is a midwife. Nannie will be with me, too." Ella smiled at her sister, who was walking beside her.

Andrew touched his wife's cheek. "Do ye want to stay behind? Some are going to. It's nice enough beside the river, and there's not a drop of dye in it." The river that flowed beside the factory where he had worked as a weaver had been dark with dye and stank from the chemicals.

"No, we'll go on with the others. Isn't that what ye want?"

"To be sure," he said.

Ella turned to her sister. "Do I not have the best husband in the world?"

"Aye," Nannie replied. But she could not help wondering if Ella's pregnancy wasn't the real reason Andrew had spoken in favor of staying. Andrew was slight, and even after the weeks pushing the cart across the prairie, he was weak from the years he had spent with the loom. His lungs still suffered from the foul air and the lint that he had breathed in the factory, and Nannie knew he was worried that he had contracted weaver's consumption. Although he would never admit it, Andrew might not be strong enough to pull the cart the rest of the way to Utah Territory and was using his wife as an excuse to rest through the winter. Nannie pondered that, hoping she was wrong, because if she was right and Andrew indeed had inflammation of the lungs, she and Ella would have the responsibility of getting the three of them to the valley.

Anne Sully knew that no matter how many others stayed behind, she and John and the children would go on, and that once they left Florence, there was no turning back. She had not even bothered to attend the meeting with her husband. Instead, she had stayed near the campfire to do the baking for the journey—the bread and corn bread, the tart and cake that she would not have time to prepare on the trail.

They had argued over whether to stay, Anne pleading her difficulty with childbirth, but John was against it, pointing out that it wouldn't be any harder for her to give birth on the trail than to do so in a squalid tent near the river, where the chill rose up out of the ground and sickened children. The little one would be healthier because it would be born in the high mountains instead of in the miasma of the river. So because she knew that John would never change his mind, Anne had ceased her complaints and given in. And strangely enough, she had felt the better for it. She told herself that she was not the only woman who would give birth on the trail. There were others with child, among them Ella Buck, the young woman she had talked with the day before who was so excited that her baby would be born in Zion—or on the way, for the vigorous exercise of walking across the prairie seemed to bring on labor. Others had delivered before their time. Ella had told her that God would take care of them because they were marching to His kingdom. Anne envied Ella her faith, even while she scoffed at its foolishness.

In fact, after her weeks among them, Anne had begun to envy all of the Saints their faith, their heartfelt, sometimes childlike belief that God had chosen them. The Mormon worship, with its uplifting songs and cries of praise, was so different from the solemn rituals she had practiced in the Church of England, just as the promise of a happy afterlife the Mormons believed in as God's chosen people contrasted with the gloomy threats of the Lord's wrath toward the sinful of her own faith, the threats of burning forever in hell.

But still, Anne could not embrace the strange doctrine of the Church of Jesus Christ of Latter-day Saints, nor the commandment that the faithful gather in the Salt Lake Valley. Many believed that they must hurry to Zion before the Lord unleashed a pox upon the earth, but if that were the case, why were the emigrants planning to start farms and open businesses? Why were the Mormons the only ones God told about the "last days"? Another missionary had said that the British Saints were like trees in a nursery. They were being transplanted to Zion, where there was room for them to grow and flourish. She had not been pleased to be compared with a sapling.

Anne questioned why the Saints couldn't forget that foolishness and just stay home and practice their religion there. If she had remained in England, perhaps she would have come round to John's faith. But she could not condone a religion that required such sacrifice—the sacrifice of her own daughter—just to gather in the mountains of America beside a dead sea. She wondered if Brigham Young were calling the people to the valley to build up his own kingdom, not God's.

"We leave in the morning, Annie," John said, emerging out of the darkness to sit down beside her at the campfire.

She had not heard him return from the meeting, and she was startled. At first, she thought to object one last time, to reply with chosen remarks about the foolhardiness of going on when they might run into poor weather, but instead, she bit her tongue. Such replies did no good and only hardened John in his decisions. "We'll be ready. The children were as sleepy as laudanum, and I put them to bed. I've prepared enough food for the next few days. Did they argufy much?"

"Oh, yes, but almost all wanted to go on. It's for the best." John put his arm around her, and his lips brushed the top of her head. "It's not been easy for you. I know it."

He had not said that before, and Anne was moved. "No," she replied, "but it's been tolerable fair." Except for Emma Lee, she thought, but she would not burden her husband with that now.

"It's a long journey, and you've given up much."

She nodded, although he could not see her in the dark.

"Are you liking the Mormons a little more?"

Anne pulled away from her husband to remove a skillet from the fire, then leaned back into John's arms. "I like the Mormons fine. It's their religion—your religion—that I have a quarrel with."

"I thought by now . . ."

Anne felt a certain sadness as she realized her husband's tenderness was not caused by his feelings of concern for her but was yet another attempt to convert her. She wondered if that would always be so, if the closeness they had felt those first years of their married life would return only if she gave up her soul to the Mormons. Then she wondered if maybe she ought to pretend to accept the church. That would not only restore domestic harmony but would keep that bothersome missionary Thales Tanner away from her. Did it matter if she lied? But it did matter. "I am pretty well worn. Let's not discuss it," she said.

Louisa had been right about Thales. The two slept outside the tent, and when all was quiet, Thales pulled her to him. She swallowed her embarrassment that someone might awaken and know what they were about—although she herself had heard other couples moving around in the night—and yielded to him, for she wanted him to need her. She listened to the snores, the sleeping cries of children, the coughs of the older people as Thales's body moved on top of hers, and at last, she felt him shudder, then move away, satisfied, and he fell asleep holding her in his arms. Louisa took her own satisfaction in knowing that she had pleasured him and that tomorrow he would be tender toward her and her family.

He is not an easy man, but he is a good one, Louisa thought. Oh, she knew that Jessie Cooper considered him overbearing and self-important and that others found him unyielding. But they did not know him the way she did. They did not hear him pour out his heart, bemoaning his weaknesses, his sins. They did not know how he worried that God would find him inadequate, how he prayed that he would be strong enough to see his hundred through to Zion, how he suffered over each Saint whose faith faltered.

She had heard her husband beg God to let him be the instrument for converting the Gentile who accompanied her Mormon husband, and knew his sense of failure when the woman repulsed him. Louisa did not understand how the woman— *Sister* Anne, she was in Louisa's mind—could live among them all those weeks and not become a convert. Now as she lay beside her husband, listening to his deep breathing, Louisa decided she would try again with the woman. Perhaps if she did not talk about religion, if she put off trying to convert Sister Anne but instead lived her life as an example of the true faith, Louisa might move her.

Long before the cornet sounded, Louisa felt Thales leave their blankets and knew he would be sorting through the belongings in the Tanner cart, a task he had put aside the night before in his desire for her. Brother Martin and the captains in charge of the hundreds had ordered the Saints to undergo another purge, to throw out everything that wasn't necessary, since each cart was now to be loaded with a hundred-pound bag of flour. Of course, that weight would lessen as the flour was consumed, but the next days of travel would be difficult.

So her husband was following his own dictate and searching for things that could be discarded, and when Louisa rose and went to the cart, she found her silver hand mirror lying on the ground between the cart's wheels. The mirror had been Thales's wedding present to her, and she protested leaving it behind, for it was her prized possession. "I can carry the mirror. I will tie a string around the handle and fasten it to my waist," she promised her husband.

"We are to rid ourselves of everything that is not necessary. What would it look like if as head of our hundred, I allowed my wife to take along such a luxury? I must set the example." He looked at Louisa, whose eyes pleaded with him, and perhaps because he remembered the night before, he added, "I shall buy you another once we reach the valley."

Louisa searched his face, uncertain. "Do they have mirrors in Zion?"

"Of course they do. And until then, you can see yourself reflected in my eyes." He leaned over and kissed her forehead in an uncharacteristic gesture of affection. "You are so pretty, you deserve to see yourself in a mirror when we get there. I think you will be surprised at how you are no longer a girl in her first bloom. You have become a woman all at once."

Louisa flushed, because Thales did not often compliment her. "Pleasing you is my fondest desire. I hope I may always do so."

"And I you," he replied, and Louisa turned away, knowing he meant what had happened in the night. She was overwhelmed by the remark, because she and Thales never discussed such things. Then her husband added, "I am hoping that before we reach Zion, there will be proof of it."

He smiled at her, and Louisa flushed. That was her wish, too, and a wish, she thought, that might have been granted already. But she said nothing, because the nausea she had dealt with each morning for the past few days might have come from straining behind the cart or kneeling beside the river with the washing, not from a child growing inside her. Although she thought she had become pregnant as far back as Iowa City, she would wait a little longer to tell him.

Thales left Louisa and her family the chore of rearranging the cart so that he could attend to his duties as head of the hundred, and the family unpacked the cart and laid out their possessions and began the difficult task of choosing what to discard. Margaret threw away her second pair of shoes, saying she could go barefoot until bad weather set in, and Louisa's sister left behind her pillow and an umbrella. Hall took a letter knife from his pocket and set it on the ground, causing Margaret to protest that its weight was of no consequence. But he insisted that if others were leaving behind their treasures, he would do so, too.

Then after the cart was repacked to Louisa's satisfaction, for in Thales's absence, Louisa, not her father, took charge of the family, she picked up the crosspiece, and her sister arranged herself behind the cart to push. Before they could get under way, however, Hall—the only man present—begged to pull the cart, and Louisa agreed. He would feel belittled if he let the women do the work, especially at the outset. Besides, he still suffered the embarrassment of having been called an apostate by his son-in-law, and he needed to redeem himself. That left Louisa free to walk beside her mother, who appeared stronger that morning because of the days she had rested in Florence.

Margaret was cheerful, too. "Once my poor feet toughen up, I believe I will do a better job of the walk than before," she confided. "I have such faith that I will reach Zion."

"God blesses us," Louisa replied. She turned to look at her mother, but instead, she caught the eye of the Gentile. "Good morning, Sister Anne," she called.

Anne was pushing her own cart, while her husband pulled it. Their son, Joe, pushed alongside Anne. The baby, Lucy, perched on top. The cart rolled along easily on the flat, dry surface, and Anne let go of it for a moment to walk beside Louisa. "Good morning, Mrs. Tanner," she replied. Louisa did not correct Anne by saying she was not Mrs. Tanner, but Sister Louisa. In time, when Anne is one of us, Louisa thought, she will adopt the Mormon form of address.

"It's a morning the Lord has made," Louisa said. Indeed, the day was dry and cool, with a feeling of fall, for it was now late August. The sun would beat down on them later in the day—that is, if rain didn't soak them—but the morning was glorious. Louisa looked across the plains at the prairie grass, dried now to a golden brown. The stalks rustled as the carts and the Saints trampled them. When we reach camp, Louisa thought, I shall gather the grass and wind it together for kindling. There were bright wildflowers among the grasses, and birds sang, their shrill notes rising above the murmuring of the travelers. The land was so different from England, but Louisa had come to love the dry air, the clean, bright sky, the openness.

Someone at the front of the train began the Mormon favorite, "Come, Come, Ye Saints," and the song spread down the line of carts as the emigrants joined in. Anne, too, sang the song, in a sweet, strong voice, and Louisa thought what a good Mormon the woman would make.

She wanted to remark on it, to say how the Mormons loved the singers among them, but she knew if she did, the woman would turn cold. So instead, she confided, "I am glad to have a chance to speak a word with you, for I should like to ask your advice."

When Anne looked at her sharply, Louisa wondered why in the world she had spoken up. Although she had not confided her suspicions to her family, she knew she should have inquired of her sister, Huldah, who had delivered two children. She lowered her voice. "I cannot ask my mother or my sister, for if I should be wrong, then great will be their disappointment." She paused, not sure how to bring up the subject. But the Saints were a direct people, so she simply said, "I believe I am with child, although I do not know for certain, and I would ask your advice."

"About what?" Anne asked.

"How I should care for myself."

Anne gave a short laugh and replied sourly, "If we were at home, I would tell you to drink plenty of milk, to rest with your feet on a footstool so that your legs and ankles would not swell up. I should advise you to engage a hired girl to do the heavy work and to take naps in the afternoon."

Louisa laughed, and in a minute, Anne joined her. "Have you any other questions I can help you with?" Anne asked, and they both laughed again.

They walked on a little, Louisa leaning over to pick a purple flower beside the trail and handing it to Anne. "Here is my thanks until you are better paid."

Anne stuck the flower into a buttonhole in her dress. "How are you feeling?"

"Very middling."

"I would tell you to rest as much as you can, then, but how can you do that when you're pushing a handcart?" She thought it over and added, "Who knows, perhaps all this walking will strengthen us. There is some talk, you know, that women should not be pampered when they are in our state, but encouraged to exercise, so that their bones will be strong and the blood will flow to the vital organs."

"If that is so, we are better prepared than any women in

the world. In any case, I believe God will see me through. And you?"

"I am not so sure. I have a difficult time with it and have nearly died."

Louisa impulsively took the other woman's hand. "I'm sorry for that."

"I will manage, I suppose. Most women have it easier," she said, as if she were sorry she had frightened Louisa.

"I'll pray for you."

Anne frowned and reminded Louisa that she was not a Mormon.

"Do you think we Mormons pray only for ourselves? I shall pray all the harder for you to show you how much God loves you. And to show you that I, too, love you," she added as she broke away to catch up with the Tanner cart, because her sister Huldah had stopped pushing and was rubbing her back.

Anne stared at Louisa Tanner as Louisa replaced Huldah behind their family's cart. With the exception of Catherine, Anne had exchanged virtually no confidences with other women since leaving England, but in the past two days, she had made two friends—Ella and the pious Louisa. She had undertaken the journey with hundreds of other women, and yet she had isolated herself. She had held herself aloof to avoid the proselytizing, and in doing so, she had robbed herself of intimacy with other women. Anne missed the connection, the sharing of confidences and complaints that only another woman could understand. After all, where was the husband who could sympathize with the difficulties of pregnancy? She would need these friendships during the miles that lay ahead on the trail—and later on, after she was settled in the valley. It would be a wise thing to make friends now.

She wondered if the plural wives in Zion were intimates with one another. She had heard that some Mormon men had taken sisters as wives and that more than one man had married a mother and her daughter. Did the women remain friends, or did that hideous system destroy their closeness? The latter was more likely, because how could you be close to a woman who shared her bed with your husband? How could you hold her in esteem after you heard your husband on the bedsprings in her bedroom? The Mormons could call it "plural marriage" or "celestial marriage" or "the principle" or anything they wanted, but it was plainly immoral. It was despicable.

At home, when she and John had talked about that strange doctrine—because by then, it was common knowledge that Mormons were polygamous—neither one of them had seriously considered that John would ever take another wife. The idea was too vile, he told her, so with all her resentment toward the Mormon Church, Anne, at least, did not have that worry. Still, once when they had argued about making the trip, Anne had lashed out, saying she supposed that once they reached the valley, he would find himself another woman, so why should she go all that way just to be set aside? Instead of denying it or defending the principle, John had stared at her incredulously, then burst into laughter, and when he was unable to stop, Anne found herself smiling a little, then laughing, too.

"You are the candle of my eye. Do you think with the wife I have, I would ever want another? Why, no woman would measure up," he said. Then he added, "Where is the woman who would agree to have *you* as her sister-wife? There is no woman alive who could best you." And they both laughed again.

Of course, she had thought a little about it, and eventually, she told John that if he ever brought home another woman, she would take the children and return to England, and no one could stop her. "No court in the land would rule in favor of such barbarous conduct," she said.

But John assured her that on that score, she could ease her mind. "I have never wanted any woman but you," he said, then added for emphasis, "and I never will."

Knowing he spoke the truth, Anne had said, "Now, if your church would rule that a woman might have more than one husband, I might look more favorably on it." But instead of laughing, John had frowned, as if she'd asked that the laws of creation be repealed, and Anne said no more about it. Still, she thought to herself, with two husbands, I might have stayed home in England with one of them.

She hurried now to catch up with John and push the cart, because Joe would be tired and want to run off across the prairie. He was a dear little boy, always helpful and full of fun, and while she blamed God and the Mormons for Emma Lee's death, she was grateful that Joe and Lucy had been spared. And there was the little one inside of her. Anne hoped that if the baby was a girl, John would agree to name her Emma Lee.

Jessie knew that Maud's ankles were rubbery and her back hurt from helping heft the sack of flour onto the cart, but the old woman didn't complain. In fact, she was in fine spirits as she walked along the trail beside Jessie, who was pushing the cart.

Earlier, the two had stopped while Maud advised a woman who had asked about a bowel complaint, since it was known among the Saints now that Maud was as good as any doctor. Maud had told her about a concoction that would give her relief and promised to mix it for her after they camped for the night. The woman went back to her cart, and Jessie and Maud dawdled, looking out over the prairie in search of herbs to add to Maud's dwindling cache.

"So many grasses and plants I've not seen before. Each has its purpose, if only I knew what it was. Look at that yellow flower as tiny as a gnat. I know God didn't create it just to be pretty. You ask Him what I can use it for," she muttered. Jessie didn't have the least idea, and if she asked God for help, she wouldn't waste the request on a flower. But then she realized the old woman was talking to Robert. Maud did that sometimes when she thought no one was listening. At first, Jessie had thought Maud's mind was half-cracked, that she had gone dotty. But the younger woman rather liked the idea that Maud's husband was watching over his wife. It appealed to Jessie, because nobody had ever watched over her.

As the two women caught up to the cart, Jessie saw that one of the wheels wobbled, and that the wheel shook even worse as they descended a hill. Ephraim, who was pulling, announced they would stop near a ravine, where there was shade for the women to rest. The Cooper vehicle was not only made of green wood but had been hastily constructed, and the brothers, Ephraim and Sutter, had to stop often to make repairs. It was a pity they had not taken Maud's cart, but by the time she joined them, her cart had been claimed by others.

"I must say, I don't mind stopping for a few minutes," Jessie said, and the two women sat in the dirt while the brothers examined the wheel. "It's the infernal dust. At home, I could take a bath whenever I wanted, as often as once a week, if I felt like it. But here with so many people, it is difficult. I wonder if we will bathe before we reach Zion. I can't hardly stand to camp near someone because of the smell of all the unwashed bodies."

"When the weather turns cold, it won't be so bad," Maud replied.

"It's the axle," Sutter called, and the two women stood, because the cart might have to be unloaded.

Just then, a Saint pulling a cart stopped beside them and offered to help. "I'm Brother Addison Gray, a carpenter by trade, and I have my tools. I believe we can strengthen your axle enough so that you can reach camp. Then we'll take the cart apart and repair it," he said. When the brothers protested that they could do it, the man told them, "Three will make light work of it. Besides, my wife, Sophia, is tired, and she would like a chance to rest." He smiled fondly at the woman beside him. So the women unloaded the cart. Then, while the men turned it over and began to work on the axle, Sophia stood beside them, watching, and so did her daughter, Emeline, a pretty, solemn girl of about thirteen.

"You are tired," Maud told Sophia.

The woman nodded. "I do poorly. I have had a hurting in my breast since before we left England, and I pray that I can reach the valley before I die."

Maud frowned. "You should not have made the trip."

"And died in England? I would not deny my husband and daughter a home in Zion."

"I have herbs to help."

"Nothing will help me."

"For the pain."

Sophia nodded and closed her eyes.

"She did not complain much," Jessie said softly.

Maud whispered, "Look at her face. She hasn't long, perhaps only days."

As Jessie stood to look at the woman, she glanced back up the trail and gasped. The others turned quickly and saw a cart rushing down the hill toward them, out of control. Its owner had slipped and fallen between the wheels of the vehicle, which passed over him, and with nothing to stop it, the cart gathered force. It wasn't much of a hill, and the cart was not going fast, but it hit a rut and was tossed into the air, smashing into the Gray cart. There was a long scream and a splintering of wood, and the women hurried over, while the Saints behind them rushed forward to help. Addison lay crumpled on the ground. Sophia crouched over him, while Ephraim was sprawled in the ravine, his left arm cradled in his right hand, agony etched on his face. "I fell on my arm. It's broke," he said. Sutter went to his brother and tried to examine the wound, but Ephraim groaned and shoved him away with his good elbow.

"If it's broke, the arm's got to be set, and it will pain him some," Maud told him. "Let me have a look at it. But first, I'll see to Brother Addison. He must be dazed."

"He's not moved," Sophia said. She herself had been hurt

when the cart fell against her, her dress torn, but, out of concern for her husband, she refused to let Maud examine her.

Maud raised Addison's head and pushed back his eyelids.

"Is he all right?" Sophia asked, wringing her hands. "He's as healthy as the fresh wind. It's such a little accident. The cart just knocked him over. He ought not to be lying there like that."

"I believe he must have hit his forehead on a rock. See it here in the road, as big as a loaf of bread." Maud laid the man's head back down and felt for a pulse, then put her ear to Addison's chest. By now, the Coopers were gathered around the prostrate man, even Ephraim, who was supporting his broken arm. And a growing number of the brethren had stopped their carts and were offering to help.

"He'll come to, won't he?" Sophia asked. "I'll pray. Emeline and I will pray." She knelt down beside the cart, her daughter next to her, folding her arms and bowing her head.

A woman took a small mirror from her cart and gave it to Maud, who held it to Addison's mouth. "I fear not," Maud said sadly. "I fear he's with the Lord."

Some of the Saints gasped, and a few knelt in the dirt and prayed. Sophia, her hands pressed together in front of her, slowly looked up at Maud. "But he was talking to these men not more than a minute ago. He can't be . . ." She swallowed. "He can't be dead." Sophia shook her head. "The accident was of no consequence."

"It happens that way sometimes," Maud told her.

Sophia looked from Maud to Jessie and said, "But you saw him. Didn't you hear him say he'd help fix the cart when we camped? Addison always keeps his word."

The woman might have said more, but all of a sudden, Emeline, who had not uttered a word since she'd stopped with her parents, took her mother's arm and tugged at her. "Mama, he's gone. He's no more with us."

At that, Sophia broke into tears, and Emeline, like a little old woman, comforted her, patting her on the back and leading her away from the body of Addison Gray. "He's in Zion, Mama. He's waiting for us there."

Sophia shook her head. "I'm the one who is not supposed to make it to the valley. Who will take care of me? Who will take care of Emeline if something happens to me?"

Maud started to say that she would, but she stopped, because she could do nothing for the woman unless the Coopers agreed to take her on. She looked at the brothers, realizing then that she had forgotten about Ephraim, who was pale now, perspiration running down his face. As she stood up to attend to Ephraim, Maud glanced at Jessie, hoping she would speak.

But before Jessie could offer, Emeline said, "I will, Mama. I'll take care of you. I'll pull the cart, and you can push. Brother Martin will assign others to help. And if God wills, then I will take care of myself."

"You're just a little girl," Maud told her.

"I'm strong. I'm as strong as a boy, and look at how many boys are pulling carts." She ducked under the crossbar of the Gray cart and stood between the traces. "Can you push a little, Mother?" she asked.

"We must load your father onto the cart," her mother said, although Sophia herself could barely stand up.

"We will do that," Jessie told her. "We'll take your husband's body on our cart, and we'll prepare it for burial once we reach camp." She examined the Gray cart and pronounced it in good condition, although the handcart that had crashed into it was smashed, and one of its wheels lay in the road.

The owner of the broken cart went to Sophia then and told her he would push her cart if he could load his things onto it. He introduced himself as Brother Prime.

Jessie knew Brother Prime and did not like him much, because he was quarrelsome. He had started the journey with his brother, who had an inflammation of the lungs, and Brother Prime had complained about having to bear an unfair share of the work. Jessie had heard him say he would not have agreed to the trip if he had known he would have to do the labor of two. Eventually, the brother could not take Prime's complaints and sat down beside the trail, announcing he would go no farther. He died in the night, and learning of his brother's demise, Prime had thrown away the man's belongings, which included a photograph of the brother's family, who were still in England, and a half-finished letter to his wife.

Now Jessie wondered whether Brother Prime would help the newly widowed woman or simply appropriate her cart. But she knew she must attend to Ephraim, so she turned away from Sophia.

Ephraim was sitting in the dirt beside the Coopers' cart, Maud leaning over him while she examined his arm, for it was indeed broken. The ends of bones poked through the flesh. She prodded a little, nodding when Ephraim winced. "It's a bad break. I can move the bones into place, but I must do it now, and it will hurt. There isn't time to find whiskey to dull the pain."

Sutter sat down beside his brother while Jessie found a stick and told Ephraim to bite on it as Maud probed with her fingers, adjusting the bones until the ends met. Ephraim grimaced, his teeth sinking into the stick as the old woman worked. When she was finished, Maud told Jessie to tear a strip off a sheet to bind the break.

"We have none," Jessie replied.

"Then a piece of petticoat will do," Maud said, and Jessie raised her skirt and tore off a strip of white.

Maud placed two sticks against the arm to keep the bones in place, then wrapped the whole in the strip of petticoat. "You mustn't use your arm," she said.

"Then how can I push the cart?" Ephraim asked.

"We'll push it. You can ride on top," Sutter told him.

"It's only one arm. God gave me two," Ephraim replied, but his face was flushed and damp. He got to his feet clumsily, then nearly fell over in a faint.

"Ride, or we'll leave you behind," Jessie said. So Ephraim hefted himself on top of the cart and lay down next to the dead man. Then Sutter pulled and Jessie and Maud pushed the cart with its loose axle to the evening's campsite.

The Saints buried Addison Gray that evening, wrapped in a blanket that Emeline had stitched into a shroud, and when the service was finished, Maud told Sophia, "You must rest and warm yourself against the night chill." She turned to Emeline. "Did Brother Addison have a coat? Fetch it for your mother."

Emeline went to the cart, then returned empty-handed.

"Papa's things are gone. That man—Brother Prime—must have throwed them out."

"Or kept them for himself. I wager he's wearing the coat," Jessie said.

Sophia started to say something, then coughed and fell backward onto the ground, knocking off her sunbonnet. Maud noticed for the first time that the woman's face was badly bruised, her hair bloody, and there were cuts on her face that had started to bleed.

"I never asked her if she was hurt. She's in a bad way. She's lost blood and is losing more, and I ought to bandage her head," Maud told Jessie, then whispered, "She was already in a bad way. I worry she will last the night."

Jessie raised her skirt. "I've got what's left of my petticoat." She unbuttoned the garment, which was ragged from the strips she'd ripped off to bind Ephraim's arm, stepped out of it, and handed it to Maud, who knelt and ministered to the woman, Emeline beside her, whimpering, "Mama. Mama." The girl was as pale as wax, her eyes wet with tears. "It's not fair, Papa gone and her dying after she walked all this way. God wouldn't do that, would He? She'll be all right, won't she?"

"We'll do everything we can. It might help if you prayed," Maud told her. Emeline moved a little so that she was on her knees, but she would not leave her mother.

Sophia weakened, and after a time, she did not respond when Maud prodded her. Jessie went in search of an elder to administer to her, but the man looked at the woman and declared he did not have faith enough to raise the dead, then left.

"Can't we do something?" Jessie asked Maud as the eastern sky turned gray with the dawn.

Maud shook her head, and the three, the two women and the girl, knelt in prayer until, just as the sun came up, Sophia died. She was buried next to Addison, following a hasty service, because the carts had to move out and departure could be delayed for neither birth nor death.

As the men shoveled dirt onto the blanket-wrapped body, Emeline began to wail. She had been dry-eyed during her father's burial. But now as the body of her mother was put into the earth, the finality of her parents' deaths weighed on her, and she threw herself onto the ground and sobbed. Jessie put her arms around the orphan, raising her to her feet, then leading her to the Gray cart. "We must move on," Jessie said, "but know the Lord is with you in your sorrow. And so are Sister Maud and I."

Prime had already thrown Sophia's things onto the ground, and he was anxious to move along. "She can push," he said, jerking with his thumb at Emeline. "I guess she's my responsibility now."

Neither Jessie nor Maud liked the looks of the man and did not want Emeline to share a cart with him. "P'raps I should move my things to the cart so's I could stay with the girl," Maud muttered, watching as Emeline shrank away from Prime, pleading, "Don't make me go with him."

"You'll do what you're told," he said.

Ephraim spoke up. "She'll travel with us. Put your things on our cart, Sister Emeline." Both Maud and Jessie looked at him in surprise, while Emeline gazed at him as her savior.

Prime glared at Ephraim, then at Sutter, but when the two men stood firm, Prime picked up the girl's clothes and thrust them at her. Emeline didn't take them, however. Instead, she turned to Maud. "Even though the church owns it, it's my cart, ain't it? It was give to Mama and Papa, so it's mine now, ain't it?"

"You can't push it by yourself," Maud told her.

"No, I can't, but if I'm to go with you and Sister Jessie, I can trade it to you for your cart, can't I? Ours is better made, and the axle ain't broke like yours, is it?"

"Your mother give it to me," the man insisted. "It's mine to keep."

"No, it's Emeline's," Ephraim said, and the others gathered behind him. They unpacked their handcart, and the man reluctantly removed his things from the Gray cart.

When they were finished, Emeline went through her mother's clothes, which were lying on the ground, where Prime had thrown them. She picked up her mother's small purse, then asked, "Where's Mama's wedding ring?" She stared hard at the man.

He shrugged. "You must have buried her with it."

"No, her hands got so thin, she feared she'd lose it, so she sewed it in the pocket of her extra dress. Here's the dress, and look, the thread's broke."

The man turned away and began packing his things on the Cooper cart.

"Indeed, sir! I believe you have the ring," Ephraim said, looming over Prime.

"I believe you can mind your own business."

"The girl is our business. You've no right to her mother's

ring. Do you want to hand it to her, or shall I search you?" Although Ephraim was weak and feverish, his voice was like flint.

"Oh, well, I didn't think anybody wanted it. I figured it was mine for my troubles." He reached into a pocket and took out a thin gold band with garnets and pearls embedded in it. Emeline snatched it up.

"Aren't you ashamed to steal something on the way to Zion? And a dead woman's wedding ring at that!" Ephraim said, his voice loud enough for other Saints to hear. "If there's a thing missing again, we'll know where to look."

Maud, Emeline, and the Coopers watched as Prime took up his cart and hurried off. Then Sutter picked up the crosspiece of the Gray cart, and Jessie and Maud positioned themselves at the back to push. Ephraim reached for a stout stick that his brother had given him and, wincing, began to hobble down the trail. But Emeline touched his arm and said, "Brother Ephraim, you ride. I'll push. I'm near full grown and as strong as a boy." Ephraim protested, but the others insisted, and Emeline, true to her word, pushed the cart Zionward.

Chapter 4

October 1, 1856

That day had been the hardest yet for Nannie Macintosh. She had pulled the cart for ten hours, for fifteen miles, while Andrew and Ella had barely pushed, because Andrew was sickly and Ella's labor pains had come on the night before. Nannie had called Sister Maud, who'd prepared a foul-tasting concoction of herbs for Ella to drink, and the pains had subsided. But there was still a danger that the baby would be born early. Sister Maud had said Ella ought to be put to bed to keep the labor from coming on again, but they might as well ask for a string of gold nuggets as for a bed in the middle of that awful prairie. And even if there were a bed, someone would have to push it.

Nannie wanted her sister to ride on top of the cart, but Ella refused, knowing the extra weight would be too much for Nannie. Besides, Ella added, she was so tired of pregnancy that she wouldn't mind the baby being born that day. "I'd rather carry it in my arms than in my belly," she jested, although the women knew that a baby arriving so early would have a hard time of it.

Before they set off that morning, Nannie had stepped inside the shafts and picked them up. Neither Ella nor Andrew had objected. In fact, both were too weak to push much, so Nannie had had to call on all of her strength to keep the cart moving, for she was too proud to ask for help. The trek that day would have been hard even if Andrew had been fit enough to pull, because they were not traveling over hardpan, but making their way through sand that sucked at the wheels, holding them down. Then it had begun to rain, not the cleansing summer mist of a Scottish day that Nannie had loved, but a hard, cold American rain that turned the road into muck that clung to the wheels, heavy as sadirons.

As she strained with the cart, Nannie prayed to God for the strength to go on. And as if given an answer of sorts, she found her mind diverted from her burden to thoughts of the Edinburgh hotel where she had worked. This time of day, the maids would be gossiping in the servants' dining room over leftover pastries and tea, some of them adding a purloined drop of sherry or whiskey to their cups. She had loved working in the hotel, the perfume the guests left behind on the towels she gathered up each morning and sent to the laundry, the sharp crack of the starched sheets as she spread them on the beds.

The job had paid well enough, and on her afternoons off, Nannie had walked through the old streets, looking at the goods displayed in the windows, sometimes entering the shops to purchase a bonnet or a scarf or the silver brooch in the shape of a thistle that she had brought with her to America, pinned to her chemise. When she'd grown tired, she'd stopped at a tea shop for a Sally Lunn with jam and a cup of tea. If she were caught in the rain, Nannie would dash back to the hotel, because she did not want her clothes to get wet. Now she glanced down at her soaked skirt, its hem thick with mud, and tightened the wet shawl over her wet hair. The dress had once been blue gingham, but the color was faded, the white dingy. What would the other maids think if they could see her now?

Hers had been a pleasant life. It would be yet if she had not joined the Latter-day Saints, but the Gospel offered far more than a good time. It offered a return to the church as it was in the days of the apostles, the true church, and a chance to make something of herself. And that was worth tramping across half of a continent in the rain. Thinking of her blessings renewed Nannie's strength, and she pushed harder, picking up the words of "Come, Come, Ye Saints" that others had begun to sing. Nothing, not the rain nor the strain on her body, could weaken her belief.

Her back, however, was not as strong as her faith, and she wondered how much farther she could pull. She asked God to give her strength, and just then, Old Absalom, the man who had spoken out in Florence against continuing the trip, came up beside her. "Ye needing help?" he asked. He did not look as if he could walk the distance, let alone pull a handcart, and Nannie thought to turn him down. As if he understood Nannie's mind, Absalom said, "I may look like a skeleton, but these old bones are plenty strong. I can match my strength against that of any man. You let me pull, Sister, and you push." Nannie relinquished the shafts, and in a moment, they were moving along as quickly as she had when she'd started out.

The dark was closing in by the time they made it to camp,

Old Absalom disappearing as soon as the cart was still. Nannie insisted that Ella and Andrew find room in the tent to keep warm and take a resting spell while she fixed their supper. It would be a poor supper, she knew, and not just because of the weather. Rations were running low. The elders had believed the Saints would travel faster, and although on some days they made nearly twenty miles, they were still behind schedule. Their food would run out if they did not cut back on what they ate. Since there were no supplies waiting along the first part of the route, rations had been cut from a pound of flour a day for each adult to three-quarters of a pound, with children getting even less. That was barely enough to keep the Saints going, and Nannie suffered more than others, since she gave a portion of her porridge to Ella to build up her strength.

Before she fixed the supper, Nannie would have to find fuel. She had not picked it up along the way because she hadn't wanted to add to the weight of the cart. So now, she was forced to search for broken brush or dried buffalo chips, those round disks of dung that the pioneers used for fuel. Even if Nannie found enough of them for a fire, they would be wet and hard to light. But she had no choice, so she drew her shawl over her head and held it close under her chin while she went in search of the animal droppings. The rain beat down on her, and she wished that she had picked up the umbrella she'd seen Thales Tanner's sister-in-law discarding in Florence. *That* was a little bit of weight she would not have minded pulling.

There was no fuel to be found near the camp, of course, since the Saints who had arrived earlier had already collected it. So Nannie wandered far out onto the prairie in her search, picking up the circles of wet dung, which stank like a backhouse.

She did not realize how far she'd walked until she turned and glanced back toward the camp, which was little more than dots of campfire under the darkening sky. She had gone such a distance and the wind blew so hard that she could not even hear the din. But that meant she would not be able to hear the blasted cornet calling her to prayers, either, and Nannie found herself smiling. The Lord moved in mysterious ways, and that was His blessing for her. She wondered if the unpleasantness she had encountered that day was a blessing, too. Perhaps God was testing her with the burden He put on her shoulders. Certainly the trip was not as easy as she'd expected when she'd agreed to go to America. There had to be a purpose to the hardships. Perhaps when the elders said that God wanted only the strong to go to Zion, they meant those who were strong in body as well as faith. Well, she was strong in both, and she would pull the cart by herself all the way to Great Salt Lake City if she had to. Nannie Macintosh would not be found wanting. She would follow the fortunes of the Latter-day faith. She brightened then, knowing it could be worse.

Then she knew it was. A man loomed out of the darkling prairie, a blanket wrapped around him—an Indian—and she shivered as she watched him make his way toward her. The Mormons had encountered Indians on the trip, men mostly, who came into the camps to trade for the little the Mormons had to offer. Some of the Saints hired Indians to kill buffalo, since they had been admonished to leave the animals alone, for fear of angering the Indians and giving them cause to attack the handcarts. The prohibition against hunting was not such an inconvenience as it might have been, because few of the emigrants—and Andrew was among these—had guns, and even fewer of them knew how to shoot a buffalo. So instead, the Saints traded trinkets and articles of clothing to the Indians for meat. It was cheap. Nannie gave a handkerchief for enough meat for a stew that lasted three days. Another Mormon she knew paid just a nickel for half a side of buffalo.

Knowing the Indians were outnumbered and had no reason to attack the train, Nannie had not been afraid of them, but instead, she had looked at them with wonderment, the men all but naked under the paint they smeared on their bodies, the few women stolid, solemn, as curious about the white people as the emigrants were about the savages. The Indian men had been fascinated by the carts, and she'd seen one or two even push them for the emigrants, although they quickly tired of the work.

Of course, the Mormons had been warned not to stray far from the main body of brethren when they traveled through Indian country, and with good reason. The leaders told stories of wagon trains that had been attacked by Indians, the travelers murdered and mutilated in a most foul manner.

Now Nannie watched with fear as the man in the blanket came toward her. She thought to run, but how could she, weighted down with her wet, muddy skirts? He would catch her in two steps. So instead, she stood quietly and prayed.

"Don't be alarmed."

Nannie realized with a start that the man was not an Indian, but one of the emigrants, who was wrapped in a blanket to protect himself from the rain.

"I saw you leave and followed you, thinking you might need help."

The voice was warm and familiar, and Nannie thanked the Lord that he had come to her aid. "I am obliged. I'm hunting fuel."

The man came close to her then and removed the blanket from his head. "I thought you might be, Sister Nan. It's dark as Egypt out here, and I wouldn't want you to be lost."

"Och!" Nannie murmured, as chilled as she had been when she had mistaken him for an Indian. She almost wished he were, because of all men in the train, Levi Kirkwood was the last she wanted to see. "Ye had no right to follow me."

"Surely you know I couldn't let you go off onto the prairie by yourself, not after you were hard-worked all day. I saw you pulling your cart. That's why I came to help."

"Ye have no business to do it."

"It is the Lord's business to help one another."

"Do not tell me the Lord's business!" Nannie said sharply. "I mislike your words and will not be preached at by ye."

"There was a time when you held my preaching dear." He reached out a hand, but Nannie only clutched the buffalo chips she had picked up and backed away.

"Aye. And there was a time when ye held me dear. But ye found another to be dearer, and ye, with all your fine manners, hae not even the grace to tell me yourself, but put it in a letter. Do not preach to me, Brother Levi."

In the dark, Nannie could not see the face of the man to whom she had been betrothed, the man who had betrayed her, but she saw his shoulders slump and his head turn back toward the camp. "I was tempted by a pretty face and golden hair. And I was found wanting. Now God punishes me with a wife who is selfish and weak in the faith and addicted to idle chatter. Not a single day passes that she doesn't complain."

"And ye want *my* sympathy?" Nannie's shawl had slipped off her head, and her flaxen hair was limp and wet, but she would not set down the disks of manure to replace the head covering. She held them in front of her to keep Levi away.

"I believe you still care for me, as I do for you."

He grasped at her hand then, but Nannie dropped the fuel she had gathered and snatched her hand away. She had dreamed about this, about Levi coming to her, contrite, confessing his mistake, asking her forgiveness, but she hadn't yet dreamed about what she would say to him, and she was at a loss for words. She wrapped her arms around herself, not sure if the shaking was due to the cold or the discomfort of standing next to a man she had loved and listening to him, or to her disgust with herself for holding on to his words.

"It had to be said," Levi told her when Nannie didn't respond.

"Why? It disna good," she said at last. "Better that ye had kept still."

"And let someone else speak for you? I have watched you, Nannie. Your faith is strong, and I admire you as much as I always have, perhaps more. You are more pleasing to me than any other female. I believe the Lord intends us to be together."

"Ye already hae a wife."

"We are Mormons."

Nannie stared at him, silent, and her silence seemed to encourage him. He added, "I have seen how your Scottish nature keeps you going. Your forcefulness will make you a good wife in Zion, because we require women who work hard. If you join with me, you will be an instrument of the Lord."

He reached out and took Nannie's filthy hand, but she jerked it away. "What are ye asking, that I be your second wife—or maybe your third one or your fourth? Do ye already hae wives in the valley? How many, Levi? Are ye asking me to become part of a harem?"

"Hush, Nannie. I have only one wife, and I want no other one but you."

"Until when? Until ye meet another who charms ye? Will ye write another letter to tell me about her?" she cried.

Levi ignored the sarcasm. "Celestial marriage is our way. You knew about the doctrine of plurality before you left Scotland. It is God's way."

"It was told that it was only for the chosen few. Polygamy is not *my* way."

"You would put yourself over the Lord?" His voice boomed out, just as it had when he had preached in Scotland and had thrilled her almost to ecstasy.

"Don't preach at me. Ye hae done me great harm with your preaching."

"Harm? My preaching brought you into the church."

Nannie could not deny it, and she felt as if she were in a battle with herself. His words of affection stirred up a torment in her, but nonetheless, she was disgusted at the idea of becoming a second wife. She had assumed when she was betrothed to Levi that he would abstain from practicing the doctrine, just as Andrew had promised when he married Ella. She had been so sure that theirs would be a perfect marriage, with just the two of them, that she had not thought it necessary to bring up the subject of polygamy. Now she wondered if Levi had expected to practice it all along.

Levi was right, of course. Plural marriage was no surprise to her. She knew it was ordained by God. What had she expected would happen when she reached the valley? Had she believed there were single men waiting to meet the emigrants, men who wanted only one wife, men looking for a girl who had a pair of red silk wedding shoes? Nannie and Ella had joked that Levi might want her for a second wife, but they had not been serious.

Now Nannie stood looking at a man she had expected to marry and heard him once again ask her to become his wife. And as shocked and disgusted as she was, she found herself considering what he had said. She looked down at her bedraggled skirt and wished she were not as wet as a sop.

"Your wife would not like it. She has a good conceit of herself, and she would make me fetch for her, would make me suffer," Nannie said, not bringing herself to say the woman's name.

"Patricia is obedient."

"Ye have just told me she is not."

Levi stiffened. Nannie could not see him well, but she knew he had drawn himself up. "She will behave herself when we reach Utah. I'll see to it."

Nannie wondered if he would take a stick to his wife or fist her. The idea made her smile a little, and then she realized that if he would strike his first wife, he would surely strike his second. "Ye would beat her?"

"I would correct her. She is too outspoken and presumes she knows too much. A woman cannot have knowledge above a man. She will learn obedience if she wants me to esteem her."

Nannie had heard about how some of the polygamous Mormon men disciplined wives who displeased them, how they shunned the women who were not obedient, did not provide for them or visit them. It was said that anyone in Utah could tell when a plural wife was out of favor, because she did not become pregnant.

When Nannie said nothing, Levi added, "I am tolerant now. She is not well."

Patricia was pregnant, Nannie realized with dismay. That was what Levi meant by "not well." If she became Levi's second wife, she still would not be the first to bear him a child. She wondered how she would feel if Levi's other wives—and there would be other wives, Nannie knew, as certain as anything—bore him children.

"Forgive my plainness in speaking, Nannie, but do you want to be my wife or do you want to marry someone you don't care about, someone who is old, with no teeth and a beard down to his knees, a man like Old Absalom? For those are the men who will be after you. The older ones have first claim." When Nannie started to protest, he said, "Yes, I saw him pull your cart today. Do you think he did it out of the goodness of his heart? You will marry, of course. Your salvation depends on it. There are no spinsters in Utah."

He took both of her hands in his, oblivious to the bits of buffalo dung that clung to them, and this time Nannie did not pull away. "I am not such a bad husband. I tell you these things so there will be no misunderstanding between us. If you accept me, you will have a husband who is highly placed in the church, one who will provide for you and cherish you. I made a mistake in marrying Patricia. I should have wed you first and taken her later. You should have had the honor of being my first wife, and for that I am sorry. But I want you to be part of my kingdom as my second wife." He leaned over and kissed her, a chaste kiss. He had never done that before.

Nannie kissed him back, then turned away.

"I consider us betrothed, then."

"I hae not said aye."

"Nor have you said no." Levi reached out to touch Nannie's cheek; then, aware of the filth on his hands, he wiped them on his pants. "We have been told by the leaders not to ask for the emigrant women before we reach Great Salt Lake City. They do not want romancings among the emigrants, since many of the elders in the valley are in the market for wives, and it is not fair that the men in the company should take their pick. So we will keep this to ourselves."

"I hae not said aye," Nannie repeated.

"It is entirely up to you, of course, but I ask you again whether you want a healthy man who loves you proper or an old one who will be unable to give you children? After all, that is a woman's purpose, is it not? It is necessary for your future exaltation." His voice was warm, not dry and dictatorial, just like his words. He kissed her cheek, then left abruptly, and without looking back, he returned to camp.

Nannie stared after him, her heart torn between marrying the man she cared for more than any other and her disgust at becoming his second wife. She had not noticed until then that the rain had stopped. She removed her drenched shawl and, picking up the buffalo chips, wrapped them in the fabric square and started back to camp. As she came close to the handcarts, she saw a figure break away from the camp and start toward her, and for a moment, she thought that Levi was returning. But the man was smaller than Levi and hunched over. In a moment, she recognized Andrew. "Did you think I was lost?" she called, hoping he had not noticed Levi returning to the encampment.

"I came to tell ye I've built a fire. A brother gave me enough chips to start it, and I've mixed the porridge. Ella is asleep and willna wake till morning. She would want ye to hae her share."

Nannie unwrapped the buffalo chips and showed the mess to Andrew. "I suppose we can use these in the morning."

"Ye've ruined your shawl," he said with more feeling than she would have expected.

"It will wash."

Andrew took the shawl. "What would we do ifna for you, Nannie? You were our strength today. Without ye, Ella and I could not have got this far. I truly believe that ye are an instrument of the Lord."

It was the second time in only a few minutes that she had been called the Lord's instrument, and Nannie mulled over the words, wondering if they meant she was pleasing to God only when she was useful to someone else.

Pushing a plow had never been as hard as pushing a cart, Jessie Cooper decided as she put her shoulder to the back of the vehicle and shoved it over a rut. Sutter pulled the cart, and the two of them traded places every so often. The girl, Emeline, pushed, too. She'd been right when she'd said she was as strong as a boy. With Ephraim riding on top of the cart now, it took all three of them to keep the cart going through the heavy sand, and Jessie was grateful for the child's help.

From time to time, Ephraim insisted on walking, with Maud holding on to him as if they were the halt leading the lame. He tired quickly, however, and little wonder, since, like the other men, he was assigned guard duty for six hours every other night. Even the sick were not relieved of their responsibilities. The lack of sleep, along with the fever from his broken arm, caused him to sweat and grow weak, so after a short time, Maud insisted he get back onto the cart. Each night, the old woman examined the arm and made Ephraim a dressing of herbs to keep the inflammation from getting worse, but both women worried. "It's not healing right. Look how angry it is," Maud whispered to Jessie after she had examined the festering wound.

"I hope his arm won't have to come off," Jessie said. "I'm bad to worry about it. So is Ephraim. And little Emeline frets about it."

"No need to worry," Maud replied quickly—too quickly, Jessie thought.

"You can be plain with me. I don't need mollycoddling words."

Maud sighed. "Then I'll be just frank. Bad as it is, the break ought to have begun to heal by now. I wish I'd brought my salves with me, but they were left in Iowa the first time we lightened the loads. I thought there'd be herbs along the way to gather, and maybe there are, but I don't know them, so they're useless to me. Most of what I brought has got used up, what with so much sickness and accidents and even childbirth." She paused. "I'm doing what I can, Sister Jessie. I know a farmer isn't much use with just one arm."

"Ephraim is better with one arm than most men with two," his sister said.

Maud smiled at her. "Your brothers are noble souls. I never met two men I admire as much. If it wasn't for them and you, Sister Emeline would be with that foul man, and I'd have been devoured by wolves."

"And we'd have starved to death without you."

They might starve to death anyway, Jessie thought as she moved on, pushing the cart. She was hungry enough to eat a rusty nail. Now it seemed they ate barely enough to keep them alive. She knew that Maud was hard-pressed to prepare a supper that would fill their bellies. The night before, the old woman had made a sort of scone cake with a pinch of cinnamon that she had received as payment for doctoring. Jessie had watched Maud cut the cake, giving the others larger proportions than her own. "You have to keep up your strength, too," Jessie chided her.

"I am not hungry," Maud insisted, and because sacrifice and fasting were part of the church doctrine, Jessie said no more. Now, watching the old woman plod through the sand, Jessie wondered if Maud was starving herself. Well, they all were, and she just hoped that God would see fit to keep them alive until they reached Fort Laramie. Mormon supply wagons would surely meet them there.

The overcast lifted, and in a moment, a ray of sun shone through the clouds. "Look at that," Jessie said to Emeline, who was beside her, pushing the cart.

The girl looked up at the bright streak and nodded, saying nothing. She had been mostly silent since the deaths of her parents, and who could blame her? She'd lost her entire family in a single day. Her grieving had turned inward. Maud had drawn her out a little and then had stopped prying, although Maud hadn't shared her reasons for letting up. Emeline seemed to connect only with Ephraim, perhaps because the one was wounded in body, the other in spirit. Jessie had come across the two sitting side by side, Ephraim saying something in his deep, rich voice, and Emeline chattering like a squirrel. Jessie listened but found they were only talking about the prairie. Ephraim's arm seemed to bother him less when he was with Emeline, and the girl, too solemn for one her age, brightened when she was near him.

"Where do you come from?" Jessie asked now, as much to relieve the boredom of pushing the cart as to get Emeline to talk. The going was slow that day because Ephraim rode on top of the cart, and others passed them.

"England."

"I figured as much, you being with us on the ship that left from Liverpool. Where in England?"

"Brighton."

Jessie smiled, because she had heard that Brighton was an enchanted place, and she had hoped to visit the seaside resort one day. "It must have been a pleasure to grow up there. Did you see the queen?"

Emeline shook her head.

"What did your father do? Did he work at the Pavilion?"

"I couldn't say."

Jessie found it strange that the girl didn't know her own father's occupation, but she did not pursue it, and instead, she asked, "Do you wish to be back there?" She knew the girl must feel hard put, trading the view of the sea for one of the prairie.

Emeline did not answer at first. Then she said carefully, "I wish to be here, with Mama and Papa."

"Of course you do. But what's done cannot be undone."

"I am better here than at home."

"You must be strong in the faith."

"I am, although I'm not knowing why God took them. He should have took me instead. They were the best people that ever lived, better 'n me. No, I'm not knowing."

"Nor am I knowing why Ephraim's arm was smashed." Jessie was sorry she had spoken, because a broken arm could not compare with the death of two souls. Then she reflected on what the girl had said and thought it odd that Emeline would find herself a poorer person than her parents. Perhaps that idea came from an earlier church she had attended, one that preached that children were born in sin. Those religions were so different from this new Mormon faith.

Emeline took her hands off the back of the cart for a moment and flexed them before she began pushing again. The girl's hands were tough, the nails broken. The blisters that had formed at the beginning of the trek had turned to calluses. The cart slowed when the girl stopped, and Jessie realized then how strong Emeline was, surprising strong for such a little thing.

"What will you do when you reach Zion? Have you thought about it?" Jessie asked, anxious to keep a conversation going, because it would take her mind off the endless miles of prairie ahead of them.

"Sister Maud says I might stay with her. She believes she'll earn her keep by doctoring when she reaches the valley. Already, I helped her birth a baby, although I had some knowing about it, because Marianna—" She stopped and added quickly, "Sister Maud showed me how to care for Brother Ephraim's arm, too, how to wrap it with herbs and the splint."

"He is grateful to you. You make things easier for him." When Emeline didn't reply, Jessie added, "It's not a bad thing to know—herbs."

"Sister Maud says herbs can heal fevers and the cancer, too."

"You would be a help to her. And it would be a good thing to have that knowing, for I think there aren't many doctors in Zion. Still, you must long for a family—parents, brothers and sisters. I know I would if I lost my brothers. Perhaps you will find someone to take you in."

Emeline turned and looked at Jessie curiously. "I've already had me a family, and look what happened. Besides, I'm near fourteen years. I'm a woman and old enough to start my own family."

"You would marry at that age?"

"Such is the fact of it."

Jessie turned to stare at the girl. She was nearly twice Emeline's age and not married, nor likely to be for some time, because she intended to set up housekeeping with her brothers. It was a strange thing that someone so much younger was thinking of marriage. "Do you have a husband in mind?" she asked.

Emeline did not know that Jessie spoke in jest and she pursed her lips together while she thought. "No to that. Brother Prime would have had me just for my handcart, and he's told me he fancies me even if I went to him as poor as a pauper."

Now Jessie let go of the cart as she turned to stare at Emeline. "Would you have him?"

"No. He is evil."

Jessie wondered about the girl, who was too young to understand about evil in men. "Why do you say that?"

"I know about such things. He watches me. He did before Mama and Papa died. Sometimes he tries to take my hand. There are men who like girls, like them younger than me, like them barely more than babies."

"How do you know about that?"

Emeline did not answer, but instead, she eyed the wheel, which had bounced off a rock. But after examining it, she announced that it was sound.

Jessie knew she should not pry, but she was curious about the girl. "You are very wise for one your age. And very worldly, I should think."

Emeline did not reply.

"Aren't you?"

"I don't know about that."

"You've seen wickedness."

"Yes."

The girl did not seem to want to talk about it, so Jessie was silent for a time. Then because she enjoyed chatting with Emeline, she asked, "How did you come to join the church?"

"Mama and Papa were already Mormons."

"Already. What do you mean, *already*?"

"I misspoke," Emeline said, not looking up at Jessie.

"Are you saying they were not your true parents?"

Emeline didn't answer for a long time. She let go of the cart and arched her back to get out the kinks. Then she stood in the road, hands rubbing her lower back, as she looked at the line of handcarts before her. She watched as the Cooper handcart rolled along ahead of her, Jessie and Sutter propelling it farther and farther away. After a time, she hastened forward to help with the pushing again. "My back's near breaking sometimes."

"Walk awhile. I can push for both of us," Jessie told her.

"Wouldn't be right." She joined Jessie behind the cart.

"The land's dry here. We're out of the sand. You can push later, while I walk."

But Emeline would not be dissuaded from her duty and shook her head.

"I intruded. I ask you to forgive it," Jessie said, anxious to mend the rift she had caused.

Emeline sighed and said, "It's known among some of the Saints, the ones from Brighton. I told Sister Maud myself, and Brother Ephraim, too. I wouldn't want him to hear the gossip and not know the truth. I thought they'd told you. Maybe I should have myself, so's you know what kind of person you taken in."

Jessie turned and looked at Emeline curiously. "Told me what?"

"The Grays aren't my parents at all. I was a stray."

"A foundling?"

"No."

"An orphan?"

"You could say it."

Jessie put her rough hand over the girl's and said, "I'm so sorry. You've lost two sets of parents. How did the real ones die?"

"I couldn't say for sure."

"*When* did they die, then?"

Emeline shrugged.

Jessie did not want to bring the girl fresh grief by pressing her, so she asked, "How did you meet the Grays?"

"The missionary. He took me to them."

"Then you had already been converted."

"I heard him on the street corner. Oh, there was plenty that made fun of him, whistled and clapped and hooted when he spoke. One as said he ought to be boiled in oil for talking about the Lord the way he did, and boys threw stones at him."

"I've heard of such things," Jessie said. "Was he discouraged?"

"Not him. It didn't bother him at all. He said the Lord would avenge him one day. I like that word, *avenge*."

Jessie did not. She thought the Saints talked too much about vengeance, but she said nothing. "Go on," she said, encouraging Emeline.

"The missionary invited folks to attend a meeting, and as I was free, I followed along. Only a few people went, and I sat on the floor behind a chair so's not to be noticed. But he knew I was there, and he said, 'Suffer the little children to come unto me.' I remember those words, although I wasn't a little child—I'd never been a little child—and I didn't think he meant me. He made me go to the front of the room and told everybody I had an old soul."

"An old soul. What did he mean by that?"

Emeline shrugged. "He asked me to come back the next day, but I couldn't. I didn't go back for more than a week, but he remembered me, and he said God forgave all my sins, and I had a plenty of them. He told me Jesus loved me, just as He loved Mary Magdalene. He said she's in the Bible, although I can't say where, for I can't read. She's one of the saints, I expect. Are you acquainted with her?"

"Of course," Jessie murmured, understanding now about Emeline. She looked into the girl's eyes, thinking they were old, too.

"The missionary, he said he was about to leave Brighton that morning I first heard him, but the Lord told him to stay on because there was somebody needed to be saved."

"And that was you," Jessie said.

"I suppose so. I surely did need to get away, not that I knew where to go. You see, I hadn't any folks since I was six and was sent out to work on the streets. Like I said, there's men that likes the girls young."

"You were on your own?"

"Oh no. I lived with Twiss. He's the man that bought me of my folks. He's the one sent me out to work. I had to give him what I earned, but he made sure I had something to eat and a place to sleep."

"And then the missionary came along," Jessie said, anxious for Emeline to continue.

"He stayed in Brighton, even when I didn't go back for a long time. When I did, he told me again that God loved me, but I didn't believe it, because nobody ever loved me before, not in that way."

Jessie did not look at the girl, because she did not want Emeline to see how she pitied her. Tears formed in her eyes, and she brushed them away with her sleeve.

Emeline did not notice. She was still for a moment before continuing her story. "I started going to that meeting when I could, until finally, Twiss followed me one night and went right there in the meeting room and grabbed me and said I had to leave terrible quick, and if I ever went back, he'd beat me till I couldn't stand up. He would have, too."

"What did the Saints do when he said that?" Jessie asked.

"They were scared, but not the missionary. He said, 'The devil goeth about like a roaring lion,' and told Twiss he was the devil and to take his hands off me or he'd be the one to get the beating. Twiss said I'd better leave with him if I knew what was good for me, but I didn't. I know he'd knock me around for sure when he caught me. He beat me bad, like he did Marianna when she wanted to stay in the room to care for her baby. Still, I just couldn't leave."

"He beat you? What a foul man!" Jessie was incensed.

Emeline pushed up her sleeve to show a scar and told Jessie, "It's worse on my back. He wanted me to steal for him, to pick the pockets of the men I was with, but I wouldn't. So he took a hot poker to me."

"And your parents—your real parents—what did they do?"

"I never saw them again, not after they sold me. Twiss said my mother died of a disease and my father got drunk and drowned in a gutter, but he was a terrible liar."

Jessie was so caught up in the story that she had forgotten to push. Now she saw that Emeline was straining behind the cart, which was stuck in a mud hole, and she put her shoulder to the back of the vehicle and pushed with all her might. When the cart was free, she asked, "Did you stay at that meeting or go?"

"I stayed. I was baptized in the church. Then the missionary took me to the Grays and told them I needed a place to live. They were as poor as me, but they took me in. They hadn't any children, so I was to be their daughter. Even though they knew all about me, they treated me like I was a solid-gold necklace and told me to call them Mama and Papa."

"The Lord must love you indeed to bring that missionary to you."

"He said I was sick in body and soul, and I rightly believe he saved my life. I'd be dead in the ground by now without Brother Thales."

"Brother Thales? He converted you? He saved you?" Jessie turned to Emeline, a puzzled look on her face. "Brother Thales Tanner?"

"The same."

Being harnessed to the cart like the oxen that pull the wagons is humiliating, Anne thought as she and Joe pushed the crosspiece. The straining had brought on cramps like labor pains, and Anne wished that John had not gone off like that. At first, she had pleaded with him to stay with her that day, and he had asked if the baby was coming. But she couldn't truthfully say it was, so John had joined the group of men in search of meat or fowl to add to their stores—an antelope, if they were lucky,

143

or a bird. Some even said that rattlesnakes were tasty, but Anne would eat her shoe first.

Besides, John was going hunting for her sake. A cup of broth—she'd pretend it was beef tea—would help restore her strength, he'd said, and they'd all longed for something to vary their diet. So she couldn't in good conscience hold him back, especially since John had been such an attentive husband in all other ways, saying that he and Joe, who was five now, could manage the cart so that she could walk. He even insisted that she ride on top of the vehicle when her ankles were swollen to the size of apples. John had pulled the vehicle the entire trip, but that morning, he'd asked if she and Joe could manage without him. And Joe had swelled with pride at his father's faith in his strength, so Anne could not very well have continued to object. She had to admit, she'd felt fine that morning. The prairie path was hard, so the going would be easier than pulling through sand or mud. The cart would just roll along. Besides, John promised to return in a few hours. Even if fatigue caused her to stop, she was assured that John would find her when he returned from hunting and take the cart the rest of the way. So Anne had given in and told him to go. She'd even kissed his cheek and said she'd have a fire waiting for him, with a kettle filled with water. It did not occur to her that John would fail to find something for their supper. He always accomplished anything he set out to do.

But straining against the crosspiece as she did, Anne was sorry now that he had gone. With the scant rations that the Saints had to endure, she'd grown weak, weaker than John and Joe, since the baby inside was nourished before she was. From time to time, she stopped to rub her tortured back or to hold her distended belly. Her ankles had swollen so much that morning that she'd had to take off her shoes and put them into the cart. Now she stopped to remove a thorn from her foot, easing it out. She had gone barefoot so often that her feet were tough, and the injured foot did not bleed, a blessing of sorts, Anne thought. Perhaps the baby would come while they were at Fort Laramie. That would be good fortune, since there would be a doctor at the fort and a bed—not a very good bed, maybe a cot with a dirty blanket or an animal skin on it, but it would be a bed nonetheless and a better place to lie down than on the ground. She did so want that baby to be born safely. She couldn't bear to lose it as she had Emma Lee.

Anne wondered what it would be like when cold weather came and she had to sleep inside the tent every night, not just the nights when it rained, as she had done for the past few weeks. She preferred sleeping outdoors, beside the cart. Although some families had individual tents, the Sullys slept in a communal tent, which was crowded, the air close, and the sounds of sleep—the grunts and snores and cries—kept her awake. Not that she slept that well on the prairie. Perhaps it wasn't just the dirt bed that kept her awake but also her pregnancy and the fear of giving birth in such primitive conditions.

Anne trudged along beside Joe, with two-year-old Lucy on top of the cart, moving slowly, watching the other Saints pass them. Many of the carts were pulled by women, because there had been deaths on the trail, not just among the frail old people and the young children but among healthy men and women, too. Some, such as Addison Gray, had been killed in accidents. Maud's husband, Robert, had just given out. Others had died from mountain fever or dysentery. Anne recalled one man who had gotten sick with the flux. His wife had begged a piece of beef, which she boiled into a tea and fed to him. Too late, the Saints learned that meat made the disease worse, and he had died. More emigrants will be taken before the trip is over, many more, she thought.

Anne worried for the safety of her children. And just as much, she feared what would happen to them if she were to die. John could not raise Joe and Lucy by himself, especially with the new baby. The Mormon women would help. Anne had seen enough of the women's kindness to know they would take care of her children. But not forever. John would have to marry again, and quickly, without time to learn much about the woman. Who knew how a new wife would treat Anne's little ones. She could be a widow with children of her own and ignore Joe and Lucy. Or she might bear John her own children, and she would prefer them to those her husband had had by his first wife. Anne had seen that at home, with the dead mother's little ones treated like farm animals, forced to do the heavy work, beaten, while the favored children were allowed to attend school. When that happened, the boys ran off as soon as they were able, and the girls married at puberty to get away from their stepmothers, trading one troubled home for another. It was not death that Anne Sully feared, but leaving her children to an unknown fate.

She and Joe stopped often to rest, letting so many carts go by that they were near the end of the train. They would have to hurry if they wanted to reach the camp before dark. Anne scanned the horizon, but there was no sign of John and the others. She had put Lucy on the ground to play while they rested, and now she lifted the little girl and set her on top of the cart again, frowning at the strain on her back. "Ready, son?" she asked as she leaned over to pick up the crosspiece. Anne grimaced at the tremendous heaving in her belly. Then, just as she straightened up, ready to push on, her water broke. "Oh!" she exclaimed, and Joe stared at her, a frightened look on his young face.

"Mama, you walk. I can pull the cart by myself," he said, not understanding what had happened. As if to prove his point, he started off with the handcart, struggling to pull it a few feet. "You see, Mama. I'm almost as strong as Papa."

But he could not propel the cart by himself. Anne thought she could push until the pains grew too harsh, and she placed her hands behind the cart and shoved. But the effort was too much, and, exhausted, she dropped down on the roadside.

"I'll find someone to help us," Joe said, looking around, but the only man in sight who wasn't pulling or pushing a cart had his arm tied up in a sling and was leaning on an old woman. As the two came alongside the Sully cart, the woman asked sharply, "Are you needing help?"

"I think I'm having the baby now."

"Your water's broke."

"It has."

"Can you walk a little farther?"

Anne shook her head. "The pains . . ." and she shuddered as one gripped her.

"Well, you've had a stroke of luck, for here is Sister Maud, who is as good as a physician with borning babies," said a woman pushing a cart. She stopped beside Maud, then introduced herself as Sister Jessie and the woman beside her as Sister Emeline. "Sister Emeline is knowing of babies, too. Shall we put you on your cart and push you to camp?"

"Dear to goodness, best you let me take a peep so I'll know how far along she is," Maud said. So the little company—Maud, Joe, Emeline, Jessie, and her brothers—arranged the two carts to give the woman a bit of shade, and privacy, too.

"My labor's always been a long one. I do very poorly," Anne told them. "I should try to make it to camp, since the baby likely won't be born till morning, maybe later." Nonetheless, she lay down on the ground and let Maud examine her.

"This one won't wait that long. It won't wait at all," Maud announced. She told Sutter to build a fire and to heat the water they carried with them in a bottle. Then she asked Anne if she had any cloths in which to wrap the little one.

"She better, as I haven't any petticoat left," Jessie put in.

Joe took out a slim bundle of baby things and handed them to Maud, who had spread her own patchwork counterpane on the ground. Anne tried to hold back her cries for Joe's and Lucy's sake, but a groan escaped her lips. "It wasn't like this before."

"Every baby has a different idea," Maud told her, motioning Emeline to her side. "See here, that's the baby's head," she explained.

"So soon?" Anne asked.

"Now you lie back and look up at the clouds, which are mighty pretty today, and push when the pains come." Maud poured a tiny amount of the water into her hands and washed them, and Emeline did the same.

Then, to distract the boy, Sutter took him to the Cooper cart and asked him to help scrape mud off the spokes of the wheels. "We have a heavy-enough load without pushing all that dirt," he said. "When we're finished, we'll clean your cart, too." Ephraim came up then and offered to look after the girl, Lucy, so that Jessie could attend the woman.

"I've seen cows and pigs give birth and think that, like as not, women aren't so different," Jessie told Maud as she knelt on the ground beside Anne.

"Not so different, but more pain. I've wondered about that. Why does the Lord love a cow more than a woman?"

At that, Anne started to laugh, but her face contorted and she bit her lip so hard that a tiny blood bubble broke out. After the pain passed, she twisted her head to look for Joe and Lucy. "I don't want to frighten them," she said.

"My brothers are tending them," Jessie told her. Then she asked, "Where is your husband?"

"He went with the hunting party. He didn't expect the baby today."

"Men never do," Maud told her. "It's my experience that they don't want to be around when the little one is born. Conceiving is for men. Birthing is for womenfolks."

A man and two women pushing a cart reached the little group and stopped, the women glancing at each other as they realized what was going on. One of them was pregnant herself, and she frowned as she approached and studied the woman lying on the ground. "Is it Sister Anne?"

"It is," Maud replied.

"I'm Ella Buck and this is my sister, Nannie Macintosh. Can we help?"

At that, Anne turned her head to the woman and reached out her hand. Ella took it as she sat down in the dirt beside

Anne. "It appears ye don't hae to wait much longer, Sister," she said.

Anne smiled a little, then asked, "Do you think the baby will be a Saint or a Gentile?"

The women chuckled. "You're the one who hasn't converted, then?" Jessie asked.

"Do you think God is punishing me for it now?"

"Converting won't help you. The Lord makes childbirth as hard for Mormons as Gentiles—or apostates, for that matter," Maud said. "Sometimes, His ways are mighty difficult for a woman to understand." She examined Anne again and said, "Now, on the next pain, you push."

While the women waited, other carts stopped, the Saints inquiring if they could help. A few of the Mormons, men as well as women, bowed their heads in prayer for Anne. "The Lord be with you, Sister," they said before they pushed on. A man ripped a piece of wood from a bush, stripped off the bark with a knife, and gave it to Maud, saying Anne could bite down on it when the pain got bad. "That's what my wife done," he added.

Two young men offered to wait so that one of them could push Anne's cart after the baby was born, but Maud told them to go on, that the birth would take time.

With the next pain, Anne pushed, and the delivery began in earnest. The head, the shoulders, and finally the rest of the body emerged, and the baby was born. "A boy! Your brother!" Maud announced, tying off the cord and handing the baby to Joe, who had joined the group attending his mother. The women finished their work; then Maud wrapped the newborn in a cloth and gave him to Anne. "Whether he's a Mormon or a Gentile, he's a fine boy," she said.

Anne smiled weakly as she held her new son. In truth, the birth had been easier than those in England, where the babies had been born on the dining room table and she'd been accompanied by a midwife and a nurse. She looked at the women around her with gratitude. For the first time since she had boarded the ship at Liverpool, she did not view the people as Mormons, but as friends, and she reached out her hand and tried to speak. "I did not think . . . because I'm not a Mormon . . ."

"Be still," Maud said. "We are a people who help one another because we love the Lord. Whether you are a Mormon or not, you are one of us."

The group broke up then, the men deciding who would pull which cart, the women arranging a bed on top of Anne's cart for her and the baby. Ella went to her own vehicle and searched through the foodstuffs for a hard candy striped in pink and white and gave it to Anne. "I've been saving this for something special. What's more special than a bairn?"

"But you saved it for yourself," Anne protested.

"The Lord provides," Ella said.

Anne put the candy into her mouth and savored the sweetness, the bite of peppermint, the sugar melting on her tongue. It had been months since she had eaten candy—not since she'd left England—and the taste brought her almost to tears. "I hope when your own time comes, the Lord will provide you with a chocolate cake."

The men lifted Anne onto her cart, and the group started off, someone beginning the strains of a Mormon hymn, which ended with "All is well." In a minute, all of them were singing along.

That night, John returned exhausted. The hunters had

stayed out all day because they did not want to return empty-handed. Nonetheless, they had failed to locate game. When he found Anne lying on a blanket next to the campfire, John knelt down and looked at his wife and newborn son with pride, but he was anxious, too. "I am right glad you are well," he said.

"We are tolerable fair, I and Samuel, if you will agree to the name. And happy," Anne replied, because she knew John worried that in her sharp-tongued way, she would criticize him for deserting her. But she did not berate him. Instead, she said, "Your people have taken care of us."

Louisa Tanner held on to one side of her father, Hall Chetwin, while her sister, Huldah, gripped him on the other, the two supporting the old man as they walked along. Margaret Chetwin was behind her husband, her hand on his back, as if to catch him if he fell backward. Huldah's two sons, Dick and Jimmy, pushed the cart, and for once, Thales Tanner, Louisa's husband, was there to pull it. Hall was exhausted but stubborn, and he refused to ride on top of the cart. He would show them that his faith gave him the strength to walk to Zion, Louisa knew. It would have been easier on the women if he had ridden, since pushing him in the cart would have taxed them less than propelling him forward on his frail legs.

"We can all push the cart, Father, if you want to ride. It is of no consequence to us," Louisa told him.

"I will walk. My faith makes me strong," he replied as he stumbled. He would have fallen if his daughter had not grasped him tightly.

Margaret patted his back, as if to right him, and said,

"There is no shame in riding, my dear." But, in fact, Margaret herself had seemed to believe that riding instead of walking was weakness. After those first few days of the journey, during which her legs nearly gave out, Margaret found her strength increasing. The family had expected her to be the weak one, had prayed for her health. And as if in answer to those prayers, Margaret's health had improved, and now she walked the trail beside her daughters, even helping to push the cart.

Instead, it was Hall Chetwin who had deteriorated. At night, he slumped to the ground beside the cart, barely able to stay awake long enough to eat his supper. Sometimes he was so weak that Margaret or one of the girls had to feed him. They encouraged him by promising that the food shortage would end when they reached Fort Laramie and found supplies waiting for them. "Just hold out a few more days, Father, and everything will be fine," Louisa told him. But despite his faith, the old man grew weaker. He was often too tired to attend the evening meetings or answer the morning call to prayers, something that did not please his son-in-law, Thales Tanner. And he could not take his turn at guard duty.

Louisa pleaded with Thales to encourage her father to ride, but Thales refused, saying, "It is his right."

"He is doing it only because of the letter you wrote. He believes he must prove to you that he is worthy of Zion."

"Zion does not care if he walks or rides."

"Then you must tell him that."

"Do not advise me, Louisa. A wife should not order her husband. Your father will be all right when we reach Fort Laramie. We will find supplies there, and he will gain back his strength."

Still, that morning, Thales had told Hall in front of Louisa, "As I will pull the cart today, you may ride if you wish. I would not hold it against you."

Perhaps thinking this was a test of his faith, Hall had replied, "I thank you, Brother, but I am hardy."

So now, Louisa all but dragged her father as the two of them followed the Tanner handcart, which Huldah and her sons pulled now. The old man had been silent for a long time. He did not grumble. He never complained. Nor did he ever ask for a bite of bread or a sip of water, although he was weak from the lack of both. So they were all surprised when he announced suddenly, "I would have a lemon pudding."

"What?" Louisa asked.

"A lemon pudding. I would have one for dinner. What would you have?"

Louisa looked at her father curiously, as if his mind had gone soft. Where in the world did he think they would find lemons and cream and sugar? And then she realized he had begun a game. "An apple tart with cream poured over it. And I would dearly like a roast goose, a roast goose stuffed with sauerkraut."

"What's this about a roast goose?" Margaret asked.

"We are planning a feast for when we reach Zion," Louisa explained. "What would you most like to eat?"

"Strawberries. I would walk a hundred miles more for a strawberry. And fresh buns, saffron buns."

Huldah joined the game. "A fish. I should like a fresh fish, fried in butter, served up with potatoes and peas."

"A jelly. I'd give my penknife for a jelly," her son Jimmy added, while the elder son, Dick, supposed he could eat an entire cream cake. "I'll give you half, Jimmy," Dick said, for the two were close fellows and always shared.

"And you, Thales?" Louisa asked, since he had not joined the game. "What would you have to eat when we reach the valley?"

Her husband turned to her with a frown. "It is a silly game. Milk and bread made with wheat flour from a Mormon mill are good enough for me. If you believe you will find roast goose and cream cakes waiting for you, you will be greatly disappointed."

"It is only a game, Thales, something to pass the time."

"Then it is a foolish game."

"I do not recall that you turned down such food in England," Louisa said, almost in defiance. In fact, she remembered, her husband had timed his proselytizing and courting visits so that he would arrive as the family sat down to dinner. Louisa had joked that Thales had married her as much for her mother's cooking as for her own piety.

"It does no good to talk about such things," Thales said, his voice only a little softer now. "You knew when you agreed to come here that you would put those luxuries behind you. It is little enough sacrifice for the Lord."

Louisa, rebuked, replied, "You are right, of course. We will give over jostling." The others, disappointed that Thales had spoiled their fun, grew silent, except for Jimmy and Dick, who walked with their grandfather now as they told each other about the cakes and tarts they would eat when they reached Zion, and bragged each would consume more than the other.

Louisa, her head bowed in meekness, went to join her husband at the crossbar.

"You must understand that the valley is a harsh place. We did not become Mormons for an easy time," Thales told her.

"I understand."

"Our reward will come in the next life."

"I told you I understand. There is no need to instruct me further in the perfecting of my character."

Thales reached over and patted her hand. "You will be a good wife."

She had much to learn to please her husband, so Louisa was satisfied at the rare words of approval. There was no further talk of food until they reached camp and the women took out their bacon, rancid now, and meager ration of flour and prepared a dinner that all of them hoped would not be their usual fare in the valley.

After consuming his portion, Hall said it had given him strength to attend the meeting that evening. So when the meal was done, the family joined the others to praise the Lord and to sing the songs of Zion, which brought them joy after the difficult days. Louisa heard the sound of a fiddle, and she watched as people swayed to the music, thinking that before they knew it, they would be at Fort Laramie and would partake of the food that awaited them there. After all, she thought, we are God's chosen people, so we should not doubt that supplies have been stored in Fort Laramie for us. Thales had told her that Brigham Young would be displeased with the complaining. Their lot had been easy, he said. After all, they had not suffered the torments of those who had been driven out of Nauvoo, but had only been inconvenienced a little by their scanty rations.

Then Thales stood up before the gathering and bore his

testimony, saying he knew the Latter-day Church was the true church, that Joseph Smith himself had told him so. The crowd murmured their approval; Thales was always an inspiring speaker. And then he said that anyone who doubted had only to look at the many miracles the Saints had experienced on their journey. Why just that day, he had thought his father-in-law, Hall Chetwin, would not make it into camp, so weak was he. Louisa listened with concern, for surely Thales would not question her father's faith now. But Thales smiled a little at her when he said he had asked the Lord to give the old man strength, and there he was, fit and healthy, sitting among them at the meeting. "Now the prospect is fair that his faith will allow him to reach Zion." At that, the Saints praised the Lord, and Hall bowed his head in prayer—or perhaps it was in embarrassment at being singled out before the brethren. When Louisa took his arm and peered into his face, she saw a look of rapture and blessed Thales for bringing that joy to her father.

As Hall left the meeting, several of the Mormons patted him on the back or smiled their approval. But Hall, humbled, kept his eyes on the ground.

"You have restored his dignity," Louisa told her husband as the two walked a little apart from the rest of the family.

"I believe he has overcome his weakness. God favors him now. If he can reach Fort Laramie, he will reach Zion."

The family went to the tent and lay down, all of them falling asleep from exhaustion. Louisa awoke just at daylight, to see her mother leave the tent. When the old woman did not return, Louisa rose and went outside, straining her eyes in the dawning light. She did not see Margaret at first, but then she spied her near the Tanner cart, sitting beside the cold gray ashes of the campfire. "You have given over knitting, Mother. You must be very tired. I will see to the fire, and Huldah and I will make breakfast," Louisa said. "Go back into the tent with Father."

Margaret appeared not to hear her.

"Mother, are you ill?"

Margaret sighed and shook her head.

"What is it, then? Is Father poorly?"

The old woman did not answer at first, and then she turned to her daughter. "He slipped from me just after you went to sleep. I have lain beside him the night long."

"Oh, Mother," Louisa said, taking the woman into her arms.

"I was so sure he would reach Zion. He wanted to go there more than anything in this world. To want to and can't is hell."

"Not hell, Mother, for he is in heaven with the Lord. He went up to Zion in peace. We will pray for the peace of him who's gone." The two women rocked back and forth until the camp began to stir, and Louisa's sister emerged from the tent.

"If only . . ." Huldah said after Louisa told her their father had died. Louisa knew what she meant; it was not necessary for her sister to finish.

The next day, on October 8, Louisa and her family and the rest of the handcarts reached Fort Laramie.

Chapter 5

October 8, 1856

The Martin Company had camped a mile east of Fort Laramie, and in the morning, Jessie walked into the military post with the other Saints. Having seen the stone castles of England, she wasn't much impressed with the ramshackle outpost. There was a motley collection of structures—a large house for the officers, two long adobe barracks, log cabins and stables, and a few other buildings. Nonetheless, she was glad to be there, because she had not entered a building since leaving Iowa City, and the coolness of the structures was a relief from the prairie heat.

Jessie quickly found the sensation of standing under a roof confining, however. The air was close, and she missed the openness of the prairie, even with its deadening heat. It had been a good time coming across the prairie, seeing the vastness of America, discovering herbs and plants and trees. But she gave little thought to all that now as she passed a group of noisy Indians lounging on the ground and inquired the where-abouts of the post surgeon. A soldier directed her across the parade ground to a hospital, and she and her brothers, along with Maud and Emeline, joined a line of emigrants waiting for medical attention.

Ephraim's arm had grown worse each day. It was black and swollen, so tender that he fought Maud now when she changed the dressings. He was weaker, too, and for the past week, he'd barely walked at all, riding on top of the cart instead. Maud had inquired about a place for him in one of the wagons, but they were full, and the Saint in charge said that as Ephraim had two good legs, he must use them. At night, Ephraim suffered such pain that he could not sleep, and he muttered and cried out, until others grumbled that he kept them awake. Sutter took Ephraim's turn at guard duty now, for no matter how sick a man was, he was expected to do his share. Jessie had volunteered to take Ephraim's turn as guard, but the leaders would not allow a woman to patrol the camp. That meant Sutter walked the campsite for six hours each night instead of every two nights, and during the day, he was so tired that he almost fell asleep while pulling the cart. He dozed off by the side of the road, and the women propelled the cart until he woke up and rushed to catch up with them.

"I believe Ephraim's arm will have to come off," Maud had confided to Jessie a few days before they reached the fort. "I do not have the skill for it, so we must pray he will last until he sees the surgeon at Fort Laramie."

"Is it that bad?"

"It is. He's dangerous ill."

So now they waited in a line on the parade ground as

the physician examined those who had arrived before them. Ephraim was not the only sufferer. Some, like him, had broken arms and legs. Others were plagued with dysentery or malaria. There were toothaches and rashes and fevers, and at least one woman inside the cabin that served as an examining room was far gone in labor. They could hear her moans.

After more than an hour of waiting, Jessie, Ephraim, and the others crowded into a little office in the building that served as a surgery, where the doctor looked at Ephraim in a detached way. As Maud told him how she had treated the arm, the herbs she had used, the doctor turned the arm one way and the other, probing, while Ephraim gritted his teeth. "It's putrefied. There is no way to save it. Smell the decay yourself," the doctor said brusquely. "I will amputate, but you'll have to wait until I've seen the rest of these people. You Saints are a healthy lot, but you've had a bad time of it. Yes, we have to take it off unless you want to meet your Mormon God on the morrow. I don't know why you aren't dead already."

Ephraim looked at Jessie and then at Emeline. "No. You won't cut me," he told the doctor. "What good am I with one arm? I'll take my chances."

"Suit yourself," the doctor replied.

"You'll do no such thing, Ephraim. I'd rather have a live brother with one arm than a dead one with two," Jessie told him.

"It'll turn me into a cripple, sitting in the gutter with a tin cup."

"Nonsense. There are no gutters in Salt Lake. We'll find work to suit you."

"What work is there for half a man?"

"Better you should have one arm than risk death," Emeline told him. "I couldn't stand it if you died, too."

Ephraim looked at her a long time before he said, "I could just as well die from the amputation."

"And you might die falling on your face when you walk out the door," Jessie said. "Life's a chance, but keeping your arm isn't. It's certain death."

"Take your choice. There are other patients," the doctor told them. "If you're of a mind to do it, wait over on the parade ground. If you're there when I finish up here, then come back, and I'll amputate. You are in a bad way. You won't live a week with your arm in that condition."

"We'll be back," Jessie said, and Emeline took Ephraim's good hand and led him to the shade of a wagon. Groups of Mormons lounged nearby, watching a formation of soldiers march. Jimmy and Dick, the sons of Jessie's friend Huldah, followed behind the soldiers, sticks over their arms to serve as guns.

When they were seated in the dirt, Jessie repeated the doctor's words. "You'll die if he doesn't take the arm," she told Ephraim. But he was stubborn and shook his head.

"What you can't do with one arm, I'll do with my two," Sutter told his brother. "There is plenty of work for a man with one arm. You can write the letters and keep the books, the way you did before. I've always hated such work."

Ephraim looked at Sutter scornfully. "I didn't come thousands of miles to scribble on paper."

"Look at Brother Paul. He has only one arm, and he can

push his cart as well as any man. He says he can ride a horse and push a plow, too," Maud said.

"I won't be a cripple."

They were all silent for a time. Then Emeline began whispering to Ephraim, her voice so low that only Jessie could hear it. "Please, Ephraim, for me. You're the only man besides Papa and the missionary that's ever treated me decent, treated me like I wasn't dirty. If you died, I couldn't go on. I'd just give up. I'd rather you had one arm to put around me instead of none." He listened to her, dejected, but finally Emeline whispered something in his ear that made him smile, and he nodded his head. Later, when the doctor came out of the surgery and beckoned to them, Emeline helped Ephraim rise.

"What did you tell him?" Maud asked the girl, but Emeline only shook her head.

Inside the cabin, they helped Ephraim climb on top of a table covered with a sheet that was none too clean and spotted with blood, and the surgeon ordered him to drink a concoction. Maud asked what it was, and he replied, "Laudanum. He'll suffer, but he'll live. Or if he don't, it won't be because of the amputation. It'll be because you waited too long."

The woman in childbirth lying on another table moaned, and the sister attending her spoke out, asking the doctor to help.

"Shouldn't you attend to her first?" Jessie asked.

"She'll wait. What's a woman in labor need a doctor for anyway?" He did not wash his hands, but picked up a saw that was splattered with gore. "Third amputation this week. One's a soldier got shot through the arm, the other a fool who let his horse fall on him. Bones sticking out every which way. If it hadn't happened a day's ride from here, he'd be dead. I took off his leg below the knee. Course, he don't much need the knee no more. Pretty funny, if you ask me." The doctor chuckled, then gave a cough when no one else laughed, and he ordered Sutter and Jessie to hold their brother down. "It'll be over before you know it," he said, and indeed, in barely a minute, he had cut through the bone and thrown the severed arm into a pail. Ephraim thrashed about, protesting, screaming, and then passed out. The surgeon folded a flap of skin around the stump and stitched it in place, then announced, "It's done. I usually get two dollars." After Sutter paid him, the doctor took Maud aside and explained how to care for the wound.

"Will he live?" the old woman asked.

The doctor shrugged. "Maybe. He's young and strong. The young ones think the Lord Hisself will reach down and cure them, the damn fools." He went to a cupboard and removed a bottle, took a swallow, and then handed the bottle around. Sutter sampled it, and so did Jessie. Maud declined, but Emeline took a turn, handing the bottle back to the surgeon. "Whiskey helps more than anything. You got any?" the doctor asked.

Jessie shook her head. "I know there's some among the brethren as have it, but I don't know who."

"You can accumulate it at the trading post."

Others pushed into the building to consult the doctor then, and the woman in childbirth began to cry out, so Jessie and Sutter carried their brother outside and laid him down in the shade, telling Maud they would stay with him until he regained consciousness. Then they would walk him back to the cart.

"We'll visit the store," Maud announced. "Come along, Emeline. You've seen your first amputation. Now we'll find out if there are herbs here to help in the recovery." Emeline lingered, but Maud took her arm firmly and said in a low voice, "We'll leave them be. It's family tragedy."

"My tragedy, too," the girl said. She accompanied Maud to the building that served as a sutler's store and waited with the Saints who were bartering for rice and bacon, biscuits and crackers, tea, saleratus, black and cayenne pepper, and candy. Maud had expected supplies to be waiting for them at Fort Laramie, but none were there, so she was not surprised that the Saints with a little money were buying provisions for themselves.

She looked at the boots hanging from the ceiling and over at the hardware—hammers and nails, iron that might be used to reinforce the wheels of their carts, spades and axes that could replace the ones they had discarded. She saw women send furtive glances at the coats and shoes, even bonnets that were for sale. But Maud knew that most did not have the money to buy anything, and even if they had, they would have had to discard other belongings, since the leaders kept strict about the amount of weight each emigrant was allowed. She and Emeline stood quietly for a moment, waiting for the Saints in front of them to finish.

Anne, the heathen, glanced down at her daughter Lucy, who was pointing at the peppermint sticks in a dusty glass jar, and whispered to her husband, "Couldn't we buy just one piece for the two children? They love it so. And maybe a bit of tea to give me strength. It might help my milk." There had been no rest for Anne after the birth of Samuel. She had not had even the luxury of riding on a cart, but had had to march with the other pioneers after the baby was born—and every day since. The handcarts did not tarry for childbirth any more than they did for death, and Anne had not fully recovered.

But her husband shook his head, saying they had no money for such, and the family left the store without purchasing anything.

Then Nannie, standing next to the counter, removed a silver brooch in the shape of a thistle from inside her dress and handed it to the sutler, who curled his lip and snarled, "What will I do with this? I've no call to stock a silver pin. It's worthless to me."

"But it's all I hae. Widna you give me something for it? We're in need."

The man, who was thin and sallow and smelled like a stable, stared at the pin, jiggling it in his hand to feel its weight. "A piece of trash. Besides, I bought one similar from a woman in the last handcart company, the one before you, 'the Willie Company,' they called it, and it's still a-sittin' here," he said. "But maybe I'll give you two bits for it—charity on my part."

"I paid a good fair price for it in Edinburgh."

"Take it back there, then."

Maud peered over the girl's shoulder at the brooch, a fine bit of workmanship. "It's worth more than a quarter."

Emeline spoke up. "It's worth a dollar. There's a Scottish soldier outside. I wager he'd pay you twice that. Offer it to him, Sister. And if he won't buy it, why, one of the soldiers' wives will want it. There's little enough of pretty things they have."

She looked around the shop and added scornfully, "And nothing here worth the price."

The sutler narrowed his eyes at Emeline. "Aye, my fine lady. Would you cheat this child, then?" he asked, referring to himself as a "child," as the old trappers did. He hefted the heavy brooch. "All right, I'll give you a dollar, but you'll take it in trade."

Nannie flashed a look of triumph at Emeline, then quickly picked out the items she wanted in exchange—butter, dried beef, a little coffee and sugar. As she turned, she asked Emeline, "Which one is the Scottish soldier? P'haps he is from my village."

"Oh, he's outside," Emeline said vaguely. "He looked like a Scot to me, but then, I never asked."

The sutler cast a cold eye at Emeline and said, "You'll not cheat me twice."

"I didn't cheat you once. You'll get a fair price for the silver pin."

The sutler ignored the girl and turned to Maud, asking what she wanted. When she told him she was after herbs, he said he didn't deal in them. "There's no call for 'em at the fort. If the surgeon can't cure a soldier, he dies. No cause to drag it out."

The crowd in the store had thinned out, and only a few Saints were left, not buying but only looking at the goods, longing in their eyes.

"You Mormons are a poor lot," the sutler observed sourly. He squinted at Emeline, who was waiting beside the counter, and asked, "You be wanting something?"

"A bottle of whiskey."

The sutler guffawed. "A tippler, are you? I guess you people ain't so high-and-mighty after all. And you just a chunk of a girl!"

Emeline did not smile, just stared at the man so long that he turned away. He shrugged and took out a bottle and set it on the counter. "That there's my best whiskey."

Emeline removed the cork, tasted it, and made a face. "I would not care to taste your worst."

He put the bottle back under the counter and removed another. "You're a particular one, ain't you?"

Not answering, Emeline took a swallow from the second bottle, then said, "For sure, it's taken from the same barrel. I've tasted better from the horse trough."

"Well, it's the last taste you'll get for free. I know your kind—taste and taste until the bottle's dry. Yah! Get on with you." He slammed the cork into the bottle and picked it up by the neck.

"How much?" Emeline asked.

"You insult me like that, I'm of a mind not to sell to you."

"You'll sell. How much?"

He shrugged. "Two dollars."

"Ha!" Emeline said. "For two dollars, I could buy a gallon of Holland gin."

"He charges the soldiers only a dollar," said a man who was watching the bartering.

The sutler narrowed his eyes at the man, who only laughed and left the store.

Emeline reached into her pocket and drew out Sophia Gray's little purse, which she had guarded carefully. But when she opened it, Emeline found it empty. The coins that the Grays had brought with them were gone. "Brother Prime's took my money," she told Maud. "He must have stole it when he tried to take my mother's ring. I never checked."

"I haven't that much," Maud replied.

"It's for a brother whose arm was just took off," Emeline said.

"Not likely. Eight bits," the sutler said, unmoved.

"Then I'll have to give this up." Emeline reached into her pocket and removed a gold ring.

"It's your mama's wedding ring," Maud said.

"Brother Ephraim needs the whiskey," Emeline told her.

The sutler reached for the ring, but Emeline held it a minute longer, gazing at it before the man twisted it from her fingers. He examined it and said, "Another gold band. I have enough for all my fingers."

"Not like this," Emeline told him. "Pure gold, the finest there is, smooth as your cheek." She studied the sutler. "Smooth as *my* cheek. And garnets and pearls set in it." She almost purred.

"Still, not worth much," he said. "But being as how your brother's in need, I'll trade it for a bottle."

"Oh, no," Emeline said, snatching back the ring. "I wouldn't trade a pure gold ring for whiskey not worth three skips of a louse. I wouldn't take less than three dollars for it."

The sutler snorted.

"One dollar for the whiskey, two dollars in trade."

"Not likely."

Emeline returned the ring to her pocket, then smiled at the sutler, smiled in a way no Mormon girl had ever smiled at him. "Come along, Sister Maud. I know a brother who'll have this ring for his wife, and he'll give me a bottle and a blanket for it." The two women started for the door.

Sandra Dallas

"Hold on," the sutler called, and Maud stopped, although Emeline did not. "I said hold on."

Emeline turned and raised her chin a little but did not go back to the counter.

"All right. This child's an old fool. I'll give you the two dollars in trade. I'll lose money on it."

"Not so's you'd notice. Why, your goods cost four times those in Iowa City."

"You think they walk here like a parcel of Mormons?"

At that, Emeline laughed. "I don't believe you'd push a handcart, old man."

"Not too old for you." The sutler laughed, too, showing rotted teeth above his gray beard.

"I'll have a little of the sugar, and a bit of cinnamon, yarn to make stockings." Emeline rattled off what she wanted, and the merchant took down the items with his gnarled fingers. The purchases totaled more than two dollars.

When the things were lined up, the sutler put his arm around them, glaring so fiercely at Maud that she stepped back. He leaned over the counter then, grinning, and said to Emeline, "Winter between here and the Salt Lake is fierce. The snow in the mountains is as deep as a horse. There's many won't survive the crossing. It's clear as gin a little girl like you . . ." He shrugged.

Emeline looked at him wide-eyed, and the old man added a stick of candy to the pile of purchases. "I shouldn't like to be cold like that," she said.

"This child wouldn't like to see a pretty thing like you get her feet froze off. The Mormons don't tell you that, do they?"

"I thank *you* for telling me, sir." Emeline looked up shyly

170

through her lashes, and the old man took down a cone of sugar.

"The Mormons don't have nothing in the way of provisions. You'd get so hungry, you'd gnaw a file."

"I wouldn't like that." She paused and smiled. "Do *you* have enough provisions?"

"You'd have fresh meat every day—and I got me some good hooch, too, seeing as you like it. So there's no need to go in the winter. You could stay till spring. You'd have a full belly." He leered at her, and Emeline gave him as beguiling a smile as Maud had ever seen.

"I am tired to death of the trail," Emeline admitted. "But I don't know you. You might be mean and stingy."

The sutler played with the gold ring, rubbed the garnets on his shirt, then set it beside the other goods. "To show you what kind of child I be, I'll give you back your ring." He pushed it toward Emeline. "I'd fancy a young girl like you to help in the store, somebody sharp as a pin. I'd make a lady of you."

"She is a lady," Maud interjected, but the old man ignored her.

Thinking over the words, Emeline cast down her eyes and slowly picked up the purchases, handing them to Maud. Then she put the gold ring on her finger. "I would like to sleep in a bed. Have you a bed?"

"Aye, and you could sleep till noon and only work a little. I would dote on a pretty thing like you. I'd be right glad for your company."

Maud spoke up. "She's rather young for that, is she not?"

"I didn't ask you, old lady. It's 'tween me and her," the

sutler snapped. He leaned over the counter and whispered, "I take in one hundred and seventy dollars a day here, and I could be generous."

"I'm beholden to those that brought me. I owe them for the food," Emeline said, glancing up at a cured ham that was hanging behind the counter. The sutler gauged her for a moment, then took it down. Emeline picked it up with one hand and the bottle with the other. "Come along, Sister Maud. My things are on your cart." She raised an eyebrow at the man, and the two women quickly left the store.

"You come on back," the sutler called.

Outside, Maud said, "You wouldn't, would you, Sister? He is a foul man."

"I've known worse," Emeline said. "I would not mind a warm bed and plenty to eat, but not with the likes of him. He's the mouse in the meal."

"He thought he could buy you up like a mule. The man was a bad lot altogether." She looked at the girl.

"I've been bought like a mule, and for a lot less."

Maud did not respond but said instead, "You gave him old Harry."

"I played him pretty good, didn't I? I wonder if he really thinks I am fool enough to go back." Emeline added, "I enjoyed myself pretty well, and we got the whiskey for Ephraim."

"It was enough to make an owl laugh."

Emeline frowned and turned to Maud. "Was it a sin? I thought not."

"No, Sister, it was no sin. More likely the Lord worked through you to give the Gentile his comeuppance." She thought that over and nodded at the wisdom of what she'd said. "Such opportunities, like the angels' visits, are few and far between. You acted rightly. And look at what the Lord made him give you!"

Like others the Sullys had encountered along the trail, the men in Fort Laramie warned them about the weather that lay ahead in the mountains. The animals' coats were heavy that fall, which meant a harsh winter. The storms that swept down the mountainsides would be too much for the Mormons in their weakened condition. "Leave the women and children, the sick," they urged. "You can go on in the spring." They should not be such fools as the Willie handcart company, which had set out days ahead of them.

Anne would have stayed, for in her weakened condition, she dreaded the endless walking and the threat of cold weather. But she knew John would not consider it, so she didn't bother to ask him. Others, whose health was weak—or perhaps it was their faith that was—succumbed to the pleadings. A few wanted to remain at the fort. "It will rain pitchforks on them, tines down, if they do," thundered a Saint. "But there will be no storm for God's chosen." Anne did not believe that, and she noted that the church had purchased one hundred buffalo robes at Fort Laramie for the hundreds of members of the company who trudged steadily Zionward.

The Saints pushed on hard after leaving Fort Laramie. The fort had been a disappointment to the Sullys, as well as to the rest of the Saints, because they'd found no supplies waiting for them. Provisions were on their way from the valley, John promised Anne. After all, he said, the handcart companies that had left early in the summer would have reached their destination and told of those following them—the Willie Company and the Martin Company just days behind it. Besides, John pointed out, the elders who had passed them in buggies and wagons on their way to the valley would have told of the emigrants' plight. So the prophet would have sent out wagons. Perhaps they had already reached the Willie Company. The first provisions would have gone to those travelers, but others would be on their way to the Martin Company. John thought the Saints would encounter them any day now. Anne was not so sure. She heard people grumbling, complaining that they had been forgotten, that they had been left to perish, and she feared it was so. This was not what John and the others had been promised when they'd agreed to go to Zion.

Anne observed that some of the Saints did more than grumble. Two men who had camped near the Sullys and had pushed a cart together from Iowa with not a word of discontent began to quarrel. One complained so heartily that they were going to die because they had been forsaken by the church officials in the valley that his partner told him, "I'll stand no more complaints against the authorities. Go and die, then." The two walked on and made camp without talking. The next morning, the grumbler did not wake. Anne thought the man might feel compassion for his friend or even praise God for having taken a faithful Saint to heaven, but the companion announced, "Let the fire of the Almighty consume the wicked."

She was not surprised when the leaders declared that all would have to lighten their loads one more time. The limit was now ten pounds for each adult, five for children. The carts were moving too slowly, and the people, suffering from lack of food and the long walk, were too exhausted to push. So John and Anne and the others went through their possessions again, putting aside not only books, photographs, toys, and mementos from home but also quilts and blankets, worn-out clothing, overcoats, even shoes. Anne stuffed her pockets with small items, donned extra clothing, then let the authorities weigh the things she had put aside to keep. Once more, they had to go through their poor belongings for discards to meet the weight limit. John attempted to cheat at the weighing-up and was chastised later at meeting and forced to ask for forgiveness. "I acted foolishly and wickedly by overloading my cart," he confessed, and Anne hated the Saints for humiliating her husband.

After all the abandoned items had been piled together, the leaders set the lot on fire, so that no one could return to claim a prized possession. Some turned away, but Anne watched as flames consumed the heap, hoping they would not need the blankets and heavy clothing that were turning into ashes.

Not long after that, she and John reached the North Platte River. The air was chill by then. In the distance, the blue-and-purple mountains were covered with snow clouds that swirled and threatened to bring down a storm. Cakes of ice floated in the river, and as the Saints made ready to cross, a sleet storm hit them like a wall of ice. The Sullys had waded the Platte before, since the trail they followed meandered back and forth across the river, but the water had never been icy like this.

John stared into the frigid depths of the river, then returned to the cart, where Anne waited, the infant Samuel bundled up in her shawl. Joe and Lucy sat on top of the cart, wrapped in blankets, and Joe announced suddenly, "Mother, the snow has come."

John looked to the north and saw the storm closing in. "It bodes no good. This won't be an easy crossing," he told his wife. "I'll take the children on the cart, but you will have to wade across."

"It won't be the first time my feet have been wet," she reassured him.

"The water is icy and deep, maybe up to your waist."

"Then we'll build a fire on the other side to dry us off."

John studied his wife a moment. She was gaunt, her face gray, and she'd lost the roundness of her figure because of childbirth, the long trek, and the meager rations. But she was resolute and no longer complained as she had during the first months of the journey. "It hasn't been an easy time for you. I wonder now if I should have insisted you come along."

He had never questioned the rightness of his decision to immigrate to the valley, and Anne studied him. "Is your faith waning?" she asked.

"Oh no," he replied quickly.

"But your decision to travel to Zion is."

He turned away and did not reply.

"Perhaps you are only being tested."

"By whom? Who tests us?" John asked. "God or the leaders? Perhaps we should have stayed in Fort Laramie or in Iowa

City and come on in the spring. It was the leaders who insisted we go on this late in the year, not God."

"How can you say that, you who have been so loyal? You have claimed that God speaks through the leaders of the church and that it is sinful to question them. Do you no longer believe that?"

"Do *you* believe it, Annie?"

Anne looked at the baby, Samuel, who had awakened and begun mewling. He was a tiny thing, smaller than her other infants had been at birth, and he did not feed well. "I don't know what I believe. I've grown fond of these people. I haven't accepted your religion. I may never do so. But I will no longer close myself off to it."

"Anne—"

"No, don't preach at me, John. I will make the decision myself."

"I wasn't going to." He gave a short laugh. "It's too cold to talk religion. We've got to cross the Platte before the storm catches us."

So John pulled the cart to the Platte while Anne, the baby in one arm, pushed. Six miles back, there had been a toll station on the river with a bridge that the Saints could cross, but none of them had the fee, so they were forced to push their carts through the water. Poised on the bank, Anne looked off in the direction of the station, thinking that if John had not given their money to the church, they could have taken their cart across the river. But she knew that even if they'd had the coins, John would never set himself above the others by using the bridge, while his fellow Saints waded through the water. Nor would she. How could she cross the river in luxury while old women like Maud, who had delivered Samuel, waded through the water?

Other carts were ahead of them on the riverbank, men shoving them off into the cold water and propelling them to the far side while their wives tied up their skirts and waded across, pushing the carts or carrying the children. John and Anne watched as a cart pushed by an old man tipped over in midstream, spilling blankets and clothing and cooking utensils. Men rushed to right the vehicle. Others grabbed for the items as they were swept downstream, but most of the contents of the cart disappeared. The man pulled the vehicle to the far bank and shoved it out of the water, then sank down, his wife beside him, and put his hands over his face.

"At least they were not injured," John said.

"Yes." Still, Anne could not help wondering how the couple would go on. It was clear now that there would be snow, and without the things lost in the water, the two old people would be hard-pressed to survive. She thought about the blankets and clothing that had been burned.

"You must look at the carts that are already across. Almost everyone made it safely. Look, people are already building fires," John told her, as if he understood her fear. "Are you ready?"

Anne smiled a little and replied, "And what if I am not? Is there a choice? Could we go back?" When John looked dejected, his wife added, "I'm only jesting. If we have no choice, we might as well endure with humor."

John took his wife's hand and gripped it hard. Then he shoved the cart into the stream and started across. The baby in her arms, Anne stepped into the water behind him and gasped at the icy coldness of it. Although she wore stout shoes, she could feel the chill like needles thrusting their sharp points into her feet, the pricks moving up her legs all the way to her back as she waded into deeper water. By the time she was half-way across, the water was above her waist, and she no longer felt as cold, because it had begun to numb her. She looked over at John, whose face was grim as he struggled with the weight of the cart. Anne walked slowly, feeling each rock on the river bottom with a foot before she took a step. She felt as if she were walking with peas in her shoes. But she was more concerned about John, worried that if the cart tipped, the children would slide into the water.

They were nearly across when the cart hit a rock and lurched. Anne reached out with her free arm as if to right it, although she was too far away even to touch it. Then as she took a step toward the cart, she slipped on the cobblestones of the river bottom. Her free arm flailed, and she tried to regain her balance, but instead, she fell backward, the water closing over her head, and she struggled not to go down. The swirling water whipped Anne's shawl over her face, smothering her, then wrapped itself around her neck as if to strangle her. As Anne clawed it away, her feet slid all the way out from under her and she fell onto the river bottom. The shawl caught on a branch under the water and yanked the infant Samuel out of her hands. Anne reached for the baby, but she could not grab him, only push him up to the surface. She found purchase and thrust her head above the water, but the baby was not in sight. John had seen her fall, had watched with disbelief as she went down, and then he'd seen Samuel pop to the surface of the water. He pushed through the water toward the baby. But the infant was out of his grasp, and with a feeling of horror, Anne watched as her baby disappeared in a swirl of water. "Samuel!" she called, and then, "Emma Lee!"

At that instant, Catherine Dunford, who was downstream from Anne, spotted the baby. Too stunned to cry out, she grabbed her husband's arm and pointed. Despite his more than seventy years, Peter Dunford had a back like an oak plank and legs as stout as stone fence posts. He had been hard-worked in the coal mines of Scotland, but through the grace of God, Catherine believed, had not contracted the miner's puff, the tuberculosis that robbed so many of his companions of their lives.

Catherine had told Anne more than once how they had heard the message that the church was building up an empire in America where men and women would no longer be tied to the drudgery into which they'd been born, where each could find work that suited. "There are no shackles in Zion. There you will breathe the pure air of the mountains and glory in the sunshine of God's days," the missionary had said. "You have endured much as the slaves of rich men. God will avenge you, and he will take you to His kingdom." Catherine had repeated the message to Anne word for word, wonderment in her voice. "Our entire family was converted. Our son is already in the valley and is waiting for us. He has written that none shall go up to Zion except the pure in heart, and no heart is purer than Peter's," she'd said fondly.

Peter Dunford's heart was indeed pure, Anne realized later, for just as Samuel rose to the surface of the water, floating like

Moses in ancient Egypt, Peter let go of the shafts of his cart and flailed through the water, thrusting himself forward to where the baby had been tossed by the water and had begun to sink again. Peter dropped into the frigid depths of the river, thrusting his arms about until he felt the infant and grasped the tiny body. Then he surfaced, gasping and coughing, but he held Samuel in his huge hand.

Anne pushed through the water and grasped her son. "You saved his life!" she murmured as the baby sputtered and then began to cry. "It is a miracle."

John came up beside them and gripped the man's arm, too emotional to speak, and the two looked at each other for a moment before Peter said, "We've got to get out of this water or God and all the angels won't save us from pneumonia."

John nodded, and he went back to his cart, pushing it to the far side of the river, where a brother helped him lift it onto the bank. When his family was out of the water, John turned back to help Peter and Catherine and the Saints with them propel their cart onto land. Then they pushed their carts a mile inland to where the main body of the Saints was camped in the falling snow. After they set up their tents, the men went to scrounge sagebrush for fuel to build a fire, and Anne carefully rubbed Samuel to warm him and wrapped him in a dry shirt of John's. Then she and Catherine wrung out the wet clothing. There was not much hope it would dry, because the sleet was coming fast now, stinging them like broken glass. It was all they could do to keep the children out of the storm.

The men returned and built a fire, and Peter, shivering because his boots and clothing were wet, collapsed onto a damp blanket that Catherine had spread under the shelter. She warmed his hands in her own and quoted fondly from a Robert Burns poem, " 'Your locks are like the snaw.' "

Anne turned aside. The scene was too intimate.

"My poor head is vexed," Peter muttered.

John, hovering over the old man who had saved his son, said, "He is not well, Anne. I'll get an elder to lay hands on him."

Anne felt the old man's forehead, which was feverish, and she went to the cart for a blanket to cover him, but there was none, because the blankets had been used to form the shelter, and they were soaked by the storm. "We must move him closer to the fire," she told Catherine, but when Peter tried to sit up, he could not. Catherine took off her cloak and wrapped it around her husband. "You do too much. You are not particular to help others."

He might have replied, "It is the Lord's work," but instead, Peter looked up blankly, his eyes red, and muttered, "Such whiteness."

"What?"

"So white." He gazed heavenward.

John returned then with two men, who anointed Peter with consecrated oil, then put their hands on him and prayed. "Lord, look down on thy servant Peter and his good works and rebuke the fever that consumes him. Cast out the Destroyer and return your servant to health," entreated one. The little group outside the tent prayed silently, but Peter did not seem to be aware of them. He looked heavenward and tried to sit up. "White feathers," he said.

"It is just the snow falling, my love," Catherine told him. "Don't ye feel it?"

"Angel wings." His speech became slurred, then he stopped speaking and made a mighty effort to get up, but instead, he fell backward onto the ground and was still.

John put his ear to the old man's chest, then rose slowly, shaking his head. Crying softly, Catherine took her husband's wrist and felt for life, but there was none. She held his hand for a long time, then gently placed it on his breast and smoothed the blanket she had wrapped around him. "He rests in peace with the Lord," she said as she put her head against Anne's shoulder.

"We are sorrowfully disappointed," Anne told her.

"As the Lord lives, I know that he is in heaven with all the angels. His good works have taken him there. And he waits for your coming," John said. Anne frowned at that, because she thought such words were little comfort to a woman who had lost her life's companion. Catherine did not appear to hear them, however. John left to join men who were already digging a grave, a large grave, because others would die before morning, and when the men were finished, they carried off Peter's body, which they had wrapped in a damp blanket. There would be a service for all the dead before the company left on the morrow.

Catherine did not follow. She had not moved from the fire since Peter sat down beside her, and now she stared into the coals, every now and then reaching for a stick to keep the fire going.

"Are you cold?" Anne asked.

Catherine shook her head.

"I am so sorry. He died because he saved my son."

"He died because he did God's work."

"He was chilled going under the water."

"It was the Lord's way," Catherine said.

"How can you be so calm?" Anne was perplexed, because if her own husband had died, she would have cried out in anguish, would have found someone to blame.

"We are taught the Lord is all-wise, although I am hard-pressed to see the wisdom in taking Peter from me. We have not been apart a single night in fifty years, and now, I don't know what I shall do. But I must trust in the Lord and hope He shows better judgment next time."

"You'll go on with us," Anne told her. She had not consulted John about that. Adding an old woman to their family would be a hardship. Catherine's belongings would increase the weight on the cart and there would be times when the old woman would be too tired to walk and would have to ride on top. But John would agree with his wife's decision. How could he not? Peter Dunford had saved Samuel from the river, and Catherine had given comfort to Anne on the ship when Emma Lee died.

Remembering that, Anne rose suddenly and went to where John had stacked their belongings. Rummaging through the things, she found a slim volume that had been slipped into the pocket of her good dress. She had forgotten about it, and in fact, if she had remembered it, she would have discarded it long since in one of the demands to lighten the loads. She knelt beside Catherine and gave her the book. "This is yours. I picked it up after you discarded it in Iowa City."

Catherine took the book and opened it, showing Anne the inscription written in a cramped hand: "To my wife, Catherine Dunford, replacing the book that well served for fifty year. Peter Dunford." Catherine closed the book and clasped it in her hands. "He gave me the first volume on our wedding day, and over the years, it was worn to pieces. This came on the day we'd been married fifty years. No possession in the world means more to me. I have been pained every day since I left it behind. She opened the volume and began to read slowly:

John Anderson my jo, John,
When we were first acquent,
Your locks were like the raven,
Your bonnie brow was brent . . .

She closed the book and finished the poem by memory.

Later that evening, John did indeed agree that Catherine would join them. She sorted through the possessions the old couple had brought from Scotland, giving Peter's warm gloves and coat to John and setting aside her husband's boots and extra clothing to be distributed among the Saints. Anne found it painful to watch the woman examine each item, recalling what had been a gift, what purchased, agonizing over which to discard. Catherine removed one item and furtively put it into her pocket, and Anne wondered if the woman would carry some memento rather than add it to the cart.

The night was bitterly cold. Snow replaced the sleet, and the Saints huddled together in the tents to keep warm. Anne slept fitfully, waking often to check on Samuel, then moving close to the two older children, who slept between her and

John. Not until nearly morning did she fall into a deep sleep. When she awoke, she saw that Catherine was gone, and Anne wondered if the woman had slept at all. Then she turned to Samuel and found him still asleep, wrapped in her shawl, a small bundle beside him. Anne frowned and rose on her elbow to look. There beside the baby's tiny hands, which were red and chapped from the river water, was Emma Lee's doll, the one Anne had discarded in Iowa City. Catherine had carried it all this way. Anne picked up the wooden figure, which was still dressed in its silk gown and wrapped in the miniature quilt that she herself had made, and clasped it in her hand, just as Catherine had done with the volume of poetry the evening before. And she wondered at the remarkable way they had kept each other's precious possessions and returned them in time of need.

Louisa and her family were among the last to cross, because her husband had put the safety of the others in his hundred before them. Thales had worked with a vengeance to get the members of his hundred across the North Platte. She could not fault him, for she saw how he helped the emigrants repack their carts to keep blankets and foodstuffs dry, pushed their vehicles into the river, and raced through the water when a cart seemed ready to tip over. He ferried an old woman across on his back, then returned to the east side of the river and took young children from a poorly loaded cart and carried them through the water. And he did not limit his aid to those of his hundred. He helped any Saint who needed him.

Louisa did not mind the wait, for she was proud of her

husband's kindness. But she was glad when, at last, Thales ordered his family—Louisa, her sister, Huldah, and their mother, with the nephews, Dick, walking, and Jimmy, on top of the cart—into the water, where they moved swiftly to the far bank, passing others as they pushed their way across the river. Even after reaching the far bank, Thales's work was not done. Scarcely was the Tanner cart pulled from the water than Thales turned again to the river, taking Jimmy and Dick with him.

Their mother, Huldah, protested. "The water's deep and much too cold for little children. They're already chilled. Besides, Jimmy can't swim, Brother Thales."

"Neither can I," he replied. "They'll stay in the shallows. Others younger are wading the river."

"They feel the cold very bad. After all, they are only eight and eleven."

"Old enough by our reckoning to be responsible. They aren't children anymore. You have been too liberal with them."

Louisa, too, protested Thales's taking the boys with him. "Do not be grumbling-angry. They have already sacrificed much in coming here."

"I have said they are to come with me. Obedience is better than sacrifice," Thales told her. "Surely you understand that." Knowing her husband was speaking of her, too, Louisa looked away meekly. But she did not leave the river. Instead, she told her mother and sister to take the cart to the camp, where she would join them later with the boys. Thales might change his mind if he saw his wife waiting for the children and let them go with her.

"Please, just this one time, can't they run around? Jimmy's afraid of water. They are just boys," Louisa pleaded once more.

She rarely spoke after being rebuked, and Thales seemed surprised as well as displeased. "I believe I am head of this family and have stated my decision," he told her. "Besides, it is nothing compared to what I put up with when I camped with the Saints at Winter Quarters. I was a boy, too."

"You were twenty. That is what you have said."

He ignored the retort and started to march the boys off, but Dick stood in front of his brother and said, "Sir, I will go, but Jimmy's too little. He won't be of much help. I'll do the work for both of us."

Thales was unmoved. "There, you can help that man, both of you," he ordered, pointing to a Saint who was struggling with a cart near the bank.

"But the water's too cold," the younger boy, Jimmy, protested, looking to his brother for help.

"I cannot but wonder if you prefer the fires of hell," Thales replied.

"Thales—" Louisa said, but her husband put up his hand to silence her.

"I'll have no more interference. You, too, must learn obedience, Louisa."

"Oh, don't preach me to death," she retorted.

She should not have spoken so, because Thales seemed angered by her defiance and demanded of Dick and Jimmy, "Are you for God?" When the two nodded, Thales said, "Then you will gladly do His work. Have faith in God, and you will not get cold."

The boys trudged off beside Thales, Dick taking his brother's hand, and went into the river, shivering and frightened, wading through the chill water to the cart that Thales had pointed out to them. There wasn't much two little boys could do, Louisa knew. They were slight, barely strong enough to help push the Tanner cart when it was on dry ground. Thales must want them to learn that helping others is a part of their religion, Louisa thought. And she knew that he was concerned about appearances. After all, what would others think if the two children in Thales Tanner's own family did not do their part? It would reflect on Thales himself. The boys' hard work would be one more proof that Thales lived his religion.

With the snow falling heavily now, the water was frigid, and the Saints dodged cakes of ice that floated in the river. The emigrants were numb with the cold, careless, and many could not feel the rocks of the river with their frosted feet. Thales seemed to ignore the cold, however, as he rushed back and forth to keep the carts from toppling over. He plucked two children from an overloaded cart so that the parents could pull it more easily, carrying the children the rest of the way across the river. He helped a couple push their cart out of the rocks of the river bottom, where a wheel was caught. Whenever someone needed his aid, Thales was there. Once, he looked over at Louisa and pointed to her nephews, who were unloading a cart so that an old man could get it out of the river. His look of satisfaction told her that he knew he had been right in insisting the boys help.

Thales was intent in examining a broken spoke, his back to Jimmy, and did not see the boy go under the water. But Louisa did, and she cried out, "Catch him!" Someone else called, "That boy's been hit by the ice!" Men abandoned their carts in midstream in an effort to save the child, who was being swept away in the current. Horrified, Louisa rushed to the river as she watched a red scarf flash through the water downstream. In a rare bit of extravagance before the journey, Thales had bought the scarves for the boys, red for Jimmy, green for Dick, confiding to his wife that the colors would stand out in the crowd, making it easier for him to keep an eye on the two.

Clutching her skirts, Louisa rushed into the river and grabbed Thales's arm. "Jimmy! It's Jimmy!" She pointed at the tip of the scarf, which moved through the water like a snake, carried swiftly, far too fast for anyone to catch the boy. Thales thrust her aside, but Louisa would not be stopped, and she followed her husband as he thrashed through the water, then up onto the bank. They would never reach Jimmy, but perhaps he would grab hold of a tree or right himself in the shallows and they would find him. In a few seconds, the scarf disappeared, and there was no sign of anyone in the churning water. The boy was gone, had sunk below the current that was the color of soot.

The two turned back and caught sight of Dick, paralyzed, staring at the spot where his brother had disappeared. Thales, Louisa behind him, made his way to the bank and tried to hold the boy, but Dick stood stiffly, resisting the embrace. "Was it Jimmy?" Thales asked, thinking, perhaps, some other boy had worn a red scarf. When Dick didn't answer, Thales told him, "It was the Lord's will."

"No it wasn't," Dick snapped. "It was yours." He started to snivel, then took a deep breath and turned on Thales. "You knew Jimmy couldn't swim. He was only a little boy. I don't care if you knew Joseph Smith. You aren't God. You don't rule everything. You had no right to make him go in the water. You killed him." The boy turned and fled up the trail to the camp.

Louisa was stunned, for no one had ever spoken to her husband that way; no Saint had ever questioned his authority. She watched as Dick flung his own green scarf onto the ground and disappeared among the carts. "Go to him," Thales told her.

"No, we must search for Jimmy. Huldah will need a body to bury."

"I'll do it, then."

"I'll go with you. I cannot face my sister without Jimmy."

Wet and cold, Thales, with Louisa behind him, trudged through the dusk, searching among the rocks and the roots of trees lining the bank. From time to time, Louisa raised her eyes to the far bank, thinking the current might have carried the boy to the other side. "I'll cross and search there," she said.

Thales put his hand on her arm. "I will do it. The sin is mine," and he went into the icy water.

The two searched the opposite sides of the river, calling out to each other from time to time, for it was growing dark and it was hard to see a small boy, let alone a person, on the other side. As she searched, Louisa pondered her husband's "sin." Thales had never doubted that he was inspired, that he did God's work, that he had been chosen to lead not only her family but the other Saints. From the day he was baptized, he had told her, he had believed he was destined for great things among the Mormons. That was why he was such an inspired missionary, why he worked tirelessly to take his people to Zion. But perhaps he was not perfect.

They had searched for nearly a mile when Louisa spotted the red scarf, caught in a branch of a tree hanging over the river. Her heart leapt at the sight of it, and she prayed that Jimmy had survived the water, had climbed out onto the bank, catching his scarf on the limb. He could be resting there, under that tree. Perhaps God was only testing her—or Thales. She called to Thales, who crossed the river, only to find that Jimmy wasn't under the tree. The scarf hung there like a banner to taunt them.

They went on together now, because it was dark and snow was swirling around, making it difficult to see more than a few feet. Louisa wondered if they had passed the boy, had missed him in the blackness. And then Thales spotted Jimmy lying in the shallow water, where ice had begun to form. Snow was falling on the boy and in a few more minutes would have covered him, so that passing by, they would have thought him only a rock. Thales knelt and picked up the body from the cold water, pausing to look into the small face for signs of life. But there were none. So with the body in his arms, Thales made his way toward the camp, Louisa beside him, her hand stroking the still face.

The two were chilled through to their bones now. Their wet clothing froze to their bodies, and they shivered as they walked beside the river, snow and sleet pelting them. How could people stand such cold? Louisa wondered. They would sleep in wet clothes, covered by wet blankets, the only warmth coming from bodies crowded into the tents. Louisa would have Thales to keep her warm, but what about Huldah? Whom did she have?

Thales began to mumble. "I did what I thought God wanted. How could I be wrong? Was it what I wanted? Did I hope to prove myself as a leader?"

"Hush," Louisa said, but Thales did not hear her, did not

seem to know she was there. He was talking to himself, not to her.

The boy's body heavy in his arms, Thales stumbled in the brush that lined the river and went down on one knee, striking it on a rock and ripping his pants, nearly dropping the boy. Clutching the body, he rose, and Louisa saw him bite his lip against the pain in his leg. She was confused now with the snow swirling around them. Which way were they going? Thales stopped a moment to get a sense of direction. They had been turned around when they picked up Jimmy and had headed downriver. The body had floated down with the current. They must go upstream, he told Louisa. So she followed her husband as he turned and headed up the river, stumbling along, her feet so cold, she could barely move them.

They came to the place where the handcarts had left the river and gone west, then followed the tracks in the snow. "If we can make it to the camp, we will be all right," Louisa said through lips so cold she could barely form the words. "Mother and my sister will have a supper and a fire."

They trudged on, heading into the storm, which howled like nothing Louisa had ever heard. She was moving slowly because her legs throbbed and her footing was unsure. She did not see the camp—the snow was too thick—but she heard it. The murmur of voices and the sound of oxen, and only when they were upon it did she see the faint yellow flair of campfires. She followed Thales slowly past the fires that the Saints were trying to keep going, until someone recognized him and pointed toward the Tanner cart, where the women were huddled beside their own fire.

Without a word, Huldah held out her arms for her son. She was a small woman, not strong, but the boy had been frail, and she took his body easily, bowing her head over his. She said stiffly, "You found him."

Thales tried to reply, but his mouth seemed frozen, and he mumbled, "Yes, we found him." He sat down beside the cart and put his head in his hands.

"Mother has taken Dick to the supply wagon. He is very angry. There is a little pancake left. Would you eat?" Huldah asked.

Thales shook his head, but Huldah had been speaking to Louisa, who was holding her hands over the feeble fire. "Give it to Dick when he comes back."

They were silent for a moment. Then Thales said, "I made him go into the river. I killed him."

"No, Thales, it was the Lord's doing," Louisa said in a faint voice.

"It was mine," Thales said, and he glanced at Huldah, who was rocking back and forth with the boy's body in her arms. "I was tempted by the Destroyer. I sent Jimmy to his death to build up my kingdom. I am sure of it. Now the Lord is pointing me hellward."

"You are the most righteous man I know. You did what you thought God wanted. You must not get into darkness over it." Louisa looked at her sister, who was absorbed in her son. "We must look on God's side. Will this not teach us a lesson?"

"What lesson is that?"

Louisa shook her head. "He will reveal it to you. You have always been His servant."

"I believe I would rather be a dog and bay at the moon than be that kind of servant."

Shocked, Louisa reached for her husband and put her arms around him. "No one blames you, not even Huldah. Only Dick, I think, and he will change in time. Draw into the fire and warm yourself."

But he would not do it. "We must find a winding-sheet." Thales took down one of the blankets that had been used to shield the carts from the storm. Then he lifted Jimmy's body from Huldah's arms and wrapped it in the wet covering. "There is a burial place already dug. I saw it as we passed through the camp." Thales picked up the boy's body and, followed by the women, carried it to the mass grave.

Chapter 6

Nannie Macintosh made her way out of the tent, past a group of Saints sleeping under a shelter. She stepped on something in the dark, and glancing down, she made out a man's arm under her shoe. She mumbled an apology, but he did not respond, and Nannie thought that she had not awakened him. Then she realized the arm was as solid as a rock. He was dead. He had frozen in the night.

She did not shudder. Just a few months ago, she would have been horrified at stumbling over a dead man, at the un-breathing quiet, but there had been so much death along the trail that it no longer moved her. Once, she had awakened each morning filled with joy. Now she was grateful just to wake at all. Nannie wondered if the man's wife felt as she did, because the woman snored beside her husband, her arm carelessly thrown across his body. Perhaps she did not know that he had died. Let her sleep, Nannie thought. The rest would do her more good than the knowledge that her husband was no longer among the living. Nannie wondered if there were others in the tent who slept that same eternal sleep.

She shivered as she walked through the snow, which was still falling. It had settled over the carts, until they appeared like great white humps of sheep, reminding her of those she had seen in the fields of Scotland. Andrew had left the cart in a protected place, and now Nannie wondered how she would find the vehicle. They all looked alike under the powdery white. Other Saints were up before her. Some had started fires with fuel they had saved from the night before, but they were hard put to keep the flames going. Men used flint to start the fires, but the women were not so adept at that and preferred lucifers. Just as soon as one flared up, however, the wind blew it out, and the women were reluctant to light another of the precious matches.

It ought to be morning by now, Nannie thought, glancing back in the direction of the river, but the dark had thinned only a little. She scanned the carts, clapping her cold hands as she looked for her own vehicle, but she could not see it in the winter gloom. She and Ella and Andrew had been among the first to cross the river, and they had left their cart near a stand of willows. They'd thought the trees with yellow leaves still clinging to the branches would be easy to spot in the morning and would give the cart a little protection, but even trees were difficult to make out in the snow now. Nannie trudged along the lines of vehicles, remembering what a soldier at the fort had told her—that people grew disoriented in the snow, confused about direction, and fell down and froze to death, although they were not ten feet from safety.

The storm did not seem to be that bad now, however. Shapes loomed up in the blackness, and as long as she could see the lumps of the carts, she would be safe. As if to assure herself she would not get lost in the storm, she touched each cart as she passed it.

A tree loomed up before her. It was too small to be their tree, but she remembered seeing it the night before, so she knew her cart was not far away. In a minute, she made out two vehicles placed so that they formed a V. Her cart had been next to them, and Nannie strained her eyes until she saw the wheels, barely visible in the dawning light.

She had left the tent to retrieve her second shawl. She'd thought about discarding it before they crossed the river, when the Saints had been told to lighten their carts again, but it was her good shawl. In Edinburgh, she had sacrificed her Saturday-afternoon tea outings with the lovely Sally Lunn buns to save her wages to purchase the garment—a heavy wool paisley with picklelike designs. She had picked the purple color so that she would be reminded of the heather at home, in case Utah failed to have the dear plants. Just the thought of the heather cheered her a little. The shawl was as warm as a blanket and not nearly as heavy. A few days before, when the Saints had been told to pare down their belongings once more, she had discarded her second pair of boots in favor of keeping it.

But she had left it in the cart and had shivered all night, even though they all slept in their shawls and cloaks now, had for some time. So Nannie had decided to retrieve the covering. She envied Ella, sleeping in the embrace of Andrew's arms. The two had kept each other warm. But Nannie had nothing to warm her except her clothing. Now she dug through the things left in the cart.

There wasn't much. The three of them had watched as nearly half of their belongings went up in flames back across the river. It had been hard for them to part with those last possessions, the things they had brought along for their new life in Zion. They no longer had luxuries such as books or mementos from home. Those had been discarded early in the trip. So the last time, they'd been forced to part with necessities. Andrew had sacrificed his gloves, Ella her second dress. Andrew had tossed Nannie's red silk slippers into the pile, but Nannie had snatched them up and tucked them into the waistband of her skirt, under her coat; she had lost so much weight that there was room for the red shoes. If she carried them like that, they wouldn't be weighed. Instead, she had discarded the boots.

Now she looked through the meager possessions in the cart, but she could not find the shawl. Had it been thrown out by accident? At the last moment, had Andrew tossed it into the pile when she wasn't looking? Or perhaps it had fallen out of the cart during the river crossing. Then Nannie remembered having seen it the night before, when they took out the cooking things. She had put the soft wool against her cheek and felt its warmth before she carefully folded it and placed it in the bottom of the cart, where it would be dry. She went through the things again, and when she still didn't find the shawl, Nannie removed everything from the cart and repacked it. But the shawl was gone. How could it have been lost? And then Nannie thought, No, it hasn't been lost. Someone has taken it. She wondered then if other things were missing, and she went through their belongings again. The rice she'd acquired at Fort Laramie in exchange for her silver brooch was gone, along with the coffee. She sank down beside the cart and began to cry.

No one paid her attention. The Saints who were moving among the carts now had their own grief, some worse than Nannie's. She thought of the little boy who had drowned in the North Platte. He was the nephew of the missionary who considered himself so high-and-mighty. And there was the old man who had died after helping the Saints cross the river. The two were buried in the same grave, left open last night because the emigrants knew others would be dead by morning. Many had died before they'd even reached the North Platte. Not long after the company left Fort Laramie, a man had sat down beside the trail and refused to move, saying he would die before he took another step. The Saints had thought he would change his mind and come in during the night, but when he didn't, a group of men went back and found the man's body, already feasted upon by wild animals.

There'd been that woman, too, who'd died in childbirth and others who'd been taken in accidents. Perhaps some had already died of exhaustions. So Nannie couldn't expect sympathy just because she'd lost a shawl and a little food. Still, even that small amount could mean the difference between life and death in the miles yet to travel to Great Salt Lake City. Without the shawl, she could freeze to death, and with their rations already reduced, the rice might have kept them from starvation. Nannie had not expected to find thieves among the Mormons.

She huddled beside the cart, the chill wind blowing snow

into the folds of her shawl and freezing the tears on her cheeks, until a man knelt beside her and said, "Sister Nannie?"

She made out the face in the wan light and replied, "Brother Levi." She had seen him the night before when he'd pushed his cart near hers. She had heard Levi's wife, Patricia, complain that she expected Levi to provide her with a fine house in Great Salt Lake City to make up for the misery she had endured on the trail. Nannie had wondered if Levi had told her he expected to take a second wife.

"We did not expect the snow," Levi said.

"We were promised there would be none."

"I wonder where the snow prophet is who said he'd eat every flake that fell. He has more than his words to eat now."

Despite herself, Nannie laughed. Levi had always made her laugh. He could be stormy and pompous, but he found humor in the most serious subjects, and that was one of the reasons she'd loved him—and perhaps loved him still. "I wonder if his courage is as great now as it was in Florence." She wiped the tears from her face with the backs of her hands.

"You bubble. You've given over crying. Is it such a hard trip?" He took her hand, and she did not resist.

"It's my shawl. I fear it's been stole."

"A shame!"

Nannie tried to be charitable. "In the Bible, Solomon says that men do not despise a thief if he steals to satisfy his soul when he's hungry."

"Solomon did not cross the continent with a handcart company. Besides, the thief didn't steal from the warm and well fed, but from others as cold and hungry as he is. I suppose it's to be expected."

"Scripture says a thief must make sevenfold restitution. Seven shawls and seven bowls of rice for every one he took would satisfy me."

The two laughed together, and Nannie realized she had stopped shivering. Levi smiled at her and said, "I am well acquainted with Brother Martin, who heads this company. I'll inquire of him if there's another shawl to be had."

"Ye'd do that for me?"

"I would not want my future wife to be cold."

Nannie blushed deeply, thinking she was so warm now that the snow would indeed melt when it hit her cheeks. She hoped Levi could not see her burning face through the falling flakes. "I've told ye I winna care to be a second wife."

"There's time for you to consider it further. We won't reach the valley for days, weeks, maybe. I believe you've already given it some thought."

He was right, although Nannie would not tell him so. She shivered, thinking it would be a long walk without a warm shawl. Perhaps she should encourage Levi so that he would find a cloak for her, but that struck her as almost as dishonest as stealing from a cart.

The sky was lighter now, and more Saints moved about the camp. Some stamped their feet and waved their arms to bring back the circulation. Others simply stood by the carts, confused and discouraged.

"Will we go aboot today?" Nannie asked, wanting Levi to stay with her, although she did not care to talk about marriage. She wondered then if Mormon men flirted when they courted their second or third—or seventh—wives. It seemed disrespectful to the others, but she supposed they all had to get used to it. Perhaps there were rules, some kind of etiquette that covered plural marriage. Who sat next to him at dinner? Who slept with him first when he returned from a trip? Who got the best dress? That last was easy to answer—the favorite, for despite the elders' insistence that each wife was treasured, each wife equal, Nannie knew that a husband must prefer one over the others. If she married Levi, which wife would he prefer—Patricia or her? Or maybe there was another woman Levi was courting, one he loved more than either of them.

The women must try to curry favor with their husband, she thought, sacrificing to give him the choicest foods, dressing shabbily so that he might have fine clothes. Perhaps they lied about each other, charging other wives with bad behavior to gain his approval. Or perhaps the wives were friends, confiding in each other, supporting one another when the husband was cruel or unfair, laughing at his pompousness and faults. Maybe they shared the work just like sisters did, one cooking, the other mending, a third tending the children. That appealed to Nannie, although it would hardly make up for sharing a husband.

"Why would we not?" Levi said now, answering Nannie's question about whether the company would travel that day. "We are safer moving along than lying about in the snow, where we could freeze."

"Nannie?" She had not seen her sister come up, and she wondered if Ella had overheard the conversation with Levi. "Brother Levi," said Ella, acknowledging him stiffly and tightening the blanket wrapped around her.

Levi bowed a little and said, "You will forgive me if I don't remove my hat, Sister Ella, for I have little enough of hair to warm the top of my head." She did not reply, only stared at him, until Levi said he must be tending to his fire. "My wife is ill. The snow drives the sick and the nervous mad, and it falls on me today to make a breakfast. I wonder if it will be eggs and a bit of meat or berries with clotted cream. Or perhaps a nice piece of fish or fresh bread toasted over the fire. Oh, to have to choose! Good day, Sisters."

Nannie laughed, but Ella only stared her disapproval at Levi's back as he disappeared in the snow. "I wonder ye can be civil to him, let alone find him amusing," Ella said.

"He makes me laugh, and I'm in need of it."

"Aren't we all."

"With new reason. My paisley shawl's been stole. And the rice and coffee," Nannie told her.

"Stole? Are ye sure, Nannie?"

"They're gone. How else could they hae disappeared? We dinna throw them out."

"Stole by a Saint? Who would hae thought such a thing? Oh, Nannie, how shall we survive?" Ella leaned against the wheel of the cart and put her hands over her face. "Perhaps it's punishment for buying such at the fort. Maybe we should hae given your purchases to the elders to share."

"No such a thing. Others bought for theirselves. I traded my brooch for the food, and as to the shawl, I deprived myself for weeks to buy it. I say find the thief and punish him. Her," she added, thinking about the shawl.

"I hope we won't be reduced to thievery ourselves," Ella told her.

"Levi says he'll find me another shawl, get it from the wagon, if they hae a store of things."

"Why would he do that?"

Nannie looked down at her hands, which were raw from the cold and snow, wondering whether to confide in her sister. "Because Levi asked me to marry him."

"Ye are saying he's contrite for abandoning ye on the day of your wedding. Well, he should be, the scapegrace."

"I mean he asked me again to marry him. He wants me for a second wife."

"Och! In the name of mercy!"

Nannie smiled weakly.

"My lord, such a nerve he has! I hope ye told him to get straightened up. To think he could ask such a thing!" When Nannie didn't reply, Ella asked, "Did ye tell him ye dinna care a button for him anymore, that ye'd prefer to be married to that old zealot in Florence than him?"

"I told him I dinna want to be a second wife."

"And certainly not to the fantoosh Sister Patricia, who wears as many petticoats as an onion has peels! You would hae to fetch and carry for her, cook her food and blacken her boots," Ella said loyally. "She orders Levi around as if she's the head of his house instead of him. Hae ye had a chat with her? She has no thoughts in her head. Why, talking to her is like talking to an empty soup bowl. Little wonder it is he's sorry he dinna marry ye. He's had these many months to regret his foolishness. Oh, I'm glad ye told him nay."

"Maybe I should consider him." Nannie turned and placed her cold hands under the clothing in the cart. "I still care for him, Ella. And I'd be better off as Levi's second wife than as the fourth wife of some Saint too old to give me satisfaction."

"Who's to say ye'd hae to marry with one?"

"It's said such has the pick of the girls, and there's not a thing a lass can do if she's chosen. I dinna want a man with a long beard and a mouthful of rotted teeth."

"Who has a long beard and rotted teeth?" Andrew asked, coming up beside the two women and putting his arm around his wife. "I hope ye are not talking about me. Did Ella tell ye she found a gray hair in my beard?"

"Not you—Levi," Ella told him. Nannie put up her hands to stop her sister from saying more, but Ella added, "He wants to take Nannie for a plural wife."

Andrew did not seem surprised. He stamped his feet in the cold and flung his arms around. "I figured as much, since Nannie is a fair girl and a few hae asked me about her." The two women stared at him, and he nodded at the truth of what he'd said. "There's others that hae claimed plural wives among the emigrants. They canna marry them now, but they hae only to arrive in the valley before the deed is done. It's said the elders in Zion will be angry that the missionaries hae taken the best women for themselves. And Nannie, as ye know, is one of the best. They were supposed to bring all the women to the valley, where the leaders could pick amongst them." He lowered his voice. "I heard one man call the women 'fresh fish.'"

"That's sinful," Ella told him.

"Not so's ye'd notice. Isnae that common sense? Look at the women that's lost husbands on the way. Who's to look after them if they dinna become polygamous wives? And what about the single women with no father or brother to care for them? It's said any woman who arrives in Zion can expect to find a husband. I'd call it charity."

"They're most charitable toward the prettiest ones, I expect," Ella said.

"They are men."

"Are ye saying Nannie should accept Levi's proposal?"

Andrew thought it over. "He is young and has a good head. He works hard and will be a good provider. And he is well thought of in the church. She could do worse." He grinned. "But if ye say by no means will you wed with him, Nannie, then we'll hae no complaint if ye choose to live with us forevermore in the valley."

With the weather so poor, Jessie had thought they would stay where they were for the day, but Maud told her they'd be less likely to freeze if they were moving. Besides, there was nothing to be gained by remaining. They had to reach the valley before the snows worsened. Better they should make a few miles each day than sit in the tents shivering. Surely Brigham Young would send men and wagons to help them. Perhaps the wagons were already on their way. So by continuing west, the Saints would meet the relief party that much sooner. And if there weren't wagons, as some feared, then the emigrants had no choice but to continue the trek on their own. Without provisions from the valley, the Saints faced certain death from cold and starvation if they waited in the camp.

Jessie listened to the words but said nothing. After all, the emigrants had been told there would be provisions waiting for them along the trail, but they had found nothing.

The Martin Company left the campsite on the North Platte,

moving slowly, stiffly through the drifts of snow that had accumulated. Jessie and her little company pushed their carts
into the white, dreary stretch of land, pushed with hands that
were already raw and frosted, their feet cold in worn boots
and shoes. Several inches of snow had fallen in the night, and
the storm had not let up. She knew that some of the emigrants
had never before encountered the white stuff, and she saw that
they at first had been enchanted as the snow covered the rocks
and the stunted grass, the sagebrush and the carts themselves,
as if the sky had sent down white feathers. But in a short time,
the delight had turned to terror at the ferociousness of the
wind and at cold that started in their hands and feet and spread
throughout their bodies. Jessie, too, was cold as she huddled
near her cart, trying to build a campfire from wet sagebrush,
and she was relieved when the leaders told them to push forward. She hoped that a day's journey might lead them to a
protected campsite.

But pulling the carts against the wind made her wish for
the deep sand of the prairies that the Saints had once cursed.
The ground was icy and steep in places, causing the cart to
slip, and rocks hidden under the snow threatened to break the
already-weakened axle and wheel. She saw entire families ma-
neuvering the carts now, fathers and sons working together to
pull while women and girls and even young children pushed.
To lessen the weight, only the very ill rode on top of the carts.
Children as young as three and four, too numb and cold to
cry, trudged beside the vehicles, and the sick who could not
find a place in the wagons maneuvered as best they could,
limping behind the carts, sometimes crawling on their hands
and knees.

Still racked with fever, Ephraim was one of those who stumbled along beside the cart. Jessie had begged for a place in one of the wagons for her brother, but she had been denied. A missing arm was not thought critical enough. So she and Sutter had lifted Ephraim onto the cart, but the way was too steep and slick, and the cart would not move under the burden. Even without Ephraim's weight, Sutter and Jessie strained against the crosspiece while Emeline and Maud pushed with all their might.

Jessie marveled at Maud's stamina, and at her courage and cheerfulness. She was aged, but she was as tireless as the others, not only preparing the meals, as was their agreement, but taking her turn with the cart, too. "There's not but little to do with the cooking now, what with only a bit of flour and salt to eat," she told Jessie. "It's not as if I had a barley soup or a leg of mutton to serve." The night before, the woman had made the rounds of the camp to help with doctoring. There were more demands on her now that the cold had come. In the beginning, she had dealt with childbirth and injuries. Now many had frosted feet and hands, and it would get worst. Fingers and toes would freeze and have to be cut off, and she had no linseed-meal poultices to help heal the injured bodies.

The Coopers were among the first to leave the campsite on the North Platte that morning. Ephraim was no help, of course, but Sutter and Jessie were strong. "At this rate, we could make it to the Great Salt Lake City in two weeks," Jessie said to keep their spirits up. That was not likely, of course, since the going was slow and treacherous, and the valley still hundreds of miles away. Even if the weather turned warm, the trek would take time, because like the weakest link in a chain, the slowest carts would regulate the speed of the entire company. Besides, Ephraim could barely keep up. He slid and stumbled in the snow, and after a while, Emeline stopped pushing the cart in order to hold on to him. It was not easy for the girl, because Ephraim was a large man. From time to time, Emeline went down in the snow when Ephraim slipped and fell against her. But she did not complain. In fact, she giggled, and her laughter caused Ephraim to smile, as if they shared some secret.

Jessie wondered what they would have done without both Emeline and Maud. She and her brothers had taken on the two as if they had been foundlings, doing their duty to help those in need. Instead, the girl and the old woman, whose strength had grown each day, had more than proved their worth by pushing the cart and caring for Ephraim. He would be dead without them.

Jessie looked over at Ephraim and Emeline now. Her brother had fallen and was sitting in the snow, Emeline coaxing him to get up, but the man would not. Jessie knew his stubbornness. The Coopers were all stubborn, and she told Sutter to stop the cart. The two of them would have to talk to their brother.

"Get up. You will freeze," Emeline pleaded.

Jessie knew Ephraim was past caring about himself, and she interjected. "Get up and go on. You cannot sit here. We have to go at once, or we will all die," she said brusquely.

"Leave be," Ephraim replied.

"Listen to her," Emeline told him. "She doesn't change her mind once she's spoke. We'll all be stopped here until you decide to go."

"That includes Emeline. Do you want her to freeze by the side of the road?" Jessie asked.

Ephraim looked at his sister sourly. "Emeline does what she likes. Don't you?" He turned to the girl.

"I won't desert you. I'll stay so long as you do."

"Then we will all surely freeze to death in this spot," Sutter said. "Jessie won't leave without Emeline, and I can't pull the cart without Jessie. We will none of us reach Zion."

"It's a hard way of serving the Lord," Jessie added. Then looking at her brother, she said, "And a hard way you have of serving us."

But Ephraim was unmoved, and they stayed where they were, the snow beginning to cover them, until Emeline spoke. "Couldn't we stop every hour for five minutes? Maybe ten? Then we'll go on another hour. That way, Ephraim can rest—we'll all rest—but we'll still keep going."

Ephraim only frowned. "How do you know when an hour's up? The clock was left in Iowa."

Ephraim did not appear to be making a joke, but Emeline laughed, and in a moment, he smiled a little and clumsily got to his feet. "You won't let me die in peace, will you?" And Emeline shook her head.

"The girl has the wisdom of Solomon," Maud muttered.

Or she is in love, Jessie said to herself. That was surely true. As they trudged along, Jessie studied Emeline, who was holding on to Ephraim. The two would marry when they reached the valley, she thought. The girl was young, far too young for marriage, but inside she was as old as Maud. She had seen more of the world than Jessie, more of the evil and cruelty, and she had been saved from it—saved by Thales Tanner, of all people. Emeline would make a good wife. She would save Ephraim from himself, from his bitterness, his self-pity at losing his arm.

The two were a good match, the brooding man and the wise little girl who had endured so much before being reborn as a Saint. Emeline had cared for him like a biddy hen, changing the dressings on his arm and giving him part of her food. It was clear she longed to do for him, but she forced him to learn to make do with one arm. And Ephraim, in turn, made the girl forget her ugly life. Emeline had told Jessie a little of it, how she had been sent out by herself to find men on the street, then forced to turn her money over to the man Twiss, who beat her if she did not bring enough. Her only friend was Marianna, a girl her own age. Sometimes, if they were lucky and made more than expected, they would go into a tea shop and pretend they were great ladies, ordering tea and mince tarts. Emeline found a bracelet in the street, which she presented to her friend, who wore it until Twiss wrenched it off her arm and gave it to his favorite. Despite her shabby life, Emeline had as sunny a disposition as any other Saint, and Jessie would not mind her as her brother's wife.

She had not thought much about her brothers marrying. The three of them had never needed anyone else. She had believed they would find a piece of ground together in Zion and farm it. She knew that someday they would marry, but not yet. Later, when the farm was thriving, when they were older and settled, they would build three houses close together—three, because she would wed, too, wed a man who was as strong and vital as her brothers. Not Thales Tanner, of course! Not any man who practiced polygamy.

Jessie's shawl had come undone, and the wind swirled it about her. She stopped pulling to wrap the shawl around herself again, and as she did so, the cart slowed, and another passed the Coopers. Jessie recognized the man—Brother Edward Tripp, a cobbler. She had met him at home when she was a girl and had taken her shoe to him to be mended. He had had curly yellow hair and blue eyes, and she had thought him the fairest man she had ever met, had dreamed of him for a husband one day. But she had been very young then, and he was much older. He had listened to her solemnly as she explained how she had ripped the bottom off the shoe, then patted her on the head and offered her a ginger drop. Jessie had been humiliated that he treated her like a child.

Now, as Edward passed by, he glanced at Jessie and gave her a nod of recognition. And was it a look of interest, too? Who could tell through the film of white? He was married. His wife and their children pushed the cart. At home, Jessie would have found such a look pert. But he was a Mormon, and Mormon men might flirt with any unmarried woman. He had gotten pompous and long-winded, if his testimonies at meeting were any indication. She would not like to be even his first wife.

It was foolish to worry about a husband now, although the subject did take Jessie's mind off the terrible cold. Some of the men she had considered, even those who were young and strong, were likely to die before they reached the valley. She might, too. Jessie hadn't thought of that before, but now she realized the weather and lack of food had taken a toll on her strength. She was no longer the sturdy young emigrant who had left England. None of them were. Even Sutter had weakened. His breath was raspy, and from time to time, he stumbled. He had been her rock and her fortress, and Jessie felt a cold place in her heart when she realized that the trek had affected that brother, too. Perhaps Sutter did, as well, because he raised his head into the driven snow and mumbled, "God be merciful to us and save us from the grasp of destruction."

Sutter rarely made such pronouncements, and Jessie shivered—and not from the cold this time. If something happens to Sutter . . . She did not let herself finish the thought. Instead, she announced that an hour had passed and it was time to a rest. "Why, I never saw time pass so fast," Ephraim joked. He would be all right, Jessie decided. It was Sutter she worried about now. Without him to pull the cart, they would all die. Something had to be done to preserve his strength. Jessie wished she could give him a cracker or a pancake, but they had eaten their rations the night before and would have nothing more to sustain them until the evening. She wondered if Maud had some restorative among her herbs, although she doubted it, because Maud's reserve was nearly depleted. Besides, it would be too much effort to unpack the cart to look for the scanty supply that was left. She looked at Sutter, then glanced back at Ephraim. Both of her brothers were sorely tried. She thought about the valley, about her cousin Rebecca, and wondered if she had received the letter Jessie had written to say they were coming. Perhaps Sutter and Ephraim could be taken into her home to heal.

Others passed the Cooper cart as the group huddled together against the cold. The Saints, their heads bowed against the wind, were too absorbed in their own misery to notice those who had fallen along the wayside. Jessie did not blame them, because she herself had paid small attention to any who were stopped, knowing it was all she could do to keep her own little band moving. She watched the emigrants, most poorly clad, one or two whose feet were wrapped in strips of canvas or sacking because their shoes had fallen away, moving like defeated men under the weight of the carts. She recognized some of the Saints, but she paid them no more attention than they did her.

Then she saw the Tanner cart, her friend Louisa, and Louisa's sister, Huldah, and their mother, Margaret, emerging like ghosts through a veil of white. A little boy plodded along beside them, and Jessie remembered that his brother had drowned in the North Platte. Had it been only the day before? The last days ran together in her mind. Jessie reached out to Huldah, who recognized her and stopped. "I am so sorry, Sister Huldah," Jessie said, wishing her mind was not deadened and that she could think of something more comforting to say.

"It was the Lord's will," Huldah replied dully.

"No," said the boy, but the mother hushed him.

"He's lost both brother and grandfather. It's not easy for him."

"Or for you," Jessie said, and Huldah nodded.

"I wish I understood the Lord's mysterious ways," the bereaved woman said.

"We must have faith," Jessie told her, thinking her words mawkish. She wondered how much faith Huldah put in the Lord now or how much she herself did, for that matter. How little comfort it must be to the woman to be told that God's purpose was greater than her son's life. Her discouragement must be profound. Huldah looked at Jessie dumbly.

"We knew the journey would not be easy," Louisa said.

She held her shawl close to her face with hands that had once been plump and smooth but now were red and bleeding.

"Uncle Thales—" the boy said, but his mother told him again to be still.

At that, Thales came over to the women, and recognizing Jessie, he said, "You have stayed strong, Sister."

She nodded, although she knew her strength had ebbed. "I am well enough, but I'm afraid for my brother Ephraim. We tried to find him a place on the wagon, but . . ." She shrugged and did not finish.

"He is better off walking. It keeps the blood going. Those in the wagon could freeze to death."

"Not everyone who's denied a place can walk. Some have to crawl. Isn't that as sure a way of death as freezing?" Jessie asked.

She had expected Thales to tell her to have faith, that lack of faith had caused their troubles. But instead, he shrugged. "I do not know."

"Not know?" Jessie was disappointed. She had expected encouragement, words of scorn, even, that he would say Ephraim was not worthy of Zion, something to anger her enough to keep her going. "I do not know" was not the response of the Brother Tanner she knew.

"My faith is not what it was," Thales said.

"You?" Jessie asked. "You who are so sure? You who've chided the rest of us for our sins, you who are the ruination of many? How the mighty have fallen."

"Jessie, don't do harm you cannot mend," Louisa pleaded. She reached out with a pale hand, the fingers like claws, and her shawl fell away from her face. She did not replace it, letting the snow fall onto her bare head instead.

"Let her be, Louisa," Thales said. "I am guilty of many sins, the worst of them pride."

"Yes, you have always been proud. Self-righteous, too," Jessie told him. "Do you admit to that?" Thales did not answer, and Jessie felt anger rise up inside her. She and her brothers had made this trek because of him. He owed her an answer. She did not care if the death of Huldah's son had affected him. There had been talk that Thales had forced the little boy into the water. She did not pity Thales for the guilt he carried. Besides, the Brother Tanner she knew would have blamed anyone before he blamed himself. "Answer," she demanded.

"You must stop, both of you," Louisa said. "Thales has endured much. He does not need your scorn, Jessie."

"And you, Huldah, do you agree that Thales suffers?" Jessie asked.

Huldah, straining under the weight of both shock and the cold, looked up, her eyes dull, as if she had been hollowed out. She said nothing.

"What you call self-righteousness, Jessie, I call a sureness of faith," Louisa said.

Jessie could not help but be touched then by her friend's belief in her husband, misplaced though it might be. After all she and her family had been through, Louisa still believed that Thales spoke for God. Jessie did not know whether it was love or stupidity that inspired Louisa, but it was not Jessie's place to question her. So she took Louisa's hand and said, "You have a trusting heart. Perhaps you are right, Louisa. I misspoke." She did not apologize to Thales, however, and when she glanced at him, she knew he did not expect her to.

"We must move on," Thales said to Louisa. "Your mother suffers from the cold." Indeed, the old woman's hands were so chilled that she no longer knit as she walked.

"And our five minutes are up," Jessie announced. Nonetheless, she waited until the Tanner cart was out of sight before she and Sutter picked up the shafts of their vehicle.

They did not make many miles that day, perhaps four or five, before Jessie, Sutter, and Maud stumbled into camp. They had left Ephraim and Emeline behind. He had fallen in the snow and could not take even one more step, so they decided that the three would push the cart to the camp, then return with the emptied cart for Ephraim. Emeline refused to leave him alone, so the others went on without her, pulling the cart another mile to the campsite. Maud remained there to hunt for fuel and start the supper while Jessie and Sutter returned for their brother. Ephraim had not moved. He sat beside the trail, covered with snow, and his brother and sister might not have recognized him, might even have thought him a log, if they had not seen Emeline jumping up and down and waving her arms about to keep warm.

"He's given up," she said. "I think he could walk if only he'd try, but he doesn't want to."

"We'll put him into the cart," Jessie said. She and Sutter lifted their brother to his feet; then, with one of them on each side, they pushed him into the cart and returned to the campsite.

Maud was gone. She had managed to build a fire from wet sagebrush and had mixed up a scone cake that baked in the kettle, the top already brown. The old woman had gone off to help someone who was sick, Jessie realized as she spread a blanket on the snow for Ephraim. Emeline lay beside him, warming his body with hers, while Sutter threw himself onto the ground, saying he was almost too tired to eat. Rest, Jessie told him. They would eat when Maud returned. Then she and Sutter set up a shelter, Sutter working awkwardly, because he had frozen his hand while pulling the cart, and it had swelled when he put it by the fire. When the shelter was ready, the four of them crawled inside.

The old woman found them like that, all of them sleeping despite the cold and the wind, and she woke them lest they freeze to death. She lifted the kettle off the fire, which had gone out, but the scone cake was nicely browned, and Maud reached into the pot for it. But the cake broke apart as she lifted it out, and the old woman discovered that someone had come by while the others slept and hollowed out the cake. All that was left for the five of them was the browned crust.

Jessie saw the dilemma and began to laugh, not a humorous laugh but a wild, uncontrolled one, and she said, "The Saints have their own thieves and hypocrites. We are no better than anyone else."

"We must forgive them. They are in the dark of their minds," Maud replied.

"But so are we."

The five of them had to make do with only a mouthful of crust apiece. They chewed slowly to make the supper last, all but Sutter, who tossed his portion into the fire, saying if that was all God provided him with, God could take it back. Then they found room in the tent and lay down, huddled against one another for warmth.

The night of October 21 was the worst they had encountered, the longest one, too. Jessie did not rest well, sleeping for a few minutes, then waking, then falling into a fitful sleep again. In the dark, she listened to the Saints cough and moan, some of them praying that they would live until dawn, others praying they would not. She curled into a ball for warmth, but that did not help, and finally she rose to her knees, determined to go outside so that she could jump and flail her arms about to warm herself. As she crawled to the edge of the tent, she touched her brother's face. She jerked her hand away, then slowly placed her palm on the face and found it cold, as cold as death itself, and she knew he was gone. She stayed there, cradling the face in her hands. She did not tell the others. Let them sleep, she thought. Nor did she cry out loud. The crying would awaken them. Instead, Jessie held her brother in her arms, rocking back and forth with him as if he had been a sick child, and let her tears fall silently, freezing on her cheeks.

She waited until strike of day, until Maud awoke at dawn, or at least Jessie thought it was dawn. She couldn't tell because the snow blocked out the early light. "My brother's dead," she whispered to the old lady.

The words awoke Emeline, who cried out, "Ephraim!"

"No, not Ephraim," Jessie said. "It's Sutter. Sutter died in the night."

"Sutter!" Maud said, as if she could not believe it.

Jessie nodded, then, realizing the old woman could not see her in the gloom, she repeated, "Sutter."

"What will become of us?"

The morning of October 21, Anne fashioned her second shawl into a sling so that she could carry Samuel across her chest as she pushed the cart. The shawl was a good one, made of the finest silk, and she had brought it along to wear into the valley. She had resisted discarding it the last time the Saints had been ordered to lighten the loads on the wagon. Now she was glad, not because she would appear fashionable when she entered Great Salt Lake City—who cared about that anymore?—but because she could use it to secure Samuel during the cold walk ahead.

"He's such a tiny thing. He can ride on top with Lucy," John told Anne, but she shook her head. Even wrapped up against the cold, the baby might freeze to death on the cart. Of course, Lucy could hold him, but at two, she was barely more than a baby herself. The girl might forget her brother or fall asleep and let him roll off. Anne shuddered at the idea of the baby sliding into the snow. What if they didn't see him fall? He would be crushed by the carts behind them or covered by the falling snow, so that when they went back to search for him, they wouldn't be able to find him. No, Anne, would keep him warm against her body.

So John, with Joe to help him, pulled the cart, while Anne, the baby strapped to her chest, pushed. Catherine pushed, too, and Anne was grateful for the older woman, grateful for someone of her own sex. Just being together offered comfort. Anne was mindful of the tragedy of the older woman's life, the loss of her husband only the day before, and she offered words of solace. But Catherine brushed them aside. "We must think about the living."

Anne had slept little the night before. Her head had pained her, and each time she'd dozed off, she'd awakened to relive the river crossing. She tried not to dwell on the nightmare of seeing her infant sink into the water or her fear that he might have drowned. Instead, she tried to concentrate on the joy of having her baby restored to her, and she reached into the blanket that was wrapped around Samuel to touch his tiny face.

The infant stirred and sent out a weak cry, and Anne held him to her breast, where he could feed, but she had so little milk. The hard journey, her weakness from both childbirth and the cold, and lack of food had kept her milk from coming in as it should, and she had nothing to give the infant in place of it. The Saints had brought along a herd of cows, but many had wandered off. Some had died from snakebite or broken their legs in gopher holes and had to be put down. The cold had taken its toll of the animals, too, and the ones that were left were as dry as Anne. She caught flakes of snow on her finger, let them melt, then put the finger into Samuel's mouth so that he could have a little liquid. He sucked on the finger, then cried his dissatisfaction, but at last, he went back to sleep.

Now, the baby cried again from hunger. Anne could not hear him over the moaning of the wind and the creaking of the carts, but she knew he was crying, because she felt him move against her in tiny, weak, protesting jerks, no stronger than those of a baby bird. As she pushed the cart beside Catherine, Anne reached into the shawl and touched the little head, stroked the silken threads of his hair. Catherine looked over at the bundle but said nothing. There were no words one could offer to a mother whose baby was starving. Anne tucked Emma

Lee's doll into the baby's arms, then covered his face against the cold, and in a few minutes, he fell asleep again.

As she walked behind the cart, Anne pondered the incident in the river. Why had her own baby been saved when others had been allowed to drown or die of cold? They were all Saints, while she was a Gentile—a heathen, in some minds. If Mormonism was the true faith, why would God save her child? Perhaps it was because John was a Mormon. But if God protected the Mormons, why had He let Peter Dunford drown? After all, Peter was among the most faithful. Why would He take her darling Emma Lee but not Samuel? It made no more sense to Anne than the other parts of this strange religion.

Or was it still strange to her? Was she getting used to the beliefs of the Latter-day Saints? Was she even beginning to accept them? Certainly not everything. She would never accept polygamy, although she had to admit that it had been practiced by the patriarchs of the Bible. And could she ever believe that after he was crucified and resurrected, Jesus had visited among the Indians, as the Book of Mormon told? The idea had struck her as ludicrous at first, but now she found herself asking why it could not be so. Was it any more absurd than Jesus being born in Bethlehem and living as a Jew? Why shouldn't He appear in the ancient Americas? It was possible, of course. He could roam the surface of the moon, if God wanted Him to.

She had asked God repeatedly to tell her if Mormonism was the true religion, and perhaps He had answered her by saving Samuel. She would like to talk that over with Catherine, who had never pressed Anne to join the church, had not chided her for her lack of belief. But talking took too much energy, and with the wind howling, they would have to yell to be heard. Besides, Catherine would consider it a poor bargain that her husband had died just so that Anne could become one of the chosen people.

They had gone a mile or two when John stopped the cart and told Anne that Lucy must walk. "It's too cold, and the snow is too deep," Anne protested.

"If she sits any longer, she'll freeze. Catherine can hold her hand," he added, for the old woman appeared done with and no longer able to push. "When Lucy tires, she can ride again." He lifted the little girl to the ground, and they watched her make her way through the snow that had been beaten down by the carts. The little girl picked up a handful of snow in her mittened hand and pressed it to her mouth. Then she lifted her face to the sky and laughed as the snowflakes tickled her face.

They kept a slow pace after that and were passed by other carts and then one of the provision wagons. "I'm going to ride," Joe announced, and before his parents could stop him, he ran up to the wagon.

"Well, my boy, you want to ride, do you?" asked the driver.

"Please, sir, I'm tired."

"Take my hand, then." The driver reached down and held on to the boy and lifted him into the wagon.

"Without him, you'll have to pull the cart by yourself," Anne said.

"He wasn't much help." John looked off into the distance to where the wagon had disappeared. "Would that we could all ride. We would if I hadn't given away the money."

"It's over and done with. I've forgotten it."

"Have you?"

"Does it matter?"

"It does when I consider what you've gone through. You've been the one to sacrifice."

"And given you a pretty bit of grief over it. But you've sacrificed, too, John. You've not had an easy time of it. We both lost Emma Lee." Anne shifted the baby's weight against her chest because the sling had caused a hurting in her back.

"But it was my decision to come to America. It is *my* church, after all, not yours. You didn't choose this way."

"But I chose you." She put her hand against the cart, ready to push, her way of telling John that she did not want to discuss the matter further. She had much thinking to do.

Of course, it was not just *his* church, because there were hundreds of other Mormons in the company. But that was not what Anne was pondering. Was it *her* church, too? Had she come to accept this strange Gospel? And was it because of what had happened in the river? She considered the event and decided that no, Samuel's rescue was not the reason to accept the Latter-day Saints' religion. Perhaps she could believe because of the people. She had come to love these Mormons who had befriended her despite her scorn for their religion. She'd been moved by their care, by their faith, by their strength under the worst of circumstances. She did not hate them. She did not hate their religion. Perhaps she could one day join them—but not today, she thought, her cracked lips breaking into a smile. Not today, for she did not care to be baptized in a river in the snow, but after she reached the valley, maybe.

In many ways, she already was one of them, she realized as she glanced at the women pushing the carts. She certainly was one in enduring hardships. For her and for others, the march had become one of almost unbearable difficulty. Anne's long skirts were wet with slush and snow, and they wrapped around her legs, making her stumble. At least she had on sturdy boots. Before they had left England, John had bought them good wool cloaks and coats, heavy shoes and boots. Anne had scoffed at such apparel, saying she did not want to arrive in the valley looking like a drayman. But now she was grateful for John's foresight. Many of the other emigrants wore threadbare clothing, their shoes were worn through, and a few had no shoes at all. Anne saw their bloody footprints in the snow. Her own feet were cold, but at least her boots kept out the moisture. She wished her skirts did the same, because the hem of her wet petticoat slapped at her legs, rubbing them raw.

She wondered if Lucy's legs were cold, too, and then she saw the child fall in the snow and begin to cry. "Carry me, Mama," she begged in a thin wail. Anne leaned over to pick up the child, but with Samuel strapped to her chest, she could not lift the girl.

"Stand, and I will hand her to you," Catherine said. "Then I'll take my turn pushing while you walk with your little ones."

Anne could barely carry the two children. Her back protested the load. But she had no choice. She would have to carry them until John said it was safe to set Lucy back on top of the cart. So she struggled through the snow with the two, falling back a little from the cart. She was not the only Saint who could not keep up. Many of the sick and elderly stopped to rest, while their carts continued. In the past few days, Anne had seen them limping into camp hours after the carts arrived. She knew some had not made it at all, and she wondered if she might soon be one of them. If she lagged far behind, would John come back for her and find her with the two children, all of them frozen to death, torn apart by wolves?

With such fears, she redoubled her efforts to move along. She put Lucy on her shoulders, but the child slid off into the snow. She told the girl to stand on a rock so that she could pick her up. She wondered if Lucy might hold Samuel and spare her the burden of carrying the baby against her chest, but the girl could not be expected to hold the infant when her own hands were stiff with cold. So Anne settled Lucy on her hip and hurried after the cart. She saw that John had stopped and was waiting for her, and when she reached him, he put the little girl on his shoulders. "You have enough with the baby," he said.

Anne was too exhausted to argue or even to thank him. She tightened the sling that held Samuel and took her place with Catherine behind the cart. At least Joe was safe, she thought. But if she and John didn't make it, what would happen to him? Surely some Mormon would take him in. They were kind people, but they were all weak and starving.

She had seen a motherless child in the camp the night before, whimpering from the cold and the death of his father. He had asked another boy for a piece of his griddle cake, but the boy had cried, "I cannot do it. I want it myself." Anne had been moved by the orphan's plight, but she had not gone to him, instead letting another emigrant take responsibility for him. If something happened to John and her, Joe might survive, but not Lucy, and never Samuel. No mother in the train had enough milk for her own infant, let alone the baby of another woman. She and John must be strong if the children were to survive.

They didn't talk, she and John and Catherine. They did not want to make the effort. Besides, their mouths seemed frozen shut. Instead, they pushed on in silence. From time to time, Anne paused to adjust the sling that held the sleeping baby, to touch the downy head and coo to the infant, but after a while, she stopped. She kept her thoughts to herself then, speaking to neither John nor Catherine. She no longer kept track of time or distance, just pushed the cart in a kind of daze, her mind as much a blur as the snow that fell. She was glad then for the cold that numbed her. Somewhere she heard a woman beg, "Get up, Davy, oh, do get up." And another time, she passed a woman who was beating her husband with a stick and crying, "Get up and go on, or we will all die," but she paid little attention, so inured was she to others' misery. They pushed on, the third mile, the fourth, and then the fifth. Anne felt no elation when they reached the camp.

John found a spot for the cart and said he would collect their provisions and search for Joe. She could start the fire with a piece of wood that John had picked up just before they reached the campsite. It was a fine piece of luck finding the branch, he said, his spirits rising. She could use sage for kindling and have the fire going by the time he returned with Joe. Dinner might be sparse, but they would be warm. He picked up Lucy and put her on his shoulders, saying to Anne, "Well, Mother, we have made it through another day, wet and hungry, I'll admit, but still here." Anne did not respond.

After her husband was gone, Anne stayed where she was, huddled beside the cart, cold and lonesome. So Catherine used a frying pan to scoop away the snow; some twelve inches of it had fallen by then. Then Catherine broke branches off a sagebrush and built a fire, which sputtered a little but kept going. Anne still did not stir and was still sitting where John had left her when he returned with Joe. "He has had a fine adventure, Mother," John said, squatting down to warm his hands over the flame.

"I sat with the driver," Joe told her. "I helped him hand out the provisions. I'd have taken extra for us, but it's not allowed. I didn't steal, Mother. I'm a good Saint."

Anne did not respond. She sat staring off into the snow until John came over to her and asked, "Does your head pain you?" She had suffered one of her dreadful headaches the week before, and the effects often lingered for days. When she didn't reply, he said, "You must stir yourself, Anne. The children need you. Catherine's making a pancake, but I don't want any. You can have my portion. Maybe it will bring back your milk."

"For what purpose?" she asked. She peeled back the shawl that she had used as a sling and showed him the body of Samuel, the boy curled up like a frosted flower, his eyes frozen shut, his tiny shirt frozen to his body. "My heart is bleeding. He died along the road. I could not bear to leave him in the snow."

John reached for the bundle, but Anne would not give it up. "We must bury him. There are others . . ." He did not finish, only looked at his wife with sad blue eyes.

"He is the second of our children to be buried without a name stone. Pray God he is the last."

In the morning, John and the other men prepared a mass grave, digging it through deep snow and frozen earth. Then the Saints brought the bodies of their loved ones, more than a dozen of them, and laid them in a row. Jessie and Emeline had wrapped Sutter's body in a blanket and carried it to the grave, and now they set it alongside the body of another, Jessie thinking the dead were laid side by side like logs in a corduroy road.

Little Samuel was the last to be placed in the grave. Anne had wrapped him in the silk shawl, and so tiny was he that he looked like a Christmas gift folded inside the bright silk. At the last moment, Anne had slipped Emma Lee's doll into her dead son's hands, along with a slip of paper with the words "This is my son Samuel Sully, who joins his beloved sister Emma Lee and all the angels in heaven." John placed the tiny body at the end of the row of dead, and the men reached for spades to cover the grave. But just before the frozen clods fell onto the bodies, Anne reached into the grave for Samuel and snatched him out. Then she placed him on the shroud containing Sutter. "He will be warmer here. He mustn't get cold," she said, and the other mourners nodded in understanding. Then she stood back with John and joined the Saints standing in the falling snow as they sang the Mormon hymns. Just before the carts pulled out, men would gather brush and throw it on top of the graves, then set it on fire to kill the scent of the bodies so that wolves would not dig them up.

When the mourners were finished, a Saint stood before them and announced that rescue teams were certainly on their way. They would arrive any day, he said, and the Saints must stand firm. "Have faith in God, brethren, and you will not take cold," he admonished. But Anne turned away. No messengers had arrived to say that the wagons had started out. For all she and the other members of the Martin Company knew, no one was aware that they were caught in the snow, that they were starving. What if people in Great Salt Lake City believe the company remained behind at Fort Laramie? she wondered. After all, if the Mormon prophet knew they were on their way, wouldn't he have sent rescuers long before?

She did not believe the words of the man.

Chapter 7

October 26, 1856

Louisa and her family, along with the other members of the Martin Company, had been snowbound for nearly a week in the gray-white mountains. Winter had come on all at once, the snow falling without letup, the wind howling down the mountainsides, the ground frozen so solid that it was almost impossible for Thales to drive in the tent pins, and when the tents were at last raised, the wind blew them down. The snow was deep and not just the Chetwins but all the Saints so weak that they could not push their handcarts farther. So they sheltered near a sandstone outcrop known as Red Buttes and prayed for deliverance. The Chetwins were fortunate that their cart had been made with a cover, so that Margaret could huddle inside, emerging from time to time to warm herself before a meager fire or to jump up and down and wave her arms to keep from freezing. "It is like a picture of hell," Huldah told Louisa.

The sisters tramped through the snow for as much as a mile from the camp, searching for fuel—juniper, called "green cedar," mostly, because there were no longer buffalo chips. Then using all their strength, they dragged the broken branches back to the camp.

Food rations had been reduced once more—eight ounces of flour a day for adults and four for children. Louisa worried that they would starve to death, that their long trip across the ocean and over the plains had been for naught. They would never reach the valley. Huldah cried as she asked Louisa if she thought they were facing death.

Each day, the family attended meeting, at which the leaders exhorted the Saints to have faith. The snow was punishment for their sinfulness, one told them. "If it were not for your transgressions, you would be redeemed from this horrid, stinking place by now," he said. Then he prayed, "Lord, let thy chastising hand be upon thy people until they learn to obey. Strike down every cursed person who will not do right."

Louisa knew that it was a principle of the church that the people must be tried by hardship and purified, a principle that some leaders never gave up expounding upon. "I am tired of these sad faces that show you are broken down in spirit. The Lord punishes us for refusing to obey divine counsel. We must become a righteous people, without spot, and blameless. The Lord will save only the pure in heart," declared one. "If you continue in wickedness as you have done, your own prayers will bring a curse upon you."

But Louisa did not believe the hardships her mother and sister faced were a result of their evil ways, and she was glad when Thales asked the Lord to forgive them their sins and stop the storms for a repentant people. "We know our nature is stormy, dark, and wicked, and we pray for thy forgiveness. I myself have done many wrong things, and I ask for thy mercy. Rebuke the storms and restore us so that we may join our brethren in Zion," he prayed at a meeting of the Saints.

Many around Louisa murmured in agreement as they stood shivering in an open area near the tents. All those who were able attended the prayer meetings, even the Saints who despaired of ever reaching the valley. The meetings gave them hope, an explanation of their plight, a way of sharing their troubles, and besides, what else was there to do in that cold place that Louisa dubbed "Camp Misery" and others called "the Snowbound Camp of Death"? Louisa stamped her feet and flailed her arms as she prayed with Thales for deliverance.

After Thales finished his testimony and his prayer, the people broke into the Mormon hymn "Come, Come, Ye Saints," with its soothing words: "If we die before our journey's through, happy day, all is well."

As she sang the words that gave her strength, Louisa studied her husband. He had changed a great deal since the death of little Jimmy. Thales no longer appeared to the people as a thundering prophet of old, preaching death and destruction to any who did not obey the Lord. He no longer spoke as if he were the voice of Brigham Young. Nor did he puff up when others asked if he had known Joseph Smith, although not many thought about such things now. Thales did not march through the camp as he once had, giving orders to his hundred, which was now composed of considerably fewer than one hundred members. Instead, he humbled himself, feeding the sick and offering to do the most demeaning chores, such as washing with snow the linen of those who had fouled themselves. He walked into the storm to search for fuel for the weary, took the watch for men who were nearly senseless, and he and Louisa sat with the dying, assuring them they would be with Christ in heaven. "Your sufferings are not worthy to be compared to the glory that awaits you," he said, trying to comfort them.

"They are like worn-out cattle, with no feeling except to eat or die," Thales told Louisa. "The thought of them unmans me. God forbid I should ever witness such scenes again."

"They knew when they left England the way would be hard. They knew not all would make it," Louisa replied. "They came of their own free will."

"Did they? Or did they come because they thought I was Moses leading them into the Promised Land? Did they willingly leave their homes for this?" He lifted his arms heavenward to indicate the snow. "Is this the better life I promised them when I said that America was the land of milk and honey, that God had set aside for them rich farmlands? It's poor steerage I've given them."

"You could not have known this would happen. You are not responsible for the storms."

"Perhaps I am. Do you not remember that I called those who wanted to winter in Iowa City and Florence apostates? I accused your own father of having not one atom of the spirit of Zion, and now he's dead, and dead because I would not let him stay behind. If not for me, he would be alive."

"If not for you, he would not be saved."

Thales stared at his wife. "Do you believe that, or are you muddled?"

"I believe that God is testing us, that He wants to make sure we're worthy of reaching Israel." Louisa tightened the shawl about her head, tucking in her hair, which was now dull and lifeless. The shawl was torn, and Louisa's hands had been too cold to thread a needle to repair it. The frayed ends whipped about her head in the wind. "We can none of us see the future, but we must do what we think God expects of us, you no less than the others. Who is to say my father would not have died in England."

"Do you believe that?"

"I have to. If I do not believe that God led us here, then there is nothing for me to believe, and I will perish unsaved." She stared long and hard at her husband, allowing herself for a moment to question his righteousness. "Do not take away our belief that we will be reunited with Father and Jimmy in heaven, that we have come here for a reason. It would be vanity for you to convince us of anything else," she begged, thinking he would argue, afraid he would tell her his ambition was gone, that he was in the midnight of his mind. Her eyes pleaded with him to reassure her that he was the Saint she had married, a man sure of his faith.

Instead, Thales regarded Louisa a moment, his eyes roaming over the once-neat figure that was now swollen in pregnancy. "I look at your face and see gold shining in every corner of it. The Lord blesses me with an understanding wife, although He knows I have not been square with her." He took off his coat and wrapped it around her.

Louisa was uncertain what he meant about not being "square," but she was gratified, at least, for her husband's faith in her. She thought to ask then if he meant that he no longer found fault with her. But she feared such a remark would sting him, and she held her tongue.

He reached out his hand to catch the falling snow and said bitterly, "Do you remember I said I would eat every flake of snow that fell?"

"Oh, I think no one holds you to that."

Thales frowned at his wife, perhaps not sure if she had made a joke, then deciding she hadn't. He said, "They say they will slaughter one or two of the oxen that have fallen and distribute pieces of meat. I'll see what they're about." He went off into the cold.

She watched as he trudged through the snow to a makeshift corral where the oxen and milk cows were kept. The Saints needed the stronger animals to pull the wagons, but many of them, like the people, were starving. The oxen could not paw away the snow to reach the dried grass beneath it, and each day, one or two fell and would not rise. So the Saints slaughtered any beast that was almost starved or was chilled to death, hitting it with hammers and hatchets and even frying pans to knock it senseless so that its throat could be cut. Then two or three men who could do butchering cut up the carcass, setting aside the tenderest parts for the leaders and dividing the rest among members of the company. Every bit of the ox was used, even the hides, which were scraped and roasted over the fire so that the Saints could chew them.

Thales returned to the campfire with the beast's head and handed it to Louisa. "We'll roast it in the campfire and turn it into a great feast. Tomorrow, we'll make a broth of the remains, and we can suck on the bones after that," she said, accepting the ox head as reverently as if it had been a suckling pig.

Louisa's nephew Dick came up to her and looked at the bloody thing that had already stained the snow with drops of red. Blood was on Thales's hands and his pants, too. "It's a damnable cow's head," the boy said with disgust. He shivered from the cold in his thin coat, and Louisa wished he had not thrown away the green scarf.

"You must not say that. This is food," Louisa told him. "It is the likeliest food Brother Thales could find."

"At home, we wouldn't eat the disgusting thing."

"We aren't at home, and we are grateful to the Lord for giving us this something to eat," his aunt told him.

"*I'm* not grateful, and I believe *you* are deluded, Aunt Louisa. We'd be at home if it wasn't for him. Jimmy would be alive." Dick jerked a finger at Thales, giving him a hard look. "We're here because he tricked us. I hate him."

"Dick!" Louisa said, shocked. "Brother Thales is a great man. He knew Joseph. Without him, we wouldn't have been saved."

"*I'm* not saved. I don't care about your Joseph, and I don't want to be a Mormon anymore. I'd rather go to hell."

Dick turned and walked away, and Louisa stared after him. "He doesn't mean it," she told Thales, putting a hand on his arm, afraid he would go after Dick. "He's not an apostate."

"He does mean it. He's a boy, and he's hungry. God knows, he has reason to hate me."

"You could talk to him. You must take him with you when you make your rounds, when you look for fuel, Thales. He is too much with us women, and he needs a man to guide him."

"No," Huldah said, coming up to the two and staring at the bloody head.

"Work will do Dick good. It will take his mind off his loss," Louisa told her sister. "Besides, Thales is the head of our family. He must decide what's best for us, all of us."

"Thales is not my lord and master. I have lost one son. I will not lose another. I will not allow Thales to put him in danger."

Thales studied her a moment before he replied, "You are his mother." He turned and disappeared into the storm, Louisa watching him, her heart cold. She had loved him for his steadfastness, his unquestioning belief that he was chosen of the Lord, and now she was not sure she knew this man.

She dropped the ox head into the snow, knelt, and started to scrape away the hair with a knife. Huldah watched her for a moment, then she, too, sat down in the snow and, using a sharp rock, began helping her sister. "Do you blame Thales for Jimmy's death?" Louisa asked.

Huldah shook her head; then, perhaps realizing Louisa could not see her, she replied, "I don't know. It's a muckle in my mind. Maybe it was only Jimmy's time. But I won't have him risk Dick."

"Thales broods, you know. It's changed him, Jimmy's death and Father's, and all the other deaths among our hundred. Thales blames himself." Louisa stopped scraping to look at one of the ox's dead eyes. She had never eaten a head before and was unsure about the eyes.

Huldah didn't respond for a long time, and then she asked, "Do you think we should have come here, Louisa? Ought'nt we to have stayed at home?" She stopped scraping to look into her sister's face.

"And not be saved?"

"We were saved at home. We could have stayed there. We didn't have to go to Zion. Or we could have come later on, after Mother regained her health. We could have come in wagons instead of with handcarts. Father would be alive, and Jimmy. Or maybe we should have stayed in New York for a year. If it weren't for Thales . . ." Her voice trailed off. Louisa would know what she meant.

In fact, Louisa had had such thoughts herself but had pushed them away until now. "Our life on earth is short. We must endure our sorrows so that we are worthy of joining the Saints in heaven." Such pious words were unlikely to give Huldah comfort, so Louisa set down her knife and put her arms around her sister. "Oh, Huldah, I know how your heart breaks. I, too, have beseeched God for an explanation, have asked him why Jimmy had to drown. But He hasn't answered me. We must believe in our hearts that He knows what's best. That's the only way we can live through this terrible time. If we lose our faith . . ." She could not continue the awful thought.

Huldah leaned against her sister and sobbed. "It is so hard, Louisa. Dick cries every night for his brother and from the cold. He blames himself. He says he should have refused to let Jimmy go into the water. But how could he go against Brother Thales, who accused the boys of being saucy, idle fellows? Grown men cannot stand up to him and tell him the error of his ways. How could a little boy do it? Dick says he wishes he could die, too."

"Jimmy's death wasn't Dick's fault."

"I know, but he won't own up to it."

"Thales should talk to him. If Dick saw how Thales himself grieves and takes the blame for Jimmy's death, I think he would feel better. Perhaps the two of them can help heal each other."

"Would Thales do that? Would he admit to Dick that he's responsible?" Huldah asked.

"I don't know, but I'll ask him."

"If he would say it to Dick, that would help, since despite what he says, Dick thinks Brother Thales is near to being a prophet and is not to blame for anything. That's why Dick takes Jimmy's death so hard. He lashes out at Thales, but in his heart, Dick believes he is at fault."

"Thales is not a prophet. If he were, we should ask him to stop the snows," Louisa said, smiling a little at her sister.

"There was a time when he would have believed himself capable of that, when he thought the heavens and the earth would obey him," Huldah replied, looking at Louisa slyly, then picking up the stone and scraping the head.

"Now only God can do that." Afraid she might have blasphemed, Louisa added, "When the Lord, who has brought us this far, believes we are chastened enough, the snow will cease."

"Does Thales say that?"

"I say that."

The two sisters began to scrape the ox head in earnest, and when they had finished, they cleaved the head with a knife and placed it in a kettle, which they set in the coals of their campfire. The head sent up the odor of wet hair and did not smell very good, but it was sustenance, and the sisters were grateful for it anyway. The two of them, along with their mother, took turns sitting with the pot, lest someone should come along and steal their supper. The wind was so fierce that some of the carts were blown over, their contents scattered in the snow. But Thales had placed rocks on either side of the wheels of the Tanner cart, and while it shook and shuddered and creaked, it remained upright.

Later, Thales returned and told them that he had met with Brother Martin and a few of the other leaders, who had discussed sending two or three of the strongest young men to the west to see if any rescuers had reached the Willie Company ahead of them. Thales had volunteered, but then, they had all decided it was better to wait. Men traveling in that whiteout were likely to freeze, and the company could not afford to lose any more. They had talked about what they would do if rescue didn't come, had asked each other what would happen if they were forced to spend the winter in that spot. But there had been no answer. The men knew that remaining where they were meant starvation. The only thing they had agreed on was to pray. Hunting for the rescuers might have been the wiser course, Louisa thought. They could have left the halt and the lame to their prayers.

The light had faded by the time Thales returned to the cart. "I have never been so tired," he confided to Louisa, throwing himself onto a blanket beside her. He closed his eyes and put his hands over them.

"Where's Dick?" Huldah asked.

"He didn't go with me," Thales replied. "I asked his help, but he told me very rough he wanted nothing to do with me."

"You should have looked after him," Huldah said, her voice rising. "Where has he gone?"

"I'll look for him," Thales said, getting up slowly because

he was exhausted. "Surely, he's with his fellows." He wrapped a scarf around his head, because he had lost his hat at the river crossing.

"He doesn't play much with the boys. He was always with Jimmy," Louisa said. "We'll all look. Mother, you keep watch over the supper." The two sisters tightened their shawls against the wind, and along with Thales, they started off, each in a different direction, calling for Dick and asking others if they had seen the boy. But most of the Saints were in misery so deep, they'd paid little attention to anyone who had passed by.

They searched throughout the camp, looking among the wagons and in the corral, thinking the boy might have huddled with the animals for warmth. The mother, Margaret, looked through the cart. Perhaps the boy had climbed inside and was under the clothing, sleeping. But he was not there.

They searched for an hour, a few Saints joining in the hunt—Emeline, the young girl who traveled with the Cooper party, and Andrew Buck, the Scottish weaver, who was accompanied by his wife and her sister on the journey. There were others, too, some as tired as Thales, but their hearts went out to a family searching for a boy. They might be starving and freezing, but they were Saints, and the sorrow of one was the sorrow of all.

Dick was not to be found, however. "I think maybe he has hidden himself or run off," Thales said when the family gathered back at the cart.

"Run off? To where?" Louisa asked, alarmed to think the boy might have disappeared in the snow.

"He would not have done so. He would not leave me," Huldah insisted, wringing her hands in her shawl. "Although he's said he wants to be with Jimmy, he knows he's all I have."

Thales proposed they search beyond the camp, but Margaret insisted they eat first to keep up their strength. She lifted the lid of the pot, where bits of meat had fallen from the ghastly skull into a broth of melted snow, and handed around spoons, because the family had discarded their bowls at the last lightening of the load and now ate from a single pot. Louisa was too agitated to eat, however, and said, "I will search one more place." The others looked at her with questions on their faces, but she would not tell them where she was going, because it was a place of no hope.

She went directly to the spot where the frozen bodies of those who died each day were lined up, awaiting burial. "I'm looking for a boy," she told Old Absalom, who was standing guard over the bodies. She did not know if he was there because he was acquainted with someone who had died or because he feared wolves would make their way into the camp and desecrate the dead.

"Look you amongst 'em," he said.

Louisa stopped beside each body, stooping down to look at the small ones, and that was where she found Dick. He must have fallen and frozen to death, or perhaps he willed himself to die, she thought. Someone had found him and carried him to the grave, where he lay in the pile of dead bodies, his arms by his sides. His eyes were closed, and it appeared he was sleeping. Louisa had not realized until she looked at him in death how Dick's cheekbones stood out in his thin little face, how his eyes were sunken in dark circles. The arms sticking out from the coat were as thin as broomsticks. Louisa cried to think how the boy must have suffered, not just from his brother's death but from the cold and hunger, that he must have been tortured by the thought of the freezing water closing over his brother. She knelt in the snow and tried to place the boy's arms over his chest, but they were already stiff. She stayed there a long time, staring into the child's frozen face until her toes began to tingle and it grew dark. Then she rose and made her way back to the cart.

Huldah and Thales stood up when she returned, neither asking her if she had found Dick, but both looking at her as if waiting for her to volunteer her answer. Finally, Thales asked, "Dick?"

"He is with Jimmy."

The boy was buried in the morning, with prayers and singing and lamentations, Thales and the women standing beside the grave, tears running down their faces. The boy was not interred alone. His body lay beside that of his mother, Huldah. She had collapsed after learning that her remaining son was gone, and she would not get up. She passed away in the evening. She and her son were among the fourteen who died that day, some covered only with snow because the living had taken their clothes.

What dismal days we are living, Nannie Macintosh thought, wondering how much longer she could stand the cold. When she could force herself to her feet, she tottered among the handcarts, wrapped in her shawl and a blanket, but she was cold, and her teeth would not stop chattering. Nor could she stop shaking.

Her feet pained her so that she was unable to walk far before she had to sit down. When the Saints were told to reduce the loads on their carts, she had discarded all but her warmest dress, but it was tattered and ripped, the hem caked with mud. Worse were her feet. She rubbed them in the snow and wrapped pieces of canvas around her boots, but her feet tingled with the snow and ice that came through the leather, because her boots were worn through and broken in places. When she removed them, she found that her stockings were bloody, and her toes seemed as frozen as the chips of ice that had pelted her at the last river crossing. She tore strips off her petticoat and wrapped them around her feet before putting her shoes back on, but that did little to keep out the cold.

Now, she sat with her feet to the little fire that Andrew had built, but she did not worry about herself. Instead, her thoughts were of her sister. Ella had turned sickly, and Nannie and Andrew were afraid that she would lose the baby. So Andrew had wrapped his coat around his wife, saying he wasn't cold, and had gone off in search of God knows what that would help Ella—fuel, food, blankets, none of which could be had. Or perhaps, he was at one of the prayer meetings. Nannie had stopped attending them because she felt preached to death, and kneeling on the ice, she told her sister, "hurt my knee bones." She thought about the things she had loved at home—the lovely teas, the mist on the hillsides, the flowers. Oh, she loved the growing things—the heather, the violets, the yellow cinquefoil and buttercups. She would plant them around her cottage in the valley—if she had a cottage. Perhaps Levi, if he were the one she married, would expect her to live in a house with Patricia. Nannie thought that Patricia already suspected Levi's intentions, because she had stepped in front of Nannie in the provision line and told her, "I come first, madam." Living in the same house with the first wife would not be easy, Nannie knew, but the decision would be Levi's, and she would have to abide by it. Levi wasn't as thoughtful as Andrew. But wherever she lived, she would insist on flowers.

During the weeks they had pushed the handcart, Andrew had surprised Nannie. She loved her brother-in-law because, after all, he was her sister's husband and he had insisted that she come to America with them. But that didn't mean that Nannie had ever believed Andrew would amount to much. In fact, in the beginning, she had worried that after years of working in a textile mill, he wouldn't be able to maneuver the handcart across the prairie. Earlier in the journey, he had even had a sick spell that all but did him in. But Andrew had strength that Nannie had never suspected. And now, as she and Ella grew weaker, Andrew became stronger, insisting that his wife ride on top of the cart when she was exhausted, telling Nannie he could pull the cart without her help when she, too, faltered. Nannie had seen him slip part of his portion of the evening meal onto Ella's plate and, on occasion, her own, and he had even shared with other Saints who were starving.

The evening before, a woman who appeared half-dead had offered him a gold locket in exchange for food. She had made the rounds of the camp with the jewelry but found no takers. Finally, she approached Andrew, begging him to give her a bit of biscuit for it. "I've had nothing to eat for two days but a little piece of hide roasted over the fire, and that I chewed until it turned white," she said. Andrew had only one biscuit, a poor thing that Nannie had made from flour and water, but he broke it in half and handed a piece to the woman. Then he'd refused to take the locket. She had sat down a little ways off, the biscuit in her hand, staring at it. She stayed that way so long that Andrew had gone to her to inquire if she was all right, and he'd discovered that she was dead, the biscuit clutched in her fingers. Such was their need that he had taken the food from the dead woman and given it to Ella.

It wasn't just Andrew's physical strength and generosity that impressed Nannie. As Ella grew weaker, she also grew discouraged, and it was Andrew who kept up her spirits, singing the songs of Zion and talking of the joy they would find in the valley. "All is well, my girls. We've a good day ahead," he told them each morning when they rose and found each other yet alive, insisting each morning that he felt first-rate. And then he found some little bit of joy in the day. That morning he had said, "The blessed snow keeps the midges away," and the women had laughed, because they'd complained about the flies that had plagued them on the prairie.

Nannie leaned over and wrapped her arms around her sister, holding her close to warm her.

"Andrew sleeps with one eye open and one foot out of bed, believing I might need him," Ella said. "Ye and he pamper me."

"Nay." Nannie gave a bark of a laugh and replied, "Your clothes are worn through. We are starving. We are freezing to death in the middle of a blizzard. And yet ye say ye are pampered. God alone knows what things would be like if ye felt neglected."

Ella laughed, too. "Ye keep me in good spirits, Nannie. I widna hae made it this far without ye—ye and Andrew. He is a good husband."

"Aye. He's better by half than any man here. If anyone can get us through to Utah, Andrew can."

Ella stared into the falling snow and asked, "Do ye think they'll come in time. Do ye think we'll be rescued?"

"Of course we will."

"What if no one knows we're here? What if they think we stayed at Fort Laramie?" When Nannie didn't answer, Ella continued: "They dinna hae supplies for us along the way. If they'd known we were on the road, widna they hae had flour and beef and blankets waiting for us?"

"I hae not come all this way just to die in the mountains, and neither hae ye. Or Andrew. Or the bairn. I canna believe it is the End of Days."

The two sat there, rocking back and forth a little, Ella hugging her belly, as if her arms could warm the baby inside her. She had been growing like Jonah's gourd vine and was heavy with child now. To distract her sister from her misery, Nannie asked, "What do ye think ye will do when we reach the valley?"

"First, I'll eat a bowl of warm milk and a bap. Then, I think, a meat pie, two of them, a whole trayful. And a cake, an entire cake. Then I'll take a lovely warm bath and put on clean clothes. Imagine, a clean dress with no tears in it. And warm slippers." She sighed with pleasure. "What about ye?"

"I'd like a Sally Lund, a warm large one with fresh-made butter, and a tattie scone. Do ye think they make them here?"

"Of course. There are Scots already in the valley. What else?"

"A piece of beef as big as my fist. And turnips, although I canna tell ye why, for I never favored a neep before. And a platter of tarts—lemon and strawberry, I think, maybe mince. P'raps a dumpling." She paused and then said, "But it's not about that I'm asking. I was wondering if Andrew has decided what work he'll do. I donna believe there are textile mills in Zion."

"If there aren't yet, there are bound to be soon, what with all the people coming to the valley. But if he canna be a mill worker, Andrew says he will labor as a carpenter."

"Does he know a thing about building?"

"No, but he dinna know about handcarts, either, and it's a fine job he's done with ours." Ella removed her shawl to fling off the snow that had fallen on it, then asked, "What about ye, Nannie? Will ye look for a husband—a young one—or do ye want to get work?"

Nannie ignored the question about a husband, for she did not want Ella to know she was considering Levi's proposal. "Right off, I should like to find a job in a hotel, someplace nice where I can wear a white apron starched stiff as a plate and pour tea from a silver teapot into china cups as thin as onion skin. Do you suppose there's such a place in the valley?"

Ella shrugged.

"If there isn't, I shall start one myself. Or maybe a shop that sells dainty sweets."

"Then I canna think but what it is a shame ye traded your silver brooch at Fort Laramie, because ye could hae sold it to open your establishment." Both sisters laughed and huddled together, Nannie wondering if any husband would ever make her as happy as Ella did. She rubbed her feet, then sat on them, hoping that would warm them.

She was adjusting her skirts and didn't see the man approach, didn't know he was there until Ella said, "Brother Levi." Nannie looked up, startled.

"Sister Ella and Sister Nannie. Are you well?" he asked.

"Nay, we're as cold as frozen potatoes," Nannie replied, hoping Levi had not sought her out to discuss his marriage proposition again. She did not want him to speak of it in front of Ella, who would be scornful. Nannie had not seen him since he promised to ask Brother Martin for a shawl to replace the one that had been stolen from her, but since Levi held nothing in his hands, Nannie supposed he had come to tell her he'd been unsuccessful. That would not surprise her, since no matter how close Levi was to the leader of their company, he was not likely to interest the elder in procuring a shawl. After all, Brother Martin had hundreds of other brothers and sisters to worry about, and any extra shawls would have been handed out long since. She had seem him, gaunt and sorrowful, and she'd wondered if he was sorry he'd been asked to head the company. "And ye, Brother Levi, are ye enjoying this balmy day?" She hoped levity might turn his mind away from marriage, if that was indeed his reason for seeking her out.

Levi squatted beside her. "I am not so well. Patricia died last night. She was buried with the others this morning. During the service, Brother Martin had to fire his shotgun at the crows to keep them from the grave."

Nannie was horrified at her light tone. She should have realized that Levi was there for a solemn purpose. "I am sorry. She was as beautiful a lass as I ever saw, so full of life." Nannie tried to think of something more to say about Patricia but was hard-pressed to remember a thing that was nice.

Ella spoke up. "I recall her at prayer meeting, how she did

sing. We've a good lot of singers amongst the Saints, but hers was the loveliest voice of all, like an angel's. And now she is with the angels. Did she suffer much?"

Nannie remembered Patricia's complaining and thought the woman suffered much even when she had no reason to, but she said, "I'm hoping she was not discomforted. Was she dangerous ill?"

"She went for a walk. I believe her mind was deranged from the cold, and she wandered away. A brother found her sitting in the snow. The wolves—"

Nannie gasped as she thought of the bodies she'd seen that the wolves had all but devoured, the ripped torsos and half-eaten arms and legs. The graves the men dug now in the frozen earth were shallow, and she knew that even if the Saints built fires on top of the graves to destroy the smell of flesh, the wolves would tear up the earth to get at the bodies. She'd heard the howls of the wolves at night, seen the animals prowling the edges of the camp, their ragged yellow teeth gleaming in the moonlight. She had not liked Patricia, had hated her, in fact, for marrying Levi on Nannie's own wedding day, but she did not wish her body desecrated, did not wish her dead, either.

Finally, Levi said, "The wolves had not found her. She looked at peace."

"Ye shall be reunited in the Lord's own due time. We'll neglect no opportunity to pray for her soul," Ella said.

Nannie frowned at her sister, for Ella was not so pious as her words. But what else could one say? She hoped Levi did not find the remarks false. "I'm sorry we dinna know. We would hae attended the service. We will pray for Sister Patricia," Nannie told him, thinking herself as insincere as her sister.

"Will you walk with me a little?" Levi asked Nannie.

"Nay, my feet . . ." she began, but Ella pushed at her and told her walking would bring the blood to her feet. Nannie was surprised, because she knew Ella disliked Levi, but maybe Ella's heart had softened at the news of his wife's death. Perhaps Ella did indeed mean those words. Whatever it was, Levi was a brother who needed consoling, so she could not turn him down.

Nannie put on her shoes, and Levi helped her to her feet, holding her up, because she had trouble standing. She realized that he was as strong as Andrew. Why was it, she wondered, that some men pulled the handcarts all day, deprived themselves of food so that they could feed their families, then died in the night, while others seemed to gain strength from the same sacrifices?

"She did not live easy, nor make it easy for me. The pretty ones are the lazy ones," Levi said as he walked slowly among the tents and handcarts, Nannie hobbling beside him. "Patricia was one to complain. She said toward the end that all she asked of the world was to be comfortably out of it."

"Hush," Nannie told him, a little shocked at his words about the dead. "Ye mustna tell me about that. Ye are distressed."

"You would not have complained. You are not lazy."

Nannie frowned, wondering if that meant he thought she was not pretty, and did not reply.

"I tell you now she's gone, you would be the first wife."

Nannie stopped, holding on to the wheel of a handcart to keep from falling. "It isnae fitting for ye to say that, Levi."

"It's not fitting that the Camp of Israel should be starved and frozen, either. If this is not a godforsaken country, it is a

God-forgotten one. These are hard days for Mormons, and we can no longer observe the conventions we once did."

"We are being tested. There's not one amongst us who's not been tested."

"So we are."

Nannie hoped that Levi would turn his thoughts away from the proposal, but he did not. "If we were at home, I wouldn't dare to discuss such a subject, with my wife still warm in her grave. . . ." He cleared his throat, and Nannie wondered if he had the same thought she did, that no one, not the newly dead nor the living, could be called warm. A giggle started in her throat at the idea, but, horrified, she coughed it down. Levi continued: "But we aren't at home, and I believe we ought to settle this thing between us. You told me you did not care to be a second wife. Now I can promise that you will be the first."

Nannie could not look at Levi. Instead, she stared into the falling snow that swirled around the carts. Except for a few green and blue shawls, red ones faded to the color of heather, everything in front of her was gray. "The first but not the only wife," she said at last.

"We are Mormons. You know it precious well we are expected to embrace the principle."

"Andrew widna. He promised. He wrote it in Ella's Bible on their wedding day. She would not hae married him otherwise."

"She is selfish. Such promises are not binding. He will change."

"Like that, is it?" she said scornfully.

Levi shrugged. "It's very well for them, then, if that's what they want. I won't promise you I won't take other wives. You know as well as I do that the prophet says it's our duty. Our salvation depends on it. No other man you would marry, if he's a good Saint, would make you that promise, either. But I tell you, Nannie, that you will be first in my heart, first in my esteem."

Nannie turned her back on Levi and put both hands on a wheel, a blue blanket attached to it for a shelter. Blue was her favorite color, because it reminded her of the sky. She wondered how many in the camp would live to see the sky turn blue again. "I was not first before."

"You're right to be angry. Only after I married Patricia did I realize what a fool I was. Not a day went by that I didn't regret that impulse. Where she would cry, you would have laughed; where she complained, you would have carried on with a smile. It was being married to her that made me realize you were meant to be my wife. When I looked at Patricia, I saw her soul was dross, but glory shines around your head."

Nannie glowed at the compliments but said, "Ye are harsh in regards to Patricia."

"I am honest."

Yes, Nannie thought, he is that, just as he'd been honest about embracing plural marriage.

"Now there is no obstacle to our being married. If I have caused you grief, I beg pardon and ask you to forgive me. Forgiveness is a part of our religion, too." He grinned at Nannie, and she could not help but smile back. "I will make it all up to you by being a good husband. Will you say yes, then?"

Nannie put her hands over her face and breathed into the wet wool of her shawl. She wondered if the cold had affected her mind, because she could not think clearly. She knew there was a reason she ought to say no, but she couldn't remember what it was. Oh, she did love Levi. There was no question of that. Her darkest hour had been her wedding day, when she'd read Levi's note telling her that he was casting her aside for Patricia. But now it was as if that had never happened. Nannie envisioned herself as she had once dreamed, wearing a wedding dress and the precious red silk slippers, the past months erased. There would be other wives. Levi had been frank about that, but there could be other wives no matter which Saint she wed. Was it better to be married to a man she loved and watch him court other women or to wed a man she didn't care about and therefore wouldn't be as hurt when he chose subsequent wives? For a little while, at least, she would be happy with Levi, and they would be together in the celestial kingdom. What was a little unhappiness in life if she were assured of eternal bliss?

She thought perhaps she ought to let him court her a little and bring her gewgaws, play the flirt, but that was what Patricia had done. Nannie was not like that. Besides, they weren't at home, but in a camp filled with dying people, where they could not go pleasuring. They couldn't walk about in the sunshine as they once had. And where would he find a trinket to give her unless he plucked a gold locket from the fingers of a dead woman? They were Saints, and such frivolity did not become them. But still, she would not say yes. Perhaps she was not really sure of him. Or it might be that she wanted him to feel a measure of the distress he had caused her. "I canna say."

"Is there someone else?"

"Och, nay." Nannie realized she shouldn't have spoken so quickly. Perhaps Levi would value her more if he thought others had sought her hand. Levi grinned at her, grinned with such self-assurance that Nannie added, "None that I hae answered aye to." She thought his smile lessened, but she could not be sure.

"Of course, there are others who would want such a beautiful girl," he said. "I may have to fight them off with a stick." He glanced at the sky and added, "Or snowballs. I suppose it is foolish of me to think you could care for me as you once did. There are many would say I'm not worthy of you, and I'm one of them."

Nannie thought her heart would swell to bursting with Levi's words of contrition, and she said, "Aye."

"You think it, too, then?"

"I didna say aye to the question of your worth. I said aye to your proposal."

Levi took her hands in his and smiled at her. "You won't be sorry. We'll work hard, both of us. Patricia could not have stood the pace, but you can. We're both strong. We can make it in Zion. You will work beside me. We may have a house made of earth bricks instead of stone, and when we go about, it will be to push a plow instead of walking down a country lane. There may be hardships, but we will know that God is on our side."

Those might not have been the expressions of love and tenderness that a young girl would cherish, but Nannie and Levi were Mormons, and the words were appropriate for Saints. Nannie had no illusions about a pampered life, and Levi was right to say he expected her to work hard. And she would.

She would be cheerful and not complain and show him how much better a wife she was than Patricia had been.

"If it were seemly, I would like to be married today. Brother Martin could officiate, although I don't believe we could have a party with cake and wine for the guests." He smiled at his little joke.

"Nay," Nannie said slowly. "We'll wait until we reach the valley. My sister's unwell. The bairn is almost here. I canna leave her. Besides . . ." Besides what? she asked herself. Was she unsure of her decision? Was she concerned about what others would think of her marrying Levi so soon after his wife died? Perhaps she wanted to postpone the wedding so that she could wear a silk dress and the red shoes after all, or make Levi wait, to worry that she might change her mind, to hunger for her. Nannie didn't know. "Besides, it's not right to celebrate a wedding now, not when people are dying," she told him.

Levi started to protest but thought better of it. A good sign, Nannie told herself. Perhaps after they were married, he would care about her feelings, would listen to her. Maybe she would not be under her husband's thumb as so many wives were.

"I will agree, if you will make it as soon as we reach Zion, for I don't care to wait," he said.

Nannie nodded, and Levi said, "I don't deserve such a good wife."

"'Tis true," Nannie said slyly. "Now I must tell Ella."

"We'll tell her together."

"Nay," Nannie said quickly, because she didn't know what her sister's reaction would be—or Andrew's.

"You think they won't approve. They don't like me."

"They liked ye fine once. They will again. Just as I love ye again."

"You never stopped loving me," Levi chided, then added quickly, "Nor I you." He put his hand over hers, and hand in hand, they returned to Nannie's cart, where he squeezed her fingers and left.

Ella, huddled beside the cart, did not look up, and Nannie inquired if she was all right.

"Just cold."

"There's news I'm hoping will warm ye as it does me."

"You will marry him, then?"

Nannie should have realized that her sister knew what Levi was about. "He's the man I love best of all others. I'm hoping ye will approve."

Ella did not respond for a moment. "If ye choose him, that is your doing. After all, ye should marry, and he is a good-enough man. But I allow I am selfish. It's not your marrying I fear; it's losing ye. What will I do without ye?"

"There's Andrew." She sat down in the snow, her feet to the fire.

"Of course, it's grateful enough I am for him." Ella looked at Nannie. "But I'm thinking there is no bond as powerful as that of sisters."

Nannie took Ella's hand and held it. "What will Andrew say aboot that, do ye think?"

At that, Ella laughed. "He's said it already. He told me in Iowa City, when he saw Levi was there, that ye would wed the lad as soon as we reached the valley. Of course, we dinna know it would be as his first wife."

The sisters sat with their arms around each other, Nannie

stirring every so often to add juniper to the fire. Once when she reached over to throw a branch on the coals, she caught sight of a woman who looked familiar, although she could not place her, and the woman did not seem to recognize her. She was resting against a cart, two young children clasped to her, sheltered with a shawl—*her* shawl, Nannie realized with a start, the one stolen from her handcart. *That* was what was familiar! At first, Nannie thought to rip the garment off the woman. After all, it was hers to claim. She had bought the shawl, kept it when she had thrown out her boots, and the woman had stolen it. But she stopped, realizing where she had seen the woman—grieving on the banks of the North Platte over her husband, who had died that day of the river crossing. She'd been left a widow, and now hungry and cold, she protected the little children as best she could under the bright shawl. Nannie settled back and watched as the family disappeared in the snow. The shawl is better used to warm the three Saints than to assure a fashionable entry into the valley, she thought, and she leaned against Ella, grateful that she had her sister instead of just a piece of cloth to warm her.

They were there, the two of them, drugged by the cold and lack of food, when Nannie heard a cry. "I see them coming. Angels! The angels have come!" screamed a woman. At first, Nannie dismissed the shouts. Several women had succumbed to dementia after crossing the North Platte. But the cry was taken up by others, so Nannie, ignoring the pain in her feet, pulled herself up. She stood holding on to the wagon wheel, straining her eyes to see through the dense fog, and then she yelled, "Riders, Ella! Three of them. Sent from the valley for sure. We are saved, Ella. We are saved!"

Chapter 8

October 28, 1856

Louisa could tell by the faces of the three express riders who rode into the encampment at Red Buttes on that late-October day that they were stunned by the suffering they encountered among the handcart Saints. She and the other emigrants had been stranded in the snow for nine days. She knew their faces were raw from the wind and cold, and that their arms, sticking out from under torn shirts and filthy cloaks, were as thin as willow shoots. Noses were frozen black, and people wrung their hands or clutched their shawls and blankets around themselves with blackened fingers that would have to be cut off. A few of the Saints were barefoot and stamped their feet to keep warm. There were bloody footprints in the snow near where Louisa stood, some from children's feet.

These people were told once that they were the spiritual favorites of the Almighty, Louisa thought, and now, they looked at the riders as if they were apparitions. Beside Louisa, her mother, Margaret, cried, the tears of joy freezing on her face. Then the old woman hobbled toward the rescuers, clasping her bare arms around one of the riders' neck and kissing him. Other emigrants too weak to stand reached out with their arms, shouting, "Hosanna!" and "Hurrah!" "Lord be praised!" and "Angels from heaven!"

"Better than angels—strong men come to help us reach the valley," said a woman. "We have given up on angels." She fell down in a faint.

Louisa knew it wasn't just the physical condition of her people and the scanty provisions—enough for only six more days—or the threadbare clothing and blankets that horrified the riders. It was the emigrants' shattered spirit. "There is some here that has the heartache mighty bad," one of the riders remarked to Louisa as he looked over the crowd of converts.

A gray-bearded Saint from Louisa's village, a man whose skin hung from his cheekbones like empty seed sacks, grasped the hem of the military overcoat worn by a rider and begged for food. A bit of bread, a piece of dried beef, an empty flour sack that could be boiled and the dredges of flour extracted to make a thin soup. It was not for himself, but for his wife, his children, he pleaded, opening his palm, which was like the hand of a skeleton. Louisa knew him as a once-proud man and a leader in the church, and he had been reduced to a beggar.

The rider turned aside and wept. He and the other two carried no food with them except for what was loaded onto a single pack mule and stored in their saddle bags, and that was not enough to feed the multitude. There will be no miracle of loaves and fishes in this desolate place, Louisa thought.

The rider shook his head at the starving Saint. "You must hold out a little longer, Brother, just two days, three at most. The rescue wagons are waiting at Devil's Gate but will soon be on their way."

"He may be dead by then, dead of general decay," Louisa told him, and indeed, the man's absent stare and countenance foretold his end. "But we have no fear of death. We are so used to looking it in the face that it doesn't frighten us anymore," she added.

If they brought few provisions with them, the riders nonetheless brought hope, telling the Saints that relief wagons were only three days away. Louisa all but clapped her hands when the leaders announced that flour rations would be increased to a pound a day from the scanty supply still in the camp. They ordered the emigrants to kill some cattle and divide the meat. "We'll move on tomorrow," Thales said, coming up to his wife. "Brother Brigham says the emigrants are to be brought to the valley. He promised that if we journeyed just a few miles each day, we would reach safety."

"Did the rescuers say why relief supplies were slow in coming? Surely they were asked."

"They were. Many thought we had wintered in Florence or even Iowa City." He lowered his voice. "A few admit it was poor planning and poorer execution. They say the prophet will flay the hide of whoever is responsible."

So the following morning, Thales urged the remaining members of his hundred on. The Saints made up a pitiful train, strung out over three or four miles. Louisa and her mother pulled their cart past old men who were dragging their vehicles behind them. Louisa all but cried when she saw children no older than Dick and Jimmy whimper from the cold as they picked up the shafts of their vehicles, which were piled with the few belongings that they had left and sometimes with a brother or sister or even a mother who was too sick to walk. Snow and mud clung to Louisa's clothes, and as the weather worsened, the snow turned into icicles, which pierced her worn dress and rubbed against her bare skin. She passed Saints who had given up and were crouched beside their carts to keep out of the wind or had sought shelter among the rocks. They had to be persuaded to keep on.

The two women maneuvered around deserted carts, their axles broken, their wheels shattered. Rather than repair the carts, a few of the Saints packed what they could carry on their backs and trudged on, abandoning the hated vehicles. Pulling the Tanner cart, Louisa walked thirty miles in two days, until at last, the Saints were met by the wagons of the rescue party, with six loads of supplies. But still, Louisa could not rest. Like the others in the Martin Company, she trudged on for two more days until, on November 2, the emigrants and their rescuers arrived at the remains of a log fort, a place known as Devil's Gate.

Gripping the shafts of her handcart, Jessie had stopped counting the steps she'd taken since their last rest. It was a game she played with herself to keep her mind off their plight. But she'd stopped counting at 403, when she felt the weight of the handcart increase and knew that Emeline had stopped pushing. The girl had weakened at the Red Buttes camp, had caught cold and maybe something worse—pneumonia, Maud had whispered, although they hadn't told the girl. Jessie pulled the cart a dozen more steps, but Emeline did not resume pushing, so Jessie stopped and looked back, hoping Emeline had not dropped into the snow. To Jessie's relief, the girl seemed all right. She stood in the road beside Ephraim, holding him up. Maud generally walked with Ephraim now, but the old lady sat in the snow. She, too, was exhausted, not only from the cold and scanty rations but from tending the Saints who needed her. Jessie wondered that the woman slept at all, and she thought that Maud must have simply dozed off. The emigrants did that, fell asleep while trudging along the road. Sometimes they didn't wake up. But Maud got to her feet and examined Ephraim's stump, all that was left of his arm, and Jessie dropped the shafts and walked back to the little group.

"I believe the cold helps it heal, but I don't know why," Maud said. "Does it hurt?"

Ephraim shook his head, but that told the women nothing, because he had not complained since Sutter died. He was coping better than Jessie had thought, no longer bemoaning his state or saying he hoped to die. He'd asked Jessie once if she thought there would be a place in Zion for a man who could add and subtract and keep books, and she had said there would. Emeline was responsible for the improvement in Ephraim's attitude, his sister believed. In fact, without Emeline, Ephraim wouldn't be alive.

Jessie wondered what had drawn them to each other. At first, she'd thought that both had been flawed, Ephraim in body, Emeline in soul, and certainly that had been part of it.

But each had found a happiness with the other beyond mutual suffering. She'd watched as Ephraim had drawn a flower in the snow and written "Emeline" beneath it.

"What's it say?" the girl had asked.

"Your name. Emeline," he'd replied. "Can't you read it?"

"Can't read."

"Then I'll teach you." And at each stop, he had written a letter or a simple word, and Emeline had copied it. Once he wrote "love," and after that, Emeline had written it at each stop.

"That was his way of saying he loves you," Jessie confided to her.

"The wonder of it, a girl like me."

Now, the dressing had slipped off Ephraim's stump, which had begun to heal. It was no longer an angry red. Still, Ephraim was weak, and it was all he could do to walk. They were all in bad shape. Only willpower kept Emeline going, and Jessie did not know how long she herself could continue, but she refused to think about that, because the others would not make it without her.

None of them noticed the rider who stopped beside them until he spoke. "Do you need a hand?"

"A left one," Ephraim said, indicating the stump.

Jessie smiled. Ephraim had been a good laugher once, and thanks to Emeline, he might be again.

"I beg pardon," the man said. He might have blushed, but they couldn't tell because his face was red from the cold.

"It's all right. Without you rescuers, I might have lost the other one. Or my life. I never saw a sight I liked better in my life than you people riding into camp, Brother . . ."

"Brother Thomas," he said.

"Can you hitch your horse to our cart, Brother Thomas?" Jessie asked.

"I can tie my lariat to it and pull it, if you and your daughter will steady it from behind. Your husband and mother can walk."

"He's not my husband, but my brother," Jessie explained. "We thought there would be provisions before now. We were told . . ." She shrugged. What reason was there to complain about the lack of planning, the lack of food and warm clothing? After all, they were being cared for now.

Thomas dismounted and tied a rope to the crosspiece of the handcart. "It should hold."

"They are poor built," Ephraim told him.

"I can see it." He mounted and walked the horse slowly until the rope was taut. Then Jessie and Emeline put their hands against the back of the cart, and with Ephraim and Maud walking behind, they started off. Thomas pulled the cart until the crosspiece fell off, and then he tried to tie the rope around the shafts, but that didn't work. "We're but a mile from the camp. Can you pull the cart on your own?" he asked. "There are others I must help, but I'll come back."

"We'll make it," Jessie said. Thanks to the horse, which had relieved her from pulling the cart for part of the journey, she felt a little rested.

"I won't forget you. I'll make sure you reach the camp," Thomas said, and rode off.

Jessie took one shaft and Emeline the other, and they plodded along, not stopping until they saw a young man who had collapsed under a sagebrush. The two women left the cart and went over to the Saint, asking if he needed help.

"Leave me alone," he muttered. "It is too much to get up."

"If you tarry, you will die," Jessie told him.

"I will die anyway. I've had nothing to eat but the straps of my boots." The man laid his head in the snow and refused to move.

"Please, it's not even a mile," Emeline pleaded, but the man only turned away.

Suddenly, Maud yelled, "Your mother is hunting you. Jump up. You must help her."

The Saint scrambled to his feet and looked around, but he could not see his parent. "Where?"

"Ahead," Maud pointed. "Hurry on before it's too late." As the lad ran off the others watched, smiling at the way Maud had provoked him. "Running will get his blood flowing, and he will be in the camp before we are," Maud told them. Jessie and Emeline returned to their cart, and late in the afternoon, they reached Devil's Gate.

Some eighteen inches of snow lay on the ground there, blown by the wind into drifts as big as hedgerows, but Jessie was used to snow, so that was not what stunned her as she reached the camp. She had expected to help set up her tent, build her own fire from fuel she'd collected on the way. So she was startled by the frenzy of activity at Devil's Gate, which was a crumbling fort made up of the remains of two walls and seven or eight log buildings. Huge fires blazed, and tents had been erected. Rescuers handed out blankets and coats, shoes, boots, and even handkerchiefs.

The members of the Cooper party pushed into the largest

of the old fort's structures to stand near a fire, but the air was suffocating inside, what with the heat and the steam from the wet clothing, and several women had fainted. So the four found a smaller fire and crowded near it, hoping that finally they would be warm. Jessie tried to think back to the last time she hadn't been cold and couldn't remember. Was it Fort Laramie or Florence? Or maybe she'd been cold ever since she left England.

"You are not going to freeze tonight," Thomas said, coming up to stand beside her. "I've been looking for you, Sister. As you can see, I've kept my promise to make sure you arrived safe. There's to be flour handed around and beef, but you must be patient. First we must ensure the fires won't give out."

"Will the Lord provide us with firewood?" Jessie asked, then wondered if she had blasphemed and if this man who had been so kind to them would be shocked.

"He will, and He will provide woodcutters to chop it for you." Thomas left to join other rescuers who were taking axes to the wall of a cabin and chopping it into firewood. Then the men handed out the logs, one to each family." Jessie and Emeline built a fire with theirs; then the two of them and Maud took off their shoes and stockings to let them dry near the flames, sitting with their bare feet to the fire.

Just then, however, Thomas returned, his hands holding something behind his back. "I've brought your supper," he said, handing a piece of meat to Jessie. "Now don't quarrel over it like a houseful of wives."

"We never quarrel among ourselves," Maud told him. And Jessie wondered if polygamous wives did indeed fight over the best cuts of meat, the cabbage without worms, the milk not yet spoiled. Perhaps in hard times, those who were out of favor received no food at all. But she did not think about such things for long. Instead, barefoot, she went to the cart for the tin plates and forks, while Emeline sharpened a stick and pushed it through the piece of meat, which she held over the fire.

"Brother Thomas, you are welcome to join us, but you must have your own plate. We are poor prepared for guests," Jessie said.

"It is little enough for four people." He turned aside to wipe his eyes, saying that a little snow had gotten into them. Then he told Jessie, "These few days are the most melancholy time I have ever passed through. I did not expect to find sharing." He cleared his throat, perhaps because such emotion was unmanly. "When the fire's gone out, pitch your tent on the spot. You won't have to scoop away the snow with a frying pan, and you will sleep warmer than you have in many nights."

"Without your help, we would surely have died. We owe our lives to you."

"Oh, damn that," Thomas replied. "We don't want any of that. You are welcome. We have come to help you."

With Lucy wrapped in blankets and riding on top of the cart and Joe and Catherine walking beside them, John and Anne pulled the cart together. Usually, Anne pushed, but the day was so cold and the wind so brutal that she was warmer beside John, and warmth seemed more important than speed. He was silent. The cold made taking a breath like breathing through a hat. Besides, the wind scattered the words. But there was little to say that hadn't been said the night they arrived at Devil's Gate. They had talked it out.

"It is too much, too much to ask of us," he'd said that evening as he dropped the shafts and fell down between them after they reached the camp.

Anne had been every bit as tired, but she'd said nothing about her state. Instead, she told him, "It is a religion that requires sacrifice. We knew it at the outset."

"Haven't we sacrificed enough—our shop, our livelihood, everything we owned, our . . ." He swallowed and added, "Our daughter and son. What more does God expect? Does He want the rest of us, too?"

"We don't know His purpose. We can only hope He has one."

"You sound like the missionaries." There was sarcasm in John's voice.

Anne shrugged and searched the cart for the tin plates, handing them to Joe and Catherine. The three began to scoop away the snow so that they could set up their tent. The process, Anne knew, might take them an hour. John watched for a moment, then got up, took out his own plate, and joined them.

"They say this is not as bad as it was at Winter Quarters," Catherine said, shaking her head to rid her old bonnet of the snow that had accumulated on top.

"Damn Winter Quarters! Those there would say that even hell could not be worse," John replied. "I believe they are poor remembrancers of past times. If Winter Quarters was this bad, the Saints would have perished and there would be no church. I am tired of hearing about Winter Quarters. But I suppose that in a year's time, those of us who make it to the valley with our handcarts will count ourselves God's anointed for having survived this ordeal. I'm sure our hardships will be magnified a hundredfold, if that's possible. Perhaps our experience will count toward the celestial kingdom."

John was bitter, and Anne and Catherine exchanged looks because the words were blasphemous and John could be censored in meeting. But Anne knew Catherine would never repeat them, and no one else could hear them with the wind howling. Nonetheless, Catherine said, "I myself do not believe it is wrong to question the church. That is how we learn. But it would be better if ye didn't voice your criticisms in such a loud voice."

"You're right. That old zealot who spoke out so strongly in favor of continuing this trip from Florence might make me sorry," John said sourly. "I've not heard the leaders pontificate much of late."

"Ye are distressed, like so many, wondering how the Lord can bring such hardship to His people, but as Sister Anne says, He has a reason. The hand of the Lord is with us yet. We would not be here if we dinna believe that."

"Where else would we be? Do you think we could turn back? That would be certain death," John said.

Catherine stopped scooping for a moment, glancing down at the red drops of blood in the snow. They had come from her hands, which were raw from the cold and ice. "There is no place for an apostate to go in this storm, and few enough places even for a believer," she agreed. "But ye are not an apostate. Ye are a man who has been sorely tried, and ye want to know for what purpose. The Lord asks much of His people, but He brings us miracles, too." John started to say something, but Catherine held up her plate, as if she knew the answer to the question he was about to ask. "The rescuers. There's a miracle. It's said that after another day, the express riders would hae turned back. But they found us. Can any question that was God's will?"

"*Are* you an apostate?" Anne asked her husband. She knew John questioned, but she did not believe he had gone that far.

"No. Oh, no. But I believe the Lord owes us an explanation, especially to you, Anne. Why must you sacrifice when this is not even your religion?"

Anne looked at her husband for a long time, for he was not one to apologize.

When Anne didn't reply, Catherine asked, "Isn't it? Isn't it her faith, too?"

John looked at the woman sharply. "You know as much. Anne is not a Saint."

Catherine didn't reply, but instead, she turned to Anne.

"I have not been baptized," Anne said.

"Would you be willing?" John asked.

"No one would be willing to be baptized in this snow."

John narrowed his eyes at his wife. "You have toyed with me these past days. Say aloud what you believe."

"I am not sure what I believe."

"Could you become a Mormon after all that's happened?"

Anne thought that over. "Perhaps I would not join your church, but I have joined your people. I don't believe I could accept these hardships if I did not admire the faith of those who experienced them. I will stay with you here, in your Zion."

John looked at his wife for a long time. "It is enough. I think I should get down on my knees and thank God, but I'm afraid I wouldn't be able to get up. Besides, I believe you would rather I scoop away snow than pray."

"Did the Lord speak to ye?" Catherine asked.

Anne turned back to the snow with her plate and scraped away part of a drift. "I'm not for sure knowing what it was. I've never seen such goodness, such sacrifice. The Saints' kindness to me knows no bounds."

"And the doctrine?" John asked. "Do you still question it?"

Lucy crept up to her mother then, and to the little girl's delight, Anne drew a face in the snow. The girl destroyed it with her hand, pushing her mitten back and forth across the face until nothing remained of it. Then she drew a clumsy face of her own. Anne added a body to it, a girl in a skirt, and the two of them laughed.

"The doctrine," John reminded his wife.

"I cannot accept it yet, cannot accept the deaths of Emma Lee and Samuel. God knows I will never accept that." She turned to look at her husband. "But I believe the Lord loves your people, that if you prove worthy, He will bless you."

"And if ye are wrong?" Catherine asked.

"Then you are wrong, and John is wrong. And so is everyone here. And we will all perish, the unbelievers included."

Joe, who had been shoveling snow beside them, listening, turned to Anne. "Mama, does that mean you are a Mormon now?"

"Not quite."

"Then I'll hope for it so you won't go to hell." He thought

a moment and added, "Papa can take Sister Catherine for his second wife."

They all laughed at that. But even if John had considered such a preposterous idea, it was not to be. Later that evening, as they ate a meal of flour cooked with a little water and a beef bone, Catherine complained of a discomfort in her chest. Anne made a bed for her under the cart, where she would be protected from the snow. But that did no good. In an hour, the old woman was dead. There was no good-bye from her, no final word. Only when Anne went to Catherine to see if she needed anything did she discover that her friend had crossed over.

She and John prepared Catherine for burial, but there was little to it, because they could spare no blanket for a shroud. John carried the body to the place where the dead were laid out, already six of them. Anne followed him, weeping, bowed down with as much grief as she had felt when Samuel died, but this time, there was no friend to comfort her. The family stood there, looking down at the body, Lucy in her father's arms, Joe with his cap in his hand, for he thought of the old woman as a grandmother.

"And what of your faith today, Anne?" John asked now as they pulled their handcart through the snow.

His wife pushed her shawl away from her mouth. "My faith in Him remains strong," she replied, then turning her eyes upward to the falling snow, she added, "My faith in some of His decisions is less firm."

"Why, you would question His sending us this snow?" John asked, grinning at his wife and placing his hand over hers on the crosspiece of the cart. It was not often in the past few weeks that they had found something that amused them.

"The snow, no. I question that He did not think to put a railroad in this place."

"I suppose He can't be expected to consider everything."

"Is He not omnipotent?"

The leaders would not have liked the little joke, Anne thought, but they would never know, and if they did, she did not care. She looked over at her husband and, observing the way the two of them pulled the cart in tandem, thought they had become one again, no longer two separate persons at odds with each other, but a couple whose purpose linked them together. Then suddenly, John let go of the crosspiece of the cart and embraced Anne. "No man ever had such a wife," he said, and kissed her full on the mouth.

That day, November 4, was the worst one Louisa had yet encountered. They had been exposed to the snow and cold for more than two weeks, and the previous day, the drifts had been so bad, the bitter wind so strong, the temperature so far below zero that they had not moved from the camp at Devil's Gate. A rescuer told her the company could not stay there any longer, and late in the morning, when the weather let up, the emigrants began to move. The captain of the rescue company felt their salvation depended on traveling a little each day, so Louisa and her mother set out once more with their handcart. There was a cove just three miles away where they could be sheltered, but to reach it, they would have to cross the Sweetwater River. Earlier in their journey, Louisa would have thought little about such a crossing. After all, they had waded a dozen such streams. But they had never crossed a river in such cold, and this would be the most difficult crossing of all.

Louisa had heard rumors that the handcarts were to be discarded and all would be taken up in the wagons, but to her disappointment, there was not enough room in the wagons the rescuers had brought for all who needed to ride across the river, and it would take too long for the wagons to cross, double back, then cross again—and again. The elders established a priority: the sick and elderly, the children and widows first, then the men, if there were places left.

Louisa begged for a spot on one of the wagons for her mother, Margaret, who, after all, was both old and a widow, but too many others were deemed in worse condition. "I can walk," the old woman insisted, as she had since the beginning of the journey, when Thales had suggested she was an idler.

"She can't. It is too much for her," Louisa told Thales.

"Then she can ride on top of our cart, and I'll pull her."

"She's too heavy. We can barely push the cart as it is."

"I will do as I say." Theirs was one of the stronger carts, made with a canvas top, and Thales settled the old woman on top of their possessions, where the canopy would keep the snow off her.

We will all find the strength to push the cart, Louisa thought. There were just the three of them now. The rest of her family—her father, her sister Huldah, and her nephews, Jimmy and Dick—were gone. Louisa wondered if those few remaining would make it to the valley—the three still living, plus the baby she carried. It might die if it were born in a camp, and so might she. She worried about how Thales would take her death. His belief in the church had already been tested with so many other deaths. And how would she go on if Thales died? She pushed the thoughts from her mind, because they were in God's hands. She prayed to the Almighty to protect them, then wondered if that did any good. After all, her prayers hadn't helped the others.

She stopped her cart to let the wagons go ahead, trampling the snow to make it easier for the converts following behind to pull their carts. The river was not far, but the temperature was more than ten degrees below zero, and the emigrants were weaker than they'd ever been, so the first of them did not reach the Sweetwater until midafternoon. Louisa watched as the wagons, filled with those who were fortunate enough to ride, crossed the river first, breaking through the thin crust of ice that had formed on the water, while the emigrants who walked behind stood on the slippery banks, looking out across the river, mustering the courage to step into the freezing water. The ford was perhaps a hundred feet wide, although Louisa could see from where the water came on the wagon wheels that it was not more than two feet deep. She watched the first emigrants push into the water, where the soft mud of the riverbed sucked at their feet and the cart wheels, and freezing water stung their bodies. Chunks of ice swept down the river, their sharp edges piercing the legs of the Saints, tearing the bare skin and bloodying the water. She stood on the bank, readying herself for their turn, for as cold as the day was, the water would be colder. She tucked up her skirts to keep the current from dragging them down.

Thales, who had been helping the other emigrants, came

up to the cart and asked, "Are you ready?" Louisa dipped her chin, too weary even to reply, and Thales stepped off into the water, his wife behind him, holding her breath in anticipation of the cold. She gasped as she felt the water on her legs, and bit her lip but did not cry out. Gathering all their strength, Thales and Louisa moved as quickly as they could before the water numbed their feet. They were more than halfway to the opposite bank, Louisa thinking how lucky they were to cross without mishap, when the cart tipped, flinging Margaret into the water.

Louisa grabbed her mother but she could not lift the old lady back into the cart, and Thales would not let go of the vehicle, for fear it would be swept down the river. "I'll drag her to the riverbank," Louisa said as she tried to maneuver her mother through the water.

But as she started forward, a man ordered, "Hold on to her while I help right the cart." He went to the back of the vehicle, and he and Thales rocked it loose from the rocks that had caught a wheel. "You push, Sister," he told Louisa. "I'll fetch the old woman across." Without the burden of Margaret, the cart moved easily then, and in a few minutes, Thales and Louisa gained the bank, where Margaret sat, shaking from the cold and wringing out her skirts.

Thales said, "We thank you, Brother—" then stopped abruptly. "Brother Thomas!"

Thomas stared blankly, and Thales said, "You don't know me, your old friend Thales Tanner? I am so much a skeleton that even my oldest friends don't recognize me."

"Heaven's mercy, Thales, is it you?" Thomas grasped the

other man's hands between his own. When Thales assured him it was, Thomas added, "You are enough to astonish a man. You were looking better the last time we met."

"As were we all. It's been a devilish trip, one to try the faith of all, myself included."

"Then it must have been a difficult time indeed."

"I'm grateful to you. These are Margaret and Louisa, my wife."

"You married in England?"

Thales nodded.

"Both wives?" Thomas asked.

Thales looked uncomfortable. "Only Louisa. Margaret is her mother."

Louisa tried to courtesy, but her wet skirts threw her off balance, and it was all she could do to keep upright.

"Two would be one too many to bring. Our enemies would make much of it," Thomas said, then added quietly to Thales, although Louisa heard, "I am discovering two may be too much anyway." He bowed a little to the women and said he must return to the river, that there were other Saints who needed help.

"I'll go with you," Thales told him.

Louisa touched his arm, while Thomas looked at him uncertainly, "Are you up to it?"

"These are my hundred, what's left of them. I must see them through."

"But you are in as poor a shape as any of them."

"I do not know why God has made them such cruel sufferers. We promised them the Lord would protect them, and look at this. It's an abomination." Thales gestured at the river, which was filled with struggling emigrants. "Perhaps the Lord should have told them to stay the winter in Iowa. I must help them across."

"You could die," Louisa said.

"She's right," Thomas told him.

"Not likely. I'm not good enough to die."

"You have changed," Thomas observed.

The only thing that kept Jessie going on that terrible journey from Devil's Gate to the cove was the knowledge that Ephraim, Emeline, and Maud would not make it if she failed. She had never been so defeated. If she could have, she would have lain down and let the snow, so white and pure, cover her like a fresh-washed sheet. She had heard it said that when you froze to death, you felt warm, and the idea of resting eternally under that white warmth tempted her. But she knew she had to keep moving. Emeline, sick as she was with fever, could barely push, and Maud and Ephraim were no help with the cart. They stumbled as they followed behind.

"The river. At last, the river," Emeline said. She had been pushing the cart with her head down and had not seen the Sweetwater until Jessie stopped on its banks and grasped her shawl to fling off the snow that had accumulated on it. The wind blew the snow sideways, and the flakes hit her neck like particles of glass. As she watched the ice in the river sweep past her, Jessie did not share the girl's joy. They would have to cross that cold swath, and Jessie wondered if they had the strength for it.

Ephraim came up beside her, and Jessie could sense his

dejection as he looked out at the Saints who were struggling in the river. They watched as a cart tipped over, spilling its contents, the couple propelling it reaching out to save their few belongings, but the items were swept away. The man stared dumbly as tin plates swirled in the water and disappeared, but the woman pulled her limp bonnet over her face, perhaps so that no one would see her tears. One of the rescuers waded through the water to the couple and helped them to the far shore.

As he watched them, Ephraim swayed a little and grasped the Cooper cart to keep from tumbling into the river. Then he looked down at the water lapping at his feet and asked, "Have we got to go through it?"

"It's not so deep. Look to the center of the river. The water comes only halfway up the cart wheels," Jessie told him.

Ephraim shook his head. He shivered with the cold and turned to his sister, his eyes feverish. "I can't. I can't go it."

"You'll make it. You've come so far."

"I can't. It's too much."

"Then I'll carry you across," Emeline said, coming up beside him and taking hold of his remaining hand.

He began to cry at that, and turning to Jessie, he said, "Look what I've come to. I left England a man, and a whole man at that. Now I'm not but a one-armed sniveling brat. I'm so weak, a girl can carry me across the river."

"No need of that, Brother Ephraim," a man said, and they turned to find Thales Tanner beside them. His clothes were wet and his face and hands were frosted. He nodded at Jessie then and said, "Sister, you have come a long way."

"Thanks to you," she replied. Her voice was dull with blame.

"I wouldn't be surprised if you hated me. Some do, you know. But don't hate God. It was men, not the Lord, who brought us to this state."

"My faith in Him is strong. I am yet a good Saint. It is my faith in missionaries that falls short."

"With good reason." He added quickly, "If your brother will climb onto the cart and you and the others will push, we can cross quickly. It is cold, but the water is not so strong as the North Platte."

"I can push," Jessie insisted, but as she took a step forward, she fell, exhausted, and could not get up.

"You look as if you could not push an ounce," Thales said. "You'll ride on the top of the cart with your brother."

"You can't push two of us. Besides, it's a temporary spell. I'll rest a moment and cross on my own." The idea of lying in the snow and letting the flakes cover her tempted Jessie once again. She would not give up but would rest for a little while.

"No, that is too dangerous. You might not rise at all if we allowed that," Thomas said. She did not know how long he had been standing behind her.

"This is an old friend from the valley, one of the rescuers, Brother Thomas," Thales said.

"We have met. I am Thomas Savage."

Jessie glanced at him sharply. "I have a relative, Rebecca Savage. Are you—"

"Her husband. So that's who you are! I've been hoping to find you. We are cousins of a sort," Thomas said. "She is so anxious to see you that she would have come along on the rescue if I'd let her." He turned back to Thales. "If you'll go ahead with the cart, Brother, I'll carry Sister Jessie across."

She started to protest. After all, Emeline was sick, too, but Thales told her, "There is no dishonor in being weak."

"In body or in spirit?" Jessie asked.

Thales did not reply. Instead, he started into the river.

"Are you ready, Sister?" Thomas asked.

"I would rest a moment."

"You haven't eaten much more than broth made from boiled leather, I'll wager. Not a nourishing meal."

"Nor a tempting one. I wouldn't feed the hogs at home what has kept us alive these last days. I never thought to envy pigs."

"You have lived on a farm, Rebecca says. Have you found a farmer on this trip who would suit you as a husband?"

"My one brother is dead. The other, as you see yourself, fares poorly. And I have the care of Maud and Emeline," she said by way of reply

"What about the girl? She could marry, too."

"She is very young."

"Young girls are desirable in Zion."

"If she marries, it will be to my brother."

"You have not answered my question."

Jessie laughed at that. "No, I've not found a man I care enough to marry."

"You will in Zion."

"Perhaps."

"My wife has told it about that you are coming. You'll have no lack of suitors."

"Most of them with a plenty of wives at home already, I think. How many do you have, Brother Thomas?"

"Two," he replied.

Jessie stared at him, for she had been jesting. She was appalled to think her cousin's husband had taken a second wife.

"I think it may be one too many, but I can't say which one." He grinned at Jessie, then picked her up. Jessie did not smile back.

Jessie felt herself relax as Thomas stepped into the river with her in his arms. "I was all in. I think I could not make it across the river without you."

"The ordeal isn't over. There's much hardship still ahead."

"There was hardship behind us."

"I am afraid, Sister, you may find it even worse going on."

And it was hard. The hardest days Anne Sully had yet spent were the five days at the cove—"Martin's Ravine," they called it, in honor of their leader, Edward Martin, although Anne wondered if he felt such a memorial was an honor. The man had been tireless in helping the Saints, as if he believed the company named for him was his sole responsibility.

The wagons carrying the sick went first, and when Anne and the other emigrants pushing handcarts arrived at the cove, just a mile beyond the Sweetwater, they found tents set up and fires blazing. But the food that had been brought by the rescuers was almost used up, and rations were reduced again, this time to just four ounces of flour per adult, two per child. During the angriest storm Anne could imagine—a rescuer told her it was the worst he had ever seen—she and the others remained snowbound in the cove. The snow was relentless, and the wind swirled it around them so that it chapped their hands and faces. They had not been able to do washing in weeks, and their clothes were filthy. So the snow mixed with the dirt on the clothing and made it muddy. Skirts and pants were always wet. The temperature reached ten degrees below zero, and despite the fires, Anne feared they would freeze to death. Some did.

Anne had seen the shallow graves where the dead were buried, because the ground was too hard for digging and the Saints themselves too weak to dig proper graves. At night, she heard the howls of the wolves that dug up the bodies, scattering the bones, leaving scraps of flesh in the snow. She wondered if the Saints would stay in the cove for the winter. "Perhaps it's better to die here where we are a little comfortable than to perish in the icebound mountains," she told John. But the leaders said as soon as the weather lifted, the company must push on. So they stayed on a day and then another, each morning carrying the dead from the tents and stacking them like logs in the snow. Anne saw emigrants going through the pockets of the deceased in search of food.

John grew morose and asked Anne, "Are we being punished for our sins?" He had gone into the hills to cut cedar for fuel with others who could walk, and now he was back in the camp.

Thales Tanner, who was standing by when the woodcutters returned, heard the question and shook his head. "What sins does your little daughter have? Or my wife or our unborn babe?" he asked John.

"You don't believe it, then, as you once did, that only those who are pure in faith will reach Zion?"

"I am not the prophet. I cannot speak for God."

"Nor do you speak for the prophet any longer," John replied. The two men watched as Anne helped a woman bathe her daughter's hand, washing it with castile soap. The girl's fingers were black, and Thales told the mother, "They will have to come off. She will lose the hand and arm if they don't, and then her life. They will have to be attended to once we reach the valley." At first, the woman stared at Thales as if she were a dumb animal, so little did she comprehend. Then she said, "I wish to God I'd never heard of the Mormons. I don't care the toss of a button for your religion anymore."

Thales did not chastise the woman, just nodded in understanding. "May God give you strength, Sister," he said, and then he stepped away, but Anne could hear him remark to John, "Many others will be maimed—in mind and in body."

"Your faith has weakened," John said. When Thales didn't reply, John added, "As my own has. It is my wife, the one some still called 'a heathen,' who keeps me in the fold. And she is not even a Saint. I insisted she come. She had always had plenty and never known hardship. We could have had a good team and a wagon, but I gave our money to the elders. This is too much for her."

"I didn't appreciate the women until now. They are strong, stronger than we are."

"But we are still their leaders. It is men who make decisions, who are head of the household. Our faith tells us that."

Thales nodded. "It's not easy for us, either."

The two men parted, and John returned to the fire. The woman and her daughter were gone now, and Anne sat with the children. Lucy slept in her lap, and Joe stared into the coals. "I'm hungry, Papa," he said when John squatted beside the boy.

"Hush," Anne said. "We will eat when we reach the valley."

"I want to eat now."

"So do I," John told him, "but there's not so much food."

"I don't want boot broth," the boy said.

"I'm making something else," Anne said. She had found two sea biscuits in the bottom of the wagon, biscuits so hard, she could not break them, even when she tossed them against the rocks beside the cart. She had thrown them into a kettle and covered them with water, and now when she lifted the lid, she discovered the pan was filled with food, almost a miracle.

Anne pitied her boy, who had been such a worker the past months. He had pushed the cart without complaint and had helped both Anne and John in camp. He'd collected fuel and tended the fire, watched Lucy, and had even tried cooking when Anne's head hurt or her melancholy over the loss of her two children was so great that she could not oversee the pot. Now Joe was starving. They all were.

But Anne was more worried about Lucy, who no longer bubbled with excitement as she had in the beginning when she spotted each tree and flower along the trail. Over the past days, she'd grown listless. She slept or else stared into the snow, her little mittened hands clenched. Anne worried about the girl's feet. John had provisioned them well for the trip, buying warm clothing, but Lucy had outgrown her shoes, and they had been discarded at the North Platte. Anne dressed her in three pairs of stockings, and at Devil's Gate, she'd torn strips off the canvas cover of a deserted cart to make the bandages that protected

Lucy's feet. As she sat beside the fire with the girl, Anne unwrapped the strips and took off the stockings to check Lucy's
feet. They were cold, but there was no sign of damage. The
toes were red, not black, and Lucy did not cry out when her
mother touched them.

John took the little feet into his hands to warm them, then
tickled them, but Lucy did not respond. "She's tired," he told
his wife.

"I hope it's only that," Anne replied. "Like all, she suffers
from cold, but she won't lose her toes." She put the stockings
back on the girl, then wrapped the strips around her feet.

The wind picked up and blew snow across the camp, sweep-
ing it sideways, under Lucy's bonnet and into her face, but the
girl only blinked. She did not cry or even put up her hands to
block the snow. John and Anne exchanged a glance, but neither spoke. In a moment, John picked up the girl and held her,
telling his wife to rest. "I'll walk with her. I think it will do
her good to move. Come along, son." He got up, and Joe stood,
and they walked from fire to fire, stopping to speak to the other
Saints.

Anne crawled into the tent and curled into a ball to keep
warm and dozed a little, wondering if more rescuers would
arrive that day or if, as was rumored, they had abandoned their
search and gone back to the valley. If that was the case, then
the handcarters would all die. There was not food enough left
for the days ahead, and many of the people could no longer
walk. She did not want to be a martyr, especially when she
was not a Mormon.

She heard John return and got to her knees and crawled
out of the tent. John was alone. "The children?" she asked,

and it hit her then that Lucy was dead, that the cold had taken her. It cannot be, she thought. God had taken Emma Lee and Samuel. He would not take Lucy. He would not be so cruel. "The children?" she asked again, her voice dead.

John looked up at her quickly. "Why, they are fine. Joe got into a snowball fight with his fellows, and Lucy jumped up and down and begged to join in. They will be here shortly." Anne saw the little girl running toward her and thought of such small acts were Mormon miracles made.

Many of the Saints who hoped to ride in the wagons were turned away. Nannie Macintosh was one of the lucky ones. She'd secured a place for the trip from Devil's Gate, across the Sweetwater, to Martin's Ravine, because her feet were so painful that she couldn't stand on them. She'd barely been able to walk the last few days to Devil's Gate, and when she'd tried to get up that morning, she'd fallen down from the pain.

"We dinna mean to leave ye," Andrew had said earlier in the day as he reached to lift Nannie into their cart. Although she weighed barely a hundred pounds—the weight of the sacks of flour the emigrants had once pulled on their carts—she knew she was too much for Andrew to push, since he alone propelled the cart. So Nannie had insisted she would find space in the wagon, and she did. Andrew carried her to the vehicle and set her down in the wagon bed, wrapping a blanket around her. "Hae a care. It is colder riding than walking, and ye could freeze."

"Shall I walk beside ye?" Ella asked, but Nannie shook her head. She didn't want her sister to know how she suffered.

Because of her feet, she had not slept the night before, and now she wondered how much longer she could take the throbbing. Ella herself was in misery, fearful she would lose the baby, and she shouldn't have to worry about Nannie, too. So Nannie told her sister to go with Andrew and said they would meet in camp. If I live, Nannie thought. She might die crossing the Sweetwater, and so great was her pain that she didn't care. She would go to heaven and live with the angels and meet the Lord, but oh, she would miss her sister. How could it be heaven if Ella wasn't there?

The wagon started off, the jolting adding to Nannie's despair. She was crowded into the wagon bed with other Saints, many in worse shape than she was. Some of them moaned. A few cried or swore, but most were stoic, for, like Nannie, they wondered if this were their last day on earth, and if that were so, they did not want the Lord to know they had spent it uttering curses and lamentations. Many were preparing themselves for heaven.

"I dare say the riding is better than walking," a woman said to no one in particular. Nannie turned to agree and saw that a bloody rag was wrapped around the woman's hand. The fingers were gone. Likely they had frozen and fallen off. The woman's nose was black, and Nannie wondered if it would have to be cut off, too.

"The Lord tries us," Nannie said.

"He tries us too much," another woman muttered. Her eyes were feverish, and when she coughed, the sound came from deep in her throat.

"Have you a potato?" asked a girl who appeared to be eight or nine years old. Nannie could not tell what ailed her.

"They were used up long since. Where are your folks?" Nannie asked.

"They crossed over before Fort Laramie. Just my brother and me's left, and he died last night. Now there's only me. He died stiffer'n a ironed shirt." She seemed to like the analogy and repeated it, "Stiffer'n a ironed shirt."

"Who cares for ye?" Nannie asked.

"Me."

"But ye are so young?"

"Who's to do for me, then?"

Nannie thought she ought to offer to take the girl in, but she couldn't walk. How could she take care of a stranger? Perhaps that was another burden the Lord had given her, and Nannie decided to speak up, but before she could, the lady with the bloody bandage said, "I will. I've lost two children and would fancy a daughter to replace them. If that doesn't suit, we'll find a home for you in the valley."

"You'd be my ma?"

"I would."

The girl crawled over to the woman, touching one of Nannie's feet in the process, and pain shot up Nannie's leg. Then the child looked up at the Saint who had promised to care of her and said, "I could be your good hand."

At that, Nannie swallowed hard, and she turned away and laid her head against the side of the wagon, and after a time, she slept. When she awoke, her hair was frozen to the wagon, and as she had nothing with which to cut it, she yanked her head until the hair broke off. They were crossing the Sweetwater then, and the jolting of the wagon on the river bottom pained her feet. She put her hand into her mouth and bit down on it until the blood ran. She knew she should take off her shoes and examine her feet, but she was afraid of what she would see. She knew her feet had blistered. But now they might be black, and Nannie would rather die than have them cut off.

When the wagon reached Martin's Ravine, one of the rescuers lifted Nannie off the wagon and carried her to a shelter to wait for Ella and Andrew. As evening came on, Andrew and Ella found her, and Andrew carried her to where the two had left their cart. She winced when Andrew set her down, and he and Ella exchanged glances before he said, "I must look at your feet."

"No," Nannie told him.

"They may be frozen."

"If they are, ye'll not cut them off. I won't lose my feet."

"Ye would die. Ye'd rather die?"

"Aye. It's no trouble to die."

"You can't, Nannie," Ella said, kneeling beside her sister.

"What good would I be without feet? Do ye think Levi would marry me then?" She had not seen Levi in two or three days, and she worried that he had taken sick or even died.

"Does Levi love ye for your feet?" Andrew asked.

Nannie did not answer, and Ella said, "I would rather hae half a sister than no sister at all."

"Would ye deny yourself to Ella?" Andrew asked. He sat down beside Nannie and removed her shoes, then her stockings, which were frozen to her feet. The feet were black and rotting.

"They'll have to be removed as soon as you reach the valley," Ella said.

"I wonder can she wait that long. Look how far the rot has gone. By then, they'd hae to take her legs, too. It must be done at once."

"Nay," Nannie said in a voice that was choked.

Andrew looked at Nannie. "Can the pain of surgery be any worse than what ye feel now?"

"Please, Nannie," Ella said.

Nannie looked at her sister, her eyes unfocused. It seemed to her as if she were someplace else, a mountain covered with heather, looking down at herself. Maybe she had already gone to heaven. But if she were in paradise, she wouldn't feel her feet, and the pain had come on in such force that Nannie wouldn't mind dying. She no longer thought what her life would be like if her feet were taken, only that she wanted the hurting to end. "Are ye terrible sure they hae to come off?" she asked. When Andrew told her he was, Nannie gave a single nod.

"I canna do it myself. I'll fetch one of the men," Andrew said, getting up. "Ella, ye must melt snow in the pot over the fire. Make the water as hot as ye can." Ella did as she was told, and Andrew left, returning in a few minutes with Old Absalom, the Saint who had spoken in favor of wintering at Florence and had been chastised for it. Ella frowned when she saw the old man and whispered, "What about Sister Maud?"

"Nannie canna be cured with herbs. Old Absalom has seen many amputations," Andrew told her.

"Done my own," Absalom said, holding up a hand to show two fingers missing." He looked at Nannie's feet, then nodded at Andrew. "She can't wait for the valley. They got to come off."

"Where do we take her?" Ella asked.

"Leave be. There ain't no surgery here." He took a bottle from his coat pocket and handed it to Andrew, who lifted Nannie's head so that she could drink. She gagged at the foul taste of the liquor and shook her head, but Absalom told her, "It dulls you some. Best to drink enough to pass out."

Nannie took another swallow, and another, while Old Absalom removed a wicked-looking knife from his belt, and taking out a whetstone, he sharpened the knife in slow circular movements, then held it over the fire to cleanse it. Ella stepped in front of him so that her sister would not see the knife, but Nannie was already drugged from the pain and the whiskey. "How long does it take?" Ella asked.

"Not a few minutes. You seen a butcher . . ." The old man cleared his throat. "Have you a needle and thread, silk if you got it?" When Ella produced a threaded needle that she had secured under the lapel of her dress, the old man said, "Hold her down now." With sure strokes, he cut through the skin and muscle and then the bone, tossing first one foot and then the other into the snow. He wrapped flaps of skin over the bones and, using Ella's needle, stitched the flaps in place.

"Is she done for?" Andrew asked.

"Ask the Lord about that. Some's so agitated, they don't care to live. They give up to dying. I seen an old woman here, Maud, that's got some herbs and such to help the healing, but the girl'll not walk. Behopes someday she'll crawl. If she lives."

At that, Ella began to weep. Old Absalom seemed uneasy at Ella's sobs and stood up. "I'll come back to ye and check."

"We haven't anything to pay ye with, but when we get to Zion—"

Old Absalom cut him off. "I wouldn't charge a Saint. 'Sides, she might curse me for what I done." He turned and disappeared.

Since she had no rags for bandages, Ella wrapped her sister's legs in her own underclothing and lay down beside her in the tent. That night came a terrible wind that blew down the tent, and Ella and Andrew dragged Nannie into the snow and huddled with her under a blanket until dawn, cooing when Nannie cried out and lulling her back to sleep. Nannie didn't wake until morning, and her first words were, "My feet pain me like fire."

Ella was startled, but Andrew had learned something about amputation and said that was a common complaint. "They're gone, Nannie."

"They can't be if they hurt."

"They were cut off last night. Dinna you remember?" Ella asked.

Nannie touched her leg through the blanket and slowly slid her hand over her thigh, down to her calf, and lower, the tears pouring down her face.

Andrew knelt beside her, taking her hand. And then he reached into his pocket, removing a small bit of purple. "Here, lass. I dinna know it was in my pocket until last night. Down at the bottom it was, caught in the seam, only a wee bit, but it will do ye." He pried Nannie's fingers open and slipped a snippet of dried flower into her hand. Then he held it to Nannie's nose, and she sniffed it.

"Heather?"

"Aye. If you can smell the heather, I think ye will make it."

Chapter 9

November 10, 1856

When the weather broke the day before, the Saints once more resumed their trek. But there had not been joy in it for a long time, Louisa thought, no singing, no praising of the Lord. She did not talk unless there was a reason, instead tramping along in the snow, dumb as a stone. The only sounds she heard from the wagons were an occasional moan or sob. She wondered where the rest of the rescuers were or even if there were other rescuers. Thomas Savage had told her the prophet had called a meeting of the Saints in the valley when he heard there were still handcarts in the mountains, and the people had responded with donations of food and clothing. Men had volunteered to drive relief wagons, she was told, although Louisa couldn't help but fear that the drivers had been discouraged and returned to the valley. Perhaps even the prophet himself had abandoned them.

She thought each day would be her last on earth and was

surprised to awaken in the morning; sometimes with a flicker of disappointment. So she walked, once more pushing the cart, placing one foot in front of the other, plodding along in an uneven line that stretched out for miles. There was no order to the march.

Almost all of the hated handcarts were abandoned now, along with the freight that had been carried in the wagons, and a contingent of rescuers had been assigned to stay behind and watch the discarded belongings throughout the winter. Nonetheless, Thales insisted they keep their cart. They had come so far with it that they would see it to the valley, he told his wife. If we live, she thought.

"Is it penance, pushing the cart now?" she had asked when she saw that others had left their vehicles behind.

He didn't answer her question, but said instead, "It is my burden. I promised to see it through."

"And I promised to stand by your side," Louisa told him, taking her place behind the cart.

"No, Louisa. You must save your strength. Walk with your mother. This is my duty, not yours."

"I am stubborn, too."

He studied her a moment. "I am not the man you think I am, Louisa. I have deceived you. I—"

"Hush. I am not disappointed in you." She knew that Thales questioned himself, but she did not want to hear it. She needed his strength, his belief in the rightness of their journey, to keep going. So in that long line of emigrants, the two silently plodded along with the cart.

"Ah, Brother Thales." Thomas Savage brought his horse to a walk and steadied the boy who rode in front of him, a child who had given out in the snow and had been sleeping under a bush when Thomas spotted him. "Why does it not surprise me that you will be the only member of the Martin Company to reach the valley with a handcart?"

Thales laughed for the first time in a long while. "My wife doesn't understand it, and I daresay I don't, either. But there is a strong desire upon me to keep it. Perhaps you can explain it."

"You don't give up. That's why you are such a good missionary. You could convert the devil himself."

"Some think the devil's mark is on me. There is more than one in this train who wishes he'd never heard me preach."

Louisa thought to speak up then, to deny her husband's words, but she held her tongue.

"And more than one still grateful for it." Thomas dismounted and handed the reins to the boy and told him to walk the horse behind the cart. He joined Thales in pulling the vehicle. "At the cove, I talked with a girl who said you had rescued her from a life of sin, Sister Emeline, by name." Louisa remembered the girl, the one Jessie had taken on.

"A sad story. Her foster parents died weeks ago, and now the man who intends to be her husband has lost an arm."

"What will become of her if he dies?"

"Some Saint will take her up. She's young and works hard and would make an excellent wife. Are you in the market?"

"No. I have troubles of my own. I believe at times that plural marriage is a hard doctrine," Thomas told him.

"I will find that out for myself one day. The woman with the girl, Jessie by name, I had thought to marry her once, but Louisa was a better match, sweeter and more obedient." He glanced over his shoulder at Louisa, who gave him a wan smile.

"I believed such with my second wife, whom I took just weeks ago, but I've learned that in polygamy, few of them are obedient and fewer yet, sweet. Is there a secret to making them get along with each other?"

"If there is, I haven't heard it. And neither has anyone else in Zion."

The two men pulled the cart together, pulled it with such strength that after a time, Louisa gave up pushing, and they didn't notice.

One evening after the Saints had set up their camp in the snow, Ella spied a lone rider coming toward them, his pack horses loaded with buffalo meat. The rider was a Mormon who had killed two buffalo, then gone in search of the Martin Company. As he stopped near Ella's cart, he said, "I wouldn't ever have expected to meet a buffalo. But you folks needed meat, and he was put in my way. When a body needs the Lord, needs something the Lord can do for him so bad that there isn't any other out, that is the time the Lord will show His face."

Declaring the meat a miracle, Ella and Andrew and the other Saints gathered around the man, shouting hosannas and crying that they were saved, although it wasn't much of a miracle, since the meat was little enough for a camp of hundreds. Besides, the rider brought news that some of the rescue parties had indeed turned back, believing the emigrants could not have survived in the awful cold. Ella clutched her distended belly and turned away.

The man said he was a surgeon of sorts, and Andrew followed him as he moved through the crowd, examining the frozen extremities of the emigrants, checking fingers and toes and hands and feet, muttering, "Dang me." Then he agreed to look at Nannie's maimed limbs, turning the legs this way and that and proclaiming, "As good as if I done it myself. It will heal right well if she lives. They'll pain her bad."

"The Lord was with her," said a Saint who was looking on.

"If the Lord was with her, she wouldn't have froze her feet in the first place," retorted Old Absalom, who had come to see his patient. "In all my travels, I've never seen worse than in this company. They've had a darksome time," he told the rider.

"Will I walk? Will ye tell me will I walk?" Nannie asked. It was more of a plea than a question.

The rider was not one to mince words. "No, but you'll crawl, and the skin flaps is better than the bone sticking out. They'll pain you less."

That evening, Andrew brought news of Levi. "I hae seen him. He's sick almost to death."

"Conscious is he?" Nannie asked.

"Aye. He asked for ye. I said ye were ill and canna be moved."

"Ye didn't tell him—" Ella whispered.

Andrew shook his head. "Nay. 'Tis not my place."

"Maybe he should know," Ella said.

"As he may not live long, I saw no reason to grieve him."

They spoke softly, but Nannie overheard them. "And if he disna live, what then? What's to become of me? Not many want a wife who canna walk," she said.

"A man who desires a wife with a sweet temper," Andrew said, uncomfortable, perhaps, that he had mentioned Levi at all.

"Any man who prizes a lass who can sew a cunning seam and cook like an angel, who would be a loyal wife and raise up children in the faith," Ella added. "Not every man looks first to the feet."

But Nannie was not comforted and turned away.

With Nannie riding in a wagon, Ella and Andrew trudged on, one day and then another. At night, Andrew carried Nannie to a fire, and the three camped together. The weather was not so bad now, although it was cold, especially at night, and the deaths continued. But there was a birth. At a campsite called Bitter Cottonwood Creek, Ella went into labor.

Andrew fetched Maud, and then thinking it would do no harm, he asked Old Absalom, too, to attend his wife. "I will help," Nannie said.

She winced at the pain, and Andrew told her they could take care of Ella, but Maud said, "I have need of her. You must rub your sister's back whilst I attend her."

Old Absalom nodded in approval and whispered, "You bring the poor girl around, Sister Maud." He watched as Maud prepared Ella, and when Andrew glanced at him as if to ask if Absalom shouldn't be in charge, the old man said, "It's woman's work. She knows better'n me. Now if the baby's born with froze fingers . . ." He looked uncomfortable when Maud frowned at him, and he did not finish the jest.

As such things went, it was an easy birth, but Nannie, who had never attended a birthing before, did not know that. Tears ran down her face when her sister cried out, and she left off rubbing Ella's back to smear her damp cheeks with her fingers. "Canna you do something?" she asked Maud.

"It's Eve's pain," Absalom said.

"Men's pleasure, women's pain," Maud chided him. "Likely the Lord got this wrong. It ought to have been the other way around."

"Women's pleasure, too, it is, old woman."

"Then ought'n men to share the pain?"

Old Absalom started to reply, but Maud shushed him and told Ella, "Push, Sister. Push."

Ella did as she was told, and in a few more pushes, the baby was born. "A girl," Maud said, and started to hand the tiny thing to Andrew. But she thought better of it and gave the baby to Nannie instead. "Tie the cord; then cover her up. You wouldn't want her to catch cold her first day on earth."

Forgetting her own pain, Nannie tied the cord with string that had been set aside, and then she tugged off her petticoat to wrap around the baby. Andrew knelt beside her, and Nannie offered him the bundle. "No, ye hold her. I'll see to Ella," he said, sitting down beside his wife. "A wee dochter," he told Ella, as if the woman didn't already know she'd given birth to a girl, "with ferntickles like you and Nannie."

Nannie looked up and exchanged a glance with Maud, for how could Andrew tell what the infant looked like in the poor light, or that she had freckles? It was hard enough to see that she was a girl. "She's a healthy child, but she ought to be after all she's been through. She walked a thousand miles before she was born," Maud said. She finished tending to Ella and sat back, telling the new mother. "You've come through fine and ought to have a dozen more." When Andrew looked up, startled, Maud added, "I mislike she would want them just yet."

Maud gave instructions about the baby, told Nannie how to care for her instead of telling Ella, and then she and Old Absalom left. "I weren't needed," he said.

"You gave comfort. It was needed after what they've been through."

"I never liked a birthing."

"I like it better than a death."

After the two were gone and Nannie had relinquished the baby to Ella, Andrew said, "I expected a lad, but right glad I am to see a lass. What will ye name her, Ella?"

"Ye'll let me choose, then?"

"Aye."

"I've thought on it a good bit, and at first, I thought to call her Miriam for my mother or Sabra for yours. Then I considered whether to name her Florence or Laramie or maybe Cottonwood to mark the journey. But now there's a better name. I will call her Nancy."

Nannie jerked up her head at that and stared at Ella, while Andrew nodded and said, "I canna but tell ye I was thinking the same."

The following day, the Saints met the first group of rescue wagons since Devil's Gate, and Louisa rejoiced with the others, especially when she assumed that more wagons were close behind. She saw in the faces of the riders the pity and awe as they stared at the emaciated people with their gray, wasted faces, hardly believing they had survived an ordeal that would have killed strong men used to the mountains.

She joined the others who crowded about the wagons as the rescuers handed out flour, dried meat, cheese, dried vegetables, bread, crocks of jam, even coffee and tea. The men distributed blankets and clothing, too—dresses, coats, hoods, sweaters, shoes, and stockings, thick blankets and bright quilts. She took a knitted blanket for her mother and a petticoat for Jessie, to replace the one her friend had torn into bandages.

Flour rations were increased, and for the first time in many weeks, Louisa did not suffer the pangs of hunger that night. She knew she would not reach the valley for many days, but at last, the worst part of their ordeal was over. From then on, she and the other emigrants would be fed and clothed. At last, Thales unloaded the Tanner cart and sent the vehicle careening down a hillside, where it crashed and shattered in a ravine.

The rescuers took charge, building fires and setting up the tents. Although she hoped the worst of the journey was behind them, Louisa knew they would still encounter frozen days, when they would shiver in the wagons and the sick and maimed would agonize over their state. And there would be more deaths, many more.

On November 24, during the last week of the trek, Margaret Chetwin did not wake up. The old woman, who had been too sick to start the journey but who had walked almost the entire way, did not live to see the valley. Louisa's grief was terrible to see, and Thales feared for her health and that of the baby she carried. "Mother was the most faithful of Saints.

How can you explain it?" she asked. She held her mother's knitting, grasping the needles with such force that the tips punctured her hands. "Why did the Lord let her suffer all this way, then stop her just outside the gates of Zion?"

"She is in paradise now, with your father. Is that not a greater glory?" he replied.

"I would rather she was with me. It was my prayer."

"But what did *she* want?" Thales asked. "Perhaps it was her prayer to be with your father, and God answered her prayer instead of yours."

"Do you believe it, Thales?"

"I do." He did not appear so sure.

"Naught but death could bring them together," Louisa mused in a voice that was plaintive and soft. "You have always spoken God's truth."

Thales turned away and did not answer.

That same last week, Levi sought out Nannie. He had been confined to a wagon in the days after Martin's Ravine, racked with fever, not sure that he would live, but he had recovered, and he came in search of his intended. Andrew had visited Levi, explaining that Nannie herself was too ill to move, and that they feared that if she caught his fever, she would die. And then there was the baby, Nancy, to consider. They would not have wanted Nannie to take Levi's sickness back to her. Levi had been too feverish to inquire what ailed Nannie. And Nannie, although she knew Levi was ill and that Andrew had seen him, did not ask about him.

Then one evening, Levi, well enough to walk now,

searched the camp for Nannie and found her sitting beside a fire, a blanket wrapped around her, her sister's baby on her lap. Levi smiled at her and said, "Such a pretty picture. Before long, I expect to see you sitting just like that with our own little one. I hope we'll have many of them to add to the kingdom."

Nannie was excited to see him, but she was uneasy. "Are ye well now?"

"Aye." He did not look well. His face was thin and white, and his beard was tangled. Like the other emigrant men, he had not shaved.

"Ye were very sick."

"That I was, but I will live, and you appear to be all right."

"I prayed for ye," Nannie told him.

"And I you." They were alone, except for the baby, and Levi took Nannie's hand and kissed her fingers. "We'll be married as soon as we reach the valley. Think you, it's only a week."

Nannie took back her hand and looked away. Her feet pained her as bad as they ever had.

"You haven't changed your mind?" When Nannie didn't answer, he added, "No, you would not be so cruel. Maybe you're upset that I haven't called on you like a lover should, but surely you knew I was sick almost to death. Didn't Andrew explain? He saw how it was with me. Not only could I not walk but I couldn't even stand. As you see, I'm better now, however." He added slyly, "Well enough to be a husband in every way."

"And glad I am for that." Her voice faltered.

Levi searched her face. "You haven't found another? You aren't throwing me aside?"

"Nay."

"Then what's wrong? I see it in your eyes."

"'Tis myself." To her disgust, she groaned from the hurting in her feet.

"Nannie, are you not yet well? You don't have a fever, do you? That's not enough to keep us apart." Levi sat down beside her near the fire. "What is it?" Then he grinned at her. "You are paying me back for not marrying you at home. Is that it? You're being coy with me? I've admitted to the mistake I made. I did not think you yet held it against me."

"Isnae that." Nannie shook her head. "Levi, I am not . . . I . . . I am maimed." Her voice broke, and she could not speak further.

Levi studied the girl, confused, and said, "I don't see it. What do you mean?"

Silently, Nannie slid up her skirt so that Levi could see her legs gleaming pale in the thin light, the stumps, bound up in strips of blanket.

"Lord's mercy!" Levi exclaimed. He stared at Nannie's legs and then turned away as if sickened. "How will you walk?"

"Old Absalom says it's likely I'll crawl."

"Crawl!"

"Oh, Levi, I'll be all right. Think how much worse 'twould be if I'd lost my hands." Nannie had not thought about such a thing until that moment.

"Dearest girl, I used to watch the way you ran down the road to meeting. You had such an air of hurry about you. Do you remember? You said you had so much to do and not enough time. You walked faster than any girl I ever saw. Why, you could run as fast as a boy. And do you remember our walks, where I told you about the Gospel? I fell in love with you then."

Nannie let out a sob. "Isnae crawling enough, Levi?"

He looked down at her legs again, and Nannie, feeling she had shown him something obscene, pushed down her skirt. "I'm the same, except for that wee part of me. Ella says ye did not fall in love with my feet."

Levi seemed relieved not to have to look at the legs. "You are all right otherwise?"

The baby mewled, and Nannie was glad to have a reason to look away for a moment. Then she replied, "In every other way." She held out her hands so that Levi could see that she had all of her fingers. Then she touched her face, "My nose dinna freeze, either."

Levi looked at Nannie's nose and nodded. "I can see that."

"There are others worse, so much worse. I am one of the lucky ones. Ella and Andrew say as much. I can cook and sew and care for babies. Have ye no care for me?" She looked down at her hands, embarrassed. She realized that she was pleading with Levi, and it disgusted her. She was still then, and turned her eyes to the top of the baby's head, wondering as she stared at the fine hair whether she and Levi would ever have a baby of their own.

Levi, too, was silent for a long time, and then he said, "You must realize it is quite a shock to see you like this. I'd thought you might die, like Patricia did. But I never thought . . ." His voice trailed off.

"Who thought any of us would be maimed like this?"

"Did you wish you had died instead?"

"Nay."

"I wonder you didn't."

"Do *ye* wish I had died?"

"No, of course not. But it makes things . . . different."

"You mean you dinna care to marry me? Do ye think I would hae cast ye aside if this had happened to ye?"

"But it didn't."

They sat there, not talking, until Ella returned, and Levi stood up, saying he must help with the wagons, that he had work to do to make up for being an invalid. "I've overstayed. I will see you again, Nannie. I promise you," he said, and hurried off.

Ella said nothing, only sat beside Nannie and took the baby and began to nurse.

"I showed him my legs," Nannie said.

Ella studied her sister's face. "And?"

"Shocked he was."

"I suppose that is the way to react when someone ye love's been hurt."

" 'Tis not what I mean."

"Nay."

"Ye are wanting to know if he still intends to marry me." When Ella did not reply, Nannie continued: "I dinna know. I could see the pity in his face. It's wondering he was about how he could be tied to a wife who had to crawl beside him, who canna help him in the fields, who canna walk to church with him. He would have to pull me in a cart—or a wheelbarrow." At that, Nannie covered her face with her hands.

Ella clutched her sister with her free arm. "It won't be easy, not for Levi and especially not for ye. But ye would make it work. There is much ye can do without standing or walking.

Besides, Levi said from the beginning that he expects to take other wives. Ye would be first amongst them. Ye would divide the work so that each wife does what suits best. Ye've a sweet disposition, and ye would keep order in Levi's house. It's something every Mormon husband hopes for. That is no little thing where many women are concerned. And ye would raise up his children. There is no reason ye wouldn't hae them yourself."

But that did not comfort Nannie, who felt so weak and feverish that she wondered if she might yet die.

On November 29, Anne counted the time until they reached the valley in hours, no longer in weeks or days. Although she rode through waist-deep snow, past twenty-foot drifts on the north sides of mountains, she no longer complained of the cold. There was a heightened sense of anticipation. A few of the Saints around her were morose and saw their arrival in Great Salt Lake City not as the entry into paradise as much as their passage from hell. These emigrants were no longer hopeful. They had lost too much, and they despaired of ever being whole again. She thought that some had already made the decision to leave the valley, to apostatize.

The deaths among the members of the Martin Company had been high. More than one in four who had started the journey had not made it, and in the Sully family, the percentage was even higher, two of six. Anne thought there would be few joyous reunions, for the survivors would bring the news of the deaths of loved ones, the details so onerous that no one in the valley would want to believe them. She was not surprised that the emigrants no longer planned a triumphal entry into Great Salt Lake City, did not talk of walking out of Emigration Canyon in their finest clothes, because those clothes were either worn-out or had been discarded along the trail. The dress and silk scarf that Anne had expected to wear for her entrance into the valley had disappeared hundreds of miles back.

John Sully was too restless to ride, so when the wagons stopped, he and Anne and the children got out to walk. "And how do you feel about us Saints now?" he asked his wife, as he had every morning since Catherine died. "Are you sure you want to live amongst us?"

Anne took a deep breath. "Now that we are here, are you wishing not to stay? Are you about to renounce the faith that once made you gladsome?"

He didn't answer, and Anne knew the question was an intemperate one. The rescuers were zealous in their belief, and although they sympathized with the handcart emigrants over their plight, they did not look kindly on those who questioned the church or were critical of its authorities. More than one of them had announced, "Any who are not for us are against us."

John didn't answer his wife's question; instead, he told her, "If the valley doesn't suit, we will talk about returning to England."

He had never said such a thing, and Anne realized he was speaking from despair. Still, it was a specious remark, because, as she replied, "And how would we do that? Don't you remember that you gave all our money to the elders?" When John failed to reply, she asked, "Did you not?"

"I held out only a small sum."

Anne stopped walking, letting John go ahead a few steps. When he realized she was not beside him, he turned and went back to her. "You had money we could have used, money that would have bought food for us, and you hid it from me?" She was incredulous.

"Where would we have spent it?"

"At Fort Laramie."

"There was no need for it there. We thought there would be supply trains. And later . . . the money was no good. People would not part with food for any amount."

"A peppermint stick. Lucy cried for it. You had no right, John, no right at all."

"No." He was too tired to argue.

"You did not trust me."

"I was afraid you would leave me if you had the money to return to England, and you are all the world to me. But now, the money will take you home, if you want to go."

"And what about you and the children? Is there enough for all of us?"

"Enough for you and Lucy. I would come later with Joe."

"Would you, or would you send me away and keep Joe for yourself?" Anne remembered how he had threatened to take the children to America and leave her behind in England.

"You think that, after all we've been through?"

Anne began to tighten the ribbons of her once-fashionable bonnet, which was torn and faded, the clusters of silk violets that once had been pinned to the side long gone. She had bought the bonnet to wear when she entered the valley, but she had need of it when her sunbonnet was lost. Now, as she yanked at the ribbons, one of them tore off. There was no needle and thread with which to repair the ribbon, and she could not wear the hat without tying it under her chin. So Anne yanked it off her head and tossed it into the snow.

John watched her, dejected, his shoulders slumped. He had lost his gloves, and his hands, once smooth enough to handle the bolts of silk cloth in the tailor shop without snagging them, were now rough, corded, dark from the sun. He had been a fine, big man when they left England, but now he was as thin as the other emigrants, his face flat and eyes sunken. There was gray in his beard, once neatly trimmed but now unkempt. Anne wondered if she had changed as much, but how could she tell? It had been months since she'd seen herself in a mirror. Her hands and arms were bony, and if they were any indication, her face must be as thin and brown and wrinkled as wrapping paper.

"I would stay in the valley," she said. "We have come this far. We must give it a chance. Besides, I am comfortable in my mind about living with these people, even if I am not ready to be baptized. Surely, John, it will be tolerable fair once we reach Zion. We'll find work, and you will regain your faith. It's natural to doubt after all that's happened. As the elders say, you have been tested, and I think we have come through. Nothing could be so bad as what we have survived."

John looked out at the mountains, white with snow shining in the sunlight, and the sight of them hurt his eyes. His pupils, when he turned back to Anne, were small and dark. "I'll listen to you now, as I should have before we left England."

Anne knew how difficult a thing it was for her husband to say that, and she only nodded. "I would ask one thing," she told him.

John said nothing but waited for her to continue.

"That you give the money to me."

"You don't trust me? You think I'd yet give it to the elders?"

Now it was Anne's turn to look away. She stared at the discarded bonnet. The wind had lifted it and blown it into a tree, where it had caught on a branch. It hung there like a dead thing. John stared at his wife a long time. Then he reached into his pocket and removed a pouch and handed it to her.

They would reach Zion the next day, Jessie expected—she and Ephraim, Emeline, and Maud. They had survived. But what would they find there? Jessie had kept their spirits up virtually all of the trip, but now that they were about to ride into the valley, she worried about what sort of life awaited them. She and Ephraim and Sutter had planned to farm, but Sutter was dead, and Ephraim had lost an arm. She was the only one of the three who could do the farmwork, and there was no way that even with Emeline's help she could break the soil and plant and harvest. She should have let go of those dreams when Sutter passed, but like the seed sacks that were still tied beneath her skirt, she had not discarded them. Now, on the eve of their new life in Zion, she had to be realistic. She had to find their future. There must be other work in the valley that they could do, but what was it?

As she sat brooding beside the fire, a tin cup of coffee the color of black ink in her hand, she saw one of the rescuers, her cousin's husband, stride past, and she called to him. "I would have a word with you, Brother Thomas."

"Sister Jessie."

"My brothers and I were farmers in England, and it was our desire to start a farm in Zion. I think we could have done that pretty nicely," she told him. "But as you know, my one brother is gone, and Ephraim, it is clearer than crystal, is not fit for heavy work. I'm not knowing what we can do. What would you advise us?"

Thomas, who had taken off his hat when he addressed Jessie, put it back onto his head and squatted beside her. "You're asking if there is work for a man with one arm, then? There is no doubt of your own future, for as a woman, you will marry."

"In time, but not now. I ask about work for all of us."

"You would indeed marry," he insisted. "There are no single women in Zion after three months' time; even the halt and the lame and the old are taken up. A farmer would be happy to have such a woman as you for a wife."

"But I might not be pleased to take him."

"Most women are not so particular."

Jessie scoffed. "If I expect to spend all time and eternity with him, I'll marry only a man of my choosing."

Thomas grinned. "Perhaps a sister with such a temper is not so desirable after all. But then, I've learned that most women have tempers—most wives, at any rate."

"And men, do they not have tempers? Perhaps you haven't observed the ones pushing handcarts who blaze out with profanity." She looked at the coffee, the worst she had ever tasted, and thought to throw it out, but she would not waste the drink, not in front of this man who must have sacrificed much to come to the aid of the emigrants.

"I concede you are right."

Jessie laughed. Despite her worries about the future, she was relieved to be putting the hardships and vexations of the past months behind her. She felt lighthearted. "I ask you if there is work in Zion for Ephraim."

"Can he read?"

"Right well, and write and cipher, too. He kept the books on the farm."

"Then Brother Brigham might use him in the tithing office. I'll ask him."

"Oh, no need. I'll tell him. Ephraim will be pleased."

"I was referring to Brother Brigham."

Jessie was startled. "You know him? The prophet?"

"Many in the valley know him. Thales Tanner is a particular favorite of his."

"I didn't know it."

"No, Thales would rather mention his connection with Joseph Smith. Surely you have heard him tell that. He likes to play brag." Thomas smiled at her as if they shared a joke.

"He hasn't mentioned Joseph in a long time."

"The trip has gone badly for Thales. He takes responsibility for the suffering of the emigrants."

Jessie nodded. "As well he should. Brother Thales is sorely disliked amongst the Saints."

Thomas studied her face. "You are not an easy woman."

The remark annoyed Jessie, but she was too weary to be cross and said only, "My brothers might be well if he had not insisted we come on from Florence."

"And the three of you, what did you want? Did you vote to winter there?"

Jessie looked down at her hands. "We did not. But we didn't know what lay ahead."

"Nonetheless, you chose to continue. Can you blame Thales for that?" He picked up a handful of snow and squeezed it, then tossed it aside.

"I'm not complaining, Brother Thomas. I'm merely saying Thales Tanner has good reason to be remorseful."

"And he's been punished. Look at the deaths in his own family."

"His wife's family. They might be alive if he had not forced them to leave New York."

"His own wife doesn't blame him. Why should you?"

"Because they were my friends. And because Louisa is a fool." Jessie thought she had said too much. If Brother Thomas were offended, he might not speak to the prophet on Ephraim's behalf. "I'll say no more of it, lest you rebuke me and say it is not my affair."

"You are a strong-willed woman, Sister. Zion has need of them."

"Except as wives, I should judge."

"Except as wives," he agreed. Thomas stood and said he would not forget to recommend Ephraim to the prophet.

Jessie, too, got to her feet, but she could not stand. She swayed and spilled the coffee, then dropped the cup. Thomas grabbed her and helped her to sit again. "Are you all right?"

"A temporary spell."

"I've seen it before. Some hold out against all hardship, then collapse when their strength is no longer needed. You must rest when you reach Zion. Rebecca will take you in and nurse you to health. She made me promise to bring you and your brothers home to her."

"I thank you for your help, Brother Thomas."

"I won't forget to talk to the prophet." He took a step away, then turned back. "And I shall keep an eye out for a deaf and blind old man who would not mind a wife with a temper."

"Please to let me know." She laughed.

At midday on November 30, four months after the Martin Company had left Iowa City, Andrew, Ella, and Nannie at last reached their destination. One hundred and four wagons filled with emigrants emerged from Emigration Canyon into the Salt Lake Valley. They cried with joy as they viewed the Promised Land, at the knowledge their dreadful journey was over and they had survived. Others around them praised God or prayed, and a few—those who still walked—knelt and kissed the ground. Ella Buck raised up her sister so that she could see the city and the mountains beyond. Nannie said nothing, simply stared, wondering if the austere settlement shielded by ponderous mountains was the reason she had made the long journey.

There was no brass band to greet them as the Saints had been promised at the outset, no songs, no flowers strewn in their path. The occasion was too solemn. Ella was surprised at the silent people who lined the streets as the emigrants rode past the temple block, where services in the tabernacle had just ended, to the tithing yard. The Saints who met them there were somber. Some had heard of the terrible suffering these people had endured. One woman told Ella that the members of the Willie Company, which had arrived three weeks earlier, had relayed tales that chilled the listeners' hearts, and they knew from the scouts who had returned to Great Salt Lake City before the Martin Company's arrival that the last group of handcart pioneers had fared even worse.

"Brigham Young was so distressed by the plight of his people that he was almost ill. He canceled afternoon worship because he says when baked potatoes and pudding and milk are needed, prayer will not supply their place. Are you needing a home?" she asked

"We will wait just a bit," Ella said, because first they needed to know what Levi had decided.

Andrew lifted Nannie out of the wagon and set her gently on a wall near the tithing office, then went off. Ella and Nannie sat and watched as Mormons came up to strangers, asking if they could give rides in carriages and wagons, even wheelbarrows, offering food and clean clothes, medicine, homes. Nannie had not expected such generosity. Nor had others who had endured the long trip with little complaint, and they broke down and cried.

John and Anne Sully stood with their children in the midst of the emigrants, a little bewildered as they watched the sickest of them being carried off. "We must find Catherine's son," she told John, inquiring of a woman whether she knew a man named Dunford.

The woman searched the crowd, then pointed him out,

and Anne hurried toward him, John and the children behind her. "Are you Catherine Dunford's son?" she asked.

The man nodded. "Are they here, my parents?"

Anne shook her head, and for the first time she could remember, she began to cry. "They are in heaven."

The man grasped Anne's hands and looked into her face. "Both? Both are gone?"

"Your father died saving the life of my son, Catherine not so long ago. She was my dearest friend. I would not have made it without her." Anne reached into the pocket of her dress and took out the book of poems. "This was her most cherished possession. I thought to bury it with her, but I have saved it for you instead."

Catherine's son slowly opened the book and read the inscription, then clasped it to his breast. "She wrote me of it. I remember the first book, as threadbare as an old shirt." He wiped his eyes with his sleeve and started to turn away. But then he stopped. "Sister, are ye in need of a home? We had a room set aside for Mother and Father, but it will be empty." He glanced at John and the children. "My son would be happy to hae a playmate, and a girl would be an added blessing."

"We are grateful for your kindness," Anne said. "We were told the Lord would provide."

"The Lord and James Dunford," he replied. "And you are Sister . . ."

"My name is Anne Sully, but I am not a sister. My husband is one of you, but I am not become a Mormon and may never become one. You may not want a Gentile living in your home."

"You were my mother's friend," he said. "That makes you sister to me."

Jessie was unable to walk and sat in the wagon, Ephraim and Emeline beside her. "Wait here," Thomas told them, and he strode off to a wagon a short distance away.

In a moment, he returned with a tall woman dressed in Mormon homespun, followed by two children and a young woman clad in finery such as Jessie had not seen since she left England. "Here are your cousins Jessie and Ephraim and their friend Emeline," Thomas told the tall woman, and Jessie recognized Rebecca. The woman reached up to clasp her cousin, and the two held each other. Then Rebecca turned to Ephraim and clasped his remaining hand. "Welcome, Ephraim." She looked around. "And Sutter?"

Jessie shook her head, and Rebecca bowed hers in sorrow. "They say many died, that those living had a cold, hard time of it, but you are safe now, and we will take you home to a supper and good beds. You and Emeline will sleep in my bed, and Ephraim can have Amelia's. She is my sister-wife." Jessie pointed to the young woman with her chin.

A look of defiance came into Amelia's eyes, and she retorted, "You will not give away my bed, Sister." She turned to Jessie. "I have not been married yet six months, and I have my pride."

The two women looked to Thomas as judge. With a glance at Jessie, he squared his shoulders. "Be still now. Hush your noise, Amelia. You would be ashamed of your selfishness if you knew how Rebecca's kin have suffered."

At that, the younger wife flounced away, climbing into their wagon and sitting down on the seat. Thomas and Rebecca helped Jessie and her brother and the two children into the back, then, seeing Amelia on the wagon seat, Rebecca, too, got into the wagon bed. When everyone was settled, Thomas seated himself beside Amelia and reached for the reins. But before he could slap them on the animals' backs, he looked at his second wife for a moment, then at Rebecca and her family, and said, "You must ride in the back, Amelia. You have seated yourself in Rebecca's place."

Maud sat down on a wall in the tithing yard, not so far from Nannie Macintosh. She could have gone with Jessie, but she knew the house would be small and cramped, that it was a hard life Jessie's relatives lived. She did not want to add to the family's burden. Someone would come along to care for her. Robert was watching over her and would make sure of it. So she sat and watched the sun cross over the Salt Lake to the west, shivering as the air grew colder. Seagulls flew in the sky above her, sending their cries across the valley. The wind picked up. Maud drew her cloak around her and peered into the sky. She had made it to Zion, made it for both herself and Robert. She knew Robert would protect her, although he might just let her fall asleep and never wake up. Wouldn't that be something! But what matter if her journey ended there?

She didn't hear the man approach, for he was always stealthy. She was not aware he stood in front of her until he spoke, "You didn't go with Sister Jessie?"

Maud shaded her eyes and looked up. "No."

"Have you found a home, then?"

"Not yet."

"I could taken ye home myself."

"You?"

"My old wife died tuthree years since, and there was only the one. Now I'm lonesome as a stray dog. I could stand the company if you could stand Old Absalom. I think we could have some good few times."

Maud thought that over for a very long time, for she had not thought to marry again. Would Robert like her to marry another? Would he object? He had always wanted her happiness. He would bade her to have done mourning him, to bide with Absalom, because he was a kind soul. Besides, she and Robert would have eternity together. So she said, "I believe I could stand you." She could stand a man who held his own against authority, who didn't belittle her skills with the herbs. She'd missed doing for a husband, sleeping against a warm body. Perhaps in the cold of winter, this man, like Robert, would whisper in her ear to stay under the sleep-warm quilts while he brought her coffee. Old Absalom seemed such a man.

She placed her hand on Absalom's ancient arm, and together, they left the tithing grounds.

Thales Tanner insisted on walking the last miles into Zion, Louisa beside him. At the sight of the valley opening up before her, the tabernacle in the distance, white mountains in the background, she dropped to her knees and prayed. Thales did not join her, but waited until she was finished. "You must show me where our home is," she told him.

Thales pointed to the south. "That way, but you cannot see it."

"I am anxious to meet your parents. I hope they'll like me. They don't know about me, do they?"

"I've told you before that I wrote no one."

"Perhaps one of the riders mentioned it to them."

"No. You will be a surprise."

Louisa had brushed her hair with her fingers until the snarls were gone and mended her clothes, so she looked as good as could be expected. "I wish I had the flowered bodice I discarded in Iowa," she told her husband. "I have always been choice of my clothes. Now look at dreary, dreary me," she chattered.

"Not as it matters," Thales told her, and Louisa was rebuked for her foolishness. Still, nothing could stop her excitement, even Thales's disheartenment. He did not seem to share her joy. He walked slowly, letting the wagons pass him, until they were among the last of the emigrants to reach the city. Louisa wondered if her husband feared censure by the church authorities for his role in the handcart disaster and if that was why he seemed reluctant to reach the tithing grounds. But it was not his fault. She would say that to them. Others would tell how Thales had sacrificed for the emigrants, how he had worked himself almost to death on their behalf, carrying the sick from the wagons to the fire each night, then carrying them back to the wagons in the morning. Why, one Saint who was dying of hunger said Thales had saved his life by giving him an onion. Thales had shared his little bit of food with others until his flesh sagged against his bones.

As they reached the tithing yard, Thales was greeted

warmly by several men who congratulated him on making it home and inquired about mutual acquaintances in England and in the Martin Company, whether they had survived, whether they were maimed. Louisa held back a little, for she was shy, and Thales did not introduce her.

And then a woman came up to Thales, threw her arms around him, and said between sobs, "I am so glad you are returned. I feared for you."

"And you are well, Tabitha?" he asked.

"I am." She smiled at him and clasped his neck again. Then she saw Louisa. She looked first at Louisa's face; then her eyes moved down until she saw her belly, which had already begun to swell. "Thales?" she asked uncertainly. "What is this?"

Thales turned and stared at Louisa for a long time, watched as her smile faded and her face took on the blank look of polygamous wives. "This is my wife Louisa," he told the woman. Then turning to Louisa, he said, "And this is my wife Tabitha."

The two women stared at each other, not with hatred or even bitterness, but with blank faces that hid their emotions. So this is what it's like, Louisa thought. She said dully, "You should have told me, Thales."

"And me. Oh, you should have written me, asked my permission," Tabitha said. She looked at her husband a long time, then turned abruptly, announcing she would get the carriage.

"Did you forget you had a wife at home?" Louisa asked when the other woman was gone.

"Sarcasm does not become you."

"Nor does lying become you."

"I never lied."

"You lied with the sin of omission," Louisa said, then cried, "Why? Why didn't you tell me? Why did you let me find out this way?"

"You might not have married me, and I wanted you to marry me."

"But you had no right to deceive me."

"You know plural marriage is our way, that I would have taken another wife one day. So what difference is it if I took her before or after you?"

"You should have told me, you who preached to me of truth and righteousness. It wasn't right. Didn't it bother you even a little bit?"

"It bothered me a great deal. But I needed your lovering. I would not have made it to the valley without you."

"And without you, my family might yet be alive."

"Do you hate me, then?"

"No."

"Then you must love me." He smiled at her in a way that had always made her glow.

"Do I?" Louisa asked. "Or do I have no choice?"

"Oh, you will adjust to each other in time. Good nature is Tabitha's normal manner, and yours, as well."

Tabitha returned with the carriage, and the three started off, the first wife on the front seat beside her husband, the second wife in the seat behind, staring at their backs.

That evening, the two wives were civil but barely spoke to each other while Thales recounted the story of their ordeal. "I might have lost my faith in myself without Louisa," he said.

"I cannot believe you would ever lose your faith," Tabitha

told him. "You have a great future in the church. Everyone says so."

Louisa rose to help clear the table and scrub the dishes, but Tabitha told her, "Don't bother. It's my kitchen, madam, and I know how everything is done."

When the work was finished, the two women sat at the table with Thales until he yawned and said he was looking forward to the first night in a bed in many months. "Louisa?" he said. She stood, and despite her unhappiness, she was glad that Thales would spend that first night in Zion with her. He walked her to the door of the bedroom she had been assigned, one of two in the house. "Good night. Look to your prayers, my dear," he said, and kissed her cheek.

Then taking Tabitha's arm, he went into the other room with her. As Tabitha shut the door, she glanced at Louisa, unable to conceal her glee. Louisa closed her own door and sat down on the bed, where Tabitha had laid out one of her own worn nightgowns. She did not see to her prayers, however. She felt dull and stupid and wondered if she would ever want to pray again. Instead of getting down on her knees, Louisa lay on the bed fully clothed until she heard her husband's boots drop in the next room. And then she truly understood polygamy.

Levi had not visited Nannie since that day when she had shown him her legs. She no longer talked about marrying him, nor did she even mention his name. Instead, she was quiet, brooding, wondering what would become of her if Levi deserted her. She did not want to be a burden on her sister, but there would be no work for a cripple other than sewing, and judging from the looks of the people in Zion, there were not many who could afford to hire a seamstress. Perhaps some compassionate man would add her to his household, a plural wife to be ignored by him and the other wives, an object of resentment and pity. Nannie wondered if she should have refused to let Old Absalom amputate her feet. Perhaps she should have taken her chances between a miracle and death.

She sat with Ella on the wall near the tithing office, staring at the women of Zion. Ella knew Nannie was waiting for Levi, and to distract her, Ella said, "Look at how many that one has." She pointed with her chin to a large man who was surrounded by half a dozen women and a brood of children.

"Are they happy?" Nannie asked.

"How could they be? I never thought about all the children. How does a man support twenty-five children?" Despite herself, Ella giggled, and as Nannie laughed, too, she thought how much she would miss her sister when the two were settled. But maybe they would not live so far from each other, and Ella could visit her every day.

Nannie was thinking about that when she saw Levi striding toward her. He looked purposeful, and she knew he had made a decision about her future—not the decision she had hoped for, because if he had, he would have sought her out earlier. Ella saw him, too, and reached for her sister's hand.

Levi stopped in front of Nannie and said, "I have something to say to you."

"I must join Andrew," Ella said, but Nannie told her to stay, and Ella, the baby in one arm, squeezed her sister's hand.

"I've done a great deal of thinking," Levi began, not looking at Nannie, but shading his eyes as he stared out over the tithing yard, which was muddy from the snow and the wagons and the people milling around. "I have asked you to marry me, and I will honor that. I will not deny you a second time. I know my duty, and I will be a man of my word."

Nannie should have been pleased, but those were not words of love. Besides, the tone was ominous, and she clutched her hands in her lap, digging her nails into her flesh.

"You must know that I cannot take on the care of a wife in your condition, not by myself. There will be other wives."

"Ye hae already said as much."

"So I'm to marry Matilda Weaver, a widow who was a member of the company. She has agreed to care for you." Nannie knew the woman—pretty, vain, not unlike Patricia. Nannie had heard her complaints from the time they left Iowa City and had seen her snatch a bit of bread from her mother's hand at Devil's Gate. She had suffered as had the others, but that had not made her more sympathetic. She would not take kindly to someone crippled.

"I'm not an invalid. I will care for myself," Nannie said.

"Not in all ways. You will need someone."

Nannie had to admit that was true. As the first wife, however, she would have some authority. She would not let Matilda rule her.

"Matilda and I will marry today. Later, when you're better healed, you and I will be married."

"But ye said I would be the first wife," Nannie cried.

Levi shrugged. "Things are different now. Can you deny it?" Nannie did not answer, and Levi added, "Those are the conditions under which we'll be married. I promised Matilda."

Nannie bowed her head to hide her tears, feeling Ella grip

her to keep her from sagging. Did she have a choice? No, of course not. She could not be a maid in a fine hotel, nor own a shop of her own. She would be a second wife in Levi's house, and with luck, she might even bear him children, although she did not know if he would want her in that way. At best, she would be cared for, and at worst, she would become a bitter, barren woman, ignored by everyone.

"In a week or two, then, you will be my wife."

Ella glared at Levi, and then she said, "Nay, Levi." She straightened her back as her eyes moved to Andrew, who had returned and was standing on the other side of Nannie.

"Are you denying your sister the right to marry?" Levi asked in a mocking tone.

"Nannie disna need my permission."

"Then you have nothing to say."

"I do." Ella swallowed and, looking directly at her husband, said, "Nannie canna marry ye, because she is going to marry Andrew. She will be his plural wife."

Andrew's face turned white, and he looked at his wife in shock. Nannie muttered, "Och!" in a strangled voice. "I widna! I widna ever! I'll marry Levi."

Ella, who had once made her husband write down his promise never to take another wife, gripped baby Nancy while she let out her breath. She continued to look at her husband for a long time before she turned to her sister and said, "Nay, Nannie, ye will marry Andrew. We hae always been sisters. Now we will be sister-wives."

Nannie shook her head back and forth. "I widna share the bed with Andrew. I canna ask you to make the sacrifice." Tears streamed down Nannie's face.

The two sisters gripped each other's hands, but it was Andrew who spoke. "I would take ye for a wife and would love ye as I do your sister," he said. "But we will wait until ye want it. Ye are welcome to bide with us as long as ye like as our sister. And if ye decide ye do not want to marry me or another, why then, we'd be pleased to hae ye as the first old maid in Utah."

The three turned as one and glared at Levi, who at last took a step backward, then two, before he turned and rushed off. Andrew picked up Nannie and carried her to a wagon. But just before Andrew set her down, Nannie reached into the waistband of her dress and removed the red shoes. Then she dropped them into the mud.

Epilogue

Anne Sully never was baptized into the Church of Jesus Christ of Latter-day Saints, although she lived with the Mormons for the rest of her life and eventually began to think of herself as Sister Anne. The Sullys went south, where John worked as a laborer, while Anne took in washing. They lived in a one-room adobe house with a dirt floor. John planted a garden each year, but it was difficult to coax crops from the hard red earth, and John was not much of a farmer. The family often went hungry.

After four years, the Sullys moved to Great Salt Lake City, where John once again set up a tailor shop. It lacked the refinements of the London establishment, but he was patronized by the new Mormon gentry, including the prophet, and he prospered. He remained a member of the Church of Jesus Christ of Latter-day Saints, although he was never again the fervent convert he had been in England. Anne bore two more children, who, like Joe and Lucy, lived to old age. Some twenty-five years after arriving in the valley, John and Anne returned to London for a visit, a trip that they cut short because both of them were homesick for the valley.

Ephraim Cooper did indeed secure a job at the tithing office. He worked there for five years before he left to join the staff of the *Deseret News,* where he became an editor. Late in life, he used the diary he had kept during the first part of the journey as the basis of a book detailing the Martin Handcart Company's ordeal, a book that became a Mormon classic. Although he was devout, he never rose in the church, in part because he refused to enter into celestial marriage. He and Emeline had five children.

To no one's surprise except Jessie's, Thomas Savage, with the encouragement of his wife Rebecca, asked Jessie to become his third wife. She refused. Instead, she became the first and only wife of a farmer who had been one of the rescuers of the Martin Company. Jessie bore him four children, all delivered by her friend Maud, who moved into the household after the death of her second husband, Old Absalom. Like Jessie and Maud, Jessie and Rebecca were lifelong friends.

Andrew Buck tried his hand at carpentering, but he did not care for it, and when a textile mill opened in the valley, he was hired. The pay was low, but Ella was frugal, and Nannie did fine sewing for John Sully's shop, and the three made a comfortable living. The women divided the housework and the care of Ella's six children, who were bemused when outsiders asked which of their father's *wives* was their mother. Nannie never married, although it was assumed by many in Great Salt Lake City that she was Andrew's second wife. Andrew attached wheels to the bottom of a chair so that Nannie could move herself about as she worked with her flowers. Her garden was known throughout the valley for its beauty.

The three died within two years of one another and were buried in a little Mormon cemetery in Salt Lake City, Ella in the center, Andrew and Nannie on either side of her.

Just a year after Louisa Tanner arrived in the valley, her sister-wife, Tabitha, died in childbirth. Louisa raised Tabitha's child, along with seven of her own. Once back in the valley, Thales Tanner's doubts about his worthiness faded, and he regained his zealousness. He rose to become one of the leaders of the church, and he was called upon frequently to recount stories of crossing the plains. He was silent about the handcart debacle, leaving the story to dissidents and apostates, for fear of bringing condemnation on the church and Brigham Young. But he told of other crossings in which he had participated, both before and after the handcart journey. And as with his story of Joseph Smith, Thales's telling of his part in the Overland Trail treks changed over the years. It was a dense listener who heard the mighty voice of Thales Tanner and did not conclude that he was a hero of the Mormon Trail.

Thales took four more wives and built homes for them, although the families gathered each Sunday at the main house, the one in which Louisa lived. As first wife following Tabitha's

Sandra Dallas

death, Louisa managed the families, assigning duties, settling complaints, quietly scolding Thales when he paid too much attention to one wife or ignored another. She was fair and evenhanded and much loved by her sister-wives. The Tanner household was considered one of the most harmonious in Zion, and skeptical Gentiles who questioned the principle were often invited to visit with the Tanners to see for themselves how successful plural marriage could be.

When the Mormon Church ended celestial marriage in 1890, polygamous men were ordered to rid themselves of all but one wife. Thales chose Louisa. "I've given it much thought and have decided I will be yours. You have been a good and faithful wife, and you deserve me," he told the woman who had accompanied him from England so many years before.

Louisa turned him down.

Acknowledgments

When I was a high school student in Salt Lake City in the 1950s, I was intrigued by the bronze statue of a man pulling a handcart that was displayed in the temple grounds of the Church of Jesus Christ of Latter-day Saints. The high-walled temple grounds in the center of the city are sacred to Mormons because they contain not only the LDS temple, which is closed to outsiders, but the turtle-back tabernacle, home of the Mormon Tabernacle Choir. But it was the heroic-size handcart statue, executed by Torleif Knaphus in 1947, that appealed to me most. The statue is of a resolute man pulling a two-wheeled cart, his wife beside him, attending to their daughter, who sits on top. A small boy pushes the vehicle.

Back then, I knew that these people, LDS converts, had piled their meager belongings into the cart and walked thirteen hundred miles across the prairie and mountains to Salt Lake City, but I did not know about their terrible journey, that hundreds had suffered and died on the way to the Mormon Zion.

Acknowledgments

The handcart scheme was the idea of the prophet Brigham Young, who became head of the LDS Church in 1844, following the murder of founder Joseph Smith. By the mid-1850s, zealous missionaries had converted tens of thousands of Europeans, mostly in Scandinavia and the British Isles. The converts were encouraged to emigrate to Utah, but many were poor and couldn't afford the three-hundred-dollar cost of outfitting themselves with a covered wagon. Let them push handcarts, Young said. Handcarts would lower the emigration cost to no more than twenty dollars, and the church would loan the converts the money. Carts would be waiting for the Saints when they arrived in Iowa City, where the train tracks ended, and way stations along the route would provide the people with supplies.

The idea was an intriguing one. Walking was no ordeal, since most pioneers walked beside their wagons instead of riding in them anyway. And there would be wagons for the sick and the infirm.

Execution of the handcart scheme proved wanting, however. Carts were not waiting, nor was there seasoned wood to build them. The converts themselves were forced to construct their handcarts, and out of green wood. The rickety vehicles, which constantly broke down, were the scourge of the trek. But that was not all. The church failed to establish way stations, and the result was starvation.

Five handcart companies crossed the plains and mountains from Iowa City, Iowa, to Utah in 1856. The first three reached Zion with relatively few casualties. In *Handcarts to Zion: The Story of a Unique Western Migration, 1856–1860,* LeRoy R. and Ann W. Hafen put the total deaths in those three companies at about twenty-five. The fourth company, the Willie Company,

338

was not so fortunate. It left Iowa City on July 15 and encountered snow, and as a result sixty-seven died, according to the Hafens.

The Martin Company, the last of the five handcart companies that year, departed nearly two weeks after the Willie Company and incurred the greatest hardships. Some 625 converts left Iowa City with Captain Edward Martin. Defections on the first part of the journey reduced the number to 575. Of that group, between 135 and 170 perished from cold, hunger, exhaustion, or a combination of the three. (Some put the figure even higher.) In contrast, forty-two members of the famed Donner Party died. That makes the Martin Company saga the single greatest tragedy in the history of America's westward expansion. *There were 96 people in Donner Party 81*

For more than 150 years, there has been a debate about who was responsible for the poor execution of the handcart experiment and the failure to send rescuers until it was almost too late. Some historians, such as David Roberts in his excellent book *Devil's Gate,* the most comprehensive history yet of the handcart experiment, blame Brigham Young. The question is an intriguing one, but since my book is a novel about the members of the Martin Company and not a factual account of the handcart experiment as a whole, I have chosen to steer clear of the controversy. My characters care more about survival than they do about assigning blame.

Within days of the Martin Company's arrival in Salt Lake, the handcart experience was being turned into legend. On December 10, the *Deseret News* wrote, "This season's operations have demonstrated that the Saints, being filled with faith and the Holy Ghost, can walk across the plains, drawing their provisions and clothing on hand carts."

But it was more than faith and the Holy Ghost that allowed those exhausted Mormon converts to drag their handcarts through rivers, snow, and freezing cold. The men who pulled the carts had courage and strength and a readiness to sacrifice. So did the women. Often pregnant, carrying little ones in their arms, the women did not give up, and, in fact, there were more deaths among the men than among the women. "Their women were incredible," wrote Wallace Stegner in his introduction to *The Gathering of Zion*. As I read Mormon history, I found it was the women whose lives haunted me.

Although I am not LDS, I found that these early Mormon women spoke to me. It is their stories I wanted to tell. I hoped to portray them not as martyrs, but as real flesh-and-blood people who found joy in their religion but cursed it, too, who starved and froze but who blessed the Lord for leading them to Zion.

In the past, church archives were generally closed to outsiders, but that has changed in recent years, and the LDS Church History Library and Archives provides access to a wealth of handcart journals, accounts, stories, and articles to researchers of all faiths, both at its location in Salt Lake City and online. I'm grateful for that trove of information and also to the librarians there who answered specific questions. I drew on many of these first-person accounts in crafting *True Sisters,* but my characters are entirely fictional.

Acknowledgments

A note on style: Once they reached America, the converts, technically, were *immigrants*. I've chosen to call them *emigrants,* as they were known in the nineteenth century. *Emigrant* is preferred by virtually all Utah historians.

I am indebted to Fred E. Woods, professor of religious understanding at Brigham Young University and an expert on the Mormon migration, who critiqued an early draft of this book, correcting misunderstandings and suggesting changes, and to Will Bagley, Utah's finest, if most controversial, historian and author of the superb *Blood of the Prophets: Brigham Young and the Massacre at Mountain Meadows.* Will not only questioned some of my research but spotted errors that would have affected the novel's credibility. Lyndia Carter, whose knowledge of the handcart expeditions is almost legendary, generously shared her scholarship. My thanks to Glen Rollins for encouragement.

My books are always a collaborative effort with my agents, Danielle Egan-Miller and Joanna MacKenzie, at Browne and Miller Literary Associates. They helped me focus the stories and decided that bittersweet endings are okay. My supportive editor, Jennifer Enderlin, tied up loose ends. And the three of them solved the thorny problem of a title for a work that had been known only as "the handcart book."

Thanks to Bob, to Lloyd and Forrest, and to Dana and Kendal, who are the reason I can write about strong women.